THE SECRET

A Love in O'Leary Novel

MAY ARCHER

Cover Art: Cate Ashwood
Editing: Sandra, One Love Editing
Professional Beta Reader: Leslie Copeland

All the good bits are theirs, and any mistakes are my own!

The Secret

Micah

Constantine Ross is a cocky, provoking little…yeah.
And I swear, I'd think that even if his family's business wasn't my biggest competition.
It's time someone taught the man a lesson or two about life.
At least that's what I tell myself when I offer him a job.
Call it my good deed for the year… maybe the century.

But now he's in my shop.
In my space.
In my every damn thought.
In. My. Bed.

And how the hell am I supposed to resist him?

Constantine

I'll be the first to admit I've royally screwed up, but what can I say?

I was a stupid teen who lost his dad and spiraled out of
control.
Almost a decade later, I'm still trying to make amends.
The last thing I need is my family's arch-nemesis wading
into my life like he's got all the answers.
Except… I really need money, and the arrogant jerk
offered me a job.

I can deal with Micah's attitude.
My attraction to him? That's different.
He's my boss, not my boyfriend.
And he's way too old for me.
But God, he's gorgeous.
Dominant.
Compelling.

I don't want to want him…
But I can't turn away.

The Secret begins in June, months before the events of *The Fall* and *The Gift*.

For those who have read those books, as well as *The Date*, I hope you enjoy getting a glimpse of those stories from a different point of view!

For those who haven't, no worries! Each book is a standalone.

Chapter One

CONSTANTINE

June

FUCKING *HELL*, the things I did for my family.

Constantine? I need you to work twenty-billion hours tomorrow, son, starting at the farmer's market before dawn, and oh, I can't pay you.

You've gotta step up, little brother. Mama keeps calling me all, "Julian, I'm worried Constantine is squandering his future." But I'm just trying to deal with my own life right now, so please handle your shit for once, okay?

Con, big bro, I know you're a man who's literally made of nothing but free time and money, given that you work two jobs and one of them is unpaid, and everyone knows you require no sleep to survive, so I need you to haul your exhausted ass over to fucking Camden in the middle of the goddamn night so you can drive my drunk—and totally underaged—carcass back home before Mama wakes up and figures out how her baby boy was celebrating high school graduation, 'kay thanks.

Those last hadn't been my little brother Theo's actual words when he called me a little after two in the morning, naturally. It had actually been more like, "Hey, um… Connie? I had like, two shots… No. Maybe like, *three* shots of Turkey? And maybe like three or six beers? I think I'm good though, because 'liquor before beer, in the clear.' *Everyone* knows that. But, like, Sam says I'm a fuckin' idiot? So what do you think?"

What I'd thought was that young Theodore needed to be ripped a new asshole, and I'd been only too happy to do it, but only *after* I'd picked his sorry ass up and taken Sam home, too. I'd been an auxiliary police officer with the O'Leary PD for way too long to do otherwise.

At least I could console myself that Theo was safely at home in bed this morning. I just wished I could say the same. I was rocking a dull headache, and my eyes felt as bleary as if *I'd* been the one drinking *three or six beers* last night, when I most definitely had not.

I glared at the sun, which was way too high in the sky, and kicked at the front tire of my ancient Civic, Bessie, who'd decided to be an attention whore at the worst possible moment. It was a sign of just how well my day was going that the sun only made my headache worse, and the tire ripped the corner of my only decent pair of sneakers.

Mother. Fucker.

A battered blue tow truck honked in a friendly way as it pulled to the shoulder of the highway in front of me, and Joe Cross opened his door and swung himself down a second later.

"Hey-hey, Connie. What's the trouble?"

Joe was fifty-something, and pretty much always had been, as far as I could recall. He was *stocky*, if we were being polite, with a beer gut that strained the front of his TB12 shirt, and I couldn't have told you what color his hair was if my life depended on it, because he'd never not worn his battered, old Patriots hat. I personally always thought he looked like Santa Claus's illegitimate, Tom-Brady-loving son or something. Nobody should have cheeks that pink.

I leaned back against the driver's door and shrugged helplessly. "It's just like I explained to you on the phone, Joe. Started shuddering, smelled like burned toast, and then it just… quit."

Joe frowned at the raised hood and the exposed engine, like he could diagnose Bessie's condition just by sight. Hell, for all I knew, maybe he could. He nodded once. "Don't worry, we'll get you sorted, kiddo."

Kiddo. I almost snorted. Right then, I felt about a hundred years old.

I leaned against Bessie's side, closed my tired eyes, and sighed as the sunlight warmed my face. Ordinarily, standing in the bright sunshine of a late-spring morning in Upstate New York was high on my list of favorite things to do—right up there with sex and a hard workout—because it was one of the few things that calmed my mind for a little while.

Today, though, it had the opposite effect, reminding me that I was late *again*, and I was gonna get reamed for it *again*, and Micah-fucking-Bloom was gonna give me that superior little smirk of his *again* from his booth at the farmer's market across from the Ross Landscaping booth. Not to mention, I was gonna have to sell a kidney to pay for my fucking car repair, and I was probably gonna get skin cancer or at least a sunburn, standing out here, because I had fuck-all control over anything in my life. My brain was buzzing like cicadas in a heat wave, and it was driving me mental.

"Turn the engine for me, Con?" Joe said, bending over the front of the car.

I inhaled sharply and nodded, then pulled open the door and twisted the key once, twice, three times.

The dashboard responded by lighting up, but the engine wouldn't turn over.

Joe made a motion for me to stop and I got back out.

"What do you think?" I asked anxiously. "Battery issue, maybe? Alternator or… something?"

My knowledge of cars was extensive, clearly.

Please be something cheap, please be something cheap.

Joe straightened and scratched his cheek with one blunt finger. "Wellll," he began.

Okay, fine. *Please be something not insanely expensive, please be something not insanely expensive.*

"Thing is, Connie, car this old?" Joe shook his head. "Could be a lotta things."

Please don't say it. Please don't say it.

"Worst-case scenario," he said slowly, sadly. "You're lookin' at a new transmission." He pulled his hat off and held it over his chest as he looked down at the engine, like he was a mourner staring down at a casket.

He might as well be. I couldn't afford a new transmission. Jesus Christ, I could barely afford gas.

White, I thought inanely. Joe's hair was white. Just like Santa.

I'm sure I looked every bit as devastated as I felt, because he attempted a smile. "I mean, it might *not* be that," he said. "Remember, that's worst case, okay? Might be some connections've gone funny. Or, ah… I don't suppose you put bleach in the gas tank?"

I squinted at him.

"You remember that?" Joe shook his head and chuckled, leaning against the car next to me. "Back when you were in high school? That little shit Trent-what's-his-face from over Camden way used to drive his Camaro like he owned the road?"

"Gaynor," I said sharply. "Yeah. I remember."

"Trent Gaynor! That's right. You put bleach in his tank!" Joe said like I hadn't been there and might not recall. "Car died a ways out on Lobelia, and Trent ended up crashing into that fence out by the reservoir. I've never *seen* a man as pissed off as Trent's daddy was over that prank." Joe laughed exultantly. "Thought he was liable to kill you."

It hadn't been a prank, per se, but the truth was a moot point when Trent's daddy was a rich lawyer and my mother was a small-time business owner.

Spoiler: Vince Gaynor hadn't killed me. What he *had* done was worse, in some ways. At least if I'd died, folks in town would've probably remembered me fondly. At least I wouldn't have had to stand by helplessly while Vince Gaynor sued my mother, ripping away everything she and my dad had worked for to line his already-plush pockets.

It wasn't exactly a fond memory.

Joe shook his head again. "Shoot. That must've been, what? Two, three, four years ago now?"

"Nine last month," I said with a sigh.

"No!" Joe sounded truly shocked. "It's never been that long."

"Yep. I was a sophomore." My teenage rebellion had peaked when I was fifteen, though I hadn't known it at the time. "So about my car?"

"Right." Joe straightened. "No bleach, then?"

Jesus. "Yes, Joe. I put bleach in my own tank so I could have the fun of calling you out here on a Saturday morning, and then the added fun of paying you to fix it."

Joe's mouth turned up on one side. "Yeesh, Connie.

Just jokin' with ya. Thought you of all people could take a joke."

That was me: Constantine Ross, king of inappropriate humor.

But it wasn't Joe's fault teenage Con had been a dumbass and that my twenty-four-year-old self was literally still paying for it. "Sorry. I'm not in a joking mood. Not exactly flush with cash right now."

"Yeah, I hear ya. Well, come on then. I'll get her towed in, and we'll see what we can see. I'll call you later and letcha know."

I nodded, because there was nothing else to do. "Mind dropping me off at Ross Landscaping first? Gotta grab the truck and I'm late for the market."

Joe chortled. "Always somethin' with you, Connie."

Wasn't that the damn truth? But you know what? Even if my life was fucked, nobody in O'Leary was gonna know it.

When life hands you lemons, you juggle those fuckers and make somebody laugh.

Joe clapped me on the shoulder and gave me a shove in the direction of his truck. "Grab the chains and let's get this show on the road."

Chapter Two

MICAH

CHRIST ON A CRACKER, the things I did to earn a living.

For two decades, I'd worked my ass off and lived on breadcrumbs so I could pour money back into Micah's Blooms.

I'd learned to deal with cranky customers and bridezillas who insisted on purple jonquils and got pissed at *me* because nature didn't provide them in that color.

Hell, a year and a half ago, I'd even moved myself and my business away from my hometown—the house I owned, the family I adored—to fucking *O'Leary*, just to be closer to the destination wedding venues that were my bread and butter.

But *nothing* I'd made myself do in the name of earning a dollar was as uniquely painful as spending my Saturday mornings at the Rushton-O'Leary Farmer's Market— hauling my plants and flowers out here every week; setting them up in an eye-catching display; marking time in this six-by-ten, three-sided event tent while exactly *zero* customers stopped by; and listening to Pete Daley and his *fucking* tribute band, the Daley News, provide live entertainment.

Kill me now.

"Thank you. Thanks, everyone!" Pete said into the microphone, his voice somehow managing to sound both far away and eardrum-shatteringly loud at the same time. "So, um, that was our ska version of 'Jeremy' by the one and only Pearl Jam, if you couldn't tell! One little announcement before we get back to the music: Callie says Abe says Parker says he'll be giving away free burger samples at eleven thirty over at Hoff's! And those things are dang good, so plan your morning accordingly!" He cleared his throat. "This next number is The Daleys' rockabilly version of the classic Ace of Base song, 'The Sign'! And speaking of signs, if you're lookin' to sell your house, condo, or double-wide, stop on by the McMenamy Real Estate booth and tell my gal Cheryl you say *hey*! One. Two. *One, two, three, four.*"

I was *not* a religious man. I'd been raised by a grandmother who'd legally changed her name to MoonFlower Bloom back in the sixties. She'd taught us that organized religion was even less trustworthy than the government. Heaven and hell, she'd said, were concepts created millennia ago to hobble the minds of the masses.

Still, as Pete launched into a twanging guitar riff that was every bit as enthusiastically terrible as I'd anticipated, I couldn't help but think hell was very, very real… and it was located right here, in the middle of Nowhere Special, New York.

I squeezed my eyes shut and bit back a groan.

This is important, Micah. Eyes on the prize. You have a plan. You need to shore up your local presence if you want to diversify and stop relying solely on weddings. You have goals to attain. You have a second location in Rushton to open. You will *do this.*

And I would, I thought, as I opened my eyes once more. Once I'd set my mind on something, I did not back down.

I looked at the empty tent across the aisle and rolled my eyes. Ross Landscaping and Flowers, my biggest competitor, had apparently decided not to man their booth today. Must be nice to have such a solidly established business that you could simply choose not to show up.

Then again, from what I'd learned of Angela Ross in the past eighteen months, she'd never miss an opportunity to commune with her fellow O'Learians, especially if it meant she—and they—could stand around glaring at anyone who dared to *look* at my booth let alone actually buy something from the competition.

No, this failure had to be on Constantine Ross, the ne'er-do-well middle son. The one with the big, blue eyes and the wide, friendly smile, the broad shoulders, scruffy beard, and bubble-shaped ass. The one who laughed and teased and flirted and made *everyone* love him, from whining children to grumpy old men, even as they shook their heads over his antics and clucked their tongues at his lack of responsibility. The one O'Learians called *trouble*, and a *menace*, and a *sweetheart*, and a *charmer*.

But if there was something charming about the man, I'd never noticed. He was an entitled man-child who'd been handed everything he needed to be successful—good looks, a job, a town so rabidly supportive it was a wonder I'd stayed in business this long—and repeatedly squandered those gifts.

He was dramatic.

And fucking *provoking*.

And yes, okay, I *maybe* noticed his ass. And his blue eyes. And his smile. But that was only because I was a red-blooded, forty-year-old gay man who'd stopped enjoying one-night stands around the time Constantine was figuring out what his dick was for. I didn't do Grindr, and I didn't waste time trolling for an easy lay at the Hive on a Saturday, and consequently, I was possibly a little…*frustrated.*

Unlike Constantine.

Who was at The Hive all the damn time.

And never left with the same man or woman twice.

Not that I noticed that either.

Constantine Ross might be extremely appealing on the surface, but there was absolutely no substance to him whatsoever.

He was a Krispy Kreme with a sassy mouth.

"I'm here! The party can now begin!" my sister Leandra announced as she hurried around the table at the front of the booth. "Sorry I'm late."

I straightened up to get a good look at her. Her long, dark hair was pinned up in buns that looked like lopsided mouse ears, and her Micah's Blooms t-shirt was rumpled and stained.

"It's fine. Everything okay with you and Gwynnie? Your text didn't say much."

"Yeah, she's fine. Home with Jared. Had to take her to the doctor, though. Four-hour screaming fit last night, which Google assured me could not *possibly* be teething since she's only five months old, but the doctor says it is." She shook her head. "Why does every single child bring some new challenge? This is my third rodeo, but every one of my girls has made me feel like a newbie."

"Didn't Cora start teething at three months?" I said, referring to our other niece. "You could've called Lauren. Aren't your super twin powers redeemable for shit like that?"

Leandra smirked. She removed the huge carryall strapped around her chest and stowed it under the table at the rear of the tent. "A few years back, when Olivia was born, Lauren told me I could call her anytime night or day. That our *twin bond* was more important than sleep, or some happy horseshit like that. But after two weeks with a newborn, I knew that was a fucking *lie* because there is *nothing* more important to a mom of littles than adequate sleep. So, twin sister or not, I won't call Lauren after eleven unless someone's hemorrhaging."

I laughed. "Okay, then you could have called Mase," I reminded her. "He doesn't have any kids yet, and he's a doctor. You know, an actual medical professional, with the fancy degrees and everything."

"Puh-*lease*. Mason is useless. He's the most laid-back doctor I've ever met. He'd be like, 'Oh, she's crying? Well, is her temperature under a hundred and seventy? Is she puking major organs? Has her head started spinning around spontaneously? No? She's fine.'" She rolled her eyes. "When he has kids, he'll be singing a different tune."

"Won't be long now, right? He and Victoria are getting serious."

"Sadly, yes." She held up a hand. "And before you get on my case about thinking no one is good enough for my baby brother, let me say that Lauren doesn't like her either, and you haven't been around Victoria enough to see the bullshit we've seen."

I gritted my teeth. Leandra wasn't wrong, but I didn't have to like it.

I'd had a great plan when I moved away. I was going to be back in Baxter *constantly*. I'd be able to take care of all the needed repairs on the rundown farmhouse I'd bought from my grandmother. I'd still be everyone's favorite Uncle Micah. I'd never miss a family dinner.

But shit had gotten busier and busier, and making time

was harder than I'd thought. If Mason hadn't moved into the house and taken it over, I'd be sunk.

"Oh, speaking of family functions," Leandra began. She ducked down to her purse and pulled out a piece of pink construction paper decorated with unicorn stickers and crayon writing. "This is an invitation to Olivia's sixth birthday party. Unicorn horns are optional, sparkles are not."

I looked down at the paper in amusement. "Her birthday's in October."

"Oh, yes. But we've been talking about party themes since January. We had to start a Pinterest board."

"I… have no idea what that means," I admitted. "But you tell my girl that I'll be there. Might require a minor miracle to get me in unicorns and sparkles, though."

"I'll tell her." Leandra grinned and set her hands on her hips. "So. What do you need me to do?"

I sighed. "You know you don't need to come. I hate pulling you away from your kids and—"

She held up a hand, palm-out. "We've discussed this. Lauren and I both like the break from our kids and our husbands. And you've done so much to help *us*—Lauren, Mase, and me—we want to pay it forward. We're proud of you."

I scratched at the back of my neck, uncomfortable with the praise.

"Maybe rearrange the bouquets out front?" I pointed toward the cellophane-wrapped flowers sitting in five-gallon buckets on the ground in front of the booth. "I kinda just threw them there earlier."

"On it. Hey, we might actually do a decent business today, huh? Now that we don't have any competition?" She tilted her head at the empty Ross booth and grinned, and I had to force myself not to look over there again.

"We're not trying to outsell anyone today. We're here to get…"

"Goodwill not sales," she recited, smiling again as she knelt down to do her work. "I know. But I've got a bit of a competitive streak. I'm like my big brother that way."

I grinned as I tweaked a display of potted daisies.

"Just FYI, though?" Leandra added. "Next time you come to a cookout, expect a family intervention."

"Pardon?"

"*Pardon?*" she mocked. "You heard me. There's no reason why you can't afford to hire another person to help you out at the shop." She popped her head up. "And I'm not talking about Saturdays, because Lauren and I have that covered. But what about all the other days?"

"I have help! Belle Porter is talented! She—"

"The lady who can only work four hours a day, four days a week? Not enough."

I shook my head. "If you only knew how hard it was to find skilled people or to train someone new. Not everyone learns about flowers at their grandmother's knee like we did."

"Oh, we learned a lot of shit at her knee, Micah, but arranging flowers wasn't part of it. You learned that all on your own, and someone else can too, while you relax. It'd be nice to see you fucking *smile* for a change."

"The cost is—"

"You forget that my husband is your accountant and I've *seen* your books. You can afford it."

"Hey! That's privileged information." I folded my arms over my chest and tried to scowl. It wasn't any more effective on her now than it had been when she was sixteen.

"And you're privileged to have a sister who hasn't shared it with the rest of the family. *Yet*. I'm worried about you! You work all the damn time. My precious babies forget what you look like."

I scowled. "That's low."

"I know!" she said sunnily. "But you know what? Forget that I care about you as a person. You're getting all these new contracts, Micah. Your business increased by a full *third* last year. You can't keep growing that way without help."

"It's under control," I told her. "I have a plan."

"Oh, gravy. You and your plans."

"Excuse me? In another six to eight months, if things keep going this way, I'll be in a position to hire a full-time person *and* keep Belle on part-time."

She shook her head. "The stress will kill you first, and I'll put 'He had a plan' on your tombstone."

I snorted. "Right under 'Best Brother Ever'?"

"Right under 'Stubborn Ass.'"

I laughed out loud. "Same difference."

"Oh my Lord!" someone yelled.

My head shot up to find Constantine Ross standing stock-still in the aisle between our tents, pointing at me and grinning.

"Ladies and gentlemen of O'Leary, the end times are upon us! Micah Bloom has *smiled*."

He was wearing his bright-blue Ross Landscaping polo, carrying a huge bucket of pre-wrapped bouquets, and dragging a cart packed with even more flowers and plants. His ink-black hair was bed-rumpled and damp with sweat, like he'd just woken up. His red-rimmed eyes and the oil smears on his shirt suggested he hadn't woken up *alone*.

How. Typical.

If I'd been smiling before, I sure as fuck wasn't smiling now.

"Mrs. O'Brien! Quick! Did you see Mr. Bloom smile?"

Con demanded of a startled, middle-aged woman wearing pink nurse's scrubs.

He set his bucket on the ground and dropped the handle of his cart so he could wrap one arm around her shoulders and extend the other one in a *slooooow* arc in front of them, like a carnival storyteller setting the stage.

"Legend tells," he said in a whisper loud enough that people at all the nearby booths turned to stare, "that when Micah Bloom's smile appears, great turmoil will sweep the land! Time will fly backward, crops will die, children will cry, men will curse their terrible misfortune, and *chaos will ensue.*"

Mrs. O'Brien shook her head, dishwater-blonde hair dislodging from her bun, but looked like she was fighting a grin. "Oh, Constantine, *really.*"

Constantine shook his head. "No, mark my words, Mrs. O'Brien! I know we all thought he was just a great, soulless beast of a man with a chip on his shoulder the size of Syracuse, but there's a *reason* no one in this town has ever seen Micah Bloom smile before. I feel a portent in the air!"

He gave a dramatic head-to-toe shudder, and I heard more than one spectator snickering.

I folded my arms across my chest, desperately unamused.

Meanwhile, my least-favorite sister Leandra was *shaking* with suppressed laughter. I glared at her, but she only laughed harder.

"Mrs. O'Brien, this is the part where you're supposed to yell, *Can no one save us?*" Constantine stage-whispered to his reluctant accomplice.

Mrs. O'Brien, who was all-out grinning now, rolled her eyes and obediently complied. "Can no one save us?"

Constantine shook his head sadly. "I just don't know. If

only I had someone who knew more about fairy tales. Someone like… *Oh my gosh*, Sivan Siegel? Is that you?"

The menace with the bubble ass moved away from Mrs. O'Brien and pointed at a little blonde girl with thick glasses standing in the gathered crowd. "You are *just* the expert I need. What can be done to break a curse, Sivan?"

Sivan looked around at the adults watching her and shook her head shyly.

Leandra leaned closer to me over the table. "Is the Ross kid single?" she demanded in a whisper. "Will he marry me?"

"He's like a dozen years younger than you, perv. And he's my biggest competitor. *And* you're married."

"*Pssht.* Details. When it's meant to be, it's meant to be. Jared will understand."

Meanwhile, Constantine, who had no right to be so damn attractive, was kneeling in front of Sivan in a way that had more than one mother in the assembled group smiling like her ovaries were imploding at the sight.

"Wanna whisper it to me?" Constantine asked.

Little Sivan nodded and bent toward his ear.

Con's eyes widened. "Oh, no! Are you sure?"

She nodded.

"Nuh-uh. *No.* That's not gonna work."

"Yeah-huh!" Sivan insisted. "It is. It's the only way."

"Only true love's kiss can break the spell?" Constantine demanded. He looked me up and down, shook his head, and solemnly pronounced, "Then we're all *doomed*."

Everyone laughed — whether at him or me or both of us, I wasn't quite sure. Leandra's laugh was loudest of all.

Needless to say, I didn't find it funny.

I had no problem taking a joke—I wouldn't have lasted long in my family if I couldn't laugh at myself, after all— but I couldn't help thinking this man-child needed to be taught a lesson in humility, and I would dearly love to be the one to give it to him.

I shook my head at Constantine slowly.

Con stood up and had the audacity to wink, his blue eyes dancing at me like we were in on the joke together, some kind of comedy act where I was the straight man.

Newsflash for Constantine Ross: I'd never been a straight man, in any sense of the word.

I deliberately looked away.

"You know," Leandra began a moment later, but I glared at her so fiercely she went back to rearranging bouquets without finishing her sentence.

I tweaked each plant on my table half an inch to the right and absolutely did *not* notice Constantine's fine bubble ass shaking to the beat of whatever new song Pete was playing as the crowd dispersed and he set up his display.

Pete's voice broke in as the song ended. "Thank you everyone, thank you. One more announcement." He gave a long-suffering sigh. "Parker says he's actually serving the burgers at *eleven*, not eleven thirty! So roll your clocks back or whatever. Alrighty! Next up is a classic tune…"

Constantine had finished setting up his booth—by which I mean throwing shit haphazardly on his table with no rhyme or reason whatsoever—and was leaning on his elbows, watching people pass by. But when Pete spoke, Con's jaw dropped, and he looked at me with eyes nearly glowing with laughter.

"Oh mah gahd. It's happening," Con said in a hushed voice. "Time is moving backward."

It was *not* funny. Provoking menace.

Meanwhile, Leandra-the-traitor snickered again.

"Are you about done down there?" I demanded, peering over the front of the table.

"Um. Yes?" she answered meekly, twisting her lips to hide her smile. "Just about?"

I noticed that Constantine, despite his cluttered table, was doing a brisk business, greeting customers by name and giving each of them a friendly grin. I'd sold exactly one bouquet in this entire morning, and the woman had been looking over her shoulder the entire time like Angela Ross might come along and accuse her of infidelity.

You're here to earn goodwill, I reminded myself. *Patience.*

While my wedding flower business and corporate clients had picked up steadily in recent months, I'd vastly underestimated how loyal the average O'Learian was to the town's established small businesses. Ross Landscaping and Flowers had been the only local option for decades, and by God, O'Learians were determined to keep it that way. Didn't matter that the Rosses didn't even *have* a storefront, so you could only buy their arrangements at the farmer's market, through special order, or in a ridiculously tiny two-foot-wide section of the produce department at Lyon's Imperial. Didn't matter that the artistry of their "arrangements" was about the same quality little Olivia produced in her dandelion bouquets.

Ross had gotten here first, so Ross was the only right choice.

There were times when I questioned my decision to move here at all. Baxter, about nine miles and six million light-years southwest of O'Leary, wasn't any larger either in population or landmass, but it didn't have the same fucking *intensity* that O'Leary brought to every-damn-thing. In Baxter, we didn't have elaborate festivals every second weekend. We didn't have live entertainment at the farmer's market because we didn't *have* a farmer's market; we bought our produce at Wegman's like normal people. We might know our neighbors, but we didn't have the whole town on speed dial, like we were all one big extended family. We didn't live and die by *who got there first*.

I sucked in a deep breath and exhaled it slowly.

Things were fine. I had a plan. Attitudes would change. I'd make sure of it.

"Hey, there."

Startled, I looked up to find a tall, bearded dude standing to the right of the table. A *customer*. And here I was, too distracted by Constantine's ridiculousness to even greet the man properly.

"Good morning," I said smoothly. "Can I help you with something?"

"Micah's Blooms," he said, pointing at the banner hanging from the table. "You're the shop in town with the pride flag hanging in front of your store?"

"Yes," I said cautiously, but the man's smile widened and warmed by several degrees.

"You have beautiful window displays."

"Oh. Thank you," I said, stunned by the rare compliment. "Can I interest you in some cut flowers? Or a potted plant?"

"Maybe, yeah. I'm Robert," the man said, holding out his hand.

"Oh, right." I nodded and shook it. "Micah." I waited expectantly. "So. A bouquet? Or a plant?"

"What do you do besides flowers… Micah?"

I furrowed my brow. "Pardon?"

Robert shrugged a shoulder all the way to his ear and tilted his head. "I mean, you can't think about flowers twenty-four seven, right? Do you like to drink coffee?" His gaze was direct, and his smile was definitely flirtatious.

"Occasionally."

Leandra popped her head up and dusted her hands on her ass. "Are you kidding? Micah loves coffee. *Lives* for coffee. Drink, drink, drink, all day long." She grinned. "Isn't that right, Micah?"

I gave the man a tight smile.

He was maybe thirty and good-looking—brown hair, brown eyes, brown beard, a nice, compact body beneath his skin-tight polo. He also seemed mature and very, very interested. There should've been no reason for me to hesitate. But I couldn't help thinking of the fact that I had no time as it was—no time for my family, let alone my friends, let alone some guy who was gonna be all demanding and whatnot.

Business first. Personal shit would come later. When the time was right. Not all of us were interested in doing things the easy way.

I gave Con a little glare, but he wasn't looking at me.

"Jeremiah! Jeremiah, get back here this *instant*!"

A little brown-haired boy giggled and grinned over his shoulder as a woman with haphazard red curls and a baby carrier chased after him. The boy ran down the aisle and ducked under the table where Con was standing.

"I'm not Jeremiah, I'm a dinosaur!" he yelled.

The mother knelt down as best she could with the bulky carrier strapped to her front. "Jeremiah! We don't have time for this! We're late as it is!"

"Sorry, ma'am, I haven't seen anyone named Jeremiah," Constantine told her. "There's just me and my pet dinosaur."

She gave a helpless laugh as she looked up at Con. "Is that so?"

"Yup. His name is Celery, because that's all I feed him, he sleeps under my bed, and he does chores all day long because that's his favorite thing."

"No, it's not!" he yelled.

"Oh my gosh! Celery!" Con peered under the table. "You can *talk?*"

I glanced at my sister, who'd stood up and was watching the display with her hand clutched to her chest like it was the most adorable thing ever. I rolled my eyes.

Jeremiah giggled. "You're funny."

"I am," Con agreed, batting his eyelashes at me from across the aisle. "All the smartest people think so. And if you come out right now, I'll give you a flower to give your mom so she won't be mad."

There was no way that line would have worked for me if I'd tried it on any of my nieces, but Jeremiah pulled himself out from under the table happily, like Con was a fucking dinosaur-whisperer, and I amended my earlier opinion.

Constantine charmed children, grumpy old men, and *dinosaurs, too.*

Unfortunately, as I watched, Jeremiah's arm bumped the table just enough that one of the ceramic pots of flowers Con had stacked there hit the dirt with a *crash* and smashed into tiny pieces. It was hard to say who was more horrified, the boy or the mother, but the mother recovered more quickly.

"For goodness' sake, Jeremiah! Look what you've done. Do you have the money to pay for this? Hmm? I *told you* to stay by me. Come here right this second and say you're sorry."

Jeremiah's lip quivered, and his eyes filled with tears.

"It's fine," Constantine told her. For possibly the first time ever, his trademark grin was gone. "It was an accident. He's just a kid."

"I was trying to teach him…"

"Sure. I know. But he feels terrible already," Constantine interrupted.

I made a motion at Leandra and then down at the bouquets. She nodded and brought one over to the boy.

"Here," she said. "Give that to your mom, sweetie pie."

The little boy swiped his nose, grabbed the flowers, and handed them over.

His mother looked from Constantine to me, then took the flowers from Jeremiah with a murmured, "Thank you, baby." She sighed. "I know it was an accident. Be more careful, okay?"

Behind me, Robert cleared his throat.

Oh. Right.

"Sorry," I told him. "Got distracted by drama. I was gonna help you find some flowers."

"No," he returned. "You were gonna agree to meet me for coffee." I lifted one eyebrow and he flushed. "At least I hope you are." He pulled a card from his pocket and set it down on the table. "Call me." He winked and walked off in the same direction as the little boy and his mother.

But as I watched him walk away, for some reason my eyes were drawn across the aisle to Constantine Ross. And sure enough, the man was hunched over, elbows on his table, watching me again.

"You see what's happening here, don't you?" he demanded. It looked like he was *trying* to muster a teasing smile but couldn't quite get there. "Crops dying, children crying?" He gave a pointed look down at the smashed flowerpot next to his table and then in the direction Jeremiah had gone. "Prophecy's getting a little *too* real. I'm starting to scare myself."

The little shit looked anything but scared. He looked fucking delighted with himself.

He frowned suddenly. "Do you remember what came next? Something with pigs or…"

I ignored him. I remembered perfectly well, but I

wouldn't give him the satisfaction of thinking I'd been paying attention.

For a second there, with the little boy, I'd thought… But no. Constantine Ross was an idiot, plain and simple.

I became extremely busy tidying the already tidy box of wrapping supplies on the table at the rear of the tent.

Leandra walked over to stand next to me. She leaned her back against the table and watched me organizing ribbons in rainbow order without saying a word.

After a minute, I let out a breath. "That kid makes me insane."

"The one who thinks he's a dinosaur?"

I shot her a look.

"Oh, the adorable-as-fuck Ross kid." She smiled brightly. "You know, I think you might be protesting too much."

I exhaled an exasperated breath. "God, no. He's ridiculous, Leandra. He's so immature." I threw a hand out in the direction of his booth. "As you've witnessed."

"He's charming!"

"*Ugh*. Et tu, Leandra?"

She snickered. "He's young!"

"So? *I* wasn't like that at his age. *You* weren't." I rubbed a hand over my forehead, fighting to encapsulate all that Constantine was. "He's a loose cannon. He just shows up as late as he wants, says whatever he wants. Bursts out with a joke or an insult and never considers the consequences. He's like… the antithesis of all I stand for."

I glanced at her and saw that she was looking across the aisle at Con, a small smile playing on her face.

"What?"

She shrugged. "Just thinking. It's funny how you deal with the bitchiest brides and grooms, all these people who act like you owe them something and expect you to kiss their asses, and you're *fine*. You're *Micah Bloom*," she said, mimicking my deep voice. "It all rolls right off you, because you've got a *plan*." She looked at me and wrinkled her nose as she grinned. "But the Ross kid tells one little joke…"

"It's not the same," I said sourly. "And it wasn't a *little* joke."

"No, it was actually a really funny and well-executed one," she said, chuckling again like she was replaying it in her mind. "The kind you usually appreciate. But you seem hell-bent on *not* finding this one funny. Why is that?"

Because being teased by the cocky little shit was intolerable? Because we were absolutely not friends? So many reasons.

I chucked a spool of wire back into the box with more force than necessary, and Leandra watched with that annoying little smile still fastened to her mouth.

A second later, she added, "You know, I did a little research on the Rosses."

"Research?"

"With the internet, Micah." She rolled her eyes. "It's a powerful form of magic that exists even in Baxter, New York."

I rolled my eyes in return. "I think I've heard of it once or twice. But there's no O'Leary TMZ. And besides, why would you look *him* up?"

She grinned. "Okay, first, I'm really proud of you for knowing what TMZ is, big brother. Sincerely. You're making strides every day. But second, why *wouldn't* I look them up? They're your biggest competition. It'd be foolish not to."

I frowned. I'd never considered that before, and it didn't sit right with me now. "Leandra, I'm not stooping to gossip and smear campaigns."

Leandra propped her hands on her hips and widened her eyes. Her little buns made her look way younger than her actual thirty-something years. "*Psssht.* Am I Olivia Pope? Are we on *Scandal* right now?"

I blinked in confusion, and Leandra grimaced.

"The TMZ reference made me temporarily forget who I was talking to. I bet you haven't watched actual TV in years, for anything other than sports and snowfall predictions, have you? Still watching your VHS tapes?"

"Leandra."

She waved a hand dismissively and levered herself up onto the table. "Fine, fine. But come on, you know I'm not gonna dig up dirt on the Rosses. *Dirt* implies a secret no one else knows, and I don't think that exists in this town. I just meant that details are important to get a read on people. Frankly, you probably should've done that before you moved here—studied the playing field, learned who the big players are, figured out your common interests, made friends."

I shook my head. "I'm not here to make friends, I'm here to—"

Leandra cut me off. "Do you even hear yourself?" she demanded. "Running a business and having a personal life are not mutually exclusive concepts."

"Wow, is this déjà vu? Because I feel like we already covered that ground this morning. Next."

"But—"

"*Next.*"

"Fine. Whatever," she grumbled. "Wait until next week. If you think I'm bad, see how fired up Lauren is about this."

"Oh, joy."

Leandra smiled. "Anyway, back to my low-key investigation. Your boy lost his dad, like, ten or eleven years ago."

"Not my boy," I replied instinctively. "And everyone knows his dad passed away. Your investigative skills aren't impressing me."

Leandra ignored me. "Constantine had to be, what? Thirteen? Fourteen? Tough age, Micah. He got into trouble a good bit. Lots of mentions of him in the police blotter. Reminded me of Mason, back in the day. You remember how he—"

"*No one* was as bad as Mason back in the day," I interrupted, losing all patience with this conversation. I pointed an accusing finger at her. "And let me remind you, Mase changed himself around *completely*, way before he was twenty. I get that Constantine's had his share of troubles. But haven't we all? Remember when MoonFlower spent all the grocery money mom sent home to buy—"

"Composting worms," we finished together.

"Or the time when you were eight and MoonFlower hid her dime bag in your doll's diaper?"

"Seven." She sighed. "I remember it was Tabitha Marie's first foray into a life of crime."

"Uh-huh. My point is, a hard childhood's not an excuse for failing to take life seriously."

"I know, Micah. But maybe—" She hesitated. "Maybe sometimes you take life *too* seriously, you know?"

"What?" The comment stung, maybe more than it should have.

"Not a criticism, just an observation." She grabbed my hand and smiled. "The kid seems nice. He's kind to children. He teases without being cruel. And I have trouble believing that anyone that nice can be the total—"

"Constantine. Luciano. Ross!"

Leandra and I exchanged a look and turned as a unit to watch Angela Ross stride up the aisle toward the Ross Landscaping booth.

"What is this I hear, about you being over an *hour late*?"

Con, who had been smiling and chatting with Henry Lattimer, stood up straighter as she approached, and Henry walked quickly away. "Mama," he said, palms out, "I can explain."

"Sure you can." She flipped her long, dark braid over her shoulder, noticed the variety of onlookers, and dropped her voice to a furious whisper... which was, nevertheless, still audible if you were standing stock-still, trying to read her lips, which Leandra and I may or may not have been doing.

"And is there a reason why you were making a spectacle of yourself in front of the entire market?" she hissed. "Caroline O'Brien told me you were a *hoot*, and Poppy tells me you've been mocking that sweet, adorable Micah Bloom!"

She made air quotes around the adjectives, but I made a mental note to find Poppy and send her some flowers.

Con looked outraged. "I wasn't *mocking* him. I was only teasing, and..." He lifted his gaze to mine before he looked away.

"*Mmhmm.*" Angela nodded. She sighed so forcefully, it was a wonder the tent didn't cave in around them. "I'm going to get the rest of the baskets from my truck and check in on Pete."

"I can get—"

"No, Constantine. You stay here. I'll be back in half an hour."

She might as well have said *think about your sins*.

Con stood to one side of the tent, seething and trying to hide it. I should have looked away, but I couldn't. I felt like I was waiting for something, though I wasn't sure what... until Constantine's stormy eyes came to mine. He set his jaw and raised his chin in challenge, which, okay, actually did raise him a degree in my estimation.

Maybe *half* a degree.

"And men will curse their terrible misfortune," I mused, quoting the end of his stupid *prophecy* from earlier. "Maybe you *are* psychic, Ross."

I'd like to say I didn't notice the way his eyes flashed hot at that, but I did, and I felt an answering tug in my gut, too, before I reminded myself who he was, and who *I* was, and all the reasons why I disliked him.

It was mostly the joy of seeing him taken down a peg that made me excited. *Obviously.*

Except Constantine didn't look cowed. Not in the slightest. In fact, his lips tipped up into a smile that widened to a grin, like the sunrise breaking over the horizon.

"Aw, Micah," he said, voice soft as velvet. "I knew you remembered."

———

MAYBE TWENTY MINUTES LATER, after a few completed sales that nearly restored my faith in humanity and a "reggae-inspired remix of "Uptown Girl'" that destroyed it again, I turned to Leandra.

"This is ridiculous. There's no need for both of us to be here. I'm gonna go grab something to eat, and when I come back, you can go home."

"Really? I was gonna duck out to your apartment to pump in a minute, but if you're sure..."

"I'm sure. I don't have any orders to do this afternoon, and I can break this down by myself." I motioned toward the plants and the buckets of flowers, which were nearly as full as when I'd arrived.

"Oh, that would be amazing!" Leandra said. "I could let Jared take the girls to the playground, as planned, and I could go home and *nap*."

I snorted, kissed her on the forehead, grabbed my wallet, and ducked out.

I scarfed down a hotdog, then bought myself a frozen coffee drink at a little booth that Moira from Fanaille was running. I sipped it slowly as I strolled back toward the tent, enjoying the warm sun and thinking about the week ahead with a little bit of dread. Leandra wasn't wrong in saying I was too busy for my own good. I was going to be flat out, between supply runs and arrangement prep in the mornings, working up quotes and meeting with clients during the day, and dealing with billing and invoicing at night. It was a good thing on the one hand, but a—

"... *Micah Bloom!*"

I was cutting through two rows of back-to-back booths, on my way back to my own, and I paused when I heard my name spoken. From where I was standing, there was nothing visible but the empty alley between the white canvas backs of the booths and the hard-packed dirt of the parking lot. There wasn't a soul in sight, let alone anyone talking to me. And I thought for a second I'd imagined it, but then the voice came again.

"Well, stop letting him bother you! The last thing we need is for people to think there's any animosity between us and *that man*."

"Even if there is?" Constantine's voice was subdued but unmistakable, and I realized that I'd stopped behind *his* booth, so the person he was speaking to must be...

"There isn't," Angela said stoutly. "Animosity means acknowledging that he's competition, and he's not."

"Come on, Mama," Constantine chided gently. "You're

kidding, right? Not competition? Weren't you complaining just yesterday about how he won that wedding contract you were hoping to get? The one for Senator Whatshisname?"

I sucked on my drink and tried not to be *too* smug about that particular win.

Marissa Corcoran, stepdaughter of Senator Marcus Turnbull, was getting married next Valentine's Day, and it was going to be the wedding of the year, no doubt. She'd opted to have it over at the Scarlet Maple Inn, one of the hottest wedding destinations in the area, and thanks to her step-daddy's need to appeal to the voters, she was committed to using only local vendors for everything from her dress to her cake to her flowers.

I'd had no doubt my designs would blow anything the Rosses came up with out of the water—they used better-than-average stock, yes, but their designs were ridiculously basic—but I also knew that an eye-catching design wouldn't guarantee me a win when Ross Landscaping had loyal supporters at the Scarlet Maple just like they had in O'Leary.

I'd needed a showstopper display at a bargain price, so I'd sourced celestial-pink roses through my floral supply house. They were gonna cost a fucking *mint*, but were sure to be eye-catching and unique. I'd also deliberately cut my bid low, so low I was going to take a huge loss on the contract because I knew the publicity I gained would be worth it.

And the strategy had worked. The bride's mother had signed the contract yesterday, and the Scarlet Maple Inn had added me to their website as the florist of record for the job.

"He didn't win it. He stole it," Angela said, "right from under our noses. You should have seen the way *that man* swaggered into the Scarlet Maple like he owned the place. He's not competition. He's a *thief.*"

"You can't steal what's not yours in the first place." Con sounded so tired I nearly felt bad for him.

Partying all night did that to a person, I reminded myself.

"And what about the contract at the Crabapple Bed and Breakfast? That *is* ours. Or it was. Dana Cobb's managing the place now, and she told me *Micah Bloom* approached them with a bid for the arrangements for the guest rooms. They haven't officially signed it yet, but it's lower than anything we can quote."

"Wait, I don't understand. How can he be charging that much less when we have our own greenhouse? Wasn't that investment supposed to cut costs?"

"It will in the long term, but in the short term…" Angela hesitated, then said firmly, "I took out some loans."

"What?" Constantine's surprise was closer to betrayal. "Against the business?"

"It was the only option," Angela said matter-of-factly. "We needed the greenhouse in order to stay competitive in the floral market."

"But why do we have to *stay* in the floral market? Why can't we focus on landscaping, like we used to when Dad was alive? Mama, I know we've talked about this in the past, but I've been doing research and I've taken a bunch of online classes. There aren't a lot of really good *local* landscape designers."

"Constantine."

"No, listen. *Listen* this time, okay? The Scarlet Maple is planning to renovate half their grounds next summer— build a wedding pavilion, a formal English garden, the whole nine yards. We could get that contract, Mama. I could work up schematics. I've been doing these tutorials and—"

"No."

"But—"

"Constantine, I said *no*. I have tried and tried to explain this to you. We have committed to a path. We can't just go around dabbling here and experimenting there. That's not how businesses run. That's not how *life* runs."

"I don't want to dabble! I want to—"

"You're not sixteen anymore," she insisted, and for the first time ever, I found myself almost wanting to defend Constantine Ross. *Immature man-child he might be, but let the kid finish a fucking sentence, lady.*

I sucked on my coffee again and rolled my eyes as the feeling passed. Leandra would kill herself laughing if she could see me now.

Con laughed humorlessly. "When I was sixteen, I spent every afternoon doing community service at the police station and every weekend working for Ross for free. The only thing that's changed is that Mitch pays me for working part-time now. So one might say I *do* live like I'm sixteen."

"You're only part-time until Mitch can get the council to approve a full-time position," Angela said, in what was probably supposed to be a comforting way but missed the mark thoroughly.

"And what good will that do Ross Landscaping?" Con demanded. "If you can't afford to pay me, you can't afford to pay someone to take my place."

Angela was silent, and Con barreled ahead. "I've already run the numbers, Mama. We'd need one more full-time person at most, if we subcontracted the excavation work. I could quit working at the police station—"

"Just leave your job at the station? Leave a job you love, and leave Mitch high and dry after eight years? Look, sweetheart," she said in a softer tone. "You know I support you and your brothers in whatever you want to do. Julian wasn't interested in anything but vet school, and I supported him, even though it would have made things much easier if he'd been interested in the business. Now Theo splits his time between landscaping and working at the hardware store, and you joined Mitch at the police station part-time, and I supported you both in those choices, even though it meant things were tight with only Jonathan and Carlos on full-time. But you need to start living in reality. We have chosen the course we're going to take and we are sticking to it."

"You chose," Con said softly.

"Pardon me?" Angela's voice was deadly, daring him to repeat his words.

Con remained silent.

"Yes. *I* chose. Mistakes have consequences, Constantine," Angela said.

"Yeah," he said sounding defeated. "I get it."

You know, I'd have liked to think I wasn't the kind of person who'd stand in the sunshine, staring at the back of a tent, listening to a conversation that was *none of my business* between two people I didn't even like.

Sadly, I was *exactly* that sort of person. And when Angela started talking again, I didn't even think about moving. I was fucking fascinated by this new side of Constantine. Hell, I was fascinated to learn there *was* a side of Constantine beneath the happy-go-lucky exterior.

"I hate fighting with you about this," Angela sighed. "I hate disappointing you. I hate that things are so close to the bone right now, and that I couldn't shield you from it like I have Julian and Theo. You shouldn't be worrying about the business."

"Of course I should. It's my job."

Angela sighed again. "You work hard, Constantine,

and I appreciate it. I wish things were different. I wish I had the money to let you run wild with your landscaping idea. Heck, I wish I had the money to *pay* you."

"About that," Con said. "At the beginning of the year, you said you might be able to give me and Theo a little something this summer, once the new contracts started coming in. Do you think—"

"Oh, Con." Angela blew out a breath. "I don't even know how we'll make payroll if—*when*—we lose the Crabapple. I'll figure it out, I promise, but I just don't see how there'll be any extra."

"Right. No, of course. I get that," he said in a tone of voice I knew and understood perfectly because I'd used it so many times myself, when I'd needed money for new jeans and there wasn't any, when I'd needed money for school fees and there wasn't any, when I'd needed money for college and there wasn't any. "Don't worry about it, Mama. I'll make do."

Recognition flashed through me like a gunshot, and for the barest second, I wished I could find a way to help him—

Uh-oh.

Oh, no.

Danger, danger, danger.

Shit, shit, shit.

I walked away slowly and made a point of emerging from the alley between the booths much farther up. I stopped for a minute to admire Ma Li's collection of stained-glass candle holders, and then stopped again to buy some rainbow chard and strawberries from the Stillkeys' vegetable stand for my dinner. I walked as slowly as possible, because I knew if I went back to my stall and spotted Constantine again, I'd have to think about the conversation I'd overheard.

And if I thought about the conversation, I'd remember the way he'd sounded.

And if I remembered the way he'd sounded, the flash of *recognition* I'd felt would spark into something danger-ously like… *sympathy*.

And if I allowed myself to feel sympathy for Con, then I'd start to remember the other things I'd noticed. Like the way he'd stood up for that little boy. And the way he looked when he smiled. And that fucking bubble ass.

And if I remembered all that, the insanely stupid idea that had popped into my head back there would become a reality.

And I'd never be rid of him.

Chapter Three

CONSTANTINE

"Hit me again, barkeep."

Jordan, who'd been tending bar at The Hive nearly as long as I'd been coming here—which was to say, for a lot longer than was strictly legal—snorted as she refilled my drink.

"I don't think I've ever seen you depressed before, Connie," she said, twitching back her long fall of sleekly curled red hair with one brightly tattooed arm. I thought, just like I'd thought for years, that Jordan looked like a pinup girl who'd time-traveled to the future and decided she liked it here. "It's adorable. You're like a bewildered little kitten."

"Just what every man dreams of having a beautiful woman compare him to. A *kitten*."

One perfectly arched eyebrow lifted and Jordan's eyes widened. "Ruh-roh. This is more serious than I thought." She leaned her elbows on the shining wood countertop and ignored the other customers vying for her attention. "Did some boy dare to reject you? Or was it a girl, you bisexual beast, you? Tell Jordan all about it, precious, and we'll come up with a plan. I'll hold your earrings."

I sighed despondently. "My sex life is the least of my concerns."

"Well, at least there's that, then, right? Cute girl at ten o'clock looks like she might have an eye for you."

I slumped against the bar and didn't bother to look. "Not in the mood."

"Whoa. That's like hearing the Pillsbury Doughboy isn't in the mood for cookies."

I smiled wanly, because I knew she expected it.

"What's up, honey?"

"Eh. Just realizing that my life is pretty much fucked."

I'd gotten a call from Joe Cross earlier. A call in which he'd told me, in the same hushed tones that a doctor emerging from the operating room might use to deliver bad news to a waiting family, "It's the transmission, Connie. I'm afraid there's nothing I can do." I swear, I'd heard the high-pitched squeal of a heart monitor flatlining, except the patient was my bank account, and there was no hope of resuscitation.

But worse than knowing *my* finances were DOA was knowing that my mother's finances—Ross Landscaping's finances—were just as fucked. Thanks to me.

Everyone in town knew the story of Con-the-dumbass and his final, terrible teenage prank. Over the years, the outrage had kind of worn off, and most people remembered the audacity of it, the stupidity of it. They laughed over it, like Joe Cross had. Not a lot of people in town— hell, not a lot of people *in my own family*—knew that the real tragedy had occurred long after Trent Gaynor's car had been towed away and turned to scrap metal. My mother had paid them off somehow and had fought tooth and claw to keep the business running. She hadn't wanted to burden my brothers—or my aunt and cousin—with it, but she couldn't help burdening me.

Which was fair, since it should have been my burden.

"It can't be *that* bad," Jordan said, tilting her head. "You're young, you're healthy, you're hot."

I mustered a smile. "Well, I mean, *that's* true," I said, and I smiled when she laughed. Deliberately playing it easy, I told her, "But I was late to the market today, and my mother ripped me a new one in front of the guy who's basically my nemesis."

"Aww," she said. "And that's what's got you down?"

"It was humiliating."

It kind of had been. Micah Bloom, quoting my own stupid lines back at me like the superior know-it-all he was, rocking on the balls of his feet the whole time and smiling that little smile that made me want to… *ugh*. That had been the bright-red cherry on the shit sundae of this day. I shouldn't have provoked him, but God, he was a tempting target, all smug and reserved and buttoned up and gorgeous and—

Oh, Lord no. All I needed was to have my fucked-up mind twist Micah Bloom into someone attractive or desirable. The very idea made me shudder.

"You're too sweet to have a nemesis, Con." Jordan ran a hand through my hair, like the sister I'd never had. "Besides, with your smile and your positive attitude, everything will work out."

I sat up straighter and gave her a grin. "Of course it will. Can't keep me down for long." But I wasn't sure how I was supposed to fight bad luck and past-Con's shitty choices.

Jordan looked at me thoughtfully. "When the Universe gives you problems, it usually gives you solutions, too. You just need to keep your eyes open."

I smiled and nodded. "You've been working on your bartender speeches, haven't you?"

She leaned in confidingly. "Little bit. I'm trying to be less fortune-cookie, more new-age. What do you think?"

"It was beautiful. Very *Chicken Soup for the Soul*."

She grinned and threw an extra handful of cherries in my drink before she went to serve someone else. I hunched over my glass again and sighed.

All around me, the bar was hopping in typical Saturday night fashion. At one end of the room, a small dance floor was packed with half-dressed guys and girls moving together in beautiful chaos, like swarms of butterflies under flashing lights. This end of the room was dominated by a large bar ringed with stools and maybe a half-dozen high-top tables. Almost every stool was filled, and still more people crowded in around us, trying to catch the attention of one of the three servers and more importantly, trying to catch the attention of whoever they most wanted to leave with that evening.

This was my Saturday night routine—head out, look cute, get picked up by the hottest and most persistent guy or gal at The Hive, fuck or be fucked, and whistle a happy tune as I drove home a couple hours later. The sights were familiar, the rhythm was comforting, the rules were simple and understood, and the expectations were *minimal*, unlike the rest of my life.

But for maybe the first time ever, the whole thing left me cold. I needed something… different. But I didn't know exactly what I needed, let alone how to get it.

And wasn't *that* the story of my whole damn life?

"Hey, cutie. Looking for distraction?"

I swiveled my head toward the blond who'd literally elbowed into the spot at my side and was now leaning said elbow on the bar, effectively forming a wall to the left of me.

"Don't think I'm distractible tonight, buddy, but thanks anyway."

"Maybe just *one* drink? My name's Tyler. What's yours?"

I looked the guy up and down. He was short, blond, and twinky, with gray-blue eyes that stood out from his tan skin. Good-looking. Very.

And I was angry at myself because this was exactly the kind of distraction I needed after today, but instead of feeling my dick plumping or my belly giving a pleasant sort of swoop, I felt precisely nothing.

"I've already got a drink, Tyler. And I've had a shit day. I'm not real good company. But thanks anyway."

"You know, sometimes when you feel least distractible, that's when you most need distraction," the guy said solemnly. "The problem is also the solution."

"Have you and Jordan been reading the same books?" I demanded.

"Huh?"

"Nothing. Listen, I admire the, uh, perseverance. Okay? But I am not in the mood for whatever you're offering." I waved a hand in the general direction of his crotch.

Tyler's eyes glinted with humor. "What do you think I'm offering exactly?" He waved a hand, copying my motion. "To suck you off in the back hallway? To take you back to my hotel to fuck?" The person on the stool behind Tyler moved away and Tyler dropped into the empty seat without hesitation.

"Yeah." I felt my cheeks get warm. "Any of those."

"Good, because I don't recall offering. I said *distraction,* not… random back-room fuckery. Do those mean the same thing to you?"

"Well…" I licked my lips, embarrassed. Actually, to me they generally did.

"Ah. One of *those*." Tyler rolled his eyes and turned toward the bar, signaling for Jordan to bring him a beer. "You need to fuck ten thousand frogs before you find your soul mate and get your happily ever after?"

I snickered. "Happily ever after? I don't know if there *is* such a thing." But I thought of my parents, and of the way Caelan James looked at his new boyfriend, Ash. "For me, anyway," I added. "I don't think *everyone* finds a soul mate."

"Well, *I* believe there's someone out there for everyone." Jordan set Tyler's beer in front of him and Tyler gave her a smile, then contemplated the glass. "A person who comes along at precisely the right time and changes the way you see yourself, the way you feel about the future… everything. I've seen it happen."

"Uh-*huh*. And you think you might find this life-changing soul mate *here*?" I looked around the overly warm room, at the group of men near us who were laughing a little too loud, at the other men and women standing at the high tables in the corners sucking down alcohol like they were hoping for a temporary transformation into someone bold and confident, at the guys and gals on the dance floor grinding with total abandon. I knew most of them by sight. I knew many of them… more intimately. And they were all lovely, *lovely* folks, but there was not a single magical unicorn among them. Still, I saluted Tyler with my drink for being optimistic enough to try. "Good luck."

Tyler snorted. "I don't need to *find* him. I already met my soul mate back when we were kids. Alex and I were next-door neighbors. Friends." He took a sip of beer. "I'm in town because I'm planning a wedding."

"Oh, yeah? Lucky you." I thought about asking who he

was using for his florist, but I realized I didn't care. That part of the business was not my arena at all.

I put my drink down again. "So you're here to… what? Preach the good news of happy monogamy to us poor saps? Remind yourself how lucky you are that you won't have to deal with scenes like this anymore?"

"Uh, no. Neither." Tyler smiled, but it wasn't a happy thing. "I'm here looking for distraction myself." He shrugged. "See, Alex is getting married next February… but not to *me*."

"Oh." I winced and sucked in a breath through my teeth. "Ouch."

"Yeah. In fact—" Tyler cleared his throat, darting a glance at me. "He's marrying my sister Marissa."

I pursed my lips for a second, trying to comprehend the enormity of *that* shit show.

"And I'm the Man of Honor. So I'm here in town helping Marissa taste cake and stuff. Helping her figure out which ones Alex would like best, since he can't be here."

"Oh, fuck. That is…" I shook my head. A guy who could still believe in soul mates after *that* was either a really good person or certifiably insane. Either way, I found myself distracted.

"I'm Constantine," I said belatedly, offering the guy my hand. "Con."

"Nice to meet you," Tyler said, shaking it gravely.

"You succeeded in distracting me against my will."

"Glad I'm useful for something." He sipped at his beer. "I love my sister, you know? But if I had to stay at the Inn and settle one more argument between her and my stepmother about chicken piccata versus swordfish gremolata, I was going to find a sword and impale myself on it."

"Thus causing a one-hundred-percent increase in the local violent crime stats. You made a wise choice."

Tyler laughed and took another sip of his drink. "So, okay, what am I distracting *you* from?"

"Oh." I waved a hand. "Comparatively nothing. Just a bad day."

"*Comparatively* nothing? I see. Because this is the misery Olympics, where only one of us can win gold?" He smirked. "It's your turn to distract me by telling me about *your* problems. Spill."

I sighed. "Look, I appreciate it, but I'm not one for oversharing. Bitching about my problems does no good."

He shrugged. "Same. I have *one* close friend, and he lives three thousand miles away and refuses to discuss my love life. But I'm literally a stranger in a bar, begging you to tell me your sob story. So why not vent, just this once?"

I narrowed my eyes. "My car needs a new transmission, my bank account needs CPR, my life needs some kind of Oprah extreme-makeover, and there's this guy who —" I forced myself to stop. "Never mind."

Tyler's eyes narrowed. "No, no. I have a feeling this is the good part. This guy *who*?"

I shook my head. "This guy who's a jerk, that's all. A superior, condescending *jerk* who can't take a joke."

"Uh-*huh*. And why's he a jerk?"

"He's not the point of this story," I said, in lieu of an answer. "Just one of many components to my bad day."

Tyler made a noise that sounded like disagreement. "You're distracting me, remember? I can't be distracted without details."

I rolled my eyes. "I teased him, he didn't like it. End of."

"End of," he scoffed. "These are not details, Constantine."

"Fine. You want the whole sordid story?" I turned toward him. "This guy is my family's biggest business competitor, right? And he's trying to put us out of business like the bad guy from that movie with the angel and the bell."

"What guy? What movie?"

"Irrelevant. Point is, he's the embodiment of pure evil, okay?"

"Pure evil. Got it." Tyler snickered. "Hiding right here…" Tyler spread his hands. "In the middle of nowhere."

"Exactly. He's also hot as hell. Green eyes. A little gray mixed in with the brown," I fingered the hair at my own temples. "Tall. Huge-ass hands. Serious as fuck."

"Huge-ass hands," Tyler repeated. "How oddly specific."

"What? No. It's just… a fact." Though thinking about his hands for too long *did* make my heart rate kick up weirdly. "He's really confident but grumpy. Never smiles, never laughs. And he's got these mind-reader eyes that can see your soul. Every terrible thing about you. He's basically like this giant calm *rock*. You know?"

"I know exactly. The friend I mentioned is exactly that," Tyler said. He paused for a second. "Except Gus isn't pure evil. He uses his powers for good. Anyway, go on."

"Right," I said, warming up to the story. Maybe venting *was* helpful. "So the first day I met him, he looked at me with those eyes and I blurted out some stupid joke— something about asking if he picked the name or the profession first. It was totally lame."

"His name?"

"Yeah, he works with plants, and his last name is…" I waved a hand. "Whatever. That's irrelevant, too. Suffice it to say, he totally threw me off balance, and ever since then, he can't even *see* me without getting pissed off."

"*Really*. And you see him a lot?"

"Oh yeah. For business things. Farmer's markets and festivals and stuff." I snorted. The shit my mother made me do.

"And he just randomly glares at you because of this one time?"

"Well. I mean. I may continue to provoke him occasionally."

"Occasionally?"

I scratched my chin. "Often."

"Oh."

"Alright, fine, pretty much every time I see him," I admitted. "But honestly, what else am I supposed to do? The guy *never* speaks a civil word to me, like I'm so far beneath his notice or something. It gets under my skin. So… I get under his." I shrugged.

"That sounds healthy."

"Hey! There's not a lot that I control in my life, Tyler. Let me have this." I tipped the last of my drink into my mouth and then fished in the glass for the cherries.

"So, is it flirtation between you two?" Tyler asked, his brow puckering. "Because it sounds kind of like when I was in junior high and—"

"No," I interrupted with a laugh. "No, no, no. Pure evil, remember? And honestly, he's hot enough that I could get over the evil if the man had a sense of humor, but no. He's about as warm as the refrigerator where my mother keeps flower arrangements. So, yeah, *no*. Hard-core *no* on the flirting."

Tyler made this pinch-lipped, lemon-sucking expression, like he was trying not to laugh.

"What?"

"Nothing! Nothing." His grin broke free. "I was just

trying to count how many times you said no. Because there were a lot. Enough to indicate, you know, denial."

"Trust me," I said, slinging my arm around his shoulder. "There's not a lot I know, but I sure as hell know when I'm flirting with someone and when I'm not. Okay?"

"Okay," he agreed readily.

"Okay! So how about you buy me that drink." I waggled my eyebrows.

Tyler twisted up his lips again, and it was kinda cute. Not cute enough that I was truly distracted-distracted, but cute enough that I could try to be, for tonight anyway. My ability to flirt with a passably cute guy like he was all three Hemsworth brothers at the same time was one of the few true talents I possessed, which is why I never left The Hive solo.

Of course, my inability to maintain any interest in them—or keep them interested in me—after the sheets cooled was why I kept coming back week after week. But that was a problem so far down the priority list it wasn't even a problem, if you know what I mean.

"Wait, just so I understand, is *this* your idea of flirtation?" Tyler gestured back and forth between us. "The arm thing and the eyebrow wiggle? Because if so, I'm not sure you *do* know when you're flirting," he said wryly.

"Hey! I'll have you know I have mad game! I never leave alone on a Saturday night. Ask Jordan."

"Oh, I believe it. But I'm guessing *you* don't generally have to make the first move."

I frowned at that. Tyler wasn't wrong. I couldn't remember the last time I'd picked someone to flirt with. I usually waited for them to come to me, and they did.

Shaking off the idea, I smiled again and batted my eyelashes. "Usually not. 'Cause I'm so pretty. Irresistible, really."

Tyler smirked and shrugged my arm off his shoulder. "Yeah, I don't think—"

Behind me, someone snorted. "Some of us are quite capable of resisting you, Ross."

I twisted around on my stool to find Micah Bloom standing between Tyler and me, looking at me with a single raised eyebrow.

I scowled.

If life were fair, someone with a stick lodged so firmly up his ass would look the part. He should be oily and sneering, hooked-nosed and dressed in black… He should basically look like Severus Snape, but before we all got sympathetic toward him.

Instead, the world's injustice was clearly displayed in the slim-fitting jeans that hugged Micah's hips so much better than his usual cargo shorts, and the oh-so-tight olive-green t-shirt clinging to a well-defined chest I'd never imagined he'd been hiding under his work shirts. His brown hair was messy, but in a deliberate way that almost highlighted the silver at his temples and the little crinkles at the corners of his eyes.

"What the hell are you doing here?" I ground out.

"Getting a drink. This *is* a bar, Ross. Not my first time here either."

As if on cue, Jordan came by to drop off a fresh drink for me and gave Micah a wide grin. "Hey, cutie. Your usual?"

I looked at Jordan in betrayed outrage and she rolled her eyes at me.

"Yes, please," Micah said. The smile he gave her in return was small but *real*. Adorable.

Annoying.

I looked away, but Tyler caught my eye immediately.

"Evil?" he mouthed, eyes wide, like maybe he understood this was the guy I'd been describing, but Micah didn't look as devilish as I'd led him to believe.

I sighed, torn between being pissed off and darkly amused. Of course my shitty day would be capped off this way. It only really needed Micah approaching me at The Hive for the first time ever, when we usually gave each other the widest berth possible.

"Sorry to interrupt your *conversation*," Micah said with a tight little smile and a knowing glance from me to Tyler and back again. He managed to make the word sound dirty, though Tyler and I had literally done nothing but talk.

Christ, he was infuriating.

"You haven't interrupted anything," I said sweetly, jumping down from my barstool. "Yet. Tyler and I were on our way out. Right, Tyler?"

Tyler's eyes widened impossibly further, until he looked like one of the creepy, doe-eyed figurines my mother used to collect, but he played along gamely enough. "Oh, yeah. Yup. We're… leaving?"

"Not so fast," Micah said, splaying one large hand on my chest, and I swear I felt the pressure of each individual fingertip through the thin material of my shirt. "I have a proposition for you."

"Hey! I propositioned him first," Tyler protested, but when Micah threw him a disdainful look, Tyler shut up.

"Not that kind of proposition." Micah dropped his hand and gave me an arched-brow, superior look that begged me to hit him. "Constantine's *really* not my type."

This was so patently obvious it should *not* have burned the way it did.

"Yes, Micah finds things like laughter and pleasure repellent, much the way vampires abhor sunlight," I confided to Tyler without looking away from Micah. "As soon as he starts to enjoy anything, his little brain shuts down and he becomes a monster."

"Like Angel's curse," Tyler whispered.

I turned my head. "What?"

Micah snorted. "Your friend is referencing *Buffy the Vampire Slayer*," he explained in a bored voice. "More or less inaccurately. And no, I'm *cursed* in other ways. Whole prophecies about me. Right, Mr. Ross?"

"Well, I got the chaos part right," I grumbled. I just hadn't imagined that the chaos would involve *me.*

"Ooookay, then." Tyler cleared his throat. He looked like he didn't know whether to be offended or amused by Micah. Join the club. "Constantine, are we going?"

"*You* can run along," Micah said dismissively. He didn't turn to look at Tyler either. "I have something to tell Mr. Ross that he's going to want to stay and hear."

It was on the tip of my tongue to tell him there was *nothing* I wanted to hear from him, but... I was only human, you know? As far as I could remember—and believe me, I'd have remembered—he'd never sought me out, never voluntarily even *spoken* to me. Was he gonna yell at me for my dumb joke earlier? Make me feel like even more of an incompetent kid? Prove himself to be even more unlikeable than I already knew him to be? He was welcome to try.

"Tyler, can I get a raincheck on that drink?"

"Uh. Yeah. Of course," Tyler said. "Give me your phone and I'll give you my number. You can text me when you get home safely."

That made me break eye contact with Micah long enough to shoot Tyler a smile. "I've known you for ten whole minutes, Tyler," I reminded him. "I've known this guy for a while." But I unlocked my phone and handed it over anyway.

"Uh-huh. But I'm not looking at you like he is either." Tyler tilted his head toward Micah as he plugged in his number.

"Like I'm a mosquito bite in an unmentionable place?" I suggested.

"No. More like it's feeding time at the zoo." He handed me back my phone.

I laughed out loud at the idea. "I'll be fine. Micah's no threat to me. Are you Micah?"

Micah ignored me.

"You boys play nice," Tyler said as he walked away.

Micah dropped onto his stool immediately, but somehow it still felt like the guy was looming over me. It made me uncomfortable—my throat tight, my stomach jumping. Just being in his presence was like a shot of adrenaline, and the fatigue that had swamped me all night was nowhere to be found.

"Okay," I said, turning on my stool to face him, trying desperately to regain the control I lost in his proximity. "Now that you've run off my new friend, *proposition me.*"

Micah smiled knowingly. "Your new friend? The flavor of the week, you mean."

"What?"

He sipped his drink. "Don't pretend like your *friendship* with that twink would have lasted for longer than the half hour it took you both to get off."

"The fuck? Judging me for the number and frequency of my sex partners says more about *you* being a judgmental asshole than it does about *me*. You don't know shit about my sex life."

Micah shrugged, a half-assed apology. "Fair."

"But for the record." I leaned closer for just a second, and he leaned in, too, almost like he couldn't help it. "I never stop at *one* orgasm," I whispered. "And it takes way longer than half an hour."

I winked, satisfied that I'd provoked him.

But Micah didn't just look annoyed; he looked *angry*. He glared at me, all heat and fire and intensity, like what I'd said was personally offensive to him or something.

I would never understand the man. *He* had no problem being rude and insulting, but when *I* teased *him*, even in a friendly way, he acted like I'd insulted his mom. Just like everyone else, he seemed to expect me to be someone I wasn't, and all I could ever do was fail, and fail, and fail.

This was nothing new. I was always too loud, too brash, too excited, too emotional, too quick to find the humor in a situation, too slow to think of the consequences, too much of everything bad, and too little of everything good. I was a recipe that never turned out right no matter how many times I'd tried to change myself, so I'd stopped trying to change myself years ago. I wasn't responsible for the way other people reacted to me, and most of the time, I didn't care what they thought.

It killed me that, of all the people in this bar, of all the people in this town, the one person determined to hate me seemed to be the one person whose opinion I cared about.

It was inexplicable.

And, did I mention, fucking *annoying*?

I pursed my lips. "M'kay, so this little glaring contest is super fun and all, but I have two brothers *and* an Italian mother. My skin is Teflon, and your death rays can't touch me. Last chance, big man. Say whatever you need to say to me, yell as loud as you want, and then leave me alone."

"Yell?" He looked honestly confused. "Why would I want to yell at you right now?"

"Who the hell knows? I can't imagine why you'd *ever* be

annoyed at me, seeing as how I'm perpetually charming. Yet you always look angry."

He snorted. "You're delusional."

I laughed shortly. "There's a new one. Honestly, you're totally disappointing me right now. What else you got?"

"You're immature as hell."

"Also not news." But it stung, coming from him. Oh, yes it did.

"You're impulsive. You don't *think*."

"Uh-huh. Get it all out." I made a gimme gesture with my fingers as I fished a cherry out of the ice at the bottom of my glass with my tongue. "I'm a terrible person. Careless. Thoughtless. I hurt people. I ruin everything." I showed him the cherry between my teeth before chomping down on it.

He scowled, either at my words or my cherry-related talents. "What?"

"Oh, don't pretend you weren't thinking it." I wiped my mouth with the back of my hand and motioned to Jordan for a refill. She rolled her eyes but complied. "Everyone in O'Leary thinks it, so you might as well say it. Teflon," I reminded him, making a sliding motion over the top of my head. "Slides right off. Tell me how badly I embarrassed you at the market, and how I'm basically an overgrown kid, and how my pranks aren't amusing. You won't hurt my feelings."

Micah was looking at me funny, doing that laser-beam eye thing again, but less like he was trying to burn me alive and more like he was trying to see through my skull. It was disconcerting and all of a sudden I was pretty sure I didn't want to stick around to hear whatever else he had to say.

"Time's up," I announced. "You've missed your window. So if you'll excuse me." I made to get off my stool, but he stopped me with one large hand on my arm.

"Constantine, I didn't come over here to trade insults with you. Or to yell at you, either."

I wasn't a small guy by any stretch—I was the tallest in our family by inches, and years of hard, physical work had given me a way more defined body than most guys got in a gym. Micah was barely bigger than I was, physically. But there was something about him, his *presence* or something, that made me stop when I could've—*should've*—shrugged him off. I looked into his eyes, which were deep green and impossible to read in the light of the bar, and swallowed hard.

I looked down at his hand. His skin was a shade darker than mine, despite my spring tan, and the hairs on his arm were gilded by the overhead lights like gold on bronze. His fingers were callused, just a little, and the back of his hand was nicked and scratched to hell. It was not a soft hand any more than Micah was a soft *man*, but for the first time, I wondered what it would feel like touching me, and I was shocked by how badly I wanted to find out.

Which was *also* inexplicable and annoying.

"So you came over for the same reason Tyler did?" I asked. I'd been going for skeptical, even amused, but my voice came out all husky and breathless and *interested*, goddammit. "Wanted to be my flavor of the week?"

He dropped my arm like it was on fire and snorted. "Hardly. I wasn't kidding before. You're not my type." Before I could react to this, he added, "I wanted to offer you a job."

I snickered, sure that had to be a joke, but he didn't so much as smile.

"A job? With you?" I belatedly snatched my arm away from him. "Are you insane?"

Micah was silent for a moment, like he was honestly considering the question, and the pulse of the music from the dance floor washed over us. "I have a lot of standing orders and a ton of larger projects in the next couple of months. Too many. And I need short-term help to fill them."

"Your business is booming? How terrible," I said, thinking of my mother's words earlier. "Go hire a new employee. Preferably someone who needs the work. Or, here's an even better idea: stop stealing Ross Landscaping's clients and stick with what you've got."

"I *can't* hire just anyone, and you know it," he said, ignoring the second half of my statement. "I need someone experienced. Someone who knows the work so I don't have to spend days training them." He angled his body toward mine and grudgingly admitted, "It's nearly impossible to find someone experienced who only wants limited hours and no benefits. You'd be perfect. In fact, you're the only person I can think of who could do it."

"How sad for you. No."

Micah blew out a frustrated breath. "Hear me out, idiot. This could help both of us."

"You'd be helping me? By giving me a job?" I laughed. "I already work *two*, but thanks anyway." I turned to leave.

"Take the job, and I'll give up the contract at the Crabapple Bed and Breakfast."

"You what?" I stared at him, sure I'd heard wrong.

"You heard me. I'll give up the contract to supply flowers to the B and B. They asked me for a bid, and I haven't submitted it officially. You come work for me, I won't. It's that easy."

I shook my head. "No way. That's..." Incredibly fucking tempting. Holy shit. It would take away the biggest worry hanging over my mother's head and help Ross Landscaping survive, at least for the summer. "Ridiculous.

You could find a dozen people who could do the work. And my schedule is insane already."

"I'm telling you, I've tried to find someone. I can't. And I'm willing to work with your schedule. I'd need your help late night, after hours, to prep things for the following day, and really early mornings, when I need to pick up supplies."

"What *is* this?" I demanded, squinting at him. "Some kind of charity thing? Some way to get me to owe you a favor? Because I don't need—"

"No! Jesus, you're suspicious. Listen, I can't handle the Crabapple job with my current staff *anyway*. You'd be doing *me* the favor."

"And having Ross keep the Crabapple as a client would be my compensation," I said slowly. "For the favor."

He nodded. "Plus, I'll pay you my standard part-time wage."

I bit my lip, thinking of all the many, many reasons I should say no.

There was a catch to this; there had to be. Micah Bloom had never struck me as a man who did nice things for free, and sure as *hell* not someone who'd do nice things for *me*.

But God, I needed the money. There was no way I'd be able to replace Bessie otherwise, and I had no idea how I was going to do *either* of my jobs without a car.

"How many hours?"

Micah smiled, recognizing this for the capitulation it was. "Maybe ten or fifteen a week."

"We'd need to keep this quiet. As in, *silent*." I could glare too, and I demonstrated it now. "If my mother hears about this, the nuclear fallout would devastate the entire Northeast." Not that I'd care; I'd already be burned to cinders.

"Fine," he agreed. He finished his drink and set the glass down on the bar. "I have a delivery at four o'clock on Monday. That's four *in the morning*," he added.

I rolled my eyes. "I figured."

"Great. Then meet me at the shop at three forty-five and we'll get started. And you'd better not tell me you were too drunk to remember this conversation, no matter how many of *these* you've been sucking back." He held my gaze as he leaned way too far into my personal space, picked up my drink, and took a sip.

Which was *rude* and not at all cute. Especially when he screwed up his face the second the beverage hit his tongue and shivered head to toe like he'd been hit with poison.

"Jesus. What the hell is this? I hate to break it to you, Ross, but Jordan cut you off. There's no alcohol in there at all. It tastes like…"

"Cherries?" I gave him a pitying look. "It's a Shirley Temple, *Bloom*."

"A Shirley Temple?"

"It's ginger ale," I explained. "With cherry syrup and—"

"I know what it *is*. I don't know why you have one."

"Uh, 'cause it's the designated-driver specialty of the house and 'cause cherries are delicious?"

Once again, Micah wore that intense, confused, nearly angry look that was pretty much his default way of looking at me, and I didn't *get* it. How did I make him so angry all the damn time?

"What?" I demanded, throwing my hands in the air. "I don't drink alcohol when I have to drive. Ever. You can call that childish if you want, but I've worked for the police department too long and seen too many cars wrapped around trees on the Camden Road to take a ch—"

Micah's hand came around the back of my neck and

pulled me forward until his lips were on mine. *Hard.* Unyieldingly hard.

But Jesus, so fucking hot.

He kissed me the way he'd touched me, the way he'd looked at me, demanding and pissed off and searching for something I wasn't sure how to provide, or if I even wanted to.

My hands flailed for a second as I was thrown off-balance—literally and figuratively—but Micah's other hand came up to grab my jaw and steady me. My lips parted for him in a way that wasn't voluntary or involuntary, but simply *necessary* and unavoidable, like breathing.

The force of the kiss blew across my brain, sending all my thoughts and beliefs and preconceptions skittering like last year's leaves, and I grabbed at his bicep for support because *holy shit*, all of a sudden I *was* intoxicated.

"You taste like cherries," he whispered as he pulled back.

I stared at him, a little breathless and a lot wary. "What…" I cleared my throat and tried again, trying desperately to be cool about this. "What was that?"

"That was a kiss, Constantine." Micah sounded bored again. His cheeks were flushed, but his eyes were already scanning the room like he couldn't wait to get away. "A one-time thing, just to seal the deal. Guess I'm your flavor of the week after all, huh?" He licked his lips slowly. "Guess you're mine, too."

He clapped me on the shoulder with enough force to make me sway and stood up. "Gotta go. See you early Monday," he said as he walked away. "Drive home safe."

"Yeah. Okay. Um. Same to you," I called, all casual and shit.

But his taste lingered on my lips, even after I left the bar.

Alone.

Chapter Four

MICAH

As I SAT in my delivery van on Monday morning with the window rolled down, watching the first hints of pinkish gray tinge the sky over the alley behind my shop, I was struggling to figure out how the fuck I'd gotten here.

I mean, not literally. I remembered every stupid moment of Saturday with blinding clarity—Constantine joking at my expense, Constantine being vulnerable when he didn't know I could hear him, the brilliantly idiotic idea to employ Constantine Ross that had leapt into my brain in a way that made me rethink all my grandmother's ideas about religion because demonic possession was *real*, goddammit.

I remembered thinking I'd talked myself out of it, too, after going back to the shop and looking around my office —at the invoices and the bills and the fucking logo with my name on it, at the pictures of my family scattered across the desk—and reminding myself that Micah's Blooms was the most important thing in my personal universe for a reason, and I wasn't gonna fuck with that just to help *Constantine Ross* of all people.

And then I remembered the way I'd somehow found myself freshly showered, standing in front of my mirror as I pulled on my t-shirt, getting ready to go to The Hive, like my body had hijacked my brain and decided to run *toward* a burning building.

With no protective gear.

And no fucking *plan*.

I sure as fuck remembered standing at a table in the corner, nursing a beer and watching a dejected Constantine out of the corner of my eye as the rational part of my brain tried to talk the rest of me into leaving—*fleeing*—before I did what I'd gone there to do and offered the man a job.

But most of all, I remembered the way I'd started noticing all this shit about Constantine that I hadn't noticed, or hadn't let myself notice, before.

Like the tiredness behind his smile.

Like the way he laughed and leaned and smiled and winked and smoldered as if he was playing a role. Following a script.

Like the way he wasn't objectively the hottest guy in the bar—in fact, the blond who'd cozied up next to him was generally more my speed: smaller, slighter, blonder, calmer, more discreet and pastel—but Con was by far the most attractive man I'd ever seen.

He had a kind of force about him, like the magnetism of a neutron star, that drew people into his orbit, closer to his light, whether he was making doomsday predictions on a sunny day, or all sad and cute and folded over the bar. He was…

Okay, fine, he was *charming*.

And that curiosity about him that I'd felt earlier in the day? It hadn't been a temporary thing. Because suddenly I was consumed by this desire to see more of the *real* Constantine. To cheer him up.

Let me break that down in case it hasn't fully sunk in.

Me. Micah Bloom. The responsible, business-focused, middle-aged guy.

Wanted an opportunity for *ongoing interaction* with Constantine. Wanted to make him *feel better*.

Him. The menace. The troublemaker. The provoker.

In short, the chaos Constantine had predicted had come to pass.

Rational-Micah had thrown his hands in the air and stomped off in a rage as I'd made my way across the room. And the demon had taken over.

I'd inserted myself between Constantine and his pet like some fucking caveman, feeling a bizarre sense of rightness settle over me the second I'd put my hand on Constantine's arm—which was the exact moment all the alarm bells in my brain *should* have been going off because the train to Good Choices had left the station, and I was not on board, but they'd all gone silent.

And then, of course, Constantine had been prickly and surprising and vulnerable and, yes, *real.* Shocking the shit out of me, assuming my opinion of him was worse than anything I'd ever thought, no matter how much he'd pissed me off. Showing me that his cockiness was the hard veneer over something really vulnerable and compelling. Drinking fucking Shirley Temples and fishing the cherries out with his tongue.

I was sunk.

He was old and young, jaded and innocent, shy and bold, fascinating as hell.

Sexy as fuck.

I had absolutely zero defense against him... as

evidenced by that mind-combusting kiss that tasted like cherries and sunlight and… I dunno. Poetry and shit.

Jesus, Micah.

Constantine had asked me the other night if I was insane for offering him a job. I could only conclude that *yes I fucking was*, because my priorities had gotten all screwed up.

I started the engine and looked at the clock. Three forty-four, and the alley was empty.

This was good, I told myself, taking a last glance at my phone. This was an opportunity to restore my equilibrium. To get my priorities back in check. If I drove out of the alley right now—

"Morning, *boss.*"

Startled, I found Constantine inches away, watching me through the open van window, a cup of coffee in each hand. His lightweight jacket was molded to his body and his hair was adorably mussed.

I inhaled sharply at his nearness.

Had I thought he *wasn't* the hottest guy in the bar Saturday night? Yeah, okay, that was a lie. He was hot as hell.

And fucking young.

And ridiculous.

And your employee, Micah, you genius.

Right. Yes. Employee. Of my *business.*

Fuck me.

"Good morning," I said belatedly. "You're late."

By exactly one minute, according to my clock.

"I was working at the station until eleven, stopped home for a cat nap, and came here." Con shrugged. "But I brought coffee." That mischievous little smile danced around his mouth. "Figured that would grant me immunity."

He handed over a to-go cup—an actual metal cup he'd brought from home, since God knew there was nothing in O'Leary open at this hour—and gave me a winning smile.

It was *thoughtful*. Really thoughtful. Another glimpse of the real Constantine, when I most needed to steel myself against him.

I made a disapproving noise and shook my head, even as I took the drink from his hand. "I know you were working last night, but that's really not an excuse. Employees should be on time. You're supposed to come when I tell you to come, not when you feel like it."

Constantine blinked and leaned toward me. "Just so I understand… are you saying you get off on people coming when you tell them to?"

I felt myself blushing as all my blood rushed to my cheeks…

And other places.

"Get in the fucking van, Constantine."

Constantine shrugged cheerfully and strolled around the hood like he had all the time in the world. He pulled open the door and dropped himself heavily into the passenger's seat. "So, is this what working for you is gonna be like? No consideration for the fact that I single-handedly saved O'Leary from a werewolf attack last night? I mean, yes, it turned out that Mrs. Quinn's werewolf was actually a stray dog in her garage, but it all could have ended in *tragedy*, Micah. And now I'm a minute late, and you're all up in my business?"

I forced myself not to think about being *all up in his business*. I also forced myself not to laugh at his story.

"It's a life lesson," I told him, all superior and conde-scending. *Honestly*. The shit that spewed out of my mouth around this guy. Mason wouldn't stop laughing for a week if he could hear me right now. "There's a right way to do things and a wrong way to do things."

Con's eyes sparkled. "You're too tall to have a Napoleon complex," he mused. "Where does all this shit come from?"

I put my cup in the cup holder. "Fasten your seat belt."

But of course, following a direct instruction was too much to ask of my new employee. He stared at me in mock concern. "Dude, I left that *wide open* for you, and you didn't make a comeback. Are you sick?"

I put the van in drive and pulled out onto Weaver Street.

"I'm attempting to be professional," I told him. "As you should. And on that subject, I wanted to apologize. For the other night."

He sipped his coffee with a little smile playing around his lips. "Which part? The part where you scared Tyler off? Or the one where you kissed me? Or the one where you offered me a job?"

"The second part."

"*Which* part?"

I shot him a glare. "I'm beginning to regret the entire thing."

"I'm just trying to communicate, Mr. Bloom. *Boss.* I just want to make sure that we have an open and respectful employer-employee dialogue going on. To be *professional*," he insisted like the fucking *menace* he was. "Which part of the other night do you regret?"

"The part where I kissed you," I said, trying to sound bored.

But just as I'd suspected, saying the words out loud brought the kiss right back to the forefront of my brain. The fucking air smelled like cherries.

"I shouldn't have done that at all, but as your new boss, especially."

"Uh-huh." Constantine twisted in his seat to face me. "Is this the part where you explain sexual harassment to me?"

"Do you have to make everything a joke?" I demanded, frustrated and aroused, and frustrated *because* I was aroused.

"Do you have to be so serious about everything?"

He sounded like Leandra, for God's sake.

And Jesus, wouldn't she and Lauren love to hear about me actually *hiring* Constantine? I vowed then and there that I was not going to breathe a damn word to either of them about this temporary insanity.

Ever.

I took a deep breath and prayed for patience. "I'm just saying, that kiss was not an accurate reflection of our relationship. It will never be repeated. Hell, I don't even like you half the time, and I know you don't like me any better."

"True." Constantine sipped his coffee pensively. "What about the other half of the time?"

"Pardon?"

"I mean"—he shot me a look that was blatantly flirtatious—"if you dislike me fifty percent of the time, what are you thinking about me the other fifty percent?"

I tightened my grip on the steering wheel. "The rest of the time, I don't think of you at all."

Constantine hooted at this. "I think you're lying. Wanna know how I know?"

"If I say no, will you shut up?"

"I know because—"

"Didn't think so," I sighed.

"I know *because*," Constantine insisted, "when I'm not hating you, I find you hot."

"Jesus."

"I know, I *know*! It's insane. I can't imagine having sex with a guy who's incapable of smiling." He pursed his lips and moved his arms up and down like a robot. "Oh. That. Feels. Nice. Yes. Just. Like. That. Ooh. Baby." He peered at me over his coffee cup. "I mean, I'll admit it's intriguing." He tilted his head to the side curiously. "Do you get angry when you orgasm?"

"Constantine."

He waved a hand in the air. "*Irrelevant*. The point is, I think the other half the time, you want me. But you don't want to want me. Because, as you said, I'm not your type." He rolled his eyes. "Which is fine, because God knows you're not *my* type, so I don't want to want you either, and the *wanting* to want is the important part. The *choice* part. The part that separates us from the animals so we don't go around humping each other all day, lovely as that sounds."

I frowned at him like he was insane because I wondered if maybe he was. Honest to God, who talked like this?

The provoking menace in my passenger's seat, that's who.

My new fucking *employee*.

Who chose to interpret my frown as confusion.

"Did I lose you? Hmm. How can I say this in small words you might understand? Oh! I know. Okay, let's say our mutual attraction is a tiny, precious seed." He made a cupping motion with his hand, sketching a seed in the air, and blinked at me solemnly. "As long as we don't plant it, it'll never grow." He wiggled his eyebrows. "See?"

Cocky bastard. I'd really like to plant my... *Ahem*. I cut

off the thought abruptly. "What I *see* is that you're delusional."

"Yes, so you mentioned Saturday night," Constantine said, supremely unconcerned. "But it's not a delusion if it's accurate."

I shook my head. I was simultaneously pissed off and entertained, which felt really fucking dangerous, so I took a cautious sip of coffee, determined to stop this entire line of conversation before I gave in to the urge to kick the man's ass… or do something else to his ass entirely.

I couldn't stop the noise of surprise when the flavor of the coffee hit my tongue. "It's black."

"Hmm? Oh, yeah. I wasn't sure how you took it, so I guessed."

"It's good. Thank you," I added grudgingly. "Good guess."

"Dark, hot, and bitter just seemed to fit." He fluttered his eyelashes.

"While yours is probably so light and sweet you can *delude yourself* into thinking it's melted ice cream."

"Hey!" He burst into laughter. "I'm still very aware it's coffee, thank you. I just don't need things to be unpleasant and painful in order for them to be worthwhile." He paused, then added slyly, "Not that I mind a little pain from time to time."

I shook my head again and locked my teeth together. God, he was impossible.

Cocky, *cocky* bastard.

"You know, FYI, your flirtation game is really weak," Con said. "Some people say mine is bad, but compared to you, I'm, like, an expert." He sounded smug.

I turned my head to stare at him and had to remind myself to look back at the road, because smug-Con was hot as hell. "That's because I'm not flirting. We're *not* flirting right now, Constantine. I thought I made that clear."

"Sure, sure." He waved a hand negligently. "I know. No, I was thinking of the other day at the farmer's market. That guy was totally trying to pick you up, and you were, like, *oblivious*."

Oh. Robert. I frowned. "That was nothing."

"Please. He was so hot for you, I could feel the pheromone shock waves all the way across the aisle."

Shock waves? "Nonsense."

"If I'd been telepathic, he would have been *screaming* his lust into my brain."

"Constantine, shut up."

"He would have laid himself down on the table by the gerbera daisies," Constantine said, sliding into the corner between the seat and the door and bending one long leg up toward the console between us, "and let you have your wicked way with him in front of the entire town."

I could feel my face going hot, and it had absolutely nothing to do with Robert and everything to do with Con's teasing humor and... okay, yes, the hairy, muscular calf exposed by Con's shorts, which was suddenly just inches away from me.

"I'm not interested in that guy." I could barely remember his face. I shoved at Con's leg. "And we are not talking about this."

"*Why* aren't you interested? How do you even know? See, flirtation doesn't have to mean anything," Constantine continued. "It doesn't have to lead to anything. Just like, one night of sex doesn't mean a relationship, and one kiss in a bar doesn't *have* to lead to something more, as you so recently informed me."

"Not. Talking."

"There's no reason why you can't chat with someone

who shows an interest in you. Because how else will you know if you *do* have an interest? You need to try people out a little, right? How'd you meet the last guy you picked up?"

I set my lips together stubbornly, but I couldn't help thinking about the last guy I'd been with—Victor, with the glasses and the button-down shirt, who'd seemed so shy and quiet when we'd met at a friend's party but had demanded to tie me down, literally, with the ropes he carried in his trunk the second I'd gotten him home.

Constantine might have a point about not judging based on appearances.

"What part of *not talking* confuses you, Ross? I'm not sure how to break it down into smaller words *you* can understand. Oh! I know. It's like, if this conversation was a tiny, precious seed? And that seed didn't *shut the fuck up*, so I *drove this van over it.*"

Con clapped a hand over his mouth. "Oh shit. You *do* have a sense of humor. It's just dark and bitter like your coffee."

I rolled my eyes, sipped at said coffee, and kept my eyes on the blacktop in front of us.

Constantine made an amused sound and sat upright again, outwardly complying, *finally*, with my instruction, staying silent and watching the trees flash by out the window... but it was too late. I was already so aware of him that his silence was more provoking than his conversation had been.

Every time he lifted his cup to his lips, it released a burst of his scent—a combination of cut grass, warm spice, and coffee that pinged every single receptor in my brain and made my gut clench. His lips were set in a small, unconscious smile and I wanted to know what the heck he was thinking about, or whether he was thinking of anything at all. Maybe Constantine Ross just had the opposite of resting bitch face. Resting… nice face?

Christ, I was *doomed*.

———

WE PULLED into the parking lot of HG Floral Supply just as dawn broke over the horizon, and I stopped in my usual spot near one of the receiving doors.

"You ready?" I demanded.

Con eyed the exterior of the building dubiously. "Yep. As I'll ever be."

"What's the problem? Suddenly remembered you're too *pretty* to be forced into manual labor before sunrise?" I asked, quoting our conversation at the bar the other night.

"No." He opened his mouth, then closed it again. "Though, you know, thanks for noticing." He framed his face with one hand and summoned a smile that was just a little too tense to be real.

"What's the problem?"

"Nothing," he began, but when I sighed loudly, he admitted, "It's just this place. Ross Landscaping used to get our flowers here, too, back in the day," he said. "But they fucked up a couple orders and were assholes about it, so I let them know exactly how I felt about them."

Meaning he'd gone off on them in an angry outburst and they refused to do business with him again. How was I not surprised?

"Well, I've never had a problem with HG Supply, and I used them even before I moved to O'Leary," I informed him. "Generally, you get out of a business relationship what you put into it. Fairness, respect, and loyalty go a long way."

"Wow. Amazing advice. Truly. I'm, like, memorizing all

these little tidbits for later." Con rolled his eyes. "My point is that Donnie and Pat know me, and they're sure as shit gonna have something to say about me *defecting* from Ross Landscaping and working for the competition. At the very least."

I frowned. I hadn't considered that. "How likely is it that they'll tell your mother, though, if she doesn't do business with them anymore?"

Constantine sighed and scratched his head. "I don't know. Safe to say they're not my biggest fans."

"Okay. So you wanna wait in the van?"

Con looked surprised that I'd offered, but I shrugged.

It *was* annoying, since the whole point of torturing myself by having Con as an employee was to actually have him do *work*, but I also wasn't quite the asshole he wanted to think I was. I'd agreed to keep things secret, and I would.

Constantine seemed to think about it, then shook his head and unbuckled his seat belt. "No, it's fine. But can we just… not stay and chitchat?"

"Chat?" I was genuinely confused. "What the hell would we chat with them for?"

Constantine snorted. "Right. Forgot who I was talking to for a second. The only person you chat with is *me*."

"I wouldn't call what we do chatting."

"Yeah? What would you call it? Dispensing valuable life advice?" He wiggled his eyebrows again. "A bizarre sort of foreplay?"

"Foreplay assumes that there'll be some form of *play*," I said, hoping desperately that I sounded bored and not at all like I was picturing that *play* in my head. "What we do is more like verbal combat."

Constantine laughed but didn't disagree.

We walked up the concrete steps to the heavy steel

door that opened into what basically was an enormous flower warehouse, and the smell, when the door was opened, was unreal. My nose started to tingle, as it often did when I first walked in, and even though I was more or less used to it after all these years, it took me a second to get my bearings.

"It's like olfactory LSD," Con grumbled, and it was so close to what I'd been thinking, I couldn't help but smile a little.

"Heya, Micah!" Pat Hudson came out of the small office near the door and greeted me with a handshake and a wink. "Making four o'clock in the morning look good, as always."

Pat was maybe a couple of years younger than me, but HG Supply was a family company, and as a distant cousin of the owner, he'd been working here for as long as I'd been in business. I'd long ago learned to ignore his easy flirtation, and he'd never pushed it.

"Donnie's got your order ready out back. Everything's all set." He looked over my shoulder to where Con was standing, and his friendly smile fell away.

"Great. Thanks, Pat." I turned to Constantine. "Wanna get started going through the inventory list with Donnie and loading it up? I have a question for Pat about a special order."

Constantine nodded, keeping his head down, and took the keys I handed him, but it was too much to hope that Pat would let it go.

I really had been foolish not to foresee this problem. There weren't many—or *any*—alternative floral supply houses in the area, and Ross Landscaping had probably been around as long as HG Supply had. Of course they knew each other. And knowing Constantine, of course they hadn't parted ways amicably.

"Constantine Ross. Well, this *is* a surprise." Pat made it clear the surprise wasn't pleasant. "Looking the same as ever."

Pat looked Con up and down, from his bed head to his bare legs. It was an oddly sexual look, and I felt the unreasonable urge to stand in front of Constantine and block him from Pat's view.

"Yeah? You haven't changed a bit either," Con said. His words were casual, but there was a tension in his body that hadn't been there before. He gave Pat the same bold appraisal, surveying Pat's carefully gelled, thinning black hair, his baggy jeans, and the thick fingers drumming against his chest, and looked decidedly unimpressed by the sight.

Pat's eyes flashed with anger. "Same cocky bastard as ever, too, eh?"

It was the exact word I'd used to describe Con myself. It shouldn't have pissed me off when Pat used it, but it did.

Con didn't reply. He turned to me and jingled my keys. "I'll get started."

"Actually," I heard myself say, "Come here just a second."

Con frowned, but let me propel him a few steps back toward the door. I could feel Pat watching us and I didn't care.

"What's the story with you and Pat?" I demanded in a whisper.

"Huh?" Con's surprised eyes met mine. "Nothing. I told you in the van, he doesn't like the way I talked to him about the orders—"

"No. The way he looked at you was *not* business, Constantine."

Con folded his arms over his chest and stood with one hip cocked out. "I think you mean the way he looked at *you*, boss," he whispered back. "There's never been anything between me and Pat but him being gross and me being completely disinterested."

I ran my tongue over my teeth, trying to decide if I believed him.

"Are you kidding?" Con straightened until he was almost my height. His eyes were bright with anger, and I realized that while I'd maybe seen him pissed off before, I'd never seen him truly angry. "Fuck you, okay? Fuck *you*. The asshole flirts with *you*, that's fine. But he flirts with me, and clearly it means I was deep-dicking him? Why? Because I have sex with a bunch of people, I clearly must have sex with *everyone*?"

I opened my mouth and shut it again.

"Micah?" Con continued in the same low voice. "One thing to know about me is that *I do not lie*. I joke, I laugh, I tease, I will piss you the fuck off—on purpose—and not even feel bad, and I do *not* always volunteer information. But I am not a liar. Whatever else I've done, I don't do that. So either believe me or don't, but if you don't, then you can keep the fucking contract at Crabapple, because—"

"I believe you." I set my hands on my hips. "I just needed to know the facts. So I could deal with Pat appropriately. Business-wise."

Now, see, *that* was what a lie looked like.

The irony was strong.

I hadn't been thinking about my business at all when I'd called Con over here. I'd been thinking of Pat's avid little eyes on Constantine, of Pat calling him *cocky* like they had this whole long history I knew nothing about, and feeling… protective. Or something.

No, seriously, *how did I get here*?

"Whatever. Hot tip," Con whispered, still looking furious. "Fairness, respect, and loyalty go a long way in a business relationship."

I rubbed at the back of my neck and said nothing. Because, really, there was nothing to say. The provoking menace was absolutely fucking right.

He brushed past me, heading for the back of the shop where the receiving bays were. I turned and watched him stalk away... and it wasn't lost on me that Pat did, too.

"So." I cleared my throat to get Pat's attention as I returned to where he stood. "Just to confirm, those celestial pink roses for the Corcoran wedding next winter? You've got a supplier and a backup supplier?"

"Told you I did."

"Okay, but this is make or break for me, so you can expect me to ask you about a dozen more times between now and then. For now, I'm going to need some more of those Juliet roses you sourced for me last winter, same peach color as before, but I only need a limited quantity, and I remember there was a minimum... Uh, *Pat?*"

Pat turned to me belatedly, his cheeks flushed. "What? Sorry, Micah. That one threw me for a loop. The Ross kid is working for *you?* How the hell did that happen? Hell froze over and no one told me? Is he giving you trouble already?" Pat nodded over my shoulder, toward the spot where Con and I had been talking.

It was on the tip of my tongue to retort that it was none of his business, but instead I cleared my throat and said, "Running late this morning, Pat. The roses?"

Pat, who seemed incapable of taking a hint, ran a hand over his mouth and darted a glance back at the place where Con had disappeared. "The kid's bad news, you know."

I'd thought so myself. Hell, I *still* thought so... kind of. And yet, I thought about the taste of cherries, and

Constantine laughing in the van, and the way he'd stood up for that little boy at the farmer's market, and what came out of my mouth was, "Constantine? He's not so bad."

"Nah," Pat said, shaking his head seriously. "That's where you're wrong. I mean, he might *look* hot as fuck, but he knows it. Bats his eyelashes, and time and time again, he gets away with *murder*. Literally." He shot a resentful glare toward the back of the warehouse.

"Literally," I repeated. "Time and time again. Because he's a serial killer."

Pat looked at me and flushed even deeper. "Well, okay, not *literally* literally."

"Is there more than one way to be *literally* something?" I mused, folding my arms over my chest.

"Point is," Pat sputtered, "he's come as close to murder as you can without actually killing someone. And it's only luck that he *hasn't* killed someone when you consider the shit he's pulled. Wouldn't trust him as far as I could throw him."

Again, not a new idea. Not something I hadn't thought myself *many* times. But Pat saying these things made my chest tight.

"I'll take that under advisement," I said, making it clear I absolutely wouldn't. "So, the *roses*?"

"Right," Pat said, moving toward his office. "Right. Come with me. Let me make a note."

When we got to his cramped little office, Pat dropped into the rolling chair behind the desk and swept aside haphazard stacks of paper to find some kind of order form, where he wrote down the specifics of the roses I needed. "I'll get that information to you next week," he promised. He licked his lips. "But look, about the Ross kid. A little friendly advice—"

I opened my mouth to tell him where he could stick his

advice when a high-pitched screech came from the far side of the warehouse.

Pat and I looked at each other, then ran.

I got to the back of the warehouse first, partly because I was faster than Pat and partly because I was more motivated. I don't know what I expected to find—*Constantine bleeding, Constantine injured, Constantine in pain*—but when I ran around the corner by the loading dock, Constantine's eyes came to mine immediately, and I saw that he wasn't hurt; he was *pissed.*

"Micah? Can you get this fool to shut the fuck up and stop trying to scalp me? Because I'm losing my patience."

Con had Donnie, Pat's short, redheaded brother, in a headlock with one arm, while his other arm pinned Donnie's arm down. But that left Donnie with one hand free—a hand he was currently using to yank Constantine's hair from his head, yelling and sputtering all the while.

"Let go of him," I told Constantine. Then more firmly, "*Now*, Con."

"But…" Con's angry eyes turned pleading.

"If he hits you again," I said, speaking to him but looking at Donnie, "I will *help you* kick his ass, so Donnie's gonna calm the fuck down. Let him go."

Constantine sighed but released the man with a not-so-gentle shove.

"What the hell is going on?" Pat demanded, still panting from his run across the building.

"It was *him!*" Donnie said, smoothing his reddened neck with one hand while pointing the other accusingly at Con. "He was being an asshole."

I tilted my head at Constantine, silently demanding answers.

Constantine huffed out a breath. "I was checking the order, as instructed." He held up a paper that looked like an HG's invoice and gestured toward the boxes on the ground. "I politely informed Donald of some errors with the order, and he didn't like being corrected."

"You informed him *politely*," I repeated.

Constantine shrugged. "Polite-ish."

"He said, 'Hey, shithead, learn to count.'" Donnie was vibrating with rage.

Constantine twisted his lips to one side and scratched at his nose. It was *not* adorable. "I could maybe have been politer."

Pat swept a hand out toward Constantine. "*This* is who you have working for you? Representing your business? Micah, honest to God—"

I ignored him. "I feel like I'm missing some details. Con, you corrected Donnie—not very politely at all—and then he attacked you?"

Constantine rubbed at his scalp and winced. "Donnie gave me the list. I told him I wanted to check it against the supplies. Which is what you're *supposed to do*." He shot Donnie a look. "But Brain-Dead over here said *you* never bother checking the inventory because you're always in a hurry and you trust them. I said *you* might be dumb enough to trust him, but *I* was here now, and *I* didn't trust him for shit." He sighed and cast his eyes toward the ceiling of the warehouse. "It sort of devolved from there. I went through the order and found several errors, which didn't surprise me in the slightest. I told Donald to correct them, and he told *me* to shut the fuck up and mind my business or he'd kick my ass."

"And I *still* say that," Donnie shouted. "It was one simple error—"

"*Ennnnhh.*" Con made a noise like a game show buzzer. "Multiple errors."

"And it has nothing to do with you at all," Donnie

continued. "Since when do you give a shit about anyone but yourself, anyway?"

"You know what?" Con said hotly. "I am really starting to get tired of people thinking they know shit about me when they do *not*. Just because your cousin was an asshole back in the day—"

"This has nothing to do with him!" Donnie yelled over him.

I whistled loudly and the sound echoed around the space. "Finish the story. Today's story," I added.

Con huffed out a breath. "That *is* the whole story. Or close enough. I told him this *was* my fucking business, so he *did* try to kick my ass, which is when you arrived." He grinned smugly and leaned toward me to whisper, "Tried but didn't succeed, though."

Donnie took a threatening step toward Constantine. "Let me try again."

"Enough," I said, loudly enough to stop Donnie in his tracks. "Apologize and we'll be done with this."

Con's wide eyes shot to me. "Oh, no. No way in hell am I apologizing to this clown, boss. I'd rather face a firing squad. *Nature* should apologize to *us* for having to put up with him."

I ran a hand over my face and heaved a sigh. "Not *you*, idiot. Donnie." I nodded toward the redheaded man. "Tell Con you're sorry."

All three men gaped at me.

Pat laughed nervously. "You're kidding, right? You heard how he spoke to Donnie. The kid was looking to stir up trouble, as usual."

"Is that what you took from this story?" I frowned at Pat. "Because from what I heard, Donnie threatened my employee and then attempted to assault him."

"Well, yes, but only after serious provocation!"

"Telling Donnie to correct an error doesn't constitute serious provocation in my book." I looked at Constantine. "Though his language was totally unprofessional and perhaps deserving of an apology also."

Constantine stared back, a baffled little frown between his eyebrows. "Okay," he said slowly. "Yeah. I'll cop to that. My mother gives me shit for it all the time. I'm sorry I offended you with my rough language, Donald."

I nodded, appeased, and turned to Donnie.

But Con wasn't done.

"I'm sorry I called you a dumbass, and an asshole, and a clown, and a sneaky little shit-for-brains. I'm sorry I told you to fuck off, and suggested that you grow a pair, and said you were a whiny bitch with a brain the size of a thimble and a dick to match."

"Hey!" Donnie scowled. "You never said that last one!"

"Oh, didn't I?" Con shrugged and spread his hands innocently. "Guess that was just in my mind."

Jesus.

"Great," I said between set teeth. "Very... comprehensive." I gave Con a glance that said we'd be speaking about this later, then looked from Donnie to Pat and raised my eyebrows expectantly.

Pat looked like he was sucking the world's most sour lemon, but he waved a hand at Donnie. "Just do it. Go on. So we can move on with our fucking lives."

"Fine," Donnie said after a brief, silent conversation with his big brother. "I'm very sorry I *attempted* to kick Constantine's ass." His tone made it clear that his only regret was not succeeding.

Constantine and I shared a look. He seemed deeply amused by this half-assed apology. I, on the other hand, was deeply annoyed. This entire morning had been a clusterfuck.

Which is maybe why asking Constantine Ross to work for me was, you know, *not a good fucking idea.*

"Super," I said. "*Kumbaya.* Now we're all friends. Donnie, Constantine informed you of what was missing from the order?" I shot a look between the men and they both nodded. "Then you can drive the missing components over to me later today. I can't waste any more time this morning." I waved Constantine toward the open loading bay. "Start putting the stuff in the van."

Constantine nodded and moved to do just that.

"Micah," Pat began in a low voice, clearly displeased by every part of this morning's interaction.

I cut him off, because I was no happier than he was. These were people I needed to work with, people I needed to rely on. People I'd always treated well and expected to treat me the same. I was angry at them for the error, I was pissed at Donnie for being an asshole, I was pissed that Pat couldn't seem to stay out of my business, I was angry at Constantine for being unable to *exist* without provoking people to violence, and I was angry with *myself.* I hadn't been thinking about my business when I jumped to Constantine's defense and I knew better.

Business was the most important thing.

"We've always gotten along just fine, Pat, and I'm sure we'll continue to. But if you have anything else to say about my new employee, I'm gonna suggest you keep it to yourself."

I walked away without waiting for his reply.

———

CONSTANTINE and I loaded the van in silence and were halfway back to town before I couldn't take it anymore. I glanced over at the passenger's seat and found Constantine staring out the windshield, arms folded across his chest like Luna, my sister's toddler.

"You know, I don't get you," I said.

"Oh, here it comes."

"Pardon?"

"I've been waiting for this lecture since you started the van," Con scoffed. He managed to sound almost amused, but his shoulders were tense and his fingers gripped his biceps hard enough that tiny white divots appeared on his skin.

I took a deep breath and struggled to rein in my temper. "I get that you and Donnie have history, but could you have kept your mouth shut for one damn morning?"

Con narrowed his eyes as he turned his head toward me. "Kept my mouth shut? And let them screw you over on your order? For real?"

"This wasn't about me and my order. You didn't start that fight because he shorted me a couple of flowers."

"*Dozens*," Con corrected.

I made a dismissive gesture, even as I made a mental note to discuss it with Pat. "Constantine, I wasn't born yesterday. If anyone in the world wants to see me get screwed over by my supplier, it's gotta be you."

"Yeah, well, enemy of my enemy is my friend, right? Lucky you, today you were less of an enemy than Donnie."

I banged my hand against the steering wheel. "Goddamn it, Constantine. For once, don't make a *joke*."

"What do you want me to say?" he demanded. The cab of the van felt smaller, nearly claustrophobic, like the air before a storm, but Constantine forced a smile. "There's right and there's wrong, Micah. It's not complicated. I don't like people to get away with things. I don't like people being shitty to other people. Not even to you."

"Really? Because you sure fuck around a lot for someone with such a finely developed sense of justice."

"Fuck around a lot? What's that supposed to mean? People who have a lot of sex are terrible humans?"

"No! I'm not even talking about actual… *fucking*," I said, though I knew that was part of it. "You don't take anything seriously."

"I assure you, I take fucking very seriously."

"Like the market the other day," I said, ignoring him. "You just *strolled* in when the morning was half-over."

"Strolled." Con laughed. "Honestly? Is that the best you've got?"

"It's indicative of a larger problem," I said, sounding all kinds of self-righteous again.

"My car broke down Saturday morning. Transmission is shot."

"What?"

"My mother has no clue. And she'd better not find out," he added in a warning voice. "She's got enough on her plate dealing with the guy who's trying to steal her contracts and run her out of business."

Fuck. This explained so much of what I'd overheard.

I ignored that too. "But the whole morning at the market, you were so—" I bit the inside of my cheek. "Cheerful. Making jokes."

"Because I knew otherwise you'd be giving me those smug, superior looks from across the aisle. And I know exactly what you'd be thinking. *Constantine's fucked up again.*"

I winced because that was pretty much exactly what I'd thought. "Since when do you care what I think?" I demanded.

He shifted in his seat uncomfortably. "I don't. I just figured I'd give you shit before you could dish it out to me. Besides, would it do any good to cry and mope around like a victim?" He shrugged. "Gotta find the happy in life or you'll spend your whole day bawling. Why not make a stupid joke and laugh off the bad stuff?"

I stared at the road silently, unable to think of a good reason, except... "You can't expect people to think well of you if you don't correct them when they assume you're a flake."

"Because I'm responsible for people's assumptions? Nah. I stopped expecting people would give me the benefit of the doubt a while ago. I, ah, got in some trouble when I was a teenager." He paused expectantly.

"I've heard that," I confirmed. "Nothing specific, though."

"Yeah, well. Someday when you're bored, I'll give you the whole story. Your opinion of me probably can't get any lower anyway." He snickered. "Anyway, when people look at me, they see that same kid. Can't blame them, I guess. Big mistakes have big consequences, and people forgive, but they don't forget, especially around here. So someday I'll be hobbling down Weaver, dying of appendicitis, and they'll be all, '*Constantine, stop joking around!*'" He laughed and shook his head. "But at least I'm pretty. So people still like having me around." He batted his eyelashes.

I made a skeptical noise.

Constantine laughed again, then sobered.

"Being serious, though. I don't like negativity. I used to have a temper. I used to get really riled. Bullshit like that back at the warehouse..." He hooked a thumb toward the road behind us. "It brings me back to that place, and I don't like it. So I focus on the positive and ignore the negative."

"Can you do that?" I asked, genuinely curious. "How?"

"Sure. Told you the other night, Teflon skin."

"Yeah, but... What happens when the thing you want

to ignore is in your own head? Not someone else's opinion, but your own?"

"When the call is coming from *inside the house*? I dunno. Never happens to me." He shrugged.

"Be serious. Teflon doesn't help you when the unhappy person is *you*."

Con smiled. "You're cute when you psychoanalyze me."

I rolled my eyes. "You're changing the subject."

"I'm focusing on the positive," he insisted, his blue eyes sparkling. "Literally, the only enjoyable part of this conversation is seeing your big, strong hands on the steering wheel and the way your face gets all gorgeous and stern when you try to figure me out." He bit his lip and his eyes went half-lidded.

My *big, strong hands* flexed on the steering wheel and I nearly groaned. Had the debacle at the warehouse today not been enough to convince me that Constantine was a distraction I could not afford?

No sexy thoughts about the cute employee, Bloom.

"Remember that conversation we had an hour ago? The one about *seeds*?" I began.

"Ah, you mean the conversation *you* didn't like and refused to take part in, because it's okay when *you* ignore things you'd rather not acknowledge?" he said pointedly. "That one?"

I cleared my throat. "The one where I said we needed to act professionally. The one where I said no flirting."

"Hmm." He cocked his head to one side. "Nope. No, that was *never* mentioned. We talked about lust and kissing. We agreed that we want each other but don't *want* to want each other. Probably because, like you said the other night, I'm not your type and you're not mine." He smiled like he knew that was a lie.

He was so my type.

"We need to make an addendum to that plan, then. No flirtation. Especially no flirtation when you're doing it just to avoid discussing something else."

"Say *plan* again," he purred. "Say *addendum*. Gets me all excited."

I shot him a look. "This is exactly what I mean. If we're going to work together from now on, there can't be this… tension thing."

His head fell back on the seat. "It doesn't have to be a big deal."

"You made your opinion on that crystal clear earlier," I reminded him. "But it's a big deal to me. Flirtation is distracting, and I can't afford a distraction. Blooms is too important."

"So, you're saying you're so focused on your business, you don't have time to flirt?" Con blinked. "Does that mean you don't have sex? Like, at all?"

"Not that it's any of your business, but… rarely." I shrugged, feeling him judging me from the other side of the cab. "And not because I think there's anything wrong with casual sex. I don't. I just prefer when it means something. And I don't have room in my life for sex that means something. Got it?"

I could feel the weight of Con's eyes on me, but he didn't reply.

"So instead, we're gonna work. And I'm gonna keep you so busy, you won't have time to flirt. I'm gonna let you process all the stock and do all the shitty jobs, so I can focus on billing and other stuff, but if you want, I'll teach you that too, because God knows, if there were ever a job for a relentlessly cheerful person, it's bookkeeping. And then I'm gonna teach you how to make a decent flower arrangement if it kills me. Or, more likely, kills *you*." I gave him a pointed smile. "Your mother's gonna wonder where your sudden talents are coming from."

He huffed.

"Only thing that sucks, really, is that I can't have you answer the phone and deal with customers, 'cause God knows you could sell ice to an Alaskan, and I could use someone to help me charm them."

I expected a joke. At the very least, I expected a smirk or a comment about me calling him *charming*. But Constantine straightened in his seat.

"Okay," he said. "I can do that."

"I know," I agreed. "I wouldn't have hired you if I thought you couldn't." Which wasn't precisely true at all, since I hadn't known him at all on Saturday. But I felt like I knew him better now.

I made the left turn onto Weaver, just a few minutes from the center of town, when a thought occurred to me.

"Still early," I said, looking at the clock. It was barely six, but the sun was already beaming through the windshield, and the world was wide-awake. "Wanna risk someone seeing you climb out of the van behind the shop, or should I drop you somewhere else?"

"I, um, parked my car over at the police station." He winced. "My little brother's car, actually. Which is only mildly mortifying."

I snorted. "Want me to drop you there?"

"Yeah. Or maybe a little farther up on Firehouse Road?"

"You've got it."

I drove a couple of blocks past my shop and took a left, then pulled into the empty parking lot of the burger place next to the police station.

Constantine reached for the door handle but hesitated. He looked back at me. "Thank you. For the *you know*." He motioned back toward the warehouse. "And the…" He motioned between us. He took a deep breath and blew it out. "And the job, frankly. Because my car's not gonna replace itself." He scrubbed a hand through his hair. "I get that you're taking a chance on me, a guy you like *maybe* half the time. And I appreciate it, even if I'm not totally sure why. I'm not gonna do anything to fuck you over. That's basically what I want you to know."

I hesitated, deciding how much I wanted to say. Part of me wanted to say nothing and just let him walk out, because that would be by far the safest bet. I'd wanted *real Constantine*, right? But now that I was seeing him, he was overwhelming.

"Well, there's right and there's wrong, Constantine," I said slowly, repeating his earlier words.

He huffed out a laugh.

I focused my gaze on the steering wheel beneath my fingers. "Besides, I might have overstated things earlier. I probably only dislike you, say, *forty* percent of the time."

Constantine laughed again. "I've gone up a whole ten percent? Was it the coffee?" He grabbed the empty metal cups from the console and shook them in my direction. "Be honest. It was the coffee, wasn't it?"

"Yeah," I agreed. "The coffee helped. But I meant what I said when I offered you this job. I really do need help, from someone I won't need to train from scratch. And I appreciate what you did for me back there, too, pointing out the discrepancies with the order. So, um." I scratched the back of my neck. "I know you said you don't expect the benefit of the doubt from anyone, but I'm going to give it to you anyway. From now on."

His expression was momentarily startled, but then his sly, mischievous smile was back.

"Oh my God. Has the apocalypse come? Tell me, Micah, is this how the end times begin?"

"Always with the jokes," I sighed. "You're the one with the gift for prophecy, remember?"

"Oh, I remember." He waggled his eyebrows. "Anytime you want the chaos to stop, I'm happy to pucker up again. *Boss*."

"Because you think *you* might be my true love?" I hooted. "Also, nice job with the not-flirting, stock boy."

He shook his head at the new nickname. "I'm a slow learner."

"No, you're a fast forgetter. Get out of my van, Constantine. I'll see you Wednesday. Don't be late."

Constantine smiled broadly as he hopped down. "God, you really want me *bad*, don't you?"

His smug little smile should not have made me want to kiss him.

"Still delusional, Ross. You should really get that checked out."

"Still *accurate*." He winked. "Have a good day, boss. And for what it's worth, I think this employment thing is gonna work out just fine."

Chapter Five

CONSTANTINE

July

THIS EMPLOYMENT THING was not working out *at all*.

When my alarm went off at three o'clock in the fucking morning for the sixth Wednesday in a row, I nearly cried.

It had all seemed so easy at first. I mean, I'd felt like I was always working *anyway*, between my shifts at the station and the landscaping work, so how bad could ten or fifteen more hours of relatively easy labor for Micah be?

Answer: very bad.

For one thing, my dumbass self hadn't taken into account that the busy season for Ross Landscaping had barely started its upswing when I'd agreed to Micah's *proposition*. Now, every day brought hours and hours of monotonous work in the hot sun, mowing lawns and spreading mulch, leaving me exhausted and frustrated and cranky.

For another thing, I hadn't considered that getting to

Micah's to make money for a replacement car... *would require me to have a car.*

So far, Theo had been pretty cool about letting me borrow his Chevy, probably figuring he owed me for keeping my mouth shut about his graduation celebration, *which he did*. But my vague excuses about having "shifts" without specifying where—not outright lies, but pretty fucking close—were starting to wear thin, and he was getting suspicious. I hadn't talked to my mother about it *at all*.

For another-nother thing? I hadn't factored in just how fucking hard it would be to go without *fucking*.

Between the farmer's market on Saturday mornings, Saturday afternoons spent landscaping, and Saturday evenings spent at the station, I didn't have time to drag my ass to The Hive on a Saturday night, let alone the energy. And consequently, said ass—along with other very crucial parts of me—was feeling very, very neglected.

Which made it super lovely to spend hours and hours working next to Micah Bloom, with his big paws, and his patient smile, and the adorable little pucker between his eyebrows, and his cedar and lavender scent, and his rusty laugh that made me feel triumphant every time I caused it, and his fucking *relentlessly* professional attitude... and... and... Yeah.

Not working out *at all*.

Because if you were thinking I'd developed a tiny crush on Micah Bloom? You'd be totally wrong. I had an enormous, humongous, *soul-destroying* crush on the man.

Turned out, when I stopped provoking him and he stopped scowling at me, we actually got along. He'd taught me shit—about taxes and marketing and stock selection—and I kept my mouth shut and absorbed it like a sponge. He'd stopped treating me like a bomb he expected to explode at any moment and set me tasks to complete on my own. He wanted me to come to him for input. He'd shown me not just *how* he crafted the arrangements he was known for, but *why* he made them the way he did. I instinctively understood concepts like space and color, layering and dimension, on a larger scale when designing landscapes, but I'd never really considered how those things should be applied on a smaller scale, or how important those details might be to a larger project.

And, I thought, as I heaved myself out of bed in the darkness and set my feet on the floor, in all that time, he hadn't made a single inappropriate gesture or said a single flirtatious word. He'd kept my secret—even down to ignoring me completely at the farmer's market every weekend—and I'd kept my promise.

No flirtation.

No kissing.

Most definitely nothing else.

I pushed myself to my feet and grabbed a semi-clean pair of shorts from the chair in the corner, navigating by the weak beam from the streetlight that filtered in between my window and my air conditioner. The poor little machine was chugging away, but it was probably as old as me and could hardly keep up with the heat wave. One of these days, I was gonna buy a new one. Something tricked out or at least, you know, *functional.*

Because I was kind of a baller these days, what with my four-figure savings account balance and all.

That was the one silver lining to all this work—I'd been earning more money than ever, and I had no time to spend it, so the balance of my new car fund was growing exponentially. Soon, I'd have enough to consider buying a replacement, and then I'd be able to quit working with Micah.

Weirdly, the thought made me feel more disappointed than relieved. Maybe because, sexual frustration aside, working at Blooms was my favorite job of the three. I was tired of doing busywork with Mitch at the station. And I was way, *way* beyond tired of doing the jobs I did for my mother—work a lobotomized baboon was capable of doing. I wanted work that used my brain. That let me *create* something rather than maintain it. I wanted Mama to—

I cracked my neck from side to side and took a deep breath.

See? This was the shit I'd been telling Micah about. Once I started thinking negative thoughts, suddenly I was all-negative, all the time. And then, before you knew it, I was an overgrown toddler having a tantrum, taking my rage out on some asshole with a Camaro. And we all knew how *that* ended up.

I shoved my feet into my sneakers and went down the hall to the bathroom to brush my teeth and push my thick, wavy hair into some semblance of order. I barely recognized the guy in the mirror. I looked exhausted and impatient and worn.

Oh, pretty Con. How I miss you.

I made my way silently down the hall, avoiding the squeaky boards in the hallway between Theo's room and my mother's. There was a certain irony in the way I was using the evasive skills I'd learned as a fourteen-year-old sneaking out to drink warm beer with my friends at Pickett's Campground, to now sneak out to work.

Alas, I was pretty sure Mama would be even less tolerant of the work than she'd been of the beer, so I was forced to sneak.

I paused near the entryway to the living room and looked at her closed door for half a second. I really hated keeping things from her, especially something like this. I knew how much I owed her, I knew how much she depended on me, and I knew how hurt she'd be if she ever found out I was working for Micah, even knowing I'd done it partly to *help* Ross Landscaping.

But then, I also felt shitty whenever she said something cutting and derogatory about *that Micah Bloom*, who was stealing all our business… but was simultaneously showing me what it felt like to have someone not automatically assume I was gonna fuck things up.

I sometimes felt like I was being torn in two when I thought about it too long, so I tried not to think about it at all.

Positivity, you know?

I'd unlocked the deadbolt and swung the front door open when my mother's disembodied voice came from the darkened dining room to my right and scared the shit out of me.

"Constantine Luciano, where are you going?"

Fuck.

"Mama?" I whispered. "What are you doing up?"

I shut the door, stepped into the dining room, and flipped on the light.

My mother was curled up in her usual seat at the head of the table, and despite the warmth of the night, she had my father's old bathrobe bundled around her. With her hair tied back in its customary braid and her hands wrapped around a coffee cup, she looked much younger than her fifty-whatever years. Even a little bit lost.

My heart lurched. "What's wrong? Is Theo okay? Aunt Teresa?"

"They're fine, honey. Everyone's fine." Mama forced a tiny smile, but it faded almost instantly, and she rubbed at her forehead like she had a headache. "You know I've always been an early riser."

I sank into the seat at the far end of the table—the seat that belonged to my aunt Teresa on big family occasions these days, but would always be my dad's seat, in my mind —and frowned. "Three-fifteen might be taking it to an extreme."

"Not when there's a heat wave going on. Gotta be productive before the sun's up." She tapped her coffee cup with a fingernail. "Oh, have you seen Julian?"

"Jules?" I looked around. "Today?"

She sighed. "In general."

"Sure. We met for breakfast before the farmer's market last weekend. Why?"

"It was so warm yesterday, I was concerned about him, but he didn't answer my calls." She sounded half-worried, half-annoyed.

"Mama, he's twenty-nine, and he works like crazy."

"So?"

"So, Julian can take care of himself. Besides, his apartment has central air and so does the vet clinic. *I'm* more likely to have heatstroke than he is. But I won't," I added quickly. "I stay hydrated. I just mean he's an adult who can take care of himself. Just like I can."

"I suppose." She narrowed her eyes and peered at me across the table. "Where are *you* headed at this hour?"

"Uh. Work. There's always paperwork to be done. Gotta get a… jump start." I swung my fist in an arc.

"You're going to the station dressed like that?" Her eyes narrowed. "Where's your uniform?"

"Oh." *Fuck.* "Mitch doesn't mind how I dress when I'm not on duty."

Another day, another secret closer to a lie.

"Hmm. Well, don't forget that you've got to head to the Aaronsons' this afternoon. They need the backyard treated for—"

I waved a dismissive hand. "I know, Mama. It's been on the calendar for weeks. What's on your mind besides Jules lying cooked to death somewhere and my lack of uniform?" I knew there was more.

Mama scratched at her ear. "One of the sprinkler systems in the nursery needs fixing. It's going to be a couple of thousand dollars."

My stomach dropped. "Thousands?"

She nodded. "I was sure it was going to last the summer so we'd have a chance to get ahead of it, but Carlos says it's a lost cause. I'm going to get another loan."

"Mama," I protested.

She held up a hand, palm out. "I'm not asking your permission, Con. It's what needs to be done, and it'll be fine."

"If you believed that, you wouldn't be stressing about it at three in the morning."

She said nothing.

"Look, I'm not a child. I keep saying this, you keep claiming you understand, but I don't think you do." I ran both hands through my hair in frustration. "We can't keep taking out loans against the business with no way to pay them."

"Yes, I'm aware of that, Constantine," she snapped. "But sometimes there's no choice unless you want to give it up altogether."

I pushed my fingers into my eyes. "Those are the choices? Throw good money after bad, or close down completely? Maybe you could let me look things over. Maybe there's a way we could cut expenses or a better way to advertise to bring in new clients. Or we could take on bigger jobs, like I've suggested in the past."

This was the part where I should have shut up.

I mean, really, that part had come the minute I sat

down, because if I'd kept quiet, I'd have been on my way to Micah's instead of digging a hole for myself. But instead, I'd opened my mouth, and suddenly the words were rolling out with all the destructive force of a runaway locomotive.

This was not the time to talk about this—literally, given that it was dark o'clock, and we were both exhausted. Plus, I'd *promised* myself after last time that I wouldn't bring up my landscape design dreams for the business again until I'd proven to her that I was responsible enough to bring them to reality, and she'd have no choice but to take me seriously. But once these words had started spewing out, once I'd seen her eyes glint the way they only did when she was *truly* angry, I knew my only hope was to keep talking. To convince her.

Because that had worked so well every other time I'd tried it.

"I have so many ideas. We could take on more clients. We could do bigger jobs, get commissions. You know, after the thing with Ms. Semple a couple of years ago—and you were right, Mama, we really couldn't have handled that then—I have learned *so* much. I've taken online courses, and I've studied extensively. And, um, recently I've been learning bookkeeping and marketing too. I could help. I *want* to help. You shouldn't have to handle all this stuff on your own when two heads are better than—"

She looked at me incredulously, and I ran out of steam.

"Constantine. Ross. I have been doing these books for *years*. I have been running this business *by myself* for years. I have been making the decisions and finding the money and keeping things afloat *for years*."

"I know," I said. "I *know*, and I hate that you've had to do that, Mama. Which is why—"

"Do you really think there's a huge pile of income I'm

sitting on that I just haven't tapped?" She sat up straight and her eyes blazed with hurt and anger. "That I'm an idiot?"

"Of course not! That's not what I'm saying *at all*," I told her. "I just think—"

"*I just think* you need to mind your business, young man. You might be an adult, but you are still my son, and it is not your job to run this company. I know what I'm doing. I've been robbing Peter to pay Paul ever since—" She broke off and shook her head in frustration. "I'll figure out a way to come up with the money this time too, alright? This is not for you to worry about."

I swallowed hard against the lump in my throat and closed my eyes.

Ever since... I'd been a little punk who'd tried to get revenge against Trent Gaynor. Ever since I'd ruined her life.

"You know, sweetie, I think I might try to head back to bed. My head's killing me." She pushed to her feet. "Don't forget the Aaronsons."

"*Jesus fucking Christ.* I said I'd remember," I snapped.

I wasn't sure which of us was more shocked by my outburst.

Positivity was a powerful drug, but always pushing away your problems had a dirty little side effect called *resentment.* There were moments when I could actually feel it, pulsing hot and angry in my gut, reminding me of everything that was holding me back from having what I wanted. This was one of those moments.

And my angry, tired, frustrated self could not back down.

"Don't you *dare* use that language with me! And don't you take that tone, either. You can be forgetful."

But I really wasn't. At all. Hadn't been for *years*. And

Micah had been right—deep down, I *was* tired of people believing I was irresponsible and dumb. I was tired of letting *myself* believe those things.

Because if Micah Bloom could give me the benefit of the doubt, why couldn't my own mother?

As calmly as I could, I asked, "Mama, when have I forgotten a job?"

Her eyelid twitched as she tried—and failed—to think of an example. "Well, I don't know. But you were late just the other day."

Oh my God.

"That was once. And it was actually more than a month ago, if you think back." I sighed. "And I was only late because Bessie's transmission died."

Her forehead wrinkled. "Your car? You said it was with a friend!"

"Joe Cross *is* a friend. And I didn't want you to worry because I'm taking care of it. I'm not the fuckup I was at fourteen."

"*Language*, Constantine."

"Really?" I pushed to my feet. "That's what you're hearing here? Me swearing? Not any of the parts about me being trustworthy? Not any of the parts where I'm asking you to trust me or the part where I'm begging to be more involved in the business?"

"I do *not* understand where all this anger is coming from." She shook her head. "You're already involved. You're an integral part of Ross Landscaping. And maybe I don't thank you often enough—"

"This isn't about me needing a pat on the back! It's about me wanting to have a say in what we do and how we handle problems." I hesitated for a second, then said, "I have a few thousand dollars saved from working overtime. I can give it to you for the sprinkler."

"You earned *thousands* working at the station? That's not in the town budget. Where'd they get the money to pay you?" She squinted at me, trying to read my mind. She wasn't nearly as good at it as Micah.

"Irrelevant!" I felt my resentment flare hot again. "I'm offering you money, and all I want in exchange is to have a voice in this business."

She set her lips, and I knew what her answer would be before she said it.

"No. Absolutely not. I'm not taking your money, Constantine, though I appreciate the offer. I truly do." She sighed so deeply the sound seemed to come from her toes. "And as far as the business goes, you don't need to *buy* a voice, for goodness' sake. It's our family company. Of course you have a say in it! If you ever want to bring me an idea—a *reasonable* idea," she added with a grin, like this was in any way funny, "I'd be more than happy to listen. I love you." She stepped forward and patted my cheek. "Stay cool today, you hear me? Hydration is key."

My stomach churned with frustration and disappointment and *anger* so vast and caustic it made my fists clench. I had no idea where to put it; I had no clue how to get *rid* of it.

This was the kind of helpless anger that had gotten me in trouble time and time and time again, until finally, I'd learned the secret to dealing with it was to never get angry.

Except here I was.

"Well, this has been a heck of a conversation, considering the sun hasn't risen, huh? I've gotta go," I told her. In fact, I was already late. "I'll see you tonight."

"Try to be home at a decent hour for once," she mock scolded. "No more overtime."

"Yeah," I agreed. "Sure."

Sometimes it really was just easier to go along with things.

———

THE SUN WAS STILL below the horizon line when I got to town. For a second, I debated parking Theo's car right outside Micah's Blooms and letting the chips fall where they might, but the last thing I wanted was *more* drama, so I pulled into a spot on the other side of the road, outside O'Leary Hardware. I *slammed* the door, and the sound ricocheted up and down the deserted street, but it wasn't enough.

I was in full basilisk mode right now. *Rip, tear, kill.*

I walked up to Micah's front door and knocked on the glass—*pounded* on the glass, really—and a minute later, Micah walked out of the back room wearing his usual jeans, t-shirt, and barely there grin.

Pretty handsome, for a guy my mother believed to be the devil incarnate.

Every time I walked into Blooms—usually via the back door he left propped open for me—I had to make a conscious effort to tamp down the *wanting*. I'd catch him sitting at the desk in his little office out back—reading glasses on his nose, tidy stack of invoices on his desk arranged by due date, another stack of orders to be filled arranged chronologically, everything stapled with stock lists and little sketches or printed pictures of arrangements, every paper littered with a confetti of multicolored sticky notes covered in his nearly illegible scrawl—and I'd become way too aware of the flow of blood in my veins and the buzzing in my ears. I'd remind myself that office supplies were not a fucking *aphrodisiac* and that Micah didn't want me anyway.

But today? Today I asked myself whether Micah actually *did* want me. Whether I could *make* him.

The thought ratcheted up the churning in my gut.

"What's this?" Micah demanded, pulling the door open a couple of inches and leaning against the frame. "We use the front door? Are we out of the closet now?"

"I've been out of the closet since I was a teenager," I told him.

"Wow, that long, huh?" Micah said in mock amazement. "A whole ten minutes?"

I gritted my teeth. "You gonna let me in? Or is there a quota of shit you have to give me first?"

"You're late."

"I know."

Micah pushed the door open, leaving just enough room for me to duck under his arm between him and the door. I walked directly to the back room, and I heard Micah lock the door behind me.

The room was familiar to me now. Comforting, in a way. But I fought the urge to kick at the furniture, just to see it smash. I was spoiling for a fight with someone. who could take it.

Or a fuck. Either would work.

I tossed my keys on the long, metal workbench in the center of the room, which was already strewn with wire, ribbons, and a half-completed arrangement of red roses and bouvardia. I leaned my palms against the cool surface and reached out a finger to trace a delicate, star-shaped flower. I wished I had something to hit.

"What's up?" Micah demanded from behind me.

I looked back at him. "Nothing. Why?"

"You're late," he repeated.

"Yeah? So?"

"So, you're always on time."

Oh, the irony.

"Singing a different tune these days, huh? This is you giving me the benefit of the doubt again, right? Keeping your promise no matter what?" I rolled my eyes.

Micah walked to the other side of the worktable and leaned back against the countertop behind him, folding his arms over his chest and studying me. "You haven't given me a reason to regret it. What's going on, Con?"

I set my teeth. I did *not* want him being nice. My body felt too big for my skin, like my anger was growing exponentially but without a target to vent it on or any way to calm it down. I was *never* like this anymore.

I pressed my palms to my eyes and groaned. "This day *sucks*."

"It's barely four hours old."

"So?" I slammed both palms down on the table with a satisfying slap. "Are you the… the… *decider of days* now, Micah? Can a day not suck without your *permission*?"

"No," Micah said solemnly. "It can't."

He was trying to make me laugh. I knew it. I knew it, and *fuck me*, I appreciated it, but I didn't *want* it. If there was ever a time I needed the man to be provoked, it was right now. I needed someone to be as worked up as I was. Someone I could punch or scream at or fuck six ways to Sunday.

So of course the man just stood there, calm as a rock in the middle of a rushing river, folding his *fucking hot* arms over his *fucking hot* chest and… Suddenly, I knew exactly how to get the reaction I wanted.

"Maybe I was late because I needed to jerk off," I said, almost like an accusation. I ran my hand down over the front of my pants and pushed against the semi-hardness there. "I'm still *young*, remember? I have needs. Especially first thing in the morning when I—"

"*Jesus.*" He rolled his eyes. "If you don't wanna talk to me, we won't talk. Don't be an asshole."

He pushed past me toward his office and his shoulder bumped mine.

Not *quite* the reaction I'd hoped for.

Not even remotely.

"You asked what was up with me," I called before turning to follow him. "So I'm telling you."

Micah sighed and sank into his chair. He picked up a pen and shuffled through the papers on his desk. "We have three arrangements to make for deliveries to the hospital this afternoon. There's a goddamn baby boom in the O'Leary area right now. Oh, and I wanted to talk to you about… What are you doing, Con?"

"Me?" I walked around the desk, leaned my ass just inches from his hand, and ran my hand up and down my stomach. "Nothing."

He leaned his chair back, threw his pen on the desk, and folded his arms over his chest again. "I swear, I thought I'd learned to read you over the past few weeks, but this?" He shook his head in exasperation. "You're gonna have to help me out. What's the exact *opposite* of horny, Constantine? Because I'm pretty sure *that* is how you're *really* feeling right now."

The fact that he was right only made me madder. "Always trying to psychoanalyze me, Micah. When are you going to learn I'm just not that complicated?" My nostrils flared. "When are you gonna learn you're not as smart as you think you are?"

"Mmm. Nah. Sorry. I'm pretty freakin' smart," he said, almost apologetically. "And I know your tells."

I snorted. "Yeah? Well, thank God one of us does. Maybe you could clue *me* in."

"Like, for example," he continued as if I hadn't

spoken. "Half the time, you don't laugh at your own bullshit."

"What?"

"You don't do and say outrageous things because you think they're funny, you do them to *deflect*. Like that, out there." He lifted his chin toward the workroom. "Like this, right now." A nod at the hand just above my waistband.

I moved my hand away and made myself laugh. "Fascinating. This erection is actually... *a deflection*? There are so many poems just waiting for me to—"

Micah's lips twitched. "*Aaaand* he proves my point."

"Oh, come on! That proves exactly *nothing* except that I'm really sarcastic. I'm told I get it from my dad, but I wouldn't know. My dad actually—"

"*Aaaand* he deflects again."

"What the fuck?" I said, leaning over so I was in his space. "It's not deflection when you don't want to talk about something. Deflection is when you're—"

"*Aaaand* he deflects once more, this time by actually arguing the definition of deflection." He paused. "So meta."

I straightened and glared at him. "People can have bad days, you know. Not wanting to talk about my troubles with *yo*, doesn't mean I'm *deflecting*."

"With me," Micah repeated. "Why is talking with *me* so bad?"

I felt my face go hot. Fucking stupid fucking *crush*. "Because you like me less than half the time, maybe?"

Micah opened his mouth, and I leaned forward to clap my hand over it before he could speak. "And if you tell me I'm deflecting again, so help me God, I will not be responsible for my actions."

I could practically feel Micah's smile grow under my hand.

"Don't do it," I warned. "I will… I will throw every single one of these meticulously organized papers on the floor."

Micah's breath was hot on my palm as he laughed —*laughed*! Jesus, I should not like him laughing as much as I did. "What's so funny? You would *hate it* if I messed up your perfect desk, so don't make me do it."

Except we both knew he could stop me if he wanted to. Could move away in a heartbeat if he wanted to. He could take everything I dished out and give it right back to me… if he wanted to.

Micah stayed where he was, watching me with those intense green eyes that just *did things* to me, and that same hot urge that had been riding me since I left the house that morning roared back, stronger than before, but different somehow. All that nonspecific anger had morphed from a simple desire to provoke a reaction into true desire.

Very *targeted* desire.

I cleared my throat as need seared through my belly. My fingers twitched against his face. "Micah? You remember when I told you that our mutual attraction was like a seed?" My voice was low in the silent room.

Micah's eyes grew wary and he shook his head slowly… but he didn't move away, and that was as good as an engraved invitation, as far as I was concerned.

I moved my hand away from his mouth, braced my palms on the arms of his chair, and bent my head until our lips were a centimeter apart.

"Constantine," he warned.

"Micah," I teased.

I leaned a little farther, closed my eyes, and pressed my mouth to his softly.

Micah froze, about as excited by my proximity as a piece of furniture. So, I kissed him again, harder, because sex was the one thing that had always been *easy* for Christ's sake, but he sat there like a block of marble, and I realized —like, *duh*—that him not pushing me away was *not* the same thing as him wanting me. And more than likely, I'd gotten it wrong again.

Oh, *God*, I was so stupid. And I'd just ruined—

As I started to pull back, Micah lifted a hand to cup my neck, his lips parted beneath mine, and his tongue came out to trace the seam of my lips. I gasped at the contact— the *oh, shit, finally contact*—and closed my eyes as the kiss burned hotter.

The hard knot of anger and confusion in my gut transformed into something cleaner, brighter, *harmless*, like fireworks flaring behind my eyelids. It was so good, not just the way the kiss felt but the way it made *me* feel—that I made this horrifying, needy little noise at the back of my throat and I *melted* into it. My arms wobbled, and I all but climbed onto his lap in an attempt to get closer.

And then Micah's free hand was on my ass, pulling me toward him, and suddenly I *was* in his lap, straddling him on the narrow rolling chair. My dick pushed against my shorts, needing more friction, and when I rubbed myself against him and found *him* hard, as well, I moaned at the sensation. I speared my hands into his hair, locking him against me as I rocked against his stomach.

Micah inhaled sharply and started to pull back, but I instinctively followed him, not wanting the kiss to end. He yanked at my hair and forced my head back.

"*Enough*," he said, his voice smoky-rough but insistent. "Enough, Con."

I opened my eyes—I wasn't really sure when I'd closed them—but the glare of the overhead lights seemed way too bright suddenly, way too intense and real, and I fought the urge to close them again as I backed off his lap and stood up.

"*Wow.*" I pushed out a breath and forced a smile. "That was good, huh? Better than the last one, even. I mean, not that I'm in the habit of comparing kisses or whatever, because that would be rude, but if I had to rate it—"

"Constantine." Micah ran a hand through his hair. "Stop."

"Stopped." I spread my hands. "Witness me stopping."

He sighed. "This was a bad idea on so many levels. I swore this wasn't going to happen again."

Like I didn't know that.

"Okay, so it's done. Over. Do we have to talk about it?" I pleaded. I rubbed my eyes and colors burst behind my lids, which was a little too close to the fireworks I saw when Micah kissed me, so I stopped immediately and opened my eyes to look at him and started ticking the reasons off on my fingers. "You're not down to fuck. Not with me. I get it. That's clear. Like, abundantly clear. I knew it. I *know* it. A bad idea on so many levels, like you said. I'm a hot mess. You only like me maybe half the time. I'm your *employee.*" I made air quotes. "I just had a moment of temporary insanity, okay? Which, if we're being honest, was bound to happen at some point because I'm *me* and you're—"

"*No.* No, Con. It's not okay." Micah pushed to his feet, and his chair went rolling back to crash into the wall as he loomed over me. "This was not bound to happen. I told you before. *Talk* to me if you want, but don't be an asshole and push this—"

"*Pssht.* Okay, wait. There are many things I'm guilty of, but those *were* your hands on me, right? You don't *want* to want me, but you do," I reminded him. "I admit that I shouldn't have done it, for all the reasons I said. But after the first second you were right there with me! I was hardly pushing you or corrupting you or whatever." I was pretty sure, anyway. *God*, let me be sure of *something.* "Right?"

Micah's eyes softened and he sighed. Like he pitied me.

I might literally vomit.

"Yes, I want you! Jesus Christ, of course I want you. Three quarters of the people on this earth want you, and if there are sentient beings in outer space, *they want you, too.* Wanting you is not the issue."

"Wanting to want me is." I rolled my eyes. "I know. I get it. *Now* can we stop talking?"

"You know what I think, Constantine?" He leaned even closer.

I rolled my eyes and folded my arms over my chest, purposely not letting him crowd me. "I know you're gonna tell me."

"I think you use sex to deflect *a lot.* And guess what? I am *not* going to be another guy you fuck around with."

He sounded so self-righteous, I wanted to hit him. And it occurred to me that never before in my entire life had I found myself painfully aroused and violently angry at the same time.

This was a special new low.

"Oh, for God's sake." I pushed at his chest with both hands and felt a rush of victory when I pushed him back a pace. "You think you're *so* smart and *so* observant, Micah? You don't know *shit.*"

He shook his head, patient and calm, like I was a little kid throwing a tantrum. His erection was still tenting the front of his pants, and mine was too, but unlike me, he was as emotionally engaged as if we were discussing cereal choices at the grocery store. How could he turn off and on like that? It was *infuriating.*

I pushed him again.

"You think you've got me all figured out, huh?"

Micah's chin went back. "A little. I think you're afraid to talk about real shit. I think you put on a mask sometimes. I think it's easier for you to pretend you don't care what other people think of you than for you to challenge assumptions."

I had no argument against any of that, and that was even *more* infuriating.

I lifted my hands to push him again, but this time he grabbed my wrists.

"I also think you'd better calm the fuck down and not put your hands on me again, Constantine."

"Or *what?*" I demanded. "You don't get to be in control of everything, Micah. You don't get to decide how I feel or how I act! And you know what? I think I scare the shit out of *you* for that exact reason."

Micah pushed me back by the wrists and I stumbled back a pace. The desk caught me in the back of the legs and knocked me backward.

"I'm not going to let you provoke me into doing something impulsive just because you're in a shit mood for reasons I can't fathom because *you won't share them.*"

I sucked in a shuddering breath and stared at him, at his set jaw, at the exasperation and concern in his green eyes. I was pushing too hard, wanting too much, always too much emotion and too little sense.

"Fuck." I was horrified to find tears stinging the backs of my eyes, and I looked away before they could fall or, worse, before he could see them. "You know what? Record this, because I'm only gonna say it once: you're right. I'm wrong." I pushed myself upright and stepped away from the desk. "And I'm sorry. I think I'm overtired. Or possibly I've been taken over by an alien." I made myself laugh as I turned toward the workroom. "Is it aliens that take people over? Or is that demons? I always forget."

"Constantine—" Micah called.

"No." I shook my head. "You want me to talk about everything that's wrong with me," I said without turning around. "But you don't get that I *can't* talk. I just… I can't fucking *talk*. I open my mouth to speak, and what comes out is a joke or something hateful."

I grabbed my keys from the workbench and kicked at the leg of the table *hard*, sending flowers and wire cutters crashing to the floor. I sucked in a breath through my nose. "I don't *know* what I think, and I don't *know* how I feel, except very tired and very, very… *angry*. So I'm gonna take my ass home—" I thought of my mother and cringed at the idea of going back to that house for round two. "Or possibly to Disney World. Or Outer Mongolia. Or outer space. Someplace not here."

I scrubbed at my eyes, trying to erase the moisture, but it just kept building. I clenched my hand around the keys so hard I could feel the metal pressing against the bumps and edges in my bones, and one of them would yield eventually, but who knew which one?

"I'll make up the hours another day, assuming I still have a—*oof*."

The breath left my lungs in a whoosh as I was suddenly pinned face-first against the stainless-steel refrigerator next to the workbench by a very large, very hard body.

"Micah?" I croaked, bucking my back. "Get the fuck off me!"

"I didn't get it." His voice was calm in my ear. "I understand now."

"Get what? Understand what? Get *off*." I tried to elbow him in the ribs, tried to squirm away, but his entire body was pushing against me and I had no leverage. He grabbed my wrists and pinned those against the cold metal, too.

"I know a thing or two about feeling like something is taking over your brain," Micah said in my ear. The fucker didn't even sound out of breath, despite my flailing, and it shouldn't have been possible, because I was nearly his size, but I was stuck to the refrigerator like a goddamn magnet. "Like, for example, when I found myself asking this pain in the ass to come and work for me, even though I wanted him and didn't *want* to want him."

Then he rubbed his erection against the top of my ass.

I had no clue what was going on right now. My cock didn't seem to care. My erection, which had nearly died away a few minutes ago, came roaring back to life.

"I wanted you to talk, because for some reason it matters that you trust me." Micah's breath was hot against my ear. "But that's what this is, isn't it? You came to me *because* you trust me."

My heart went *skip-thump-skip*, and my breathing picked up like I was running when I hadn't moved a muscle. His fingers twitched against my skin and his chest pressed against my side.

"What do you need, Constantine?" he demanded, his voice low and intent.

I looked over my shoulder and found his eyes, those laser-beam eyes, focused right on me, reading the truth before I could even utter it. "I don't *know*," I whispered miserably.

Micah nodded once. He spun me around and pressed me against the refrigerator once again. The metal was cold against my back, even through my shirt, and I sucked in a ragged breath. In one fluid movement, Micah grabbed both my wrists and pinned them to the door above my head, while his knee shoved between my thighs, pushing my legs apart.

"You stay right there," he warned.

"What? No." I struggled against him. "This isn't—"

"You stay," he growled again, pushing my wrists harder. "Where I put you. And for once, do as I say."

"Fuck. You." I yanked against his grip, which was iron-hard, and ignored the pleasant swoop in my belly. "I'm not a *child*."

"You're not a child," Micah agreed. "But you're gonna listen to me, and I'm gonna take care of you. And then we're gonna talk."

He bit at the hinge of my jaw and my back bowed off the fridge in helpless arousal. My cock was rock-hard, harder than I could ever remember it.

"I want to be fucked," I insisted. "Hard and fast. That's what I want. To get out of my head for a minute."

"To be used up?" Micah demanded. "For me to use you to get off?"

"Yes! Yes, exactly," I nearly sobbed in relief. "Exactly like that. Rough and messy. Right now."

Micah transferred my wrists to one hand and shifted his weight so he was leaning against me, trapping my right leg between both of his. His free hand gripped my chin, and his thumb dragged back and forth over my mouth, catching on my bottom lip.

"This mouth," he whispered. "This mouth is *indecent*. The shit you say to me, Constantine. The way you tease. I've wanted to slap this mouth. I've wanted to kiss this mouth."

I whimpered and darted my tongue out to wet my lips, wetting his thumb not-so-accidentally in the process. His pupils dilated, and he ground against my hip in a slow circle, letting me feel his hardness, but otherwise didn't move. His thumb kept brushing against my mouth until every single nerve ending was standing at attention, every electron in every molecule in every cell of my skin was charged and waiting to combust.

"Come on," I whined. "Micah, for God's sake, do something."

Micah smiled a little and shifted his fingers back to my hair.

"Do *something*?" he repeated, like he was tasting the words as he spoke them. "I think I *am* doing something. I'm appreciating you. I'm *savoring* you, Constantine. Nice and slowly. And I'm making you take it."

He gripped my hair in his fist and forced my head to the side, baring my neck, and ran his teeth over the tendon he exposed.

"Ahhh!" My hips punched into the air, seeking friction where there was none to be found.

"You might have noticed, I'm not twenty-four. I've learned to take my time, to enjoy things. You need something, baby? I'm gonna give it to you. But I told you, I'm not one of your anonymous fucks. You're gonna know *exactly* who you're with, every minute. This is going to happen *my way*, or it's not going to happen at all. You decide. Right now."

He licked a path from my collarbone up to my ear and gnawed lightly at the lobe. I squeezed my eyes shut and nearly cried from frustration. I bit my oversensitized lip and whimpered.

I needed more action and less thought. More speed and less savoring. Already, I could feel my anger morphing, twisting, becoming something less like a fire and more like a flood, and I didn't know how to hold it back. When he actually put his hands on me, I thought I might drown in the riptide.

But Jesus, I wanted him. I *needed* his hands on me. If he walked away right now, I wasn't sure I could survive that either. So I picked the lesser of two evils and whispered, "Your way."

Micah huffed out a breath. "Damn straight." He brought my wrists down to pin them on either side of my waist. "Don't move unless I tell you to."

I leaned my head back against the refrigerator and watched through half-lidded eyes as he sank to his knees in front of me.

Oh mother of God.

He unbuttoned my shorts in record time, helped me kick off my shoes and socks, and stripped down my pants and briefs. I had this one second where I thought this would be exactly as fast and simple as I wanted it to be. But the second I was naked from the waist down, he stopped again.

"Oh, Con," he breathed, staring at my erection like it was a work of art as he ran his hands up the front of my thighs. "*Christ.*"

He braced his hands on my hips and looked up at me, green eyes dark with *wanting*. I had to swallow hard.

I was no stranger to blowjobs, giving or receiving. And not to be crass, or whatever, but it would take more than my fingers and toes to count the number of people I'd had staring up at me while they sucked my dick over the years. Every person had a different technique, some were better than others, but there wasn't a single one I could really *remember*. They'd all sort of blurred together.

But having Micah on his knees, staring at me in that reverent, intense way? This was the best blowjob of my life, and his mouth hadn't hit my cock yet.

He gripped the base of my erection and stroked it once with exactly the right amount of pressure. That, just *that,* and I let out a long moan and leaned heavily against the door. He chuckled.

"God, you're so responsive."

"Not living up to your fantasies?"

Micah hummed, neither agreement nor disagreement. "You're assuming I've let myself have fantasies?" Micah licked at the crease where my leg met my torso.

"Hunh-unh."

"Because if I did, I wouldn't have been able to work with you. I wouldn't have been able to stand across from you at the farmer's market every week and pretend I didn't see you." He pushed my thighs farther apart and caressed my balls with his free hand while he whispered his words into my skin. "How'd you put it before? I'd have pushed you down on my table, right on those fucking potted daisies, and taken you in front of the whole town."

My head fell back to *thunk* against the door, and I felt my dick pulse in Micah's hand. I didn't think that had ever happened before.

"But this is so much better, isn't it, Con? Now I can take you apart piece by piece, and no one will see it but me." He flicked his tongue over the tip of my cock.

"Oh my God," I breathed.

Micah chuckled again, his breath ghosting over my skin. "Look at me, Constantine. Watch me."

He waited until my eyes met his, until our gazes caught and held, then he licked a stripe up the length and swirled around the head.

"And you say *my* mouth is indecent," I croaked. "Shit, Micah." My palms flexed against the door, needing something to grip onto. Grinning, Micah picked up one of my hands and moved it to his head, forcing my fingers to close over his hair, like he could read my fucking mind. Like he really *did* know what I needed.

Nope. I definitely wasn't gonna survive this.

Micah sucked the head inside his mouth and then *he* was the one moaning as he swirled his tongue around it, like he'd been teasing *himself* for ten minutes instead of me. I clenched my hands more tightly in his hair and his eyes blazed with approval, so I moved my hips just a little and then a little more, loving the sounds he made and the way his fingers were leaving bruises on my hipbones.

"That's it," he said hoarsely, pulling off with a wet, popping sound that echoed in the otherwise silent room. "Give it to me. Hard as you want. Because you know I can take it."

Fuck. Fuck. *That* was exactly what I needed. And exactly what I wanted, too.

I nodded and Micah grinned up at me, fierce and *proud*, and I understood that there was no place else he wanted to be right then, no one else he was imagining in my place. This, right now, was for me specifically. For *him and me* specifically.

I tried to be gentle as I guided his mouth back to my cock, respectful of this gift he was offering me. But when he parted his lips and looked up at me again, when the warmth of his breath hit the skin he'd already dampened with his tongue, gentle ceased to be an option. I wanted to take, and own, and *mark*.

That was *my* dick leaving a sticky trail of precum against his stubbled chin. *Me* who was going to own that mouth. *Me* who was gonna mess him up. *Me* Micah had gotten on his knees for. *Me* he didn't want to be gentle. *Me* who was going to lose my mind.

Me he was provoking, as surely and deliberately as I'd ever provoked him.

He sucked me all the way to the back of his throat with a grunt, and I gripped his hair with two hands because it felt so fucking good, the sensation ricocheted up my spine and down my legs. I thrust into his mouth over and over again, faster and faster, and Micah loved it, his eyes telegraphing that he was every bit in control here, no matter who was on their knees for whom. He was giving me this because he wanted me to have it.

I slapped my palms against the refrigerator, my arms braced wide like some kind of sacrificial offering, and let the pleasure consume me—pleasure so vast and deep that there was no room inside me for impotent anger, or doubt, or embarrassment. My heart stuttered, my chest clenched tight, and when I screamed Micah's name and shot down his throat, the release was way beyond physical.

I lost a little part of myself to Micah Bloom right then —opened myself to him in a way I didn't think I could undo—because I'd just shown him all the worst pieces of me, the ugliest, most vulnerable, shameful parts of Constantine Ross, and instead of rejecting, or dismissing, or mocking them, he'd transformed them into something beautiful.

I tapped his shoulder to get him to stand up, though my breathing was still ragged, and my mind was spinning, and I wasn't sure my legs were going to hold me, because that was how this game was played, you know? Tit for tat, and now it was my turn, and that was okay because I wanted it.

But Micah didn't jump up to take my place. Instead, he ran his tongue over my cock with that same patient reverence as before and slowly pulled my underwear and shorts back on. I bent to grab my shoes and socks, but he batted my hands away so he could do the task himself. My breathing stuttered again.

When he finally did lift himself to his feet, he didn't move away, and he shook his head when I reached for the waistband of his pants, despite the fact that he was *insanely* hard.

He leaned against me, pressing me into the refrigerator with his body again. This time, I didn't fight his hold.

All the fight had gone out of me.

He pressed his lips to the pulse in my neck and it was… *God.* I didn't know what to do or say. I was good at sex, right? It was, like, my *one thing.* And Micah had changed the rules and left me wrong-footed even in this. Still, my hands clenched in the fabric of his t-shirt because I couldn't seem to let him go.

"I can hear you thinking," he said, his voice sounding wrecked but amused. "You ready to talk yet?"

"All this to get me to talk?" My own voice was hardly more than a croak. "I feel like if more therapists offered this service, American mental health would—"

"Constantine." Patient, gentle.

"Especially if you were the therapist, because I have to say you've got skills like *whoa*—"

"Constantine." Still gentle. Less patient.

I sighed and told the top of his head, "I'm kind of an idiot."

"Uh-huh."

I slapped his flank. "You're supposed to disagree."

"Uh-huh," he said again, more gently. "Why are you an idiot?"

I shrugged. It was too silly to even articulate. *I had a fight with my mother, and I was having a hissy fit-slash-existential crisis. Typical Wednesday.* Definitely the way to reassure the guy who'd just given you the most epic sexual experience of your entire life that you weren't just a one-time thing, right?

Oh fuck. I was more messed up than I'd thought if I was already wanting a repeat. I really *was* an idiot.

When I remained silent, Micah sighed and pulled away. "Come on." He wrapped an arm around my waist and tried to steer me toward the back door, but I resisted.

"Come where?"

"Oh, *now* you're suspicious? You beg me to fuck you over the counter, but God forbid I want to take you out for coffee, because *that's* when shit might get weird?"

I looked at his face. His mouth was red and puffy, but his eyes were shining.

"Come on," he repeated, and this time I followed him without a word.

Chapter Six

MICAH

I HAD to bite the inside of my cheek to keep from groaning as I led Constantine out into the alley. Of course, *now* the man was compliant and silent, wearing the little half-smile that had started making my stomach flip at some point over the past month.

Have you ever felt like a part of you—the rational, sensible part of you—was watching from a distance in horrified fascination, perhaps eating popcorn, as the irrational, idiot part of you was about to make a Very Large Error?

Yeah, me neither, until Constantine and I had crashed together a few weeks ago at the farmer's market. Ever since, there'd been this other thing—this very irrational, needy *other thing*—making all my decisions.

Constantine's hair was a little damp, like he'd been sweating—like I'd *made him* sweat—and I couldn't help walking a little more closely behind him and resting my hand on the small of his back. I inhaled deeply, and I could smell him on me, or me on him, and it made my blood pound with something that was beyond protective, it was downright *possessive*.

I led Con around the delivery van, which was parked closest to the door, and pulled open the passenger's-side door of my silver pickup. He seemed surprised, maybe because we'd never gone anywhere in my personal vehicle together, but then, this was hardly the biggest employer-employee line we'd crossed today. *That* had happened sometime when I was kneeling on the hard, linoleum floor of my own fucking store, swallowing his load.

I adjusted my hard-on and tried to regain just a tiny bit of the self-control I used to think was ingrained in my bones.

Con didn't say a word as he climbed in, just gave me this grateful, sheepish little smile that sent a bolt of need flashing through me and seared away even the hope of my erection deflating. I waited until he got his seat belt on, gave him an encouraging smile, then closed his door... and froze.

Why was I acting like this was a *date*? Was it not bad enough that I'd already crossed a billion lines, messed up my priorities, left my work unfinished so I could help my employee through his mental crisis with some *sexual healing*? Not good. Not good at all. In fact, this was way more troubling than anything else that had happened that morning.

Getting on my knees for Con was not a big deal, in and of itself. Every guy knew orgasms were a handy alternative to a fistfight when your blood was running too hot to talk sense into yourself, and if a blowjob was a symbol of commitment, then Constantine would probably be engaged to half the state.

But the other shit? The part where I'd needed to make sure Constantine knew exactly who was worshipping his cock, who was swallowing his cum? The part where I wanted him to trust me? That was the part I had to put a leash on.

Or maybe a noose.

I'd told Constantine weeks ago that I didn't have room in my life for sex that meant something, and that hadn't changed. Sure, I'd *thought* about this, even if I'd told Con I hadn't. Hell, I'd jacked off thinking about this. I mean, Jesus, look at the man. But attraction did not equal action. It most certainly did not equal *feelings*. And even if I *were* insane enough to go and grow some fucking feelings, why *Constantine Ross*, a guy I wouldn't have trusted to piss on me if I was on fire two months ago?

Maybe Constantine was right. Maybe I wasn't as smart as I liked to think I was.

But did that realization stop me from climbing into the driver's seat and heading southwest out of town with a very clear destination in mind?

Hell no. Barely slowed me down.

I was so lost in my own head, it took a minute to register that Constantine was *still* silent ten minutes later, which was so unusual that I wondered if he'd fallen asleep. But when I turned my head, I found him watching me steadily.

And yeah, that look did crazy things to my stomach.

I cleared my throat. "Nothing to say for once? Not a single demand to know where I'm taking you? No jokes or provocative statements or random bits of trivia to share?"

"Not a damn thing." He sounded drugged, but his smile widened a little. "I'm kinda fucked out."

"Well, I guess I've found an effective way to shut you up."

I hadn't known Constantine was capable of blushing the way he did.

"I guess you have. Keep that in your back pocket," he

said lightly. The leather seat squeaked as he turned his head away. "For future reference."

Future reference.

Both of us recognized the implications of his statement at the same time. I swiveled my head to look at him at the exact moment his eyes opened wider, and I saw him hesitate before turning back toward me.

This was the moment when I should conjure up that stuffy, self-righteous tone that used to slip out so easily when Con was around, and clarify exactly how meaningless this morning had been.

What came out of my mouth was, "I'll definitely keep it in mind."

I gripped the steering wheel more tightly.

"But since you're *inviting* questions," Constantine said, sitting up and sounding slightly more awake as I turned off the highway and into the tiny town of Parsa. "Where *are* we going?"

"First we're getting coffee. At an all-night diner called Dillard's."

He frowned. "Never heard of it."

"No reason you should, unless you hang out in Parsa and have a thing for sub-par pancakes. Coffee's really good though."

"I don't think I've ever stopped in Parsa at all."

"Then this," I said, as I pulled to a stop in front of the diner, "is going to be a morning of new experiences for you." For both of us.

I left him in the truck and went inside to get a couple of coffees and some muffins, then drove us through another few miles of endless, relentless trees, and pulled over by a small wooden sign that said *Paston Marsh Overlook.*

"Come on," I said, just as I had earlier. I handed him the white paper bag of food and one of the coffees.

"Come on *again?*" he demanded, sighing lavishly like he was totally put out and then grinning a second later. "Where are we going this time?"

The grin kinda killed me, because I could tell it was genuine, not just him putting on a happy front, and—

And *Jesus*, I was some kind of Constantine Ross expert now, able to determine the type and sincerity of his grins? This was getting worse and worse.

Con pushed his door open and jumped down, then turned back to look at me. "Uh. You coming too, big guy? Or was the plan to dump me here with just enough food to survive and see if I could make it back to town?" He shook the paper bag.

I blinked. "Yeah, right," I said, recovering myself. "There'd be no challenge in that. You'd bat those pretty eyelashes at the first person to drive along, whether it was a minivan-driving mom or good old boy in a pickup, and you'd be back in O'Leary before I was."

Con's smile widened. "Aw. You think my eyelashes are pretty?" He fluttered them, and a helpless laugh was torn out of me.

Well, fuck.

Okay, then, I thought, as things settled into place in my mind. *Bad bet or not, Micah, you're in this.*

I stopped at the bed of the truck and took out a heavy blanket, then pointed to a break in the trees. "We're heading over there. There's a path that leads to a board-walk and an observation area."

Constantine cast a deliberate look at the forest that stretched along both sides of the road. It was still half-dark under the canopy of trees, and it felt like there wasn't another soul for miles. "Observation of what?"

I came around the truck and shoved his shoulder gently to get him moving.

The thick stand of trees petered out a few feet back from the road, as I'd known it would, and gave way to an enormous field of marsh grass. The dirt path we'd been walking gave way to a high boardwalk that stretched over the marsh, and at the end of the boardwalk was a large, rectangular deck that floated like an island in a sea of grasses.

"What is this place?" Con's voice was awed as he took in the sight. "It's like a… a lake, but with grass instead of water."

"Mmhmm. This is Paston Marsh, the birdwatching paradise of New York. Or at least of Parsa."

"God, my brother would love it here. Jules," he added. "He's the town veterinarian, and he's all about the nature shit."

"His office is practically next door to the shop. I know who he is." I set my coffee on the rough decking and spread out the blanket in one corner, then lowered myself down to sit with my back against the railing. "And you're kind of right about the water. The Mud River empties here, so the ground's really boggy."

"The Mud River?" He turned to look at me, amused. "I can't decide if that's the best or worst name ever."

"I didn't name it, Constantine. Some mapmaker two hundred years ago did."

"But couldn't they call it something a little more *uplifting*?"

"Maps, not known for their *positivity*. What use is a map that tells you what something should be? Better to call a thing what it *is*."

Con snorted. "Dear God. That's the most Micah thing you've ever said." I wanted to ask him to explain what *that* meant, but he continued. "How'd you even find this place?"

I stretched my legs out in front of me. "I didn't. Jonny —er, my grandmother's lover—used to bring me here. I grew up in Baxter, not too far that way." I pointed left, indicating a spot five miles past the horizon.

"Your grandmother's *lover*." He came and took a seat near me, set the bag and his coffee in the center of the blanket, and copied my position, leaning against the railing near me, but he kept his knees bent and his sneakers flat on the deck. "Calling a thing what it is again?"

"I guess. That's what she used to call him. *Them*. My grandmother didn't believe humans were meant to be monogamous." I took a sip of my coffee, trying not to notice how mouthwatering Con looked in the early morning light. "She was a free spirit. A hippy, more or less."

"Seriously? *Your* grandmother was a hippy?"

I turned to look at him. "Could you not guess that from my playful, laid-back nature?" I rolled my eyes. "Thing was, she didn't believe in other zany societal strictures either, like regular meals, or bedtime, or calling her *Grandma*, or not growing marijuana in our backyard and using it to barter with our neighbors. So I may have become a bit *particular* about things, thanks to MoonFlower."

"*MoonFlower*." Con digested this for a minute. "Must've been great when you were a teenager, though. No one to yell if you missed curfew or got caught drinking."

I shrugged, thinking of coming home to find a new guy in the living room who'd be "staying with us for a while," and wondering how we'd make the food stretch.

"You either become the person who raised you or you become the complete opposite, I guess. And we know which one I was. My little brother, on the other hand..." I shook my head. "Remind me to tell you that story someday."

"Where was your mom?" Con paused and bit his lip. "I mean, you don't have to tell me if it's really painful or..."

I played with the lid of my coffee cup and considered that for a second. I never talked about this shit. But that was mostly because no one ever asked.

"She lives in Schenectady. Manages a hotel there. My dad left when my mom was pregnant with my youngest brother, and there was no way she could handle all four of us on her own, so she sent us to Baxter. She used to send home money every month." Not enough. "She's still there, but she's more like a distant cousin than a mom. We exchange cards at Christmas." I shrugged again. "What can I tell you?"

Con stared at me like I had three heads. "I cannot imagine having a mother who wasn't all up in your business. Like *all* up in your business."

I laughed. "Yeah, Freedom Bloom is no Angela Ross, that's for damn sure."

"Your mother's name is *Freedom*?"

"God, the weirdest things shock you. Yes. What sort of name do you expect from a woman named MoonFlower? Mary Sue?"

"Wait, her name was MoonFlower *Bloom*?"

I snorted. "She picked the *Bloom* to go with the Moon-Flower, Con. She loved flowers, so she changed her name." Then, I added in a sourer tone, "The rest of us just got stuck with it."

"Oh my God. So the first day we met, when I asked you—"

"If I'd picked my name to go with my profession or my profession to go with my name? Yeah, hit a little close to home."

Con kept staring at me, so I shoved his shoulder.

"Quit it."

"Sorry. It's just… if you told me you came from Mars, I'd have less trouble believing it. It's fascinating. You're… fascinating." He looked away, blushing.

"If I had a nickel for every guy who said that," I teased.

Con looked at me speculatively.

"I'd have exactly one nickel. Drink your coffee." I nodded at the cup sitting on the blanket.

It was oddly liberating, telling Constantine all this. Strangely *good*. And I hoped it would inspire him to tell me his own story when he was ready. But for now, I leaned back against the railing and let the silence of the place, broken only by bird calls, wrap us both up.

"Sounds a little like the beach, doesn't it?" Con said a few minutes later. "With your eyes closed, the wind in the grass kinda sounds like waves."

"Uh-huh." I opened my eyes to find Con with his head resting against the wooden railing, all calm and comfortable. He looked like he was freakin' meditating, glowing like a Greek god in the pink-orange sunrise.

Desperate anger, to consuming lust, to sleepy satiation, to total contentment. I'd never met anyone who could shift as quickly as Constantine did, once he finally let himself feel things.

"You know, I've never been to the ocean," he volunteered a few minutes later. "But I've been to Lake Ontario a bunch. When I was a kid, my dad used to take us in the spring sometimes, before the busy season. Road trip all the way to Charlotte just to get frozen custard at the pier."

"That's a nice memory."

He nodded. "Always wanted to see the ocean though."

"So go. It's only six hours away."

Con shrugged and sipped at his coffee. "Opportunity never presented itself."

"Opportunity?" I laughed. "It's an ocean. You don't need an invitation."

"Mmm. This is good," he interrupted, taking another sip of his drink. "Perfectly light and sweet. Much like myself." He pressed a hand to his chest and grinned. "Thanks for remembering."

I shook my head. I'd never met anyone who avoided talking about shit with the same skill Con did either.

I reached for the bag and removed a muffin. "One of these days, I'm going to get a truth out of you," I warned him. "It's going to be epic, and I'll never let you live it down."

I carefully peeled the wrapper from the sides and set it on my knee like a plate, then split the muffin precisely into quarters.

Con frowned. "What's that mean? I always tell the truth."

I shot him a sideways glance. "Not technically lying isn't the same as volunteering the truth."

"Wow." Con grabbed a muffin from the bag and lifted it to his mouth to take a huge bite, all in one smooth motion. "That was deep, Micah."

I shook my head again and took another bite of muffin, washing it down with my lukewarm coffee. It was unreasonable to be disappointed that he didn't want to share. If there was one thing I'd learned in my forty years, it was that you could only lead an unwilling person so far. It went against my nature to just give up, but if Con didn't want to talk, he wouldn't. Whatever life-changing realizations *I* had been coming to about my attraction to Constantine, didn't mean *he* was feeling anything—

"Okay, fine. My dad died when I was fourteen," Con said in a rush. "Not exactly a state secret."

I turned my head against the railing and looked at him, my heart kicking up. "I've heard that. Must've been hard."

Con nodded. "It was sudden. Don't know if you knew that part."

I shook my head.

"Heart attack. He was really young. And that's part of why I started *acting out*." He sounded like he was quoting someone from long ago. "You know about all that."

"Not really, though." He gave me a skeptical look and I shrugged. "Did you draw dick pics in a bathroom stall? Did you get a girl pregnant? Did you have a chicken race and someone went over a cliff? How would I know? Hardly anyone in this town talks to me, besides you."

"A chicken race. Off a cliff?"

"Never seen *Rebel Without a Cause*? James Dean?"

Constantine shook his head slowly.

"Oh, God, you're missing out. James Dean in black leather is… very *inspiring*." I waggled my eyebrows. "I have it on tape—watched it like four hundred times when I was a teenager. You can borrow it."

"I can borrow… the tape?" He bit his lip and his eyes danced. "Like, an actual tape that you need to rewind? If I wave it near my laptop, will it sync?"

I sighed. Like I needed a further reminder of the difference in our ages. "Never mind, millennial."

He leaned over and pushed at my knee. "We can watch it together sometime."

"Don't placate me, youngster."

Con laughed and gave me a sly smile. "See, *that's* not what you were saying an hour ago." He took another bite of his muffin.

I rolled my eyes. "Let's get back to Con's teenage rebellion."

Con groaned and heaved a sigh that mingled with the wind brushing through the grass. "Must we?"

"No," I said with a shrug. "I'm not gonna push you to talk. I'm not gonna push you to do anything."

He rolled his eyes. "The guilt. The *guilt. It crushes meeeee.*"

I put my hand on his leg and squeezed gently to get his attention. "That's not guilt, Con. That's honesty."

He looked at me and sucked in a breath through his nose, then let it out slowly. He licked his lips.

"The thing is, it's weird to talk about because I've never met anyone I had to *tell* about it. You know?"

"Yeah." I thought of my family bullshit. "I know exactly."

"And it's also weird because it feels like I'm talking about some… *other person* who did these things. Drinking. Fighting. Drinking, *then* fighting. Driving without a license. It was only maybe ten years ago, but I look back and think *who the fuck* was *that kid?* But it was me. There's a record at the O'Leary Police Department that says so. Fingerprints." He held up his outstretched palm and gave me a rueful smile that faded quickly into a wary expression.

"What's that look for? You think I'm going to judge you?"

He arched one eyebrow.

"Okay, yes, fine," I admitted. "I *did* judge you, before I knew you. But this teenage stuff doesn't shock me. I'm telling you, my brother Mason was the same."

"Yeah, what did he do?" Con asked hopefully.

I threw a piece of muffin at him. "That wasn't even a *subtle* attempt at deflection."

Con caught the muffin in midair and popped it in his

mouth. "Mmm. Why does someone else's food always just taste better?"

I flipped him off, and he laughed harder.

"Why do I put up with you?" I asked the silent morning.

"My pretty eyelashes?" Con suggested.

"Must be. So, okay, you were a teenage rebel, playing chicken, car crashes, blah blah."

I turned my head in time to see something flash over Con's expression, chasing away all the good humor. Something like fear. Something like *guilt.*

"Wait, *was* that what you did?"

Con sighed. "Kinda. Not exactly."

"Okay," I told him, no longer playing around. "For once, just tell me the truth without me having to drag it out of you."

Con swallowed, staring at my face. Then he settled himself back against the railing and lifted his face to the sky.

"Once upon a time, there was a boy named Constantine."

"The handsomest boy in all the land," I supplied. "I get it."

"Nah." He glanced at me and shook his head soberly. "Short, scrawny. He hadn't grown into his eyelashes yet. But he was maybe the angriest boy in all the land. He had a great older brother who sacrificed all kinds of shit for him. A younger brother who looked up to him. A mother who loved him. But all he could see was what he *didn't* have anymore and how *unfair* the world was for taking his dad away." Con glanced at me again. "Constantine was a naïve boy."

"Constantine was a grieving boy," I corrected. "Keep going."

"Hmm. Well, in his preteen brilliance, Constantine figured there was no point in playing by the rules. His father had followed rules. Ate oatmeal every day, even though he hated it, because he wanted to keep his heart healthy, and in the end, it didn't matter even a little, so why bother?"

A flock of birds took flight from the grass nearby, their wings beating in a synchronized rush loud enough to startle both of us.

Constantine grinned. "See what I mean? You can't predict what's going to happen, so why make a plan in the first place?"

"I get it."

"*You* do? The man who has a plan for everything?"

Except for you, I thought, but what I said was, "I do have a plan for everything because life's unpredictable, so I try to control as much as I can." I shrugged. "It's basically an equal reaction in the opposite direction."

"We're mirror images, then." He turned toward me and leaned forward to lift my left hand off my lap, then shifted so we were palm to palm. "I move my right hand, you move your left hand?"

But instead of moving my hand at all, I threaded our fingers together and squeezed slightly, halting this happy little tangent.

"So rebellious Constantine wants to Hulk-smash the world," I prompted.

He sighed and looked up at the sky. "You suck."

"As you found out just an hour ago," I agreed.

Con snorted.

He didn't let go of my hand.

"Yeah, okay. So, one day Hulk-smash-Constantine picked a fight with the wrong guy. The richest kid at my high school. Drove a red Camaro. Total entitled punk, but his father was a big-deal lawyer. We played football together, and one time he… I dunno. He pissed me off." Con shifted, stretching his legs out before folding them again. "Made some stupid, shitty comments about a girl I… *liked*, so I went all avenging angel and poured bleach in his gas tank while we were partying that night."

"Bleach. In the gas tank." I wasn't sure if I was horrified or impressed.

"Ironically, something I learned about on a science show," Con said. He turned toward me. "Which should really be a warning to parents about the dangers of educational television, if you think—"

"Constantine."

He pushed out a breath and collapsed in on himself a little, looking back out over the marsh. "His engine stalled, which was what I'd expected. But when it did, he lost control and ended up getting in an accident." He winced. "Crashed into a fence. Coulda died. So could the people in the car with him. *Reckless endangerment*, you know?"

I closed my eyes as understanding dawned. "So this is why Pat at HG Supply tells me you're the next thing to a serial killer?"

Con laughed and rubbed a hand over his eyes tiredly. "He said that?"

"Wanted to warn me off you." I squeezed his hand. "We see how well that worked, huh?"

"Yeah, well, you're maybe the only person who *didn't* listen. Money talks, and big money talks *loud*." He picked at the last crumbs of his muffin. "They wanted me arrested. Jailed. Tarred and feathered. Walking the plank. Whatever. Mitch was a friend of my dad's, and he said there wasn't enough evidence to press charges for reckless endangerment. But the kid sued. Or, I mean, his dad sued my mother." He shot me a glance. "Couple of minors, you know?"

I nodded.

"I never got the exact details of how they settled things. It was a long time before my mother could *look* at me, let alone calmly explain shit." He cleared his throat and pulled at the legs of his shorts. "Is it getting hot out here?"

"No. Keep talking." In actuality, now that the sun was mostly up, it was getting *very* warm, but I needed him to finish.

"That's pretty much it. Mama managed to keep the house and the business, but all her savings, all the money from my dad's life insurance, were gone. We were screwed. Julian, ah—" He broke off and wiped his forearm over his forehead. "No, but seriously. Heat wave, Micah. We should—"

"Julian what?"

Con blew out a breath. "Julian switched colleges so he could be closer to home. To be closer *to the family*. And, I mean, no one ever said, and he never complained, but it was basically so he could babysit my ass." He picked at the fraying edge of his shorts. "Mitch made me do community service at the station, and that turned into me working for him part-time now. Kinda out of pity and kinda because he genuinely likes me, I think. And I spent the rest of my time working for Ross Landscaping since my mother had to cut expenses and couldn't afford to pay someone."

"So you worked for free?"

He nodded. "Yeah. Not *free*, though. It's more like I'm making up for what she lost thanks to me. Which makes sense, you know? And it works out fine. Except when my car breaks down and I have nothing saved." He gave me a broad grin. "And then I have to accept the first job some asshole at a bar offers me and, well, here we are."

I couldn't smile back, though. My mind was spinning a little, trying to take this in, trying to reconcile it to what I'd overheard at the farmer's market weeks ago. "Your mother *still* makes you work for her for free as punishment?"

"What? No!" Con said, turning toward me fully. "No, no, no. You have the wrong idea. It's not a punishment, it's more like family duty. To keep the business going. Er. I mean, to keep it profitable and competitive." He winked. "Now that there's a new florist in town."

I frowned. "Did they put a lien against the business? In the lawsuit?"

He shrugged. "I told you, I don't know details. I don't think so? The kid and his family moved out of town that summer, but Mama's still trying to dig out from under. I'm guessing she'd like to retire at some point, you know?"

"No," I said honestly. "I *don't* know. I mean, I'm not a lawyer, but this happened years ago, so unless they got a judgment against the business or against your mom or something, the business should be turning a profit. That's how business works. Did she have to take out loans, or—"

"I don't *know*," Con said again, more impatiently this time. "It's none of my business."

I peered at him. "Well, except it is your business. *Literally*. It's your *family*'s business."

"It's my business to keep Ross Landscaping running," he retorted. "To make up for what I did. Mistakes have consequences. Big mistakes have big consequences."

"You keep saying that. I do not think it means what you think it means."

Con huffed out a laugh. "Did you just *Princess Bride* quote me?"

"Con, even jail sentences have end dates, unless you murder someone in cold blood. You were a kid. Your mistakes should propel you on to bigger and better. To do something constructive."

"Yeah, well, maybe it will. But I've gotta do my time first," he said stubbornly. "Make amends."

"For how long? Ten years? Twenty?"

"Maybe, yeah," he shot back. "Until my mother gets back to where she was. Until she gets to a point where she can trust me again."

I shook my head, stunned. "Trust you to *what?*"

"Well. I have this idea," he said slowly. "A possibly stupid but really exciting idea that I want to expand the landscaping side of the business. Do bigger jobs, design jobs, like the kind we did when my dad was alive but… even bigger. My mother was never into that. Like, *at all.* Which is why we focused more on the floral side of things and… You know what? Talking about Ross stuff with you crosses all kinds of lines." He waved a hand in the air. "Maybe we should—"

I snorted. "You think I'm going to use this information for corporate espionage? How? I swear, I have zero interest in branching into landscape design. And I have no interest in destroying Ross Landscaping either."

More to the point, I had a definite interest in Constantine Ross.

He hesitated, then said, "Well, the thing is, right now we're committed to the flower business. Like, hardcore committed. The shit with me had some far-reaching repercussions, beyond *just* the financial. Vince—the lawyer—he had a lot of friends and family in the area, and after… everything… they didn't like me much. We lost some clients and had to deal with lots of bullshit from our suppliers."

I closed my eyes as facts clicked into place. "Like HG Supply."

"Like HG Supply," he confirmed. "Pat and Donnie are Vince's cousins or something. Anyway, we always had a little nursery, for landscape stock, but we built hothouses and stuff. We grow most of our own floral stock now, too, which is *awesome*. But it required, you know, investment."

"A *lot* of investment," I corrected.

I'd considered that move myself, but I knew I wouldn't be able to afford it for *years*, and I had *lots* of things to put in place before then, like having multiple, fully staffed shops open, a significant uptick in my corporate clients, and a fifty percent increase in my net profits.

I remembered overhearing Angela talk about taking out loans to build the greenhouses, and a mental picture was starting to come together. I wasn't sure I liked the image I was seeing.

I also wasn't sure how to point it out to Constantine or even if I should. A blowjob and single deep conversation didn't give me that right.

"So there's not a lot of, you know, flexibility, money-wise, to move into landscape design. It would be a risk. And *I* know I could make it profitable. But my mother's not as confident as I am. She thinks I'm gonna fuck it up. Which, based on past experience, I don't blame her for." He hesitated. "But this morning, I got a little, tiny bit… frustrated."

"A tiny bit."

"A lot, then. It was just impatience. And resentment, because it felt like things weren't changing. I couldn't see past it."

"You were stuck in your head."

"Yeah. Last time I felt anger like that…" One side of his mouth quirked. "A Camaro paid the price."

More like, Constantine had. And still was.

"Maybe I need to take up kickboxing," Constantine mused.

"Or maybe you need to take some steps toward actually changing things instead of just waiting. There are lots of ideas you could consider for Ross to start moving in that direction. You could pull back on—"

Con held up a hand. "No. No business advice, please. Look, it's enough that I just spewed all this to you, especially since I'm already walking a fine line just working for you. And I want to trust you. I mean, I *do* trust you. Personally. But…"

"But professionally, I need to butt out." He was right. I knew he was. But it still stung.

He shrugged. "You wanna tell me all about the finances at Blooms?"

"You help me do bookkeeping!" I protested.

"I help you organize and pay invoices. You wanna show me your profit and loss?"

I ran my teeth over my bottom lip.

"Thought so. There are lines we can't cross." He shrugged. "It's cool. We just ignore the shit we don't want to discuss and move on."

I snorted. "That's the most Constantine thing you've ever said to me."

He grinned, and his gaze turned playful. "But since there are certain lines we've *already* crossed…" He glanced at my crotch and wiggled his eyebrows. "I have a debt to pay."

I sat upright and collected our trash. "That's not a debt, Constantine."

"Well, no. I mean, I know I don't *have* to do anything. *Duh*. I was just thinking it was really quiet out here, and I really appreciate everything you've done for me this morning. The… the thing in the back room earlier and the… you know." He made a motion with his hands at the blanket and the breakfast spread out on it. "The coffee."

"The blowjob, you mean? And the conversation?"

"Yes." His gaze was frank and sincere. "Both." He frowned slightly before he recovered his smile.

"So say, '*Thank you, Micah.*'"

"Huh?"

"Not everything is transactional," I said, pushing to my feet. "Not every mistake requires you to kick your own ass for a decade. Not every blowjob requires an equal and opposite blowjob."

He stared at me with this bewildered little frown on his face, like a kicked puppy. "Wait, are you mad?"

"No." *Yes.*

"Is it because I wouldn't talk about finances?"

"No." *Also yes.*

Except that wasn't true either. It didn't bother me that he was being loyal to his family, because no one got that better than I did. *No one.* It was more the reminder that there *was* this line between us, this no-man's-land of divided loyalties. And however attracted I felt to him, however strong the urge to pick him up and take him back to my apartment and kiss the shit out of him might be, I couldn't do it.

Plus, I really didn't want to be another debt Constantine owed.

"It's just that those flower arrangements aren't gonna make themselves. You know?"

"Oh." Con got to his feet, too. "Shit. Yeah. You're behind now, aren't you?" He pulled his phone from his pocket to check the time and winced. "I could stay late and help—"

"After sunrise? When anyone could see?" I knelt to roll up the blanket and tried to rein in my shit. "It's fine, Con. Belle will be in. We'll get it done."

He grimaced. "I feel bad that—"

"Constantine," I said, straightening up and grabbing

his wrist. "*Everything* I've done today was something I did because I wanted to. You don't need to feel bad about it. You don't need to repay me for it. It was *my* choice." I lifted one eyebrow. "I like you. It's that simple."

"I don't—" He shook his head. "I don't get why. I'm sorry. I know I'm being weirdly ungrateful or dense or whatever. But like, two months ago, you hated my guts for no reason. Now I dump all this shit on you, shit that has made lots of other people think really badly of me, and you're like, '*Oh, it's fine, Con! I like you!*'"

I chuckled, almost against my will. He was so fucking cute. "Okay, first, I have never sounded like that in my life. And second… I only ever disliked you half the time. Remember? And now it's, like, twenty-five percent of the time. Tops."

"Because I'm pretty?" Con looked at me with a soft little smile dancing on his lips, his blue eyes filled with the same vulnerability I'd seen there earlier, and I sucked in a sharp breath.

Jesus fuck, the man was a walking wet dream. His hair was mussed around his head, the dark strands glinting in the sun, and I wanted to run my fingers through them so badly I ached. I wanted to kiss the shit out of him. I would happily have gone to my knees for him again.

And again.

And again.

And I wanted to *scream* in frustration, because if I made the slightest move toward him right now, he'd melt for me. I knew he would.

Which is exactly why I couldn't.

If Constantine wanted me, he'd have to make the first move.

"Yeah, Con." I tucked the blanket under my arm. "'Cause you're pretty."

"And I'm growing on you."

"Like black mold," I agreed.

He smiled again, mischievous now, quicksilver and real.

God, the protectiveness I felt was *insane*. And I wanted to protect him, not because he was weak or stupid, not because I pitied him, but because he was really fucking brave, and smart, and he knew what it meant to sacrifice for his family.

I remembered telling my sister that Con was the antithesis of everything I was, but maybe Con had gotten it right before when he said we were more like mirror images. An equal and opposite match.

I cleared my throat as I realized I'd been staring at him for way too long.

"Come on," I said, walking past him down the boardwalk.

"Always with the *come on*," Con protested, but he followed me back to the truck and let me drive us back to reality.

Chapter Seven

CONSTANTINE

August

Micah Bloom was going to kill me.

Not in the literal, stabby kind of way—though, knowing me, it was only a matter of time before I provoked the man to homicide. No, this was more of a death-by-sexual frustration thing, a slow, choking thirst that got worse every single day.

Today was especially bad.

The O'Leary Summer Picnic—not to be confused with the weekly farmer's markets, or the Fourth of July fireworks out at the lake, or the giant Labor Day cookout sponsored by the town council—was in full swing on this sunny August morning. The air smelled like grilling meat and fucking *rang* with children's laughter as O'Learians celebrated the fact that the sun had appeared to scorch us, before winter came back to bury us alive again. And here I was, manning the booth for Ross Landscaping, as I would until I was older than Ms. Semple at the antique store and crankier than Henry Lattimer.

If I lived that long.

If the sight of the gorgeous, sexy man directly across the aisle—the man currently laughing with one of the sisters I'd never met, over some joke I'd never hear, and looking like the world's coolest, most refreshing drink of water on this hot summer day—didn't make me crumble to dust first.

I was thinking of carrying a note in my pocket saying, "It's Micah's fault!" That way when the police were called to the fairgrounds to examine the shriveled, desiccated corpse of the man who used to be cute, sexy, *fun* Constantine Ross, they'd know exactly who was to blame for my demise.

"What are we looking at?" said a voice in my ear.

I was so startled, I bumped into the table, rattling the display of miniature clay pots, soil, and sunflower seeds I'd set up to show the kids and adults the joys of gardening, since today wasn't about selling but about giving back to the *community* and blah blah blah.

I turned and glared at my little brother. "Theodore, one of these days—"

Theo grinned unrepentantly. "I was *gonna* say, I brought almost all the little plant pots from the trunk." He hooked a thumb over his shoulder, toward a handcart that was loaded with cardboard boxes, bags of potting soil, and a battered old cooler full of drinks. "I was *gonna* ask if you needed help setting up your little craft DIY. But now I'm wondering why we're staring at Micah Bloom," he said in a stage whisper. "I didn't know your hate-on for him was as bad as Mama's."

"It's not," I protested, squatting down and opening the boxes, so I could pretend to count the pots I'd already counted. "And I wasn't staring. I was lost in thought."

Not a lie. I hadn't *meant* to stare. And I was most definitely lost in thought. Thoughts of Micah in his tight shirt. Of Micah kissing me, both times. Of Micah's hands, which were my kryptonite. Thoughts of Micah's laugh, which I heard more often these days. Thoughts of Micah's steady eyes meeting mine over the workbench as I helped him with some project or other. Thoughts of how fucking patient he could be when he wanted to be, like that morning at the marsh.

Thoughts of how the man hadn't made one single move in my direction since that day, and how everything had somehow gone back to business as usual. Thoughts of how I was gonna kill the next person who asked me, "What's wrong, Con?" if I didn't get some sexual relief really fucking soon.

"Sure you were," Theo agreed. "And I'm sure he was staring back at you for the same reason. That makes sense."

"Don't be ridiculous." I couldn't really see Micah from this angle, but that didn't stop me from unconsciously shooting a glance toward his table. "He wasn't looking at me. Probably at our booth. Wondering how it'll look when he puts us out of business and plants a flag here instead. Because we're *enemies*. Obviously."

Theo sighed and plunked his ass down on the cooler right beside me. "I turned eighteen last month, you know."

"'Course I know. I got you that band t-shirt and a gift card to Burger Geek."

"That's not what I meant." He pursed his lips. "Look, I have eyes in my head, okay? I see things."

My heart kicked up. "Like, dead people? Are we in that movie with the creepy kid?" I lowered my voice to a whisper. "Am I Bruce Willis?"

"Never mind. I don't know why I bother," Theo said, getting to his feet. "You need help, or what?"

I immediately felt bad and pushed against Theo's knee for him to sit back down. "Sorry. *Sorry*. It's recently come to my attention that I maybe have an issue with, um, deflection."

"You think?" Theo snorted. He narrowed his eyes. "How'd this come to your attention?"

I shrugged. "A friend pointed it out."

"Yeah, right. You don't *have* friends, Con."

"Hey!" I protested, because seriously, *what the fuck?* "I have *tons* of friends, asshole."

"You have guys you're friendly with. Not the same."

"I'm friends with Jamie Burke and with Silas Sloane. And this guy, Tyler, I text occasionally. And um…" I drew a blank. "Jordan! Over at The Hive."

"Okay, Jamie is Julian's friend, and you basically only see him when you're together," Theo ticked off on his fingers. "Silas is your coworker at the police station. I don't know Tyler, but occasional texts are not friendship. And Jordan pours you cherry Cokes."

"Shirley Temples."

"Whichever. Those aren't *friends*. Dude, even *I* know the difference. I have Sam and Rae and Dante who've always got my back and call me on my bullshit. Who calls you on your bullshit, Con?"

"Well." I smoothed my eyebrows with my fingertips and stood up. "Okay, then. I'm a friendless loser. This has been a great brotherly conversation, Theodore. Gee, I am *so* glad Mama asked you to help out here this morning. Why don't we do this more often?"

"Real talk? There's something going on with you, Constantine. You've been borrowing my car almost daily for two months, and you haven't been happy in at least that long."

"You're barking up the wrong tree. I mean, spending

every *minute* of every Saturday morning in this goddamn booth doesn't exactly fill me with glee." I glared around at the three canvas walls and studiously avoided looking toward the front and across the aisle. "But I'm *fine*."

"You wanna play it that way? Okay." He shrugged. "You're not, though. And maybe Jules hasn't been around enough to see it the past few months, and maybe Mama doesn't *want* to see it, but I see it. So what I'm trying to say is that I'm here, if you wanna talk. Or if not… I hope whoever this *friend* is keeps calling things to your attention. 'Cause you're, like… a really good brother. And you *should* be happy. Okay?"

Theo looked uncomfortable, but *Jesus*. What kind of balls did it take to actually say real shit like that *out loud*?

"Am I dying?" I demanded. "For real? Because I was pretty sure I was dying earlier, and now I'm starting to wonder if maybe I imagined it into reality. I do that sometimes."

"I don't think being an idiot is fatal."

"Sexual frustration might be." *Fuck*. Had I said that out loud?

I groaned and pushed my hands through my hair, sitting back down on the cooler Theo had vacated.

"Really? *You?*" Theo folded his arms over his chest. "No fresh meat at The Hive these days?"

"I wouldn't know," I said. "I haven't been there since the day my car broke down."

"Months ago? But you can use my car. I honestly don't—"

"Nah. It's not that," I said. "I appreciate it, though. I just haven't… wanted to go, I guess. I haven't had the time or energy."

"For *sex*?" Theo demanded. He likely wouldn't have

been as shocked if I'd announced some kind of religious conversion. "Why?"

"I don't know, man. I'm as shocked as you. Maybe this is adulthood or something."

Maybe it was that I'd become fixated on sex with one particular guy, who wasn't showing the first sign he was interested in making it happen.

Theo looked over at Micah's booth again. "Or something," he agreed. "Oh, FYI? Micah's *still* looking this way, and he definitely wants to plant a flag in *something*. It's making me a little uncomfortable and a little turned on."

"What?" I jumped to my feet. "I'm gonna kill him." Micah couldn't even *see* me when I was sitting, which I knew since I couldn't see him, and if he was shooting sex looks at my little brother…

"He's not even there, you asswipe." I turned from Micah's booth, where Micah's sister stood alone, and glared at Theo. The fucker looked way too smug.

"Hmm? Weird. I could've sworn—"

"Theo," I began. "I don't know what you think you know, but…"

"I don't think I know anything," Theo said, all innocent. "Except that hate is, like, one *teensy* step away from love, and hate sex can be fun."

"I'm not having hate sex with Micah Bloom," I whispered hotly. "I'm not having *any* sex with *anyone*."

An unfortunate, painful truth.

"Maybe that's your problem," Theo challenged. "Maybe you need to take the bull by the horns. Reach out and take what you want for once."

"I have!" I said. "I do!" *Sometimes*.

"You know, some guys really like it when you make the first move."

"I do not want to know how you know that,

Theodore," I said. "But seriously, you need to keep your theories to yourself. Mama already laid into me a couple months ago just for acknowledging Micah's existence, and I—"

Theo set his hand on my shoulder and his eyes, the same sharp blue as Jules's and mine, turned serious. "Constantine, *chill.* I know you think I'm still nine years old or something, but I'm not. I know how to keep secrets, and I can keep yours, too. Okay?"

I wasn't sure I *was* okay with it, but I didn't really have a choice.

Fortunately for me, a whole group of people came by the booth then—some kids who wanted to plant sunflower seeds and a bunch of teenagers who wanted to shoot the shit with Theo—which succeeded in distracting me from both the conversation *and* from Micah.

When the little kids were gone, I wiped my hands on a towel and grabbed a water bottle from the cooler.

"I think there's one more box of mini plant pots in your trunk," I told Theo. "Can you handle things here? Mama's coming when she's finished with her meeting, which should be in a couple hours. And I'll have my cell. You can call if you need me."

Theo looked around at the total lack of people approaching the booth, then shared a commiserating eye roll with his friends. "Yes, Con. If there's a mad rush of people dying for a free potted seed and I just can't handle the stress of it all, I'll call you."

His friend Dante snickered and looked away.

I dropped my head to my chest. Was I doing to Theo what Mama did to me? *Gross.*

"Sorry," I said. "I really do appreciate your help this morning." I hoped my glance conveyed that I meant the pep talk as well as manning the booth.

"If you wanna thank me, buy me a burger," Theo said with a grin. "Extra—"

"Ketchup," I finished. "I know."

I decided it would be easier to get the burger first and then haul the box from the trunk, so I headed for the food area, guzzling the water as I went. And since I was feeling a little brotherly guilt, I decided I'd stand in the massive line at the Burger Geek booth. I was not above buying Theo's silence with his favorite burger.

I smiled to myself at the brilliance of this plan, and got in line behind Lisa "The Dragon" Dorian, the town's librarian, who immediately turned her gimlet gaze on me.

"You seem chipper today, Mr. Ross," she said, like my smile had personally offended her.

I smiled even more widely. "What's not to be chipper about, Ms. Dorian? The sun is shining. The whole community of O'Leary has turned out for this magnificent festival. *You're* here, wearing that delightful outfit."

She was wearing head-to-toe red, white, and blue, like Uncle Sam with frizzy hair and reading glasses. And Jesus, once I thought it, I couldn't *stop* seeing her as Uncle Sam, right down to her deep-set eyes and beaky nose. I bit my lip to stifle a laugh.

"Some people don't understand the importance of these festivals," she said severely. "As a part of our agricultural heritage. Young people in particular want everything to be a party."

I nodded, not offended in the slightest. The thing about The Dragon was that she disliked everyone and everything exactly the same, and once you realized this, it was hard to take anything she said personally.

But not everyone knew this about her, including the person standing in front of her, who turned around and stared down at her with scathing green eyes.

"You know, I sometimes find that people take things *too* seriously," Micah said. "I've been accused of it myself." His eyes came to mine. "Morning, Mr. Ross."

"Mr. Bloom," I said, my heart rate picking up.

Fucked-up as it was, this was the first time he'd acknowledged me in public in months—since the day I'd teased him at the farmer's market, right in these same fairgrounds—and just hearing him say my name in that deep, formal way made me shiver despite the hot sun.

"Micah Bloom," Ms. Dorian said, her eyes pinging back and forth between us avidly. Whatever my mother thought, no one in O'Leary was unaware of our rivalry, and I imagined The Dragon wanted to stir up trouble. "What are you offering at your booth today?"

"My sister Leandra and I are giving out a gerbera daisy to everyone who stops by," he said, and I froze, remembering our stupid conversation in the van about those daisies and my suggestion about what could be done on them.

Great work, Constantine. Even flowers made me think of sex now, which was really fucking dangerous, given my job.

"Daisies," Ms. Dorian said, surprise and approval in her voice. "Excellent, summery choice. Or were you perhaps harkening back to Fachanan O'Leary, the founder of the town, and his wife, Margaret, commonly known as Daisy?"

Micah blinked, then blinked again. "I… I have to admit that's just a happy coincidence," he said. "But I've recently developed a special appreciation for gerbera daisies."

And then he shot me a look that lasted no more than an instant but told me he remembered the same conversation.

*God*damn*. Did he deliberately try to make me crazy?

"Do you have any flowers, Constantine?" Ms. Dorian asked.

"No," I said. "No, we're, uh… harkening back… to the… agricultural heritage… of the town with a seed-planting demonstration," I said smoothly. I sketched an oval in the air. "*Tiny seeds*. So full of… *promise*."

Micah's eyes narrowed.

"You Rosses always add a nice variety to the festival," The Dragon said. "Don't you think, Mr. Bloom?"

Micah turned around to move forward in line but spoke over his shoulder. "Oh, yes. Constantine is all about variety. Something new every week." He shot me a glance. "Isn't that right?"

I narrowed my eyes. Was he talking about…?

He winked and my eyes opened in shock.

For weeks—fucking *weeks*—the man hadn't so much as alluded to sex around me. He'd shot down every silly innuendo and returned to being professional and kind, and it had *killed* me. I'd really thought something had changed out there at the marsh, but apparently, I'd misread him. Again. We'd worked together mostly in silence because I couldn't think of a damn thing to say that wasn't me blurting out, "Oh, Jesus, you're hot," and begging him to fuck me.

But now suddenly he'd decided to be all flirtatious and innuendo-y right here? In front of The Dragon? And he said *I* was provoking? Dude, I was provoking like a cute and tiny puppy. *He* was provoking like a ballistic missile launch.

He gave me a bland look and added, "I know you pride yourself on always having…*fresh stock*."

I summoned my brightest smile. "Nothing wrong with trying new things, Mr. Bloom. Better than letting your stock get *old* and *stale*, right?"

"Of course," Mrs. Dorian said importantly. "People expect freshness."

It looked like Micah was biting the inside of his cheek, and when his eyes met mine over The Dragon's head, it felt like we'd formed a bridge of understanding across the churning waters of insanity that was life in O'Leary.

God, I hated him sometimes.

"Mr. Ross always delivers freshness," Micah agreed solemnly. "Sometimes I look across the aisle at the Ross booth and think, '*So. Fresh.*'"

Unbelievable. But Ms. Dorian smiled like she still thought we were talking about flowers.

"Right back atcha," I said. "Really. *Insanely*. Fresh."

Micah turned around to order his burger and Ms. Dorian patted me on the shoulder. "So good to see you becoming friends and putting aside your rivalry for the good of the community," she said.

"Oh, Mr. Bloom and I aren't rivals," I said brightly. "I like to think we inspire each other."

Ms. Dorian frowned and turned around just in time to order her own burger. I ordered Theo's, dumped half a pound of ketchup on the thing, and started walking back to the booth along the path on the far side of the festival, near the vendor parking lot where we'd left Theo's car earlier in the day.

It was hot as hell. The sun was nearly overhead now, and beneath the smell of fried food, I could smell the grass practically cooking beneath my feet. In the distance, sunlight glared off the cars in the parking lot, and a part of me wanted to just get in Theo's car and drive away— from the festival, from the town, from my past, from *myself.*

I wasn't as surprised as I should have been when Micah caught up and casually strolled alongside me, close enough that I'd be sure to notice him and far enough away that no one would think we were walking *together*.

"Walking fast, Con," he said around a mouthful of burger. "Trying to escape?"

You have no idea. "Gotta give Theo his lunch."

"Ah. And here I thought maybe you were stomping off because you were annoyed at me for earlier. Not as fun being provoked as it is doing the provoking, hmm?"

I huffed out a breath. He wasn't wrong. "Was this really the best forum for that kind of banter, Mr. Bloom?" *When you could have picked literally any other time, any other day, ever?*

"Maybe your impulsiveness is rubbing off on me."

I shot him a heated look and kept walking.

"*Tsk tsk.* Ms. Dorian would be so disappointed. Friends don't look at each other like they're plotting murder, Constantine."

I kept walking.

"Like they're wondering what their friends' livers taste like with fava beans," he continued.

"Oh, please."

"Like you're Liam Neeson and I kidnapped your daughter."

I paused and looked at him. "Is this what it's like dealing with me?" I demanded. "A relentless barrage of one-liners that aren't nearly as funny as you think they are?"

"Nah." Micah shoved his empty burger container into a trash bin. "Your one-liners are way worse."

I snorted and resumed walking. "Well, at least *I* have the eyelashes to look cute while doing it," I informed him. Though, honestly, Micah didn't need to bat his eyelashes. He was plenty cute already.

And that was the problem.

My problem.

"Wow. Look at that face! Tell me what unspeakably terrible thing I did to earn that anger," he teased.

I clutched the cardboard container with the burger more tightly in my hand and came to a full stop in the middle of the path.

The man was constantly saying he wanted honesty from me, right? For me to tell him the truth? Well, okay then. *Watch out, Micah.*

Micah walked two paces past me before he realized I'd stopped and turned around to look at me in confusion. "You alright?" His eyes lost their humor as he scanned my face. "I was only joking."

He glanced around us, maybe wondering if there were people nearby. It was good that one of us was being careful, but this corner of the grounds behind the tents was fairly deserted, with no witnesses but the delivery vans and trucks and cars the vendors had used to haul their stuff.

"You wanna know what you've done?" I said. "You've made me *like you*, Micah. You made me like you when it would have been much easier for both of us if I kept *disliking* you the way I should. And then you just walked away. I mean… not literally, but in every way that was important."

Micah's eyes widened. "Wait. What?"

"You made me *want* you," I accused, kind of half-desperate and half-angry. I took a step forward and jabbed a finger at him. "And you even made me *want* to want you. So now I can't stop thinking about you *all the fucking time*, and it's driving me insane. I haven't been to The Hive in weeks. I go from job to job to job, and I keep thinking about *you*."

I poked him again and then stared at my hand in horror. "Look at me right now! I'm getting *pissed*. Over *nothing*. Again! You make me insane." I ran my hand through my hair so I wouldn't be tempted to touch him again. "I don't like it."

The two of us stood there for a long minute, staring at one another, breathing heavily. Then, finally, Micah spoke.

"Maybe you just don't want to like it," he whispered. His tongue traced the corner of his lips and my eyes fixated on that spot like it was a big black X on a treasure map. "You make me insane, too."

"Oh, right," I nearly yelled. "*Right*. That's why you haven't said a single thing about that day in the back room? Haven't so much as held my hand since we left the marsh? Haven't talked to me about anything more important than whether I like the look of penny gum with hydrangeas?"

Micah's eyes darkened. "Are you fucking kidding me? Jesus, Con. I was trying to be *nice*. I was trying not to put pressure on *you*. I was waiting for you to decide what you wanted. I've been right here all along, just—"

"Constantine Ross!" my mother yelled from the parking lot, and the sound was like a blast of hot air rolling over us.

Micah closed his eyes and muttered, "Fuck."

I closed my eyes and pressed my lips together. *Why why why?*

"What is the meaning of this?" she demanded as she stepped closer. "*Fighting*? In the middle of the festival? For God's sake, Con."

"I wasn't fighting!" I said. And I really fucking hated how childish I sounded—how childish *I felt*—having to defend myself. "We were having a discussion."

"I saw you push him," she said through clenched teeth. "We will discuss this later." She glared at me, a promise in her eyes. Then she turned to Micah. "I apologize for my son's behavior, Mr. Bloom. Constantine gets overly emotional at times and says things he doesn't mean. Enjoy the festival."

Micah looked from my mother to me. I have no idea what he saw on my face—some delightful little combination of shame and horror, no doubt—but whatever it was made his eyes flash with anger and his face turn beet red.

"I don't require an apology," Micah said.

"Pardon?" My mother narrowed her eyes.

"I said, I don't require an apology. Constantine did nothing wrong." She tried to interrupt, but he talked over her. "Not one single thing, Mrs. Ross. We were having a conversation. It became heated, as conversations between adults often do."

"A conversation about what?" she demanded, looking from Micah to me and back again.

Micah looked at me, swallowed, and looked back at my mother. "About the use of penny gum with hydrangeas."

I rubbed a hand over my eyes. I wanted to laugh and cry at the same time.

"*Penny gum?* What in the world would Constantine know about penny gum?"

"Plenty," Micah said hotly. "Turns out, Constantine knows a lot more than I gave him credit for. A lot more than *most people* give him credit for. He's intelligent and has good instincts. And I will never expect an apology from him for expressing his feelings in a forceful way."

Micah's eyes met mine, and I had to look away to catch my breath. I didn't think anyone had ever spoken up for me that way. Not even *me*.

I could feel my mother's curiosity rising, could practically hear the thoughts in her mind as if she was projecting them—*How would he know Con's intelligent? Clearly they've had more than one conversation!*—and I didn't give a shit. Micah's words were like a shot of whiskey, warming me from the inside out, and helping me locate my backbone, which seemed to disappear whenever my mother was around.

"And frankly," Micah continued, his voice soft and steely at the same time, "if I wanted or needed an apology for anything Constantine had done? I'd ask *him* for it, Mrs. Ross. Not you. Because he's a grown man, and you don't speak for him." His eyes caught mine and held, then he nodded once. *Point made.* "You two have a good day."

He turned and walked away, leaving me stunned and gaping. And I was pretty sure he took another piece of me with him.

His words were like tiny little bombs, tearing down walls in my mind that I hadn't even known I'd erected, making me see things I'd consciously avoided for a long time… nine years to be precise.

Better to call a thing what it is, Micah had said, and maybe, in this way, he was right.

I'd been afraid for a long time. Afraid, because I'd thought I had nothing left to lose after my dad died, and I'd found out how wrong I was when the Gaynors went after my family. Afraid, because *Jesus*, how could my mother ever forgive me for what I'd done? I'd hoped to win back her respect by being an obedient child.

But I wasn't a child.

And I couldn't live scared forever.

My mother straightened her spine to her full five feet three inches. "*That man* is—"

"Right," I interrupted. "Everything he said is one hundred percent accurate."

"What? Nonsense. I was stepping in to *help* you, not because I don't think you're a grown man, Constantine." She rolled her eyes. "I gave birth to you, you know. I remember every detail."

"Answer me this," I said softly. "Would you ever get in

the middle of a conversation between Julian and, say, Caelan James? Even if it looked heated?"

"I… might," she said, and I had to laugh, because actually, that was true. God love her, she totally would.

"Okay, better example. Would you automatically go up to Cal and apologize to him for Julian getting upset?"

My mother frowned and toyed with the end of her long, black braid, which was as good as an admission.

But I had no clue where to go from there, except to say, "So please don't speak for me again, okay?"

She frowned. "Alright. I—" She shook her head no, then said, "Yes."

"Thanks. Listen, I've gotta go grab a box from the car. Give this to Theo?" I thrust Theo's burger at her, and she took the cardboard container instinctively. "I'll be along in a minute."

I maybe should have felt more victorious as I walked to Theo's car and grabbed the box of clay pots from the trunk, but I mostly felt unsettled.

I slammed the trunk closed and walked back toward the booth, thinking about Micah defending me and Micah flirting with me and…

"Micah, you're gonna scare children with that face," a woman's voice said from inside Micah's booth as I passed behind it. "Why is the Ross woman trying to kill you with her eyes?"

I stopped in my tracks and nearly laughed out loud because I knew the exact faces Micah's sister meant—both Micah's and my mother's.

"She saw me and Constantine having a… a heated discussion down by the parking lot."

"You and the Ross kid? What the heck did *you two* have to discuss?"

She sounded truly mystified, and I realized that when

Micah had decided to keep my *employment* a secret, he'd kept everything about us a secret, even from his family.

Which was a good thing. *Obviously.*

A very good thing.

"Leave it, Leandra."

"*Oh my God!* Oh my God, you're *blushing.* Do you have a crush on the Ross kid? When I told you to get to know the local competition to help your business, Micah, I didn't mean you should get to know him in a Biblical sense!" Her laughter rang through the air. "This is taking your devotion to the business a little too far."

Get to know the local competition?

"You're insufferable, you know?" Micah said. But he didn't contradict her.

I stalked around the side of the tent and across the aisle and set the box on the table at the front of the booth. Theo was alone inside, munching his burger.

"Mama gone?"

"Went to see if Julian was at his table, I think," Theo said. He licked ketchup off his palm and frowned. "Everything still *fine?*"

"Yeah. I'm just… I need to go. Right now."

"You on call today?" Theo demanded. "Mitch call you in?"

I made a noncommittal noise. "I'm taking the car," I said as I walked away. "Call if you need me."

"Con, are you sure you're okay?" Theo called, but I ignored him.

I really, *really* hated people asking me that.

Especially when it was so clear to me and everyone else that I wasn't.

I took the long route back to the parking lot—the one that didn't lead past Micah's booth. My brain was stumbling, trying to make sense of what I'd overheard, which didn't mesh in any way with what I knew to be true about my relationship with Micah. But then again, what the fuck was our relationship? Why did he blow hot and cold and claim he'd been waiting for *me* to make a move when he *had* to know I was interested?

Didn't he?

Or was it like this thing with my mother, where I'd stopped myself a hundred times from telling her how I felt, when getting her to see my point was as simple as speaking up?

I wasn't sure, and the way my mind kept whirling over it was frustrating as fuck. I could feel that old anger, the kind that scared me, churning in my gut, and I really needed to get away from here, to do something hard and physical and cathartic.

"Con?" Micah called from behind me. "Constantine, wait up!" His voice was closer, like he was jogging.

"No time," I yelled, picking up my pace. "Busy now."

"Stop," he said, right behind me.

Without a thought except the need to avoid this conversation until I was calm again, I took one of the paths into the woods at my right.

Once upon a time, when I was a kid, I'd camped in these woods with my Boy Scout Troop. The trees weren't dense, not like they were out by Pickett's Campground, where you could walk for hours without finding a sign of civilization and possibly tumble down a rock face or into a fucking waterfall if you weren't careful. Here, there were low stone walls crisscrossing the forest, signs that someone had once cleared this space. Farmed it. Made it a part of *O'Leary's agricultural heritage.* But somewhere along the way, they'd stopped trying. And the forest had restored the natural order of things and reclaimed its territory.

"Con, what the hell?" Micah called. "You're mad at

me for what I said to your mom? Okay. Tell me so. Explain it to me. Yell at me. Tell me your side of the story. But don't avoid me. Stop *running*."

"You are telling *me* to stop avoiding things? For fuck's sake, Micah," I called over my shoulder. "I need a minute. Go away."

"A minute for what? To convince yourself you shouldn't have said what you did back there by the parking lot? To figure out twenty-seven new ways you can deflect and pretend it never happened? You can tell me anything. You know that."

I stumbled over a tree root and swore as Micah grabbed my wrist and steadied me.

"Listen," he said. "I didn't know she was coming by just then. I swear I didn't. Just let me explain."

"Jesus Christ. You've done nothing but lie, and you expect me to trust you? No more explanations. No more stories. I'm done with…"

He kissed me. No games, no hesitation, no questions. Just his lips on mine, his fingers wrapping around the back of my neck, and the tiny, needy moan coming from the back of my throat.

It was tempting—God, so tempting—to let myself get caught up in it, but my mind was still racing, my heart beating inside my chest like a trapped bird, and I couldn't give in to it. I couldn't.

I pushed him back, *hard*, and took a giant step away… *right into a fucking tree branch.*

"Ahhh!" I grabbed at my head, where I'd managed to clock myself, like a fucking idiot who'd never been in the woods before. I was losing control—maybe it was already gone—and I hated this feeling. Hated that it always seemed to happen around Micah.

"No more," I said softly, holding out my palm to ward him off. "Just no more. It's done."

I turned and stomped back the way I came.

A second passed. Then ten or fifteen. I was almost sure he was going to let me go, which was what I wanted. What I needed. It *was*.

But when I heard him yell, "*Fuck!*" and stomp after me, I knew I'd been lying to myself again, because my stomach twisted and something settled in my chest and I… stopped trying to walk away.

"Con." Micah stopped a few paces behind me. "Look, I'm not going to touch you, okay? But what you said back there… I haven't lied to you. So whatever thing you've built up in your mind, whatever you've tried to convince yourself is the truth, you're wrong. I… care about you."

I lowered my chin to my chest and breathed in and out. "I know," I said.

He paused, like my admission surprised him and he had to regroup, which was good since it had shocked the shit out of me, too.

I knew it was true, though, the same way I knew I liked football and that my mother, for all her faults, would take a bullet for me any day of the week.

"What did you mean?" Micah hesitated. "About me lying? Because everything I told you—"

"I heard what your sister said," I told him without turning around. "That she'd told you to get to know the competition."

"That was… that was a *joke*, Con. One she made way before I knew you. Before I offered you a job."

I nodded and ran my fingers over the sore spot on my face. "Yeah. I couldn't quite talk myself into believing it either. I think my powers of deflection are fading." I wasn't sure if that was a good thing.

He stepped closer. I could hear his feet crunching in the carpet of pine needles. "Is your head okay?"

"Yeah." I turned around and dropped my hand so he could see it. "Not a fatal wound."

He cupped my jaw in his hand and frowned at the injury. My heart skipped a beat.

"You know, I'm kind of a mess, Micah," I said. "It's worse than I thought."

His fingertips brushed over the bump. "Nah. Not as bad as you think. You'll be okay, Con."

"I didn't mean my head."

"Neither did I," he said, and he wrapped his free hand around the other side of my jaw. "I was waiting for you to tell me you wanted me. I didn't want to put any pressure on you or to make you think that you owed me something."

"That's stupid."

He laughed. "Yeah, well."

"And then you decided to flirt with me in front of Ms. Dorian?"

Micah blushed, just a little, and his fingers tensed on my neck. "Watching you talk to Theo, watching you talk and laugh with people... Look, I'm not a possessive person. But I..."

I licked my lips. "But you want me."

He laughed and bent his forehead to mine. "Yeah."

"Well. Just so there's no doubt? I want you, too."

Micah grinned. "You going home?"

I'm going wherever you're going. "Yeah. I'm, uh, off until tomorrow afternoon. You?"

"I've gotta get back to the booth for a bit," he sighed. "I'm so tired of these damn festivals. Farmer's markets, the spring... thing."

"Lilac Day," I supplied.

"That's the one. They all blend together."

I'd been thinking the exact same thing earlier, but suddenly, I had a new fondness for the stupid, unending festivals that had set Micah across the aisle from me.

"They're each unique and vastly different," I informed him. "*Vastly*."

"Enlighten me."

"I couldn't possibly. You'd need to stick around O'Leary long enough to appreciate the differences yourself."

"Just so I understand, a Ross is telling me to stick around O'Leary?"

I grinned. "This Ross is."

His mouth hovered over mine, and I wanted him to kiss me again—soft, slow, hard, fast, however the fuck he wanted. But instead, he murmured against my lips.

"You know, it's been a while since I was at The Hive."

I frowned. "Uh. Okay?"

"Not since the time I was there with you."

"Oh." I blinked. "Me neither."

"Yeah? Meet me there tonight, then? Around eight."

My pulse raced. My breath caught. "I *might* consider it. If I don't get any better offers."

I could feel his responding grin against my lips. "Still deluded, Constantine," he whispered.

But I was thinking that maybe for the first time in weeks, I was starting to see things clearly.

Chapter Eight

So, it was possible the whole *date* thing was going to be harder than I thought. In fact, it was possible I was having a mild panic attack over it, which was so unlike me that rational-Micah was sitting in the corner with a jumbo popcorn watching me hyperventilate.

"You've got this, Bloom," I told myself as I sat on the bed in my jeans and nothing else and stared at my open closet. "All you need to do is grab a shirt and get in your car. It's that easy, buddy. It's Constantine, for God's sake. You know him. You've talked with him. You've *blown him.* The ice has been well and truly broken."

Except... well, that was kind of the problem, wasn't it? This wasn't me going to The Hive to have a couple of beers and get sucked into the throng on the dance floor for a minute, or to throw darts with some of the regulars and smirk at the guys who preened and pouted and fretted about who they'd be taking home. This was me *being one of those guys.* This was me already knowing exactly who I wanted to take home tonight.

I felt like a virgin at this because I was.

The phone rang as I was contemplating whether a second shower—to wash off the flop sweat that had accumulated after the first shower—would be a good idea, and it was really indicative of my state of mind that I just clicked Accept without even looking at the screen to see who it was.

"Yeah?"

"Um, whoa. Holy naked flesh, Micah. Warn a girl!"

I sighed and pulled the phone away from my ear, scowling at my sister. "You FaceTimed me?"

"You didn't notice?" Lauren laughed. "Okay, Leandra said you were being *very un-Micah* today. I've gotta admit, I thought she was exaggerating, but if anything, she was underselling it."

I rolled my eyes. "Yes, yes, giggle all you want. Get it out of your system. But I've gotta go. I have… plans." I heaved out a breath as nausea clogged my throat.

"Wait!" Lauren yelled waving her hand. "No, don't go. Talk to me. What's going on, Micah? Are you okay?"

"Yes, of course. I'm fine."

"Yeah, yeah. You're always fine, even when you're not." She narrowed her eyes. "Are you sick?"

"No." I huffed out a laugh and wondered if vomiting on camera would ruin my credibility forever. "I'm going out."

She blinked, and I could see her sitting down on her living room sofa and pulling a flannel blanket over her shoulders. "*You* are? On a date?"

Did she have to make it sound so ridiculous? "I guess. Yeah. Kinda."

"You don't *know*? Are you meeting someone at a prearranged time and location for the purposes of a sexual or romantic tryst?"

I sighed impatiently. "Yes."

"Then it's definitely a date."

"Super. Okay, call you tomorrow."

"No, wait! I need more information. Who are you going out with? Where are you going? What are you wearing?"

I rubbed a hand over my face. "I'd really rather not get into it."

"Then let me make some guesses." She grinned, pulling her hair into a bun on the top of her head. "You're going out with the Ross kid, aren't you?"

I narrowed my eyes. "So you and Leandra have already hashed over this, too, I see."

When I'd gotten back to the booth at the festival, Leandra had demanded to know what the fuck was going on. I'd tried to put her off, which was really foolish, in retrospect. Telling either of my sisters I didn't want to talk about something was like waving a red flag at a bull because it confirmed there was, indeed, something to talk about, and the inability to let go of a subject was genetically programmed in the Bloom DNA, like somewhere in our evolutionary history we'd been closer to Dobermans than monkeys.

"Um. I don't suppose you'd accept psychic twin powers as a plausible reason for my knowledge?"

"Yeah, I don't suppose I would."

"Come on, Micah. We're concerned about our big brother, that's all! And Leandra's not the only one who's noticed something different. I've stood next to you in that stupid booth at the farmer's markets every other week, and I've seen the way you stare across the aisle at him when you think I'm not looking. At first, I thought it was your usual, you know, beef with the Rosses."

"My *beef* with them." I laughed helplessly. "How old are you?"

"I have children," she shot back. "It's important that I stay relevant."

"Right."

"But it wasn't that," she continued. "So I started to wonder. I mean, you're gay. He's hot. He's *young*."

I made a gagging noise. "You make it sound so…"

"Normal? I mean, there's nothing wrong with finding someone attractive. But that's not what it is, is it? Or not just that. It's more than a crush. And it's all complicated by the whole mortal-enemies, Romeo-and-Romeo vibe you've got going on."

Uh-huh. And there it was. The biggest problem with this evening, laid out flat.

"Lauren, if I weren't running late, I would really love to have a heart-to-heart right now. We could braid each other's hair and paint each other's nails—"

"Ha. You would hate that. Now, if Chris and I were having a problem, you literally *would* come here and braid my hair if I asked you to. I know that. But talking about yourself? Asking for *my* help? No."

"Bullshit."

"Bullshit right *back*. Only reason you let me and Leandra help at the markets is because we forced you to by threatening to both show up *with our children* every week."

I said nothing because I had a vague recollection of that being true.

"So prove me wrong," she said. "Let me help. Go ahead and tell me what's going on with you and the Ross kid."

"Can we stop calling him a kid?" I grumbled. "His name is Constantine, and he's twenty-four."

"Holy shit. That's even younger than I thought!"

"Thank you. Hanging up now."

"No! Stop! Sorry. Sorry, it's just that you caught me off

guard!" She opened and closed her mouth for a minute, then finally admitted, "I'm still off guard. Twenty-*four*?"

I ran a hand over the lower half of my face. "Still not helping."

"And do you like him? Does he like you? Are you hooking up? How long has this been going on?"

"Yes. I think so. It's complicated. Since June, I guess."

"*June*?"

"I don't know." I blew out a breath. "I can't remember when I stopped noticing him because he was a pain in my ass and started noticing him because I…" I shook my head and bit my tongue.

"Uh-huh. The way Leandra tells it, you've been extra hard on the ki—*Constantine* for a while." She arched one eyebrow and blinked at the screen.

"Maybe I was. We got to know each other over the last few weeks because he was helping me out at the store—"

"He what?" she demanded.

"It's a long story."

"And I have nothing but time."

"Well, I *don't*." I dragged a hand through my hair. "I have to meet him in half an hour, and I haven't picked a shirt because I realized about ten minutes ago that I don't even *like* any of my shirts. My white button-down is too tight. The green one makes it look like I'm trying too hard. The striped one looks like I'm a mid-nineties Garth Brooks groupie, which is a reference I don't even think Con will *get* because, as you so helpfully pointed out, he spent the mid-nineties *being born*. And I have no idea what I'm doing here, except that I really like this guy. I *like* him, Lauren. I genuinely enjoy spending time with him and hearing his opinions on things. And I like the way he challenges my ideas and makes me laugh at myself. And I feel incredibly protective of him, not just because he's hot or because I think he's a kid but because he's *special* and he's been bruised a lot, but he's still trying to figure shit out and not make excuses, and I don't feel like I need to be so fucking perfect when he—" I caught myself, heaved a giant breath, and finished lamely, "when he's around."

Lauren stared at me through the phone and I tried to summon a smile.

"This is me talking," I told her. "Aren't you glad you asked?"

"Yes," she said solemnly. "Yes, I am. And, Micah? If Constantine Ross is the one who made this happen, I will love him forever."

"Made what happen?"

She grinned sympathetically. "Made you panic. Made you messy. Made you human. Made you stop pretending that you know all the secrets to life."

"Are you kidding? I've *never* thought that. I'm clueless."

"With this kind of stuff, we're all clueless," she said way too happily. "You just don't know it because you've never really let yourself be into someone this way. It's always been Blooms and the family, the family and the shop."

"Because those are my priorities."

"Except, Micah—I say this with love, okay? So please, *please* take it with love—we don't need a guardian anymore. You raised us when MoonFlower was..." She shook her head dismissively. "Being MoonFlower. Making daisy chains and giving Mom's money away to every old guy with a sad story. You got us through. Hell, you bought her house as soon as you could, just so we wouldn't have to worry about being homeless the next time she forgot to make the payments. You were our *rock*. You still are. And you are *determined* to make Micah's Blooms into this floral *empire* because you're gonna make sure we *never go hungry again*." She brandished her fist to the sky like Scarlett

O'Hara in a messy bun. "But we don't need you to be our parent anymore, you know? We need you to be our brother. And we need you to be happy."

"I am happy," I said, stunned. "I'm perfectly—"

But I thought of Constantine this afternoon saying, "I'm a mess, Micah," and how fucking brave he'd been to admit that, and I sighed.

"I'm not *un*happy," I said instead. "Honestly, until recently, I never even noticed anything was missing."

"And now you have. And it's Constantine Ross." She widened her eyes gleefully.

I made a little noise and admitted out loud what I'd more or less accepted in my own mind since back in July. "Yeah. Yeah, it looks like it might be Constantine Ross."

———

HALF AN HOUR LATER, I walked into The Hive, wearing my green button-down and still rolling my eyes over Lauren's pep talk, which had mostly involved a walk down the dark and seedy parts of memory lane.

"You can do this, Micah. Walking into the emergency room after the police called to say Mason was injured, when you didn't know if he was alive or dead, was *hard*. Taking Leandra to the hospital when Luna came early and Jared was out of town was *hard*. Going on a date with a guy you like who already likes you? Not even in the same realm as hard… *Heh*. Although a certain thing might *get* hard if you work it right, which—"

I'd ended the call before she could choke on her own laughter, but shockingly enough, I actually *did* feel better. At least I had until I got out of my truck and heard the pounding bass coming from inside the single-story clapboard building.

Of all the stupid places to suggest, why had I picked the scene of Constantine's thousand-and-one hookups? Why had I picked the one location in a ten-mile radius where there were bound to be dozens upon dozens of guys who were younger, hotter, less type-A, and less *me* than me?

I set my teeth as I walked through a small crowd of men and women smoking cigarettes at the corner of the building. Lauren seemed to think it was fucking adorable that I was suddenly cracked open by this thing with Con. *Messy*, she called it. *Human.* I called it needy and insecure and disgusting.

But, you know, buy rational-Micah another bucket of popcorn and settle in for the show, because in spite of all the reasons I should have stayed home, here I was anyway. And I wasn't leaving alone.

I pulled the door open and walked in, letting my eyes adjust, because it was somehow darker in here, with all the colored lights, than it had been in the parking lot.

It looked like every Saturday night since I'd started coming here. Same crush of bodies on the tiny dance floor, same group of lonely hearts hanging in the shadows, same group of older guys playing darts in the corner... same group of guys hanging at the bar around Constantine Ross, who was talking to Jordan and drinking his fruity concoction.

Good God, the man was insanely gorgeous. Dark hair effortlessly messy, pine-green t-shirt molded to shoulders and arms that rippled with lean muscles, dark jeans cupping his ass, blue eyes crinkling as he laughed at something Jordan was saying. All of *that* was the same as the last time I'd been here, too. But as my stomach clenched and my fingers ached to touch him, I realized exactly why I'd wanted him to meet me here.

Because tonight, I knew he was leaving with *me*.

I was a goddamn genius.

I walked up behind Constantine and caught Jordan's eye over his shoulder. "Evening," I said.

I could tell by the change in Constantine's posture that he'd heard me and that he knew exactly who was behind him, but he didn't turn around.

"Hey, cutie," Jordan said. "Your usual?"

I nodded, thinking a beer was exactly what I needed right now. "Oh, and get my friend a refill, too." I put a proprietary hand on Con's left shoulder. "In fact, make it a *double*."

Con looked up at me. "A *double*." He whistled softly. "You sure know how to get a guy's attention."

Jordan grinned as she filled a glass halfway with cherries and syrup topped off with a squirt of ginger ale, then slid it in front of Constantine.

"So," I said, leaning into his side as I grabbed my beer. "You come here often?"

"Pretty often." Con brushed his hair out of his eyes, and his shoulder brushed my chest. "Haven't been around in a while, though."

"And you've been missed," a guy on the other side of Con said. He wore a snapback hat, and his eyes were half-lidded, either out of some misguided impression that he was being seductive or because he'd already had too much to drink.

Con didn't even glance his way.

"Scene getting tired?" I asked, casting an eye around the place and letting my gaze linger meaningfully on snapback dude. He flushed and looked away.

"Not really. Just busy," Constantine said, sipping at his drink through a straw. He twisted so his upper body reclined back on the bar while his legs were still turned to the side. It did *amazing* things to his shoulders and abs. "You know how it is. Work, work, work."

I winced. "Sounds rough."

"You have *no* idea," Con sighed. "My boss can be so difficult."

"Bosses *suck*." The blond on my other side piped up. "I'm Thomas, by the way, Constantine." He smiled widely, but Con seemed not to notice. "We met here a few months back. Do you re—"

"Thomas, there is *no one* who sucks harder than my boss," Con said, looking at me all the while. His eyes flared with heat, and my cock stirred in my jeans.

"Rides you hard, does he?" I said, all fake sympathy. "On your ass all the time for every little thing?"

Con pursed his lips and made a sound of disagreement. "No. I can't say that. To be honest, he ignores me a little too often. He's shit at communicating his *desires* and expectations." He fished a cherry out of the drink with his straw, then eyed me steadily as he placed it on his tongue.

"Maybe he expected you to come to him. For clarification, I mean. About those desires and expectations. To show initiative and a willingness to… *progress*."

"Hmmm. See, I think he could have tried a little *harder*. To not let things… *slide*. It's important for a boss to run a tight ship. "

I inhaled sharply. Things were getting tight, alright.

"Have you thought about finding a new position?" I suggested. "I have experience managing people, and it seems to me a guy like you could probably *fit in* just about anywhere."

"You think?" Con's eyes glowed blue. "Means a lot that you say that. Are there any particular *positions* you think I'd be suitable for?"

His knee pushed against my leg in a way that probably

wasn't noticeable to anyone around us—though Snapback and Thomas were still acting like they were part of this discussion—but was definitely noticeable to *me*. My hands twitched with the need to touch him.

"I could help you!" Snapback said, leaning closer to Con. "My uncle owns a rug cleaning company!"

Constantine's lips twitched but his gaze didn't move. "That's tempting. Do you have a better offer?"

"Funny you should ask. I know of a couple openings you could *fill*." I rubbed my thumb over my bottom lip. Con's eyes locked onto my mouth. "Why don't we talk about it privately?"

"I'm intrigued," Con said. "But you're gonna have to tell me more. Last time I accepted a job at this bar, it didn't work out so well."

"No? That's too bad."

"Benefits were decent, but there's no *upward mobility*." He sighed. "Though, I mean, he did tell me I wasn't the right *type* for the job from the beginning."

How the hell had I never noticed how absolutely filthy employment talk could be? Yet another life experience I could thank Constantine Ross for because I was pretty sure I'd spring wood for the rest of my life when hiring staff.

"That won't be a problem. You're definitely the right type for the... *positions* I'm thinking of. And these positions I'm thinking of involve *longevity*. Excellent benefits. Bonuses for *hard* workers. If you're *up* for the challenge."

"Really?" Con's lips twitched. He straightened and then stood so his body was nearly pressed against mine. "You know, if I want something badly enough, I'll figure out how to get it. I never back down from a challenge. "

"Neither do I," I said softly. Con's eyes said he was counting on it.

"You're not leaving, are you?" Snapback said, interrupting the moment.

"He's leaving," I confirmed, not looking at the idiot.

Thomas snorted. "That's not up to you. You're old enough to be his dad and not old enough to be his daddy."

My jaw locked. "I suppose that's true."

Con finally turned his head to fully acknowledge Thomas with a look hot enough to singe paper… and not in a good way. "Then it's just as well I'm not looking for either one, isn't it?"

To me, he gave a sultry smile. "Come on." He grabbed a handful of my shirt and towed me away from the bar.

"So you're the one leading the way this time?" I said, low and amused as I followed him to the dance floor.

He looked back over his shoulder. "You complaining?"

I wasn't. Not even a little. I wrapped my arms around Con's waist as we reached the crowded dance floor and pulled him back against me.

Christ.

The way we fit was fucking sublime. *Perfection.* He was nearly my height, and my rapidly hardening cock ground against the top of his ass with every sway of his hips, every pulse of the music. He threaded our hands together, right and left, then pulled my right arm up across his chest, locking us in place. He leaned back, letting his head rest on my shoulder, and we moved together as one song bled into another and another.

Everything with Constantine was new and different. Not the dancing, but the synchronicity of our movements. Not the way he pressed his body against me, but the way he did it with total trust. Not the bump and slide that let my conscious thoughts fade and my instincts take over, but the way it didn't feel like losing myself in the rhythm, but like finding myself with Constantine.

With *Constantine*, who was my exact match in so many fucking ways.

The hand I had wrapped around his waist slid lower, so my thumb was tucked into his waistband behind the button of his jeans and my fingers were splayed against the hardness beneath his zipper. My breath hitched.

"*Fuck*," he breathed as I lowered my lips to his neck and licked a path to his ear. I worried the lobe with my teeth. "Micah." He squirmed against me and turned around.

Constantine's eyes were liquid, endless, trusting, which ratcheted up my own arousal to a fever pitch. There was no question of what he wanted, no question of *who* he wanted. He slid his arms up my chest deliberately and locked his wrists behind my neck, claiming me like he had back at the bar. I'd seen him aroused and needy, I'd seen him *want*. But I'd never seen him possessive before. I'd never seen him *take*.

Jesus, I thought, *I could live on this look for the rest of my life.* And the thought made me stick my hands in the back pockets of his jeans and pull him even closer so I could grind our cocks together.

He sucked in a breath and his eyes sharpened, focused. He pulled my head down.

"We're leaving," he said in my ear. "As in *now*."

I pulled back and licked my lips. "Yeah? I was thinking the back hall is closer." I nodded my head in that direction. "We could discuss employment opportunities. You could show me your skill set in certain areas… or I could demonstrate what's expected of candidates for the position. In case you forgot the example I provided last time."

He bit his lip and pushed his fingers into my hair, tugging the short strands *hard*. "I have a very different position in mind, Micah Bloom. And the back hall wouldn't be appropriate for this demonstration."

My heart slammed against my chest and I could feel adrenaline flood my system.

"Your car or mine?"

"Yours." He leaned closer, so I could feel his warm breath on my lips and practically taste the cherry sweetness of his mouth. I knew as soon as our lips met, this pent-up electricity between us was going to explode and destroy any last vestige of control I possessed. For once in my life, I didn't care.

At the last minute, he seemed to change his mind and he closed his teeth over my bottom lip instead. I groaned at the sting.

"Your truck has much more room to maneuver," he said, and before I could process what he meant, he'd hooked his finger in the front loop of my belt, and he was pulling me across the floor again.

When we reached the cooler air of the parking lot, he dropped his hand.

"You're gonna need to take a step away." His voice was raspy and he reached down to adjust himself in the dim yellow glow of the street lights. My cock throbbed against my zipper with painful intensity in response.

"Over there." I pointed toward the side of the building.

The same group of smokers stood in the shadow at the corner of the building, maybe a little drunker now, definitely a lot louder. One of them, an older guy I'd shot darts with once or twice, stepped forward and gave Con a bleary smile.

"Leaving early tonight, Cinderella? Clock ain't even struck midnight yet."

"Night, Stu," Con said shortly.

"Aw, not even time for a chat? Never seen you this

eager before," the man chuckled. "Musta found you a Prince Charming instead of a pumpkin." Stu's group laughed uproariously, like his nonsense was hilarious.

Con stopped short, looking a little bewildered.

I walked right into him, pressing myself against his ass, and he shivered. "Ignore them unless you're rethinking the back hallway," I warned.

Con looked at me over his shoulder. "Not a chance. I have plans."

Then he pulled away and marched to the passenger's side of my truck.

Plans. I nearly groaned. It had been a long time since I'd let anyone lead the show, especially when it came to sex. But then again, I'd never let myself want anyone with this kind of ferocity either. And I knew without a doubt that whatever Con wanted, I wanted too.

WE CLAMBERED up the stairs from the back alley into my one-bedroom apartment over the shop and burst through the door into the kitchen like we were racing. Con stopped in the middle of the room and spun to face me, his chest heaving like he'd run way more than a single flight of stairs.

We stared at each other for a beat, tension arcing between us like electric currents so the air nearly crackled with it. The light in here was hardly better than outside—just one anemic bulb under the microwave lit the space, but it was enough to see Constantine clearly. His eyes were wild and his hair was a mess, probably because he'd spent the entire ride home gripping it like he knew if he didn't hold onto something, he'd be grabbing onto *me*. Ordinarily I'd have taken the opportunity to give him shit about it, but I couldn't because I knew exactly what he was feeling, and I knew if he'd unleashed it then and there, we'd've ended up wrapped around a tree.

Now, though, there was nothing to stop us, and still, Con stopped.

"Con, are you—"

"Water," he croaked out at the same time.

"What?"

"A glass of water. Please?"

I blinked. "Yeah. Uh." My cock was so hard, I could barely remember what water was, let alone how to obtain any. I stared blankly around the kitchen with its pale-yellow cabinets and wooden countertops like I'd never been here before.

Con snickered and clapped a hand to his mouth. "I'm sorry," he said when I looked at him. "Sorry. Just. I need a minute, or it's gonna be over too fast and I… you look so fucking cute." He laughed again helplessly, even as he pushed his hand against the front of his jeans.

I stalked forward, crowded him up against the wall, and, without a word, took his mouth in a swift, hard kiss that knocked the breath from both our lungs as our tongues tangled together.

He pushed me back. "I changed my mind," he said. "No waiting. Bedroom. Now."

I led him through the tiny living area, which held a small folding table, two chairs, a sofa, and a television set propped atop a bookcase I'd rigged out of cement blocks and reclaimed wood, then into my room. I flipped up the light switch to reveal a queen-sized bed, hastily made up with a plain navy comforter, a pair of nightstands I'd brought from my grandmother's place, and a hanging mirror.

"Do you *live* here?" Constantine said, stepping into the room behind me. "I've seen jail cells better tricked out."

"You really want to talk about my style of decorating now, Ross?" I demanded.

"This isn't a style. This is an absence of style," he teased, because he was Constantine and he couldn't *not*. But then he yanked at my waistband to pull me closer and kissed me while he attacked the buttons on my shirt.

"What can I tell you?" I said breathlessly when he finally released my mouth. "I save my creativity for the flowers." I yanked his shirt up, pulling it loose from his pants. "And for other things."

I drew his t-shirt over his head so fast I heard something rip. I opened his jeans and pushed them down over his hips just an inch or two, then took a second to look down and admire the picture he made, all those acres of smooth skin on display. He was so fucking *gorgeous* I had to bite my tongue against the avalanche of words that popped into my brain.

Constantine didn't seem to have that problem.

"I want you," he said.

"Same." I reached around him to clutch his ass and tried to haul him against me, but his hand on my chest stopped me.

"I mean, *I want you*," Constantine said. His blue eyes lit up the entire room, and his hand trailed around to cup *my* ass in demonstration.

I felt my lips part in surprise.

"Unless you're not into that," he amended quickly. "I mean, it doesn't have to be…"

"No! No, I'm into it! I'm *very* into it." Understatement of the millennium based on how hard my cock was pulsing. "I just haven't done *that* in a while. Not in years." A *decade*, even. I hadn't wanted to. But it shocked me how badly I wanted it right now. How much I wanted him to *claim me* right now, just as he had back at the bar.

"I haven't done it in a long while either," Con said softly. He slid his hands up my torso, from my stomach up to my chest, and then sideways so this thumbs brushed my nipples. "But tonight, it's all I can think about." His eyes were filled with naked longing.

He kissed me again and pushed the shirt off my shoulders as far as the elbows, then used the ends to pull me flush against him with my arms trapped at my sides. "I can be a very good boss, Micah," he said. "Definite management potential right here."

The heat of his skin against mine was enough to steal any other words I might have said, and that was fine, since my mouth got pretty busy after that, licking at his lips, learning the precise texture of his scruffy jaw, and figuring out the exact spot below his ear that made his knees literally go weak.

Constantine finished stripping my shirt off while he kissed me. Both of us stepped out of our shoes, and he even kicked out of his jeans, so by the time he pushed me down on the bed and straddled my hips, pushing my wrists into the mattress on either side of me, he was wearing nothing but a pair of tented boxer-briefs and an expression that would tempt a saint to sin.

News flash: I was no saint.

"How do you want this?" he demanded. "Slow and sweet? Fast and hard?" He explored the tendon in my neck with his tongue and traveled south, alternately biting and sucking on seemingly random patches of flesh, like he was as eager to map my body as I was his.

"However you want it," I said quickly. "Either. Both. Just soon." I was fucking *aching*—aching to come, aching to be filled—and I pushed against his hold on my wrists, ready to take matters into my own hands.

Literally.

With a final push, like a warning to stay still, he let go of my wrists, sat back up and smiled, as mischievous and provocative as I'd ever seen him. He shook his head.

"I'm afraid that's not good enough, Mr. Bloom. You're *deflecting.*"

He unbuckled my belt, flipped open the button of my jeans, and let his fingers run up and down the hair of my happy trail.

"*Shit.*" I grabbed his thighs to hold him in place and lifted my hips off the bed, needing his hand just an inch or two lower.

He grabbed my wrists and pushed them down by my shoulders, leaning his weight into the hold. "Tsk tsk tsk. Insubordination on your first day?" He shifted his legs so that his shins pinned each of my thighs to the mattress as he hovered over me. "Is this the way you want to start your job?"

Before I could say anything, he undulated like a snake, rubbing his hard cock against my stomach in the world's most erotic punishment.

Fuuuuuck.

He moaned, and I writhed against his hold, frustrated beyond belief, and so tempted to just overpower him, to roll him over and take that smirking mouth, slap that gorgeous ass, swallow that perfect cock down my throat like I had once before, except this time because he *wanted* it as much as he needed it.

It would have been so easy for me to do that, and both of us knew it. Instead, I surrendered to the frustration.

Well. Sort of.

"Fucking *fuck me*, Constantine," I ordered, throwing my

head back against the pillow. "Weren't you the one who was *dying* back in the kitchen?"

He bit my chin, scraped his teeth over my Adam's apple, sucked a spot at the base of my throat. "I got a second wind."

He stroked his cock along my stomach again, and then again, and then a hundred thousand more times until he was moaning with every thrust, until I could feel the dampness in his underwear, until my own cock was being *strangled* in my pants.

"You're a fucking *menace*," I bit out. "You live to provoke me."

"And you live to let me," he said happily. Holding my gaze, he slowly and deliberately rubbed himself against me once more… but then he froze, holding himself above me with his teeth sunk into his bottom lip, his eyes squeezed shut, and his jaw tight. I realized immediately what had happened, and I felt my lips stretch into some parody of a smile.

"Aw. What's the matter, Constantine? Did you finally push too far?" I taunted, still breathless. "You gonna come in your pants?"

He trembled above me for two long beats, then his eyes opened. "Nope. Gonna come in *you*."

Fuck. Constantine wasn't the only one who pushed too far and lived to regret it, because that comment had me gritting my teeth as my thighs clenched.

Con backed off the bed and stripped the rest of my clothes off before I even knew what was happening.

"*Yesss*," I hissed in relief as my cock was released. I expected to feel his weight settle over me once more, and when it didn't, I opened my eyes to find Constantine standing by the bed staring at my cock and biting his poor, abused lip like he couldn't decide what he wanted to do first.

Meanwhile, his own erection was bobbing in front of him, pointing straight at my groin, like a divining rod showing the way. Even though this was Constantine's show, I couldn't help reaching out a hand to caress the smooth tip and catch the drop of wetness gathered there.

Con shuddered and sucked in a breath.

"I know you get off on plans," he said as I stroked him gently. "So let me explain what's gonna happen now. Ready?"

I raised one eyebrow and looked down at my cock, which was literally throbbing in time with my pulse. "If I were any more ready…"

"You're going to turn over for me. You're going to get on your hands and knees."

I swallowed. "I can do that."

"Don't interrupt," he said, and I shut my mouth obediently, because this confident, bossy version of Constantine was a fucking revelation. "I'm going to get you ready, and I'm going to recite some state capitals in my head while I do, because *holy fucking hell*, Micah, you are the hottest thing I've ever seen."

I laughed, turned on and charmed and amused all at the same time. "You're cute."

His eyes found mine. He grabbed my hand and pulled it away from his dick. He looked a little overwhelmed, a little bewildered, completely consumed with desire, and one hundred percent sincere. "*The. hottest. thing. I've. ever. seen.*"

Jesus. When he said it like that, it was hard not to believe him.

"And then, I'm going to fuck you, and it's going to be glorious."

"Yeah, it will."

"But you're not going to come," he continued, and my eyes narrowed.

"Yeah? Good luck with that." I thought back to that guy—Jesus, I couldn't think of his name, I couldn't even remember his face—who'd wanted to tie me up all those months ago and nearly laughed.

"You're not going to come," he repeated. He guided my hand to my cock, and with his fist over mine, stroked up and down. My eyes slid shut again, and my breathing stuttered. "Because when I'm done, I'm going to turn you over and take you in my mouth, and you're going to come down my throat. Okay?"

Was that an actual question? "Fuck yes."

Con bent close to my ear. "I do appreciate a cooperative employee," he purred, nuzzling his nose into my neck.

"Payback will be a bitch, Constantine."

He pulled back and grinned sharply. "I'm counting on it. Now, turn over."

"So I guess we're going with hard and fast," I said as I turned and arranged myself on my hands and knees, as instructed. "Supplies in the right-hand drawer, by the way." I nodded toward the nightstand.

"You sound so disappointed," Con said as he threw a foil packet and a bottle of lube next to my knee. He climbed onto the bed behind me and ran a hand up my back, caressing the skin between my shoulder blades. "I can slow things down."

"Con—"

His fingers brushed over my hole, and I broke off with a curse. He drizzled a stream of lube over my ass that made me shudder and fist the sheets in my hands. If just that light touch was driving me crazy, the actual prep was going to...

"*Fuck*," I bit out as his finger slid inside, and I took a breath as I struggled to accommodate the intrusion.

"Micah," he moaned, leaning down to bite my cheek. "You're so damn tight."

"*Years*," I reminded him as he moved his finger in and out.

"I know," he said softly, and I could tell he was really pleased to be the exception to the rule.

He prepped me slowly, carefully, and that care was, in a weird way, every bit as hot as the action. Every once in a while, his cock brushed against my ass, and he moaned, letting me know he found it every bit as hot as I did.

By the time he'd added a second finger, then a third, he was rocking against my ass regularly, leaving damp trails on my skin, and I was ready to explode. "Constantine. *Now*. Please."

He grabbed for the condom, and I grabbed for a pillow, dragging it up and burying my frustrated moan in it. "Now. Fucking *hurry*."

Constantine's lubed cock ran against the seam of my ass, and his fingers dug into my hips with bruising strength, holding me in place and reminding me that I was not running the show right now.

"I'm enjoying the view," Con said softly. He trailed his fingers down my back like he had earlier, and it was fucking *torture*. Did he want me to beg? *Would I?*

"You're so gorgeous, I just want to appreciate the moment." He brushed his fingers over my ribcage and down to my ass, spreading me so that his cock could rub against my hole.

Oh, God. "Appreciate me later," I suggested. "Next time."

Constantine stopped moving. "Later when? Tonight?"

I craned my neck to look over my shoulder. "Do we

need to schedule an appointment? Because I left my phone in my pocket, and I'm a *tiny* bit busy ri—*Fuuuuuck!*"

I clutched the pillow tighter as Constantine's cock breached my ass and kept clutching it as he worked his way into me with tiny, controlled nudges.

"Oh, Micah. So good," he moaned.

I grunted a sound I hoped conveyed agreement because Constantine felt fucking incredible inside me, stretching me, *owning* me. I remembered the sting and burn from the last time I'd done this, but the discomfort was negligible. In fact, I welcomed it, welcomed the reminder that Constantine and I were both doing things we didn't often do.

With every stroke, he proved just how much we'd both been missing by sticking to the things we knew.

Constantine changed his angle, tagging my prostate, and I cried out, because suddenly I was *thisclose* to the edge again. I planted my elbow in the bed so I could reach down and jerk myself.

"Don't you come," Constantine said, punctuating each word with a thrust that made me moan. "Remember the goddamn plan."

If I'd had the breath I would have laughed. "Nothing between you and me goes to plan."

He gripped me under the arms and tugged, pulling me upright with him *allllll* the way inside me. He set his teeth to my shoulder. "When you like the result, you can't criticize the process."

I moaned as his hand trailed down to stroke me just enough to tease without providing any relief.

"Any more opinions you'd like to offer, Micah? Any more critiques or comments?"

"No."

Have I mentioned that this confident side of Constantine was really doing it for me? Because it was *really*, seriously doing it for me.

"Good." He pushed me back down to my elbows and then pushed on my shoulder blades until I had my face pressed to the mattress. Then he really started to move.

Holy shit. The sounds Con made were the sexiest thing I'd ever heard in my life—little, breathy half moans that came faster and faster as his hips picked up speed. I couldn't ever remember *needing* to come as badly as I did just then, but I swear, I needed him to come even more.

"So good," I told him, squeezing my eyes shut. "God, Constantine."

"You like it?" he challenged.

"I *love* it. And I'll love it even more when you come for me."

"Mmmph."

"Come for me. Come *in* me. Now, Con."

Another breathy moan, longer this time. "You just can't stop, can you? So. Damn. *Bossy.*"

But he set his hands on the top of my ass, his fingers slipping on my sweat-soaked skin, and moved faster, *harder*, so he was stroking my prostate with every thrust, until finally he froze behind me in the same way he had earlier, his body completely locked down as he came with a wordless cry.

Dying of frustration as I was, I still hated the feeling of him pulling out of me. But then suddenly I was flat on my back and he was crouching between my spread legs. I opened my eyes and blinked, because even the low light was such a shock after having my eyes closed so long, and it made everything feel like a dream—distorted and unreal.

His eyes met mine, still hot with arousal, as he grabbed the base of my cock and licked a path from my balls up the underside.

"No teasing," I begged. "Please, baby. Take it. Take it all."

And wonder of wonders, he *did*. He sucked me all the way to the back of his throat, and the hand he'd splayed across my abdomen twitched and clutched at me, like even taking this much of me inside him wasn't enough. That was when I lost every vestige of control I'd managed to maintain.

His lips slid up, and I yelled. His lips slid down, and I groaned. I bucked my hips ferociously, my fingers threading into his dark hair to hold him in place, as his mouth brought me wave after wave of pleasure. My head was tilted back as far as it would go, and I was *thrashing* with the need to come.

And then the hand Con had wrapped around my dick moved lower, and he speared his fingers back inside me, taking me from the inside and the outside at the same time.

"Constan*tine*!" I screamed, and I exploded inside his very willing mouth.

We both collapsed where we were, graceless and cum-drunk. Con's head rested on my right thigh and he panted against my skin. I slung one forearm over my eyes, which were honest to God *wet*, like I'd actually shed a tear without knowing it because the sex was just that good. With my other hand, I absently stroked Con's wavy hair and let my mind drift.

That hadn't just been *good*; it had been phenomenal. Beyond anything I'd experienced or expected or even, honestly, thought sex *could* be, maybe because it was messy and honest and *human*, like Lauren had said.

And okay, I was *so* not thinking about my sister right now.

Constantine yawned, and I tugged on a lock of his hair. "Come up here," I said.

He shook his head. "I have to get cleaned up in a minute, or else I'll fall asleep." He grinned ruefully. "Falling asleep at the drop of a hat is one of my talents these days."

I combed my fingers through his hair again, and he arched into the touch like a cat.

"One of *many* talents," I teased. "Some I never would have guessed at."

His smile widened and dimmed at the same time, and it was almost like watching him pull on a mask. "Oh, well, *yeah*. Obviously. Sex is definitely my primary talent. And I practice at it." He moved his head off my thigh and sat up, leaving me chilly. "Bathroom out there?"

Without waiting for a response, he walked out of the room, and a second later, I heard the door close in the little bathroom next to my room.

I frowned. *What the fuck?* I pushed myself up in the bed and scrubbed a hand over my face. What had just happened? What was I missing?

The toilet flushed, and Con reappeared. He stood in the doorway for a half-second and looked at me uncertainly, all his earlier confidence gone, then he gave me that same fake smile and reached for his underwear.

"This was great." He rolled his eyes and cleared his throat. "I mean, *duh*. Obviously. But I can't thank you enough for the... *you know*." He motioned toward the kitchen, the back door, the world beyond. "And this." He nodded at the bed.

"The best night I've ever spent at The Hive?" I suggested. "The most mind-blowing sex of my entire life?"

His eyes met mine, and he frowned, like he wasn't sure if I was being serious. And suddenly, I got it. I *really* got it on a gut-deep level, for the first time ever, even though he'd practically *told me* in so many words months ago.

Constantine Ross thought sex was pretty much the only thing he was good for.

In my defense, the entire concept of that was so foreign to me, it's no wonder I hadn't been able to grasp it. Even back before I *liked* him, I'd seen that he was intelligent and witty and sly, and I'd known he was funny, even when I'd wished that humor wasn't directed at me. But someone had done a number on Constantine, and now he couldn't see any of it clearly.

My heart twisted, and for one second I flailed, too. Just how fucking deep did I want to get here? Just how much was I willing to risk on Constantine?

Stupid question.

"Come back to bed," I said as he shook out his jeans.

He glanced up at me in surprise. "You ready for round two already, stud?" He looked at my cock, which was still lying happily sated against my leg, and then back at my face.

I laughed. "You remember I'm forty, yes?"

"Yeah."

"So talk to me about round two in a couple of hours. Maybe in the morning. Come back to bed," I repeated.

"I… did you want me to stay the night?"

"Yes, unless you'd rather not. Did you think this was a onetime thing?"

He blinked, which was like a giant neon sign flashing *yes*. "I wasn't sure."

"I'd really like you to stay. Or, if not, I'll drive you back to your car, and I *will* check my phone and schedule a time for us to do this again later. Assuming you want to."

He cleared his throat again. "Sure. Yeah. I'm down to stay over." He frowned. "Why are you looking at me like that?"

"Because I'm still not sure you're getting me," I admitted. I swung my legs off the bed and braced my elbows on my knees. "This is not a onetime thing, meaning I don't just want to have sex again *tonight*, but I'd like to have sex with you on a regular basis. A regular, *monogamous* basis."

His lips parted, but no sound came out.

"A regular, monogamous basis where we also talk. And have meals. And hang out. And… honestly, I don't know what else, because I have about as much experience with this shit as you do, so we can kind of take it from there."

"Oh." He cleared his throat once more. He looked wary.

"Wow. Do you actually need that drink of water now?" I demanded. "Or are you trying to figure out how to tell me no? Because you can just tell me flat-out. No harm, no foul. You won't hurt my feelings," I lied.

"No! No, that's not… I want that. I… haven't had sex with anyone since… Way before the time in the workroom and… I don't want anyone else."

I sucked in a breath and told myself not to read too much into those words, but I couldn't help it.

"Good. Same here. So, *now* can you come to bed?" I demanded.

Con grinned and tossed his jeans on the floor, where they remained for the rest of the night.

And most of the morning.

Chapter Nine

CONSTANTINE

September

"I LIKED IT. Did you like it?" I demanded as we drove away from the little cul-de-sac in Piermonte, nearly ten miles outside O'Leary, and the little blue Honda parked in the driveway there.

"Told you I liked it when we were test-driving it," Micah reminded me with a smile, but I was still buzzing from the excitement of finding a car after weeks of looking, and I couldn't keep quiet.

"Low miles. Only four years old. Totally within my budget. Guy can deliver it this week." I ticked the items off on my fingers.

"Don't forget the faint air of butterscotch from the little old lady who owned it." Micah grinned over at me from the driver's seat as he navigated his truck down the side streets that led to the highway. "What's not to love, baby?"

I grinned back, feeling my face heat. The *baby* was a throwaway comment, not a declaration of anything, and I knew it, but it gave me this little *zing* every time he used it. Combined with one of Micah's rare grins, combined with the golden beauty of a September Sunday, and I could feel it lighting me up from the inside out in a way I had no desire to fight.

Of course, some of that peaceful mood might also have been because I'd spent the night at Micah's place, eating pasta and binge-watching *Man in the High Castle...* sort of. Micah, who'd already watched all three seasons, had agreed to rewatch the series starting from the first episode, and in gratitude, I'd cooked homemade baked ziti that would've made even my Nonna Bettinelli ask for seconds.

But after we ate, I'd teased Micah that with conflict resolution skills like these, our relationship was bound to get boring as fuck pretty quickly, and the man had *not at all predictably* taken that as a challenge to demonstrate just how *not*-boring things could be. So, as a result, I *still* hadn't actually seen the entire first episode.

But I'd been sloppy-grinning all day long.

"I do not trust that face, Constantine," Micah teased.

"What face?" I said innocently, lifting my hands to frame my cheeks. "*This* face? This sweet, innocent face?"

"That face means trouble."

"Trouble? God, that sounds so negative. No, this is the face of a man who just bought himself a car, *with cash money*, and is having it delivered this week." I grabbed the papers I'd set on the dash and shook them like maracas.

Micah snorted.

"This is the face of a guy who's out with his... his *man*, enjoying the day," I said, only stumbling the tiniest bit over the lack of suitable word to call him since every other relationship-y word sounded either overly juvenile for a guy over forty, or very, very committed.

"*Trouble*," Micah said again. "The kind of trouble that's gonna have me pulling over to the side of the road before I wreck us."

I felt my heart kick up and made myself study my fingernails nonchalantly. "Pssht. Like *I* am to blame for *your* utter lack of control."

He picked up my hand and interlaced our fingers so his warm, callused palm rested against mine atop the center console. "Turns out, I really like your kind of trouble."

Yep. That did it. My heart was chugging like I was pushing the truck instead of riding in it.

God, I was so gone for this guy. I was pretty sure I was way beyond "*like*." Even "*crush*" was like a distant planet I could only make out with a telescope. No, I was pretty sure I was in completely new territory altogether here, and it wasn't remotely comfortable. So, of course, I had to make a joke.

"Wait," I teased in a hushed voice. "*Wait, wait, wait.* Micah Bloom, are you saying that you don't dislike me *at all* anymore? Because last I heard, you flat-out hated me a full twenty-five percent of the time…"

"Jesus."

"… and if you're telling me that you don't dislike me *at all* anymore…"

"I think I spoke too soon," Micah said, but it seemed like he was struggling not to laugh.

"Nope. No take-backsies. You *like* me." I clasped my hand—as well as his—to my chest in rapture. "What tipped the scales?" I demanded. "I'd say it was the eyelashes, but those aren't new. Was it the blowjob this morning? Because that's not exactly a new thing either."

It *so* wasn't. I'd had more sex in the last month than I'd had in a year, and I hadn't exactly been spending my Saturday nights on the couch with Ben and Jerry's before

Micah, so that was saying something. Turned out, I was pretty fucking insatiable where Micah was concerned, and miracle of miracles, Micah seemed to feel the same way.

"Pretty sure it was the ziti that sealed the deal. That shit was *delicious*." He wiggled his eyebrows. "If you'd cooked for me months ago, this all could have gone so differently."

I snickered, and he tightened his fingers around mine.

It was enough to make a guy start thinking thoughts.

"You coming to Hoff's to watch football later?" I asked, trying to be all casual. "It's a town-wide thing. Everyone's welcome. Might be the last time I get to see you for a couple days since Mitch has me doing overnights tomorrow and Tuesday."

"What's his name getting drunk and needing to be hauled in to sleep it off again?"

"Jamie Burke," I said sadly. "And I seriously hope not, because dragging him out of the bar all the damn time is getting old. I wish I knew what was going on with him." God knew he wasn't talking to me or Julian about it. I sighed. "So. Football *yes?*"

"Football *no*." Micah's mouth twisted with regret. "I've gotta get started on some stuff for the week. Belle informed me Thursday that she's cutting back her hours now that summer's over."

"Cutting them back? You didn't tell me that."

"I meant to mention it last night, but something else came up." He arched an eyebrow at me, but I refused to be distracted.

"I thought she only gave you sixteen hours a week as it was."

"Mmm. It'll be ten, starting tomorrow. Leandra's gonna come help if her mother-in-law can babysit. I really need to find someone full-time."

"I'll come in more often. Now that I'll have the car, working early morning shifts will be even easier." Did I know how to earn the boyfriend points or what?

But Micah didn't smile at my generous offer. Instead, he shifted in his seat and wrinkled his nose. "Actually, I wanted to talk to you about that."

"About the morning shifts?"

"About you working for me." He hesitated. "You needed the job to save money for your car, right? And now you've got it?"

"Yeah." In fact, I'd saved up enough to pay cash for the car *and* have a bit left over. "But I'll keep working as long as you need me. It's not exactly a hardship to see this face in the morning." I lifted our joined hands to nudge his chin.

He drew our hands to his mouth and bit my index finger lightly. "I appreciate that, Constantine. But, uh. What if I wanted you to *stop* working for me?"

"You're firing me?" I demanded, drawing my hand away.

"No!" He pushed a hand through his hair, messing up the brown and silver, making it look way sexier than he had any right to be. "Or actually, yeah. I guess I am. It's complicated."

"Complicated? How?" I demanded. "I hardly ever give you shit anymore. And if this is about that time last week when I distracted you while you were paying invoices—"

Micah snorted. "I will never complain about *that* kind of distraction, Con."

"Then what?"

He blew out a breath. "You know how we sometimes play boss and naughty employee?"

"And you shut me up when I get mouthy? *Oh*, yeah. I know."

Micah gave me a sidelong look. "Not helping. The point is, that makes it weird for me being your *actual* boss."

I frowned. "I am perfectly capable of keeping those things separate. I know you'd never actually make me—"

"This isn't about you," he interrupted. "It's about me, okay? It's about me not liking to make my *boyfriend* load the van or process stock or hose out the fucking buckets for money. It feels wrong. And, then…"

He kept talking, and I'm sure he was saying some seriously brilliant, important stuff, but I'm not gonna lie. My mind had stuttered to a halt at *boyfriend*, and anything he said after that was irrelevant.

Micah, who called things what they were and not what he wanted them to be, had called me his boyfriend. Right then, I was soaring ten feet above the truck.

"Yeah," I whispered, interrupting his explanation.

He gave me a wary look, like he wasn't sure what I was agreeing to.

I cleared my throat. "No, that's very understandable. So I quit. Effective immediately." I grinned. "Because firing your *boyfriend* would be a really shitty thing to do, FYI."

Micah grinned. "I suppose it would."

"Maybe I could volunteer until you find someone, then." I took his hand in mine again. "It's the boyfriendly thing to do. And I'm sure you could find some form of non-monetary compensation."

The road widened into two lanes, and Micah moved right to take the on-ramp to the highway when movement on the left side of the road caught my attention.

"Actually," Micah started to say, "I was thinking you could use that little bit of free time to work on your own business—"

"Stop! Micah? Is that a person dressed up as a dancing tomato?"

"Uh." Micah squinted through the windshield. "I think he or she is meant to be an apple. Sign says Bartlett Estates U-Pick. Oh, and they have cider donuts." He turned excited eyes to mine. "Little-known fact: the only thing I love more than baked ziti is cider donuts."

"Then, by God we need to get us some." I pointed at the apple-man. "*Onward.*"

"You're crazy," he said, even as he waved to the apple guy and turned left onto an unpaved road that led up a grassy hill.

"*Crazy. Trouble.* Your flirtation game has *not* improved, Bloom," I grumbled. "Your loving little compliments make me sound like a psychopath stalker."

"Aw, Con. But you're *my* psychopath stalker." He shot me a glance that was warmer than sunshine. "And I seem to have developed a hard-on for crazy, too."

I slid my hand over to rest high on his thigh. "Do you mean that literally?"

"Keep your hand there for about thirty seconds and see," he suggested.

But as soon as Micah's truck crested the hill, I forgot all about his suggestion. I forgot about sex and my new car and my own damn *name* because the sight before us was just that beautiful.

"Is this real?" I asked, squeezing Micah's leg. "Am I dreaming?"

Micah laughed. "Unless you dream of fruit trees, I'm gonna say it's not a dream."

But it wasn't the trees, or not *just* them.

The road ended in a little parking lot where five or six other cars, including a couple of minivans, were already parked. To the left, there was an orchard—rows upon rows of trees, each labeled with a white sign indicating the varieties of apples and pears that grew there. But it was the sight on the right, beyond a low stone wall, that drew my attention.

There was a modest two-story house—not much bigger than the one I'd grown up in—covered in weathered gray shingles, and surrounding it on two sides was a garden.

A *glorious* garden.

I was out of the car before Micah turned it off.

"Look at these beds," I said, pointing excitedly. "See the way they used reclaimed fieldstone to build them up? That will last for *years* with hardly any maintenance if done correctly. Pebbles for the paths. And check out the plant choices—delphiniums, salvia, pink asters, wolfsbane. Perennials," I told Micah, like he didn't already know. "But so carefully chosen so they'll bloom from spring right on through to fall."

Micah came up behind me and rested his hand at the small of my back. "A true three-season garden."

"Exactly," I sighed happily. "In the back there? That whole row that's just starting to turn red are burning bushes."

"Looks like it," Micah agreed. "It's spectacular."

"And in a couple weeks, it'll be even better," I said.

"That it will." A woman on the other side of the wall stood up and dusted her dirty hands on her equally dirty jeans. She was maybe thirty, but it was hard to tell since her face was absolutely covered in freckles. Her curly, caramel-colored hair blew in the breeze like dandelion fluff. "I'm Iris Bartlett." She extended her hand. "My brother and I run this place."

"Con Ross," I said, taking it.

"Micah Bloom." Micah nodded.

"You guys here for apples and hayrides?"

"I'm here for the donuts," Micah said. "Pretty sure we're gonna be standing here looking at the garden a bit longer first though."

She grinned. "Look as long as you like. Always happy to have a fellow gardener around. Oh, and if you have any questions about the orchard or permaculture and have an hour—or three, not kidding—to spare, my brother Watt's around, too. You might have passed him on the way up."

"Was he the apple?" Micah asked.

"No." Iris laughed. "That's Watt's son Jack. He's ten. Watt claims he's already done his time in the apple costume, and it was time to pass the torch to the next generation." She winked.

But I didn't care about her brother or the apple-guy… er, apple-*kid*. "So, permaculture in the garden, I get. But in an orchard? Does that mean staggering the trees with nitrogen-fixing plants? Is there a way to do that without sacrificing design?"

The woman blinked and her brown eyes warmed. "Oh, man. I changed my mind. Do *not* engage Watt, or he'll hold you hostage forever. You know, he was thinking of holding classes on Saturdays this winter, kind of discussing the topic. Personally, I wasn't sure how much local interest there'd be. But if you're up for it, I could send you some info—"

I swallowed and bit my lip. Saturdays meant festivals, sometimes followed by a shift at the station. "I don't know. Maybe he could send me some literature. Websites or books I could—"

"Con's interested," Micah interrupted, pulling me in closer. "He's definitely interested."

I turned my head to look at him. "Yeah, but I've got to—"

"You'll figure it out," he interrupted. "When you want

something bad enough, you'll figure out how to get it. Right?" He raised one eyebrow at me significantly.

My cheeks heated at the memory of the last time I'd spoken those words, back at The Hive last month.

My *boyfriend* did not play fair.

"I guess so," I agreed.

"Totally none of my business," Iris said, "but how long have you guys been together?"

"Uh." I looked at Micah. Since June, when he kissed me? Since August when we first had sex? Since ten minutes ago, when Micah had called me his boyfriend? "It's complicated," I finished.

"Isn't it always?" She smiled. "Come on and I'll take your contact info."

Later, after Iris had not only taken down my email address and information but had also given us a couple of free tote bags and pointed out the rows they were harvesting this week, Micah and I strolled through the trees hand in hand for a few minutes before he pulled me to sit on the grass beneath the low-hanging branches of a pear tree.

The dappled sun was warm on my skin through the fabric of my t-shirt, but the breeze was cool, and the air smelled sweet, like apples and possibilities.

"You know, I've lived in O'Leary my whole life, and I never knew this place existed. Never knew Paston Marsh existed either. Or that diner with the good coffee. It's funny how much you miss, even when it's right there waiting for you." I moved closer so my shoulder knocked against Micah's. "Thank you for that."

"Don't thank me," he said, all gruff and adorable. "I like discovering things with you. Even shit I've already seen looks different with you there."

"Because I'm *trouble*," I reminded him. "*Crazy*."

"You're not gonna let that go, huh?"

"Hmm. No." I rested my head against his shoulder.

"So I probably shouldn't remind you I once called you a menace?" His arm wrapped around my waist and held me tight. "Or said that you live to provoke me?"

I laughed. "The last one's true, so I can't argue. And besides, you *like me*, despite all that. So who's really the crazy one here?"

Micah smiled. "Oh, it's me." He kissed me swiftly. "Definitely me."

We sat together in silence for a minute, then Micah said, "You know, you told me you were interested in landscape design. I had no idea just *how* interested."

I grinned. "Is the level of my obsession scary?"

"Not even a little. But…" He took a deep breath, like he was steeling himself to say something. "It makes it hard to understand why you're working part-time at the police station and part-time mowing lawns when *this* is what you need to be doing. Design jobs. Building huge gardens. Learning about permaculture."

I dug the toes of my sneakers into the soft grass. "Well, we've talked about why I can't go after big dreams right now. But I'm totally stealing the Barretts' planting scheme for next spring, especially if we're still doing the exterior planting for the Crabapple." I smiled up at him. "Think I could take pictures on the way out? Maybe if you posed in front of the garden—"

Micah squeezed my waist tighter, interrupting me. "Okay, back up. This is not a big dream. This is not you saying, 'I want to play the kazoo at Madison Square Garden.' This is you realizing that you have something you're very interested in, which you also have experience with and a talent for. It drives me crazy that you won't make this happen."

"But you have a hard-on for cra—"

He shook his head. "Nope. Not jokey time right now, Con." The *stop deflecting* was subtle, but it was there.

I sighed. "Look, you don't get my situation with my mother. Maybe I haven't explained this properly. I've discussed my landscape design idea with her on *many* occasions over the last couple years. She's not convinced it's the right thing to do."

"But—"

"You know Pearl Semple?" I interrupted. "Miss Pearl, from the antique store?"

Micah frowned. "I think so. Older woman? Kinda… mean?"

"Yeah." I smiled fondly. "She's kinda cranky, but she's always been sweet to me. Anyway, she's got this huge Victorian right on the edge of town, and maybe two years ago this past spring, she wanted something special in her side yard, something in keeping with the style of the house, right? I knew *nothing* about this stuff at the time. Hadn't even considered it. That was my dad's thing, you know? And that whole part of the business died along with him. But like I said, Miss Pearl's always been nice to me, so I did a bunch of research online, took measurements, and sketched it all out for her. The wrought iron fence, the crushed stone path, the fountain, the low hedges. She already had a rose garden, but she wanted a bunch of other flowers, too—chrysanthemums and marigolds and cockscomb, and big hydrangea bushes for cutting. So I told her how they needed to be laid out, how to get the height she needed and all that, you know?"

"I know exactly what you mean. And now that you describe it, I know the house you're talking about, too. You designed that?"

"No. I mean, *yes*, but not officially. She, um, loved the

design. She wanted me to do it. *Us* to do it," I clarified. "Ross Landscaping. So, I talked to my mother, told her I had a design client all lined up, I was ready to jump in with two feet. But she said no. Too much work, not enough experience. '*Ms. Semple deserves a professional, Constantine.*' And my mother was right."

Micah set his jaw. "She wasn't. You *are* a professional."

I appreciated his words, but there was something about his attitude that nevertheless pissed me off. He was listening, but he wasn't hearing me.

"No, she *was*. At that time, anyway. Because yeah, I knew exactly what Miss Pearl's garden needed, but I had no clue how to make it happen. I had a vision, but I couldn't run pipe, or install fencing, or handle the ins and outs of dealing with subcontractors. It was really disappointing, but I wasn't prepared. And my mother knew it." I blew out a breath. "So, I learned. I studied. I took online classes. Now I *do* know how to do those things. I just have to be patient and prove it to her."

Micah shook his head. "You don't have to, though. That's what I'm trying to tell you. You don't have to wait for some magical, mystical time when she gets on board in order to start doing the things you want to do. You can take out loans. I could help you."

I turned to him, shocked. "Help me with *loans*, sugar daddy?"

Micah's eyelid twitched, and he hesitated.

I laughed out loud, immeasurably relieved. "Yeah, no. That's not us. You don't feel comfortable having *your* boyfriend clean out the buckets, Mr. Bloom, and I'm sure as shit not taking money from *mine*."

"Get it on your own, then. If you've got a good plan, banks will——"

"I know," I said, holding up a hand to stop him. "Look,

I know I could. But meanwhile, my relationship with my mother would be fucked for the rest of eternity. And it wouldn't be Ross Landscape Design. It wouldn't be a part of something my dad created. So is it worth it to do that, especially given all I owe my mother? Is it really necessary when I could just… wait?" I ducked my head to catch Micah's eyes. "This is me being mature and responsible, Micah. Patient. Which is hard for me. But this is my choice. My timeline. My family. And," I added jokingly, "you have no clue what my mother is capable of when it comes to holding a grudge." I fake-shuddered.

Micah stared at me for a minute, his jaw working. I could practically see him fighting back the need to speak. I summoned a smile, one I hoped conveyed how much I didn't want him to be pissy, as well as how sincerely I did not want to discuss this topic right now.

Or ever again.

After a moment, he closed the distance between us and captured my cheek in his hand.

"I'm starting to think *you* don't know what *you're* capable of, Constantine, because it's more than you give yourself credit for. You don't have to prove anything to me or anyone else. But at a certain point you have to decide if you're going to live forever as the guy people think you are, or show *yourself* that you're worthy of something different."

He pushed to his feet and dusted off his jeans, all casual.

Meanwhile, I sat on the ground, staring at the spot where he'd been sitting, thinking *Oh, shit*. He'd razed me to my foundations and built me back up again all at the same time.

My stomach trembled violently, and I was pretty sure sweat was breaking out on my forehead, which made sense because there was some kind of seismic activity happening in my brain, too—tectonic plates shifting and realigning, old bridges collapsing, and little islands springing into existence in its wake. My mind vomited the word *love* into my consciousness before it blue-screened completely and panic took over.

Was this love? I'd sort of imagined love as a pleasant experience. Hearts and flowers. Unicorns. Possibly rainbows. Was love supposed to make every nerve in your body dance like you'd stuck your finger in a light socket and adrenaline race through your bloodstream like a T. rex had appeared on the horizon? Did love root your feet to the ground and make your fingers cold and then hot and then cold again?

Because if so, it was a wonder they let just *anybody* at this shit. They had age requirements for alcohol, licenses for guns, and prescriptions for fucking *birth control*, but apparently, any old idiot could wander out into an apple orchard and find himself electrocuted by love with no recourse whatsoever.

It was monumentally terrifying.

Micah bent down and kissed me softly, then pulled me to my feet. "Have I broken your brain?"

I nodded.

"Just think about it, okay? No pressure." He grinned. "Now, let's find some damn donuts. Because I know you're dying to talk my ear off about permaculture, and I'm gonna require sustenance if you expect me to listen."

I tried to speak, but no sound came out, so I cleared my throat and tried again. "Fuck that. If you think you're eating *all* the donuts, Bloom, you have another think coming," I said, though it came out all weak and reedy and weird.

Micah looked at me with those gorgeous, mind-reading eyes and gave me an amused smile, like maybe he saw my terror and saw my deflection, too. Like the crazy and the trouble really didn't bother him one bit.

"Race you!" he challenged, but in the end, I'm pretty sure he let me win. And for a second, I could almost let myself believe that everything between us, this whole *crazy*, secret, beautiful thing between us was something *real*. Something that could exist outside of the shadows.

Chapter Ten

CONSTANTINE

October

"Jules!" I ran out of Goode's Diner after my brother, following him as he zigzagged down the sidewalk, through the parked cars, and across the street to his clinic. "Julian! I'm talking to you!"

I knew he heard me, but he didn't even slow down, and I kinda couldn't blame him. Jules—the responsible Ross brother, the professional, not-troublemaking Ross brother, the *boring* Ross brother—had just stood up in the diner in the middle of our usual Saturday morning breakfast and announced to the entire fucking town that he was dating a guy none of us knew. When my mother found out—which she absolutely would, within minutes, thanks to the O'Leary gossip network—there was going to be hell to pay, and he knew it. When he'd pushed himself away from the table, I'd thought he was gonna vomit, and for maybe the first time ever, I had total sympathy for the man.

Somehow, Julian and I had been living parallel lives, *both* of us hiding our relationships. What were the chances?

And how the *fuck* had that happened?

I put my hand on Julian's shoulder as he pulled his keys from his pocket and unlocked the clinic door.

"Con, I can't talk now," he said. "I've got to get ready for Lina Davenport, and…"

I stepped inside after him and locked the door behind me. "And first, you have to explain what the hell is going on."

"Do I? I really think it's self-explanatory." Jules was defensive, *guilty*, and I got that. Oh, God, I got that.

"You're dating the man in the woods," I said, mostly to confirm that I hadn't somehow misheard.

He sighed. "Could you make him sound slightly less like the killer from some '80s slasher film? His name is Daniel."

"Fine, then. Daniel."

"Is it really so hard to believe?" he demanded. "No, you know what? Don't answer that."

I couldn't have answered him if I wanted to. This guy who *looked* like my capable, professional big brother—the guy who'd practically never gotten in trouble in our entire lives, the man who'd been my rock after all the Trent Gaynor bullshit—had melted down into this frantic, raving mess.

"Since when do *you* keep secrets, big brother?" I demanded. But what I really wanted to know was why I'd never seen this side of him before and how we'd grown so far apart without me even realizing it. We had breakfast on a weekly basis, but I guess maybe we didn't talk about the right things. The important things.

"Constantine, really. If I told you or Theo that Daniel and I were hanging out, you'd tell Mama."

I snorted because Julian had absolutely no idea just how much I kept from our mother on an hourly basis. Like the fact that I'd woken up in Micah's bed this morning, and since Theo had taken over my shift at the farmer's market and the weatherman had predicted a washout for the afternoon that would cancel all my landscaping jobs, I was planning to spend the rest of the day in the back room at Blooms, watching Micah work. Or like the fact that my mother had conveniently heard from someone at Marybeth's Salon and Spa that I was dating a girl over in Rushton I'd never even *met* before, and I hadn't attempted to correct her because it was way more convenient for her to think this unknown woman was the reason I didn't make it home most nights.

"No, don't make that face," Julian said. "You totally would. Not intentionally, maybe, but it would have slipped out. And you *know* the next time she was pissed at Theo and telling him to be more like me, he'd totally have thrown it out there."

I pursed my lips. Julian had no clue who I was. Not really. And I was pretty sure he didn't know Theo all that well either. It was kind of sad.

But then he whispered, "I just wanted something to be… *mine*," and I had to take a deep breath because *oh yeah*. I got *that*. Parallel lives, right down to the lies.

Right down to the utter impossibility of telling the truth.

I scratched my chin. "Not gonna be *just yours* anymore." Which was exactly what would happen if I told my mother about Micah. Even though keeping it a secret was getting harder and harder by the day.

I'd started consciously subduing my happiness whenever I walked into the Ross Landscaping office or sat down for dinner, just so my mother wouldn't get suspicious and call me on it, and I wouldn't have to lie outright. What kind of a life was that?

And when did a secret become a lie?

Julian sighed. "Daniel's going to be *pissed*."

I snickered. "You don't think he's gonna enjoy having folks speculate about when you two will get married or what you'll name your kids?" He looked horrified, so I added, "I'm kidding. People aren't likely to talk to him. I know Si and Everett like him, but he's not exactly friendly."

"You've got to tell people to stay quiet," Julian begged. He flopped down into one of the plastic chairs in his waiting area. "Just for now."

Hilarious. Did Julian really think anyone in the whole world listened to me?

"I can try. But they're gonna be more eager than ever to know what makes him so special *the* Doctor Julian Ross is dating him, when no one even knew the dude was gay." Just like everyone would want to know what the fuck *Micah Bloom* saw in an immature idiot like Constantine Ross. "They're gonna want to know how you got together and whether it's serious. And that's just the people in town. Mama is… God. She's gonna birth kittens when she hears." I wasn't sure whether I was talking about Julian's secret or mine. Maybe both.

"I know."

"Like, she's not gonna know whether to give you her pissed-off face or her disappointed face or her you-made-me-cry face. She's gonna tell you Dad would be rolling in his grave." I shuddered. "It's gonna be *biblical*." It would be like my worst teenage disappointments all over again.

Ugh.

"Thank you, Constantine. I'm aware."

I snapped out of it long enough to blink at him, to really see all his annoyance and fear, all his worry about what it would mean to disappoint Mama. Julian, for all his maturity and fucking *professionalism*, had no clue what it would be like.

"Nah, bro. You *think* you know," I said, not without sympathy. "But you've always been her favorite. Hell, you've always been this *town's* favorite. Take it from Constantine-the-Hellion, the higher you are, the harder you fall. People are still talking about shit I did in high school."

People still thought I was that guy. Mama for *sure* thought I was still that guy.

"I haven't done anything wrong," Jules insisted, like I was gonna condemn him or something.

I laughed. "Yeah, I doubt Mama will see it that way. But listen to me." I grabbed at his wrist. "When she gives you shit, and she will, push back. Hear me?"

It was a lesson I'd learned really, stupidly late. As in, *two fucking months ago*. I'd sort of expected some negative fallout from her regarding the way we'd left things after the fair and… nothing. She'd gone on as if nothing had happened. And I sure as hell wasn't gonna push the issue.

"Yeah. Okay." Julian practically rolled his eyes.

"I'm serious, Jules. You know how much I love her, but Mama will smother you if you let her."

"Easy for you to say. You've done your own thing all your life, but I…"

Done my own thing? Was that really how Julian looked at it? He sounded almost *admiring*, and how fucked was *that*? He'd gotten it totally ass-backward. *He* was the one who'd done his own thing, going after the career he wanted, moving out of the house like he wanted, never feeling like he owed someone the very breath in his lungs because he'd screwed up so badly.

For a second, it was on the tip of my tongue to tell him just how wrong he was, but then I saw his eyes—the same blue my dad had shared with all three of his sons—and I realized just how badly he was freaking out.

And things hadn't always been easy for Julian either.

"You had to switch colleges and move home after Dad died," I said softly. "Had to be a surrogate father for Theo and me." And we both knew how shitty *that* had been. "Had to sit through a billion of my high school football games even though you barely understood what was going on." I chuckled a little and gave him a smile. He really *had* been an excellent, excellent brother. Still was. "You had to put that convertible of yours up on blocks and never drove it again. But you don't have to give this up, too. Take a stand, Jules."

It was the pep talk I would have given myself under different circumstances. Like, in a world where the guy I was dating wasn't *literally* the guy my mother blamed for most of her financial problems and wasn't sixteen years older than me to boot. In a world where I wasn't still trying to live down my past, and he wasn't hyper-focused on his business, trying to build a future.

In a world where Micah and I could really be together.

"Hey. Which of us is the older brother?"

"There's never been any doubt about that, Jules. But there are a couple of things I do better than you. Knowing how to be happy is one of them." Knowing how to fake it, anyway, which was pretty much the same thing.

Or had been.

Until recently.

"Okay, I've gotta get home," I lied. "Mama's got me doing a couple landscaping jobs this afternoon." I snuck a glance out the front window, hoping to see darkening clouds out there.

"That's odd," Jules said, frowning. "It's too late in the season for mowing and too early for leaf cleanup."

I rolled my eyes. Julian didn't get involved in the landscaping work anymore, and I knew for a fact that Mama had never mentioned a word to him about her finances because she knew responsible Julian would do something drastic to fix it for her, and it wasn't his problem to fix.

"Gotta keep up with Micah's Blooms," I said lightly. "How dare someone else start a business that competes with ours, right? Now we work twice as hard for half the money."

Julian stood up and shook his head. "Such a hellion, you are. Tell me again about the joys of irresponsible living?"

"I blame you," I said, knocking my fist into his shoulder, "for being a good role model."

I took a step toward the door, then turned back.

"Listen, I'll do what I can to get people to shut up." Micah said I was good with people. Convincing. "I'll tell them *it's complicated.*" I grinned. "Theo said even old Hen Lattimer from the hardware store is on 'The Facebooks' now, so he'll get it."

"Thanks. I appreciate it. Now I've gotta talk to Daniel. After I take a look at Macarena, of course."

"It's gonna be okay, Jules." I gave him what I hoped was an encouraging smile. "If he's a decent guy, he's not gonna be nearly as upset as you think he will just because you spilled the beans while trying to save his reputation."

It seemed so simple and straightforward.

Probably because I didn't have to live it.

My phone buzzed in my pocket, and I took it out, checked the screen, and nodded goodbye as I stepped outside onto the chilly street.

Micah: *Heard there's rain coming. See you this afternoon?*

I bit my lip as an excited little bubble rose in my throat. God, this was *bad*. So, so bad.

One stupid general text about *nothing*, and I was standing on Weaver Street, all weak-kneed and wanting.

The trouble was, my situation was nothing like Julian's. Unlike Jules, I didn't have an entire lifetime of good-son brownie points that I could use up if my secret romance ever came to light. And also unlike Julian, my career goals hinged on my mother's goodwill. If I ever wanted to convince her that Ross Landscape *Design* was a good investment, I needed to keep doing exactly what I was doing— working hard, staying quiet, not complaining, and keeping my relationship with Micah Bloom very, very secret.

And maybe that was fine. I mean, Micah had sure as hell never said anything about taking our relationship public or wanting us to be more than we were. We were together, no doubt, but Micah's first commitment was to his business. And I was okay with that. Mostly.

Con: *Yes.*
Micah: *Excuse me. Is this Constantine? Constantine Ross?*
Con: *Lol. What?*
Micah: *Because I just asked you a direct question and you answered it directly, so I want to know who you are and what you've done with my boyfriend.*

I knew I was grinning like a lunatic, but I couldn't help it.

Con: *Sure you don't want me to keep replacing him? You must have a hard time keeping him in line.*
Micah: *I'm gonna show him exactly how I keep him in line this afternoon. I'm in the mood to be bossy.*

I stuck my tongue firmly in my cheek.

Con: *Really. Do tell.*

My cock stirred in my jeans, and I looked down the street to the far end of the town center, where Micah was right now. So close and yet so far.

Micah: *I'd love to. Unfortunately, I'm at the farmer's market, standing across from YOUR MOTHER.*

I grinned.

Con: *Please tell me you've accidentally cast longing looks in her direction.*

He didn't reply, and I burst out laughing, right in the middle of Weaver Street. Rena and Dana Cobb, who were emerging from the bakery next door, turned in my direction. Dana's hands were wrapped around Rena's arm like they were two lovebirds on a stroll, which I guess they sort of were, even after a billion years of marriage.

I'd always thought the two of them were sort of a strange pair. Rena, an artist with short, grayish hair, and a stocky build, was known for her sharp humor and her love of shocking people—most recently, with the giant phallus sculptures she'd, erm, *erected* at their farm outside town. Dana, meanwhile, was at least a decade younger and four inches taller, with blonde hair she wore in a cheerful ponytail and an endless supply of patience, which she needed as manager of the Crabapple Bed and Breakfast.

"You're like a breath of spring on a cold day, Constantine," Dana said with a wink. "Isn't he, Ree?"

"Mmm," Rena said, looking amused. Dana seemed to take this for agreement.

"That's why I like you, Con," Dana continued, smiling warmly. "You always try to be cheerful, no matter how hard things get or how gray the sky is. Best way to go through life. Isn't it, honey?" she asked her wife.

I wasn't sure I agreed with her assessment, but before I could say anything, the phone in my hand vibrated audibly.

Rena's lips twitched as she glanced at it, then up at me. I clasped the phone to my chest protectively, even though I knew there was no way she could see who I was texting.

"I guess even naturally cheerful folks sometimes need a reminder to smile every once in a while, eh? And better still if they turn your engine at the same time?" She wiggled her eyebrows.

I felt myself blush and I wondered for a moment if maybe Rena had X-ray vision.

"*Rena!*" Dana said, slapping her wife's arm in mock outrage.

"*Dana!*" Rena teased back, wrapping her arm around the blonde woman's back and looking up at her with a fond wink.

Dana sighed. "I'm taking you home before you cause any more trouble."

Rena grinned. "See what I mean, Con?" She made a noise like a revving motor and let her laughing wife tow her across the street to their SUV.

I shook my head as I look down at my phone.

Micah: *All I can say is, she nodded at me and didn't even scowl. I don't know how to interpret that, except if I don't show up later, it means we've run off. Or she killed me.*
Con: *The second one is more likely. You're a troublemaker.*

Micah: *Thanks to your influence.*
Micah: *Oh, great. Now Leandra wants to know why I'm laughing at my phone. Apparently, this is suspicious.*

I snorted, even though he couldn't hear, and I thought of Rena and Dana.

Con: *Maybe because you used to be a man with no sense of humor who'd glare at me across the aisle?*
Micah: *I had a sense of humor. I just didn't find you funny.*
Con: *You didn't WANT to find me funny. But you did.*
Micah: *Still deluded. Later, babe?*
Con: *Count on it.*

———

But of course, the fucking rain didn't come that afternoon. It didn't come while I was cutting grass or when I'd stopped by to re-seed the Osmans' front lawn. Didn't come until I'd parked the truck outside the Ross Landscaping office, turned in my paperwork for billing, and jumped in my new car to head back to town.

Then it had poured.

Of fucking course.

Con: *Be there in five. Hope you're home! lol.*
Con: *You are still home, right?*
Con: *Micah?*

Awesome. I sighed and slid the phone away.

I drove down the darkened street, past the empty fairgrounds where the market had been, and the yellow, nighttime glow of the shop in the center of town. Jamie Burke had made a comment at breakfast about this being the perfect weather to stay home, and it seemed like maybe the rest of O'Leary felt the same way, especially since the storm that had held off all day was coming down in sheets now.

Shit. Where to park? I sure as fuck didn't wanna park all the way down at the station; I'd drown on the walk to Blooms. So I drove around the block, down Firehouse, and into the back alley that ran behind the stores. I pulled into a spot behind Spinning Jenny's and called it good.

I noticed Julian's old car up on cinder blocks behind his clinic, but his SUV was gone. *Likely out with his boyfriend.*

Micah's truck and the van were parked in his spots, though, which meant he'd probably been ignoring me. Maybe he was more annoyed at the change of plans than I'd thought.

Double awesome.

I locked my car and darted through the rain to the back door of Blooms. I raised my hand to knock… and found the door was already open, just a crack.

Okay, so at least he was expecting me.

Shivering, I stepped into the back room. All the lights were off. The metal table in the center of the room reflected the low light from outside.

"Micah?" I took a step into the room, and my sneakers squeaked against the floor. My jeans were damp against my legs and water ran down my hair into the collar of my sweatshirt. "Where are—?"

The door slammed closed behind me, and the light from the stairway leading to Micah's apartment turned on.

I whirled around, my heart racing, and found Micah standing there, arms folded over his chest, watching me. He was wearing jeans and the olive-green t-shirt he knew I liked best—the one that fit across his broad chest like a second skin and made his eyes stand out.

I nearly swallowed my tongue.

I was also so startled I clapped a hand to my bosom like I *had* a fucking bosom.

I scowled and snatched my hand away. "Jesus. What's with the drama?"

"You're late."

Heart still pounding like I'd been jump-scared *because I had*, I riffled my fingers through my wet hair. "Yeah, I know. I texted you earlier that I wasn't gonna be able to—"

Micah took a step forward. "You're late."

I blinked and took a second to finally, belatedly, notice the expression on Micah's face—the heat in his eyes, the set of his jaw. A chill chased up my spine that had nothing to do with the water.

Micah had *said* he was in the mood to be bossy.

"Who cares about a few minutes here or there?" I demanded, playing my part. "Not a big deal, man."

Micah's eyes glinted with approval. This was exactly the way the game was played. "Put your hands against the wall," he commanded.

I laughed, and I didn't even have to fake it. God, I loved this. "Or what?"

"Or I'll *make* you," he said in a low voice that was way too pleasant to bode well for me.

Hell, yes.

I laughed again. "You're joking, *boss*."

"Oh, I assure you I'm not, Mr. Ross." He shifted his weight, bringing his face into the light, and *fuuuuuck*. Micah hadn't shaved today. The beard burn tonight was going to be very real, and I craved it. "I thought you enjoyed your employment here."

I felt my lips twitch even as my stomach curled pleasantly. Micah was so fucking right that this was a hundred times better knowing he wasn't my boss anymore… but he had been once.

"Micah…" I took a step toward him. "You don't mind if I call you Micah, right?" He quirked a brow but I didn't wait for him to reply. "Micah, surely there's been a misunderstanding. There must be some way I can make up for my lack of… *punctuality*."

He scratched at his jaw, and the rasping was loud in the otherwise quiet room. I could hear the refrigerator motor kick on.

This was the time when he'd suggest *exactly* how I could make it all up to him… on my knees. I gave him a knowing smile and reached for his belt…

He spun me so fast I saw stars, until I was cheek-to-the-wall, with both of my hands pinned against the small of my back.

This was *not* the usual script.

"Was there something else you were thinking of, Mr. Bloom?" I breathed. "Some other way I could…"

"Oh, Constantine," he said, disappointment in his voice. "You think you can wriggle out of things this easily? I was expecting you earlier."

I blinked. *Not at all* the usual script.

"You know why I wasn't here," I said, confused. "I had to work."

"No excuse. Just as I thought."

I laughed.

"I needed this ass earlier," he continued, transferring his hold on my wrists to one hand. "I had *plans* for this ass earlier."

Saliva pooled in my mouth. "You could still—"

He ran a hand down over the ass in question, and I gasped in a breath.

"And I think you need to be taught a lesson."

"A l-lesson?" I stammered. I cleared my throat and tried to speak like I wasn't turned on and nervous at the same time. "What kind of lesson?"

He squeezed my ass harder, then slapped it once, barely a tap. "The kind with a little pain. I heard once that you didn't mind a little pain, Mr. Ross."

The sound of my heart knocking against the wall had to be audible to somebody besides me, it was beating that hard and fast.

"That—" My voice came out a croak. *God.* "Was a joke."

"Was it?" Micah didn't sound surprised. The fucker sounded amused. "Well, guess what?" He leaned in closer and his nose nuzzled my neck, just behind my right ear. "This *isn't.*"

He flicked his tongue against the shell and sucked the lobe into his mouth and my hips bucked back against him. He pulled my hip back and let his hand caress my stomach beneath my sweatshirt. Then his fingers drifted lower, finding my erection and rubbing it through my jeans.

My head went back against his shoulder and I moaned.

"Interesting," he breathed in my ear. "That's a hell of a giveaway. I think you might not have been kidding after all."

He flipped open my button one-handed—dexterous fucker—and yanked down my zipper. I could feel the wet material of my jeans, weighed down by the cell in my pocket, slide down the curve of my ass.

"Do you agree to my terms, Mr. Ross? To continue your employment."

I took a deep breath. There was no one I'd ever trusted quite the way I trusted Micah and sure as fuck no one I'd ever wanted this much.

"Yes, Mr. Bloom. I understand. Anything to keep my job."

His smile was like Christmas. He removed my shirt in record time and pushed my jeans and boxers down over the curve of my ass.

"So, once again, hands against the wall, Mr. Ross. Don't make me ask you a third time."

I was shivering hard now, chilled from the rain and hot with arousal, but I braced my hands against the wall obediently and shuffled my feet back. My feet were apart, and my jeans were hanging around my thighs as I braced for whatever was about to happen.

But I wasn't prepared to feel his fingers gliding over my ass slowly and reverently like it was the first time he'd seen it when it was definitely, *definitely* not.

"What are you doing?" I demanded as goosebumps raced up my spine. "This isn't punishment."

"So smooth," he said, almost absently. "Do you know, your ass was one of the first things I noticed about you?"

"I thought it was my sassy mouth," I snapped, looking over my shoulder.

He slapped my right cheek, just once, hard enough to shock. I sucked in a breath as my erection pulsed.

"That too," he agreed in that same absent tone, and he went back to trailing his fingers up and down, up and down.

I shuffled my feet. My skin stung but only the tiniest bit, but the rest of me was flushed warm and I felt… exposed.

"You can get on with it any time now," I informed him.

Micah slapped my ass again, this time once on each cheek. I inhaled sharply and faced forward, watching my fists clench and unclench as I tried to find purchase against the smooth wall.

"Stop talking, Ross."

"What if I *like* talking?" I demanded hoping it would earn me another slap… anything to stop him from staring at me and taking his own sweet time.

But just then my cell phone rang. Micah's fingers paused in their exploration.

"You should get that," he said.

I laughed. "You're out of your mind. Ignore it."

He didn't, though. In fact, he trailed his fingers down my inner thigh and bent to grab my fucking phone from my pocket.

"Would you look at that?" he said, all innocent. "It's Julian."

I turned my head to look at him again with narrowed eyes. "Honest to God, I don't care if it's that Nigerian prince finally calling to give me my millions. Shut it off."

Micah smiled and held the phone over my shoulder. "You said you wanted to talk. So talk while I touch you. And when you're done with your call, I'll take you upstairs and fuck you."

I held his gaze for a second. There was a trick here, I knew it. But I slid my thumb over the screen to accept the call.

"Jules? Everything okay?" I demanded.

Micah's hands coasted up and down the naked skin of my back in an extremely distracting way before coming to rest on my ass again.

"Yeah, I'm fine," he said. "Where are you?"

"I'm, um… out. Why?" Micah's fingers slowly pulled my cheeks apart, and I glared at him over my shoulder and tried to step away.

He held me in place.

"Because I just got home and saw your car parked

behind the laundromat, but you're not there," Jules said, like this should've been obvious.

And damn it, maybe it should've been. What the hell had I been thinking?

"Oh. Right," I said. "Duh. Yeah. I parked behind the laundromat because I… Because I…"

Micah's finger coasted over my pucker, and I sucked in a breath.

"Stop it!" I hissed over my shoulder.

"Who are you talking to? Oh, Jesus. Constantine, are you with a hookup right now?"

"What? No!"

"Because I don't mean to be a buzzkill, but is the alley behind the laundromat really the safest place to meet? It's dark, and you should really—"

"I'm not hooking up," I said, as Micah snickered. His finger ghosted over my hole again, but this time it was wet.

Lube? Where had the fucker gotten lube?

I couldn't bring myself to care as he pushed a fingertip inside me.

"*Hunhhh.*"

"Oh, shit," Julian said. "Are you working at the station? Oh, is Si around? Because I wanted to thank him, for earlier. I know he was trying to calm me down at the diner and—"

"He's not—" My voice cracked as Micah's finger kept pushing, just the tiniest bit at a time, and his other hand came around to fist my cock.

Fuck.

"Silas isn't here right now," I said in a rush. "I'm actually super busy, though, Jules, so—"

I'm pretty sure I sounded like I was being tortured which, let me tell you, is exactly what it feels like when your boyfriend is jerking you and you have to pretend he's not.

"Ah, well. I'll catch him later. I wanted to thank *you* for earlier too. For the pep talk."

"Okie doke," I said inanely, pounding the side of my fist against the wall in frustration. Micah's teasing was both too much and not enough. "That sounds nice."

"Um. Con? You sure you're okay?"

"*Peachy!*" I all but shouted as Micah's entire finger penetrated my ass. "So fucking *peachy*."

Micah chuckled.

So did Julian. "That kind of night, huh?"

"Yeah," I said desperately. "That kind of night. That kind of *existence*."

Micah's finger moved in and out of me in time with his stroking of my dick, and I almost incinerated from the pressure of trying to stay silent.

"*You are so dirty*," I said over my shoulder.

"You are so hot," Micah whispered, jacking me twice as fast.

I sucked in a breath and bit back a whimper.

"God." Jules snorted. "So true."

I had to shake my head to remember what the fuck *he* was talking about.

Julian sighed like he was about to launch into a story, and honest to God, I wanted to be a good brother, but not *now*.

"Jules, I've gotta go."

"Yeah, okay. Just to say, you were right about standing up to Mama." Julian's voice was firm. "She doesn't get a vote about who I date. She called me earlier, as expected, and I stood up to her. More or less. Told her Daniel and I were together. So thanks for that."

Behind me, Micah froze, his hand still wrapped tightly around me, his finger still inside me. I wasn't sure if that was better or worse. *Fuck*.

"Really," I said before he hung up. "You don't need to thank me."

The second the call disconnected, I pushed off the wall and turned to face Micah.

"What the hell was that?"

Micah pursed his lips. "Fun?"

"That was *torture!*"

Micah reached behind me and grabbed two handfuls of my ass. "*Please.* Real torture would be if I didn't finish what I started," he said smugly. "Which can be arranged."

"What did Julian want?" he asked, like a man just making polite conversation.

"He wanted to talk about his new *secret* boyfriend—"

Micah looked surprised, and I nodded. "It's an epidemic around here. But I don't want to talk about Daniel and Julian right now."

"No?"

I kicked my shoes and socks off, wriggling my toes against the cold linoleum, and let my jeans fall the rest of the way to the floor before kicking them off too.

"No. I think I've earned my job, Mr. Bloom," I informed him.

"Do you?"

"In fact," I said, getting close enough to bite his lip. "I think I've earned a raise."

He laughed, then grabbed my hair, threading his fingers into it so he could bring me in for a kiss that melted my brain… along with any will to resist him.

"Okay, fine, I'll do anything," I admitted. "I'll do anything you want me to do, Micah."

Micah pulled back and ran his thumb over my bottom lip with unexpected seriousness. "I don't want you to do anything you don't want to do, Constantine. You know that, right?"

I blinked, then frowned. "Did I somehow indicate that I wasn't cool with everything up to now?" I grabbed his free hand and ran it over my erection. "Like you said before, this is a hell of a giveaway."

Micah licked his lips. "That's not what I—" He broke off and shook his head. "You know what? Never mind. You have a raise to negotiate, and I'm more than willing to listen."

But a few minutes later, when we were up in his bed and he was sinking inside me, negotiating was the last thing on my mind.

"*Jesus*," I groaned as he reached for my cock and started stroking me in time with his thrusts. "Faster. I'm so fucking close."

"I was thinking," Micah began, but I cut him off by surging up and grabbing his face in both of my hands.

The movement made me clench Micah more tightly inside me and I had to bite my lip before I could manage to whine, "Whatever you were thinking, save it for next time. I've had enough experimentation for one day, boss."

Micah laughed. He also picked up the pace, his hips thrusting harder, his hand jerking me faster, until both of us came with an endless, agonized cry, wrapped around each other.

We lay there for a long time afterward, my head on Micah's chest as he drew shapes on my back. I listened to the thud of his heart with one ear and the sound of the rain with the other.

It should have been soothing.

It *was*, in a way.

But it also sounded a lot like time ticking down on an invisible clock.

All this secrecy was like a land mine we danced around every day. Micah was careful not to push me. I was careful to *never bring it up*—because not talking about my problems had always gone *so* well for me in the past—and there were times I could almost convince myself it wasn't a big deal.

But every time I felt myself falling further, every time I lost another piece of myself to him, every time I realized just how fucking much he was coming to mean to me and how important this relationship was, it scared the shit out of me.

I knew Micah cared about me, and God knew, nobody understood sacrificing for business goals like Micah did. But that didn't mean he wanted to sign up to be *my* sacrifice. He was a forty-year-old, successful businessman, who deserved so much better than waiting for me, hiding our relationship, just so I could realize my dreams for Ross Landscaping, when I knew he had dreams of his own.

Julian had come clean about his romance—had stood up for his man in front of my mother and the whole goddamn town—and here I was, still pretending.

But what the hell was I supposed to do? Give Micah up? My arms tightened around him involuntarily at the very idea.

I was supposed to be good at this part, you know? The sex. The easy, *uncomplicated* sex. I was supposed to be better at not turning *for now* into *forever.* But then I went and fell for Micah, the guy I wasn't supposed to have, and now suddenly I was starting to question things I'd never questioned before, like how much of my future I was willing to give up to pay for my past.

But long before I'd come up with an answer, Micah's steady heartbeat lulled me to sleep.

Chapter Eleven

MICAH

"I still can't believe you made me wear this," I grumbled as we pulled into the long, unpaved driveway outside the house that would forever be my grandmother's, even though she'd died years ago and I'd technically bought the place from her even before then. My brother's and sisters' cars were already parked there, along with a couple of other cars I didn't recognize. "I look ridiculous."

"True or false: This is a unicorn party."

I sighed and looked out at the backyard, which had once been a gigantic organic garden, but was now a patchy green lawn covered with a castle-shaped bounce house, a long pink table, and a battalion of screaming kindergarteners, all wearing headbands with horns.

"True." I unbuckled my seatbelt. "For a six-year-old."

"And, true or false: You are Olivia's favorite uncle."

I looked across the console at the man who made my whole body *thrum* every time I caught a glimpse of him.

"Really depends on what Mason got her for a present. Six-year-olds are very straightforward like that, and their memories are short."

Constantine laughed. "Well, I'm telling you, you get bonus Uncle Points for the shirt."

"Selling my dignity to buy a little girl's affection might be a new low for me."

"Nonsense. You're selling your dignity to beat your brother. Take it from me, that's always worthwhile." He grinned and leaned toward me across the console. "Plus, have I mentioned I think you're hot as hell?"

"In this shirt?" I raised my eyebrows and looked down at the dark blue fabric.

"In any shirt." Con pressed a quick kiss to the corner of my mouth. "Or no shirt. Especially no shirt."

I grabbed his chin firmly between my thumb and forefinger. "If you get me hard before we see my sisters…"

Constantine's eyes flashed. "You'll what?" He yanked away, still grinning. "Once again, I am not responsible for *your* lack of control, Mr. Bloom. Now set a good example and try to have fun. Tiny people are about to overtake us."

Sure enough, a unicorn horde led by my niece Olivia was swarming the car. I pushed my door open and Constantine did the same.

"Happy birthday," I said, bending down to give Olivia a hug.

"Hey, Uncle Micah." She wrestled out of my grasp a mere second later and looked past me to where Con was rounding the hood.

"Are you Constantine?" she demanded.

Con's smile froze. "Um. Yes. You're Olivia, right? Happy birthday. Thanks for letting me come to your—"

"My mom says you're gorgeous," Olivia informed him, hands on her hips.

"Oh." Con blushed furiously. "Well. I've never officially met your mom, but um, that's nice of—"

Olivia cocked her head. "You do have *very* pretty eyes."

"You really do," another little girl I didn't recognize said.

Constantine shot me a wide-eyed glance.

"You really do," I said mildly.

Con glared back.

"Well, *my* mother says you're a magician." My niece Cora pushed through the crowd of little girls and gave Constantine an up-and-down as faintly disapproving as anything the O'Leary librarian had ever dished out. "Is that accurate?"

Con looked at me again, and I shrugged, though I was pretty sure I knew exactly what she was talking about, since Lauren had started calling Constantine "The Miracle-worker" in our conversations, and no matter how many times I'd told her that things with Con and me were complicated, she'd refused to accept it.

"You just laugh so much now, Micah. It's like he's unlocked something inside you that lets you really enjoy life in an uninhibited way. I didn't know that was possible."

Neither did I. But with the laughter came this other, sadder emotion. Like I was grieving for something I hadn't lost yet.

"No," Constantine told Cora. "Sorry, not a magician."

But I inhaled sharply, because the smile he gave her *was* magic, and it made me want to forget all the very real issues that would prevent Con and I from ever making this *thing* between us into something really permanent.

"You're wearing a pink shirt with a dancing unicorn," my nephew Killian told Con, with his uncanny gift for stating the obvious. "Also, I'm six, like Olivia, but I am going to be seven in four months because I am *older*. By a whole grade."

I pressed my lips together and leaned against the car door as Con nodded gravely. "I'll remember that. And yes," he looked down at his shirt, "this unicorn is dabbing on the haters who think unicorn shirts are ridiculous, because unicorn shirts are cool." Con turned his head to smirk at me. "Right, Micah?"

I smoothed down the front of my own shirt, which had a simple outline of a unicorn against an orange and yellow background. Or, as Constantine called it, "Literally the only unicorn shirt on the entire internet that you would ever wear because it looks a little like the Pink Floyd logo." He was absolutely right.

"Yeah," I told Killian. "Unicorn shirts are cool. Do I get a hello?"

Killian ignored me, his attention solely focused on the newcomer. He pushed his glasses up the bridge of his nose and pushed overlong blond hair out of his eyes. "You can use my Stomp Rocket," he told Con matter-of-factly. "Because I like you."

Get in line, kid.

"Wow," Con said. "I don't know what that is, but *yes.*"

"Killian Michael DiMastrio, you'd better not have brought that Stomp Rocket when I specifically told you to leave it at home." Killian's eyes went wide with guilt as his mother approached, and he melted back into the crowd of children.

I laughed out loud.

Lauren, who was dressed in a long black-and-white unicorn-print shirt and leggings, detoured around the crowd and wrapped her arms around Constantine's waist like she'd known him for a hundred years. Con gave me an amused glance over her head as he returned the hug.

"Um. Hi. Lauren, right?" he guessed.

"Yes! God, sorry." Lauren pulled away. "I'm Lauren. And my mischief-makers are Killian and Cora." She pointed at her children. "And I am *so* excited that you're here!"

"Thanks for inviting me."

"*Inviting you?* We told Micah he wouldn't get so much as a Christmas card if he didn't bring you with him."

She wasn't joking; she'd said exactly that. I didn't figure she'd actually follow through with it, but at a certain point it would have caused me more trouble to explain why I couldn't bring him than to just bring him.

Plus, I wanted him with me. *Always.* Everything was better when Con was there. It was as simple as that.

"Out of my way, unicorns!" Leandra, dressed in a sparkling shirt, pushed through the assembled children so she could get to Con also. "I'm Leandra, mother of this one." She laid her hand on Olivia's shoulder. "As well as two others who are napping. Are you overwhelmed yet? Have we overwhelmed you?"

"Nah, I'm very un-overwhelm-able." Con embraced her too, and Leandra gave me a smug smile as she released him.

I was *seriously* amused that neither of my sisters and only one of their kids had greeted *me* but were clustered around Constantine like he was an *actual* unicorn I'd brought along for show-and-tell.

I couldn't blame them on the one hand, but it made me uneasy, too.

Olivia would probably still be asking about Constantine the unicorn at her sixteenth birthday party, and I couldn't foresee a future in which I knew the answer to that question.

Fucking depressing. Yay, unicorns.

"Micah!" Mason approached through the side yard. He was wearing fitted khakis and a V-neck sweater that would have looked more appropriate at an upscale brunch than an outdoor kids' party.

I opened my mouth to give him shit when I saw the woman clinging to his arm. Victoria was wearing a pale orange sweater dress with a drape-y neckline, a plethora of bracelets that clinked as she moved, and short, pointy-heeled boots that sank into the grass as she walked. Her long, blonde hair curled in loose waves around a face dominated by huge brown eyes and perfectly pouty lips.

I was one hundred percent gay—after one disastrous attempt at dating the lovely Miranda Fulmer in high school, I'd known for sure—but even *I* could sense how sexy Victoria was, like a ghost of a thing I might have felt, had my biology been other than what it was. And like my brother, I'd probably have done a lot more than wear prissy sweaters to keep her happy, too.

I'd never understood why Lauren and Leandra didn't like her.

Mason and I shook hands, and I kissed Victoria on the cheek.

"Victoria, so nice to see you. You look lovely," I said, and she blushed prettily. "And it's nice of you to host the party," I told Mase. "You probably didn't realize you'd be stuck with upholding this tradition when you decided to move in last year, huh?"

"But soon it'll be someone else's turn," Victoria said, smiling. "Won't that be nice?"

"Pardon?" I looked at Mason in confusion.

"Nothing," Mason said quickly, giving Victoria a look that made her roll her eyes. "I'm always happy to host, you know that."

I frowned. "If you'd—"

"So, he's cute," Mason interrupted, nodding at Con. "And clearly the twins approve."

"Nice that they approve of someone," Victoria sighed. "I'm starting to take it personally."

"Oh, babe. It's not you," Mason said. "It's just that they're, you know, overprotective. They'll warm up to you."

"It's been eight months," she reminded him. "It took them eight *seconds* to like *him*." She tilted her head in Constantine's direction.

"Yeah, Con's a charmer," I said, turning to watch Constantine also. He was standing in the middle of the herd of unicorns—and their mothers—who were peppering him with questions, and I could sense that same neutron-star magnetism that had pulled me toward him working on everyone else.

He was so freakin' gorgeous.

I was so freakin' screwed.

"I keep hearing that he makes you laugh," Mason said, smiling. "And I heard he was a troublemaker back in the day, which means I automatically feel a certain kinship with him."

I snorted. I watched Con shake hands with Leandra's husband, Jared, and grin at ten-month-old Gwynnie, who looked like she'd just woken up. The baby immediately stretched out her arms to Constantine, who took her with ease, smiling all the while.

"The man can charm *anyone*," I said, grinning despite myself. "He's got them eating out of his hand."

"That's a good thing," Mason said.

"Mmm." It wasn't quite agreement, but I hoped he wouldn't catch it.

"Isn't it?" he pressed, totally catching it.

"Yeah. I mean, yes. Of course. I just... I don't want anyone getting too attached." *Except me; I was pretty sure it was too late for me.* "We're just dating. It's a casual thing. He's young."

"Huh. Babe," Mason said, turning to Victoria, who was examining her nails. "Could you give us a minute?"

She looked up and narrowed her eyes. "What? Seriously?"

"Brother talk," Mason said. "Please."

"Sure. Why don't I just toddle off and amuse myself while you keep your family things to yourself? God forbid that *I* be involved in family things, or I might start to get ideas, right?"

Mason winced. "It's not that, baby. It's just—"

Victoria held up a hand. "I'll go *amuse* myself with Constantine. Might be a novelty to talk to someone *charming.*"

She stalked off… as much as a woman tottering in high heels could stalk.

"Mason. Did your girlfriend just tell us that she was going to go flirt with my boyfriend?"

"Nah. I mean… Victoria says things like that, but she doesn't mean anything by it," Mason said. He added a moment later, "I don't think."

"Lovely. Anyway, if you sent her away so you could grill me, you shouldn't have bothered." I headed past him into the house after giving Constantine a wave to let him know I was going. "I don't want to talk about Con."

"The more you deflect, the more convinced I am," Mason warned.

I stopped dead in my tracks on the front porch. "*I* do not *deflect.*"

"Well, now *that* is interesting," Mason said.

I sighed as I pulled open the screen door and stepped into the little entryway. "You've done an amazing job on this place," I said, looking from the yellow hallway lined with pictures that led back to the kitchen, to the wide wooden staircase that had recently been refinished. "It didn't look this good when MoonFlower first moved in."

"That's a separate issue," Mason said, waving his hand. "Back to the *troublemaker*."

"He's gonna be coming inside any minute now," I warned.

"Great. Let's cut to the chase. Leandra says you're in love with him. I said no, but now I'm starting to wonder. Which is it?"

"I'm not—" I began. "I—"

"Wow. *Wowwww*. Leandra was right. Goddammit. Glad I didn't bet money."

I scowled. "No. That's—"

"Please, keep digging your hole deeper." Mason leaned against the archway to the living room. "I'm not the one whose boyfriend will be coming in any minute."

I groaned. "There are… issues."

"Pretty sure every relationship has issues. Next."

"Oh, you're a relationship guru now? No, these are insurmountable issues."

"Pretty sure everyone with issues thinks their issues are insurmountable, until they find out differently. *Next*."

"I know Leandra already told you all this, but fine. *Fine*." I rolled my eyes. "No one in O'Leary knows Con and I are dating. His mother hates my guts because I'm her biggest business competition. Constantine's dream is to take over their family business, and she won't let him because she thinks he's irresponsible and because their finances are tight. But, he craves her approval, so he thinks if he works hard enough and keeps her happy, she'll eventually give in. *And* he thinks he owes her, because he's somewhat responsible for their financial circumstances, though I swear there's some mismanagement going on there, too. Long story longer, if he brings me to Thanksgiving dinner in a couple of weeks…"

"She'll be pissed," Mason concluded, scratching his chin. "I see."

"Thank you." I rolled my eyes.

"That's gonna present some challenges. Con's going to have to take a stand. For the future, I mean."

"You're cute, assuming there'll be a future."

"You don't think he'd fight for you?"

"I think… no. I don't think he would. And you know what? I wouldn't *want* him to," I said, my gut twisting as the truth of it sank in. I leaned back against the wall by the stairs. "What we have is awesome. It's amazing. We like each other a ton. The sex is off the fucking charts. We make each other laugh. We cheer each other on. But you're talking about him giving up the dream of running his family's business. The business his *deceased father* started with his mom back in the day. The business he's worked for *without pay* for a fucking decade because that's the kind of dedicated, hardworking person he is. I mean, come on. Con and I have been dancing around this for weeks. We're getting deeper into this… relationship thing… but I know it's gonna kill me when all this comes to a head because I only see two options, Mase. One where Constantine gets everything he's dreamed of, and one where he ties himself to a guy he's been dating for a hot minute—a guy who happens to be sixteen years older than him—and regrets it bitterly."

"No third option, huh?"

"Not that I can see."

"That's dumb," he pronounced. "Let me diagnose you

right here and now. You are a fucking idiot. You have the ideal relationship," Mason demanded. "You're best friends and also have hot sex. What more do you want?"

"I dunno." I leaned back against the staircase bannister and honestly considered the question. "I think there *is* something more, though. Some crucial component. Like, being someone's priority. Knowing you're the most important thing and they care for *your* happiness as much as their own, but that's okay because you care for *their* happiness as much as your own, so it all evens out."

Mason's green eyes widened. "Oh my God."

"What?"

"You! You just explained to me what love is. In *multiple sentences*. Of fucking... *flowery prose*."

"Jesus."

"No, don't roll your eyes at me! This is a big deal. This guy has shaken you up. I like it."

"Why do people think it's a good thing to be shaken?" I demanded. "Believe me when I tell you I was perfectly content being confident and in control."

"Meh. Fuck contentment. Ride the roller coaster."

"Right. Thank you. Spoken like someone who's never ridden it."

Mason took a deep breath and looked out the door toward where he'd left Victoria. "I don't know," he said. "The way you talk about Constantine... I don't know if I ever have."

I sighed. "In the end, it doesn't matter. I told you before, I wouldn't want him to choose me. That would be the *wrong* choice."

"Of the exactly, precisely *two* choices that you have."

"I can tell you have a point. Make it."

"Okay, here it is: There is a third option. Decide right

now, *right here and now* at this fucking unicorn party, that you're in love with him. Then move heaven and earth to figure out a way you can be happy together. And don't tell me," he said, holding up a hand when I would have interrupted, "that Con will have to sacrifice something to love you. *Boohoo*. Life is all about choices. Not all of them are mutually exclusive, but some of them are. There is no *wrong* choice except to just drift along and let life make the choice for you. You've been finding your own path since you were *seven*, Micah. Ask yourself why it's so damn scary to do that now."

I stared at Mason like he was a dangerous creature, because right then, he was. Tossing out solutions, peddling hope.

The voices from outside were getting louder, indicating that the party was moving inside. Mason dragged me into the living room and spoke quickly. "Put him first, right? That's the Micah Bloom philosophy of love."

"Do *not* call it that."

"Show him that he's important. Show him that you're all in. Show him that you're choosing him. That you want him. And then talk to him about what he wants."

"Show him that I *want* to want him," I said slowly. I blinked. "I… think I can do that."

Mason smiled. "I know you can."

"Mase?" Victoria called.

"In here," Mason said. "Just showing Micah the renovation work."

Belatedly, I looked around the room and actually noticed the work he'd done. New windows, fresh paint, a pristine white ceiling where a rust-colored water stain had been for decades.

"Mason, seriously, this is incredible. When you suggested living here rent-free in exchange for fixing the place up, I'd sort of expected you to slap some paint on the walls, maybe peel off that hideous paper MoonFlower liked in the kitchen. This is hardcore." It was *excessive.*

"Realtors are gonna salivate," Victoria said, stepping into the room.

"Victoria," Mason said in a warning tone.

Lauren, her husband Chris, and Leandra stepped in, too, along with Constantine.

"What's up?" Leandra looked worriedly between me and Mason. "Oh! Are you doing this *now*? I thought you said you'd wait until spring. Jared's outside alone with all the kids."

Mason sighed and gave me a guilty look. "I *was* going to wait. Until the work was done."

"Why wait?" Victoria stepped forward and wrapped her arm around Mase's waist. "Why not get it all settled right now?"

"Get what settled?" I demanded, looking from Mase to Leandra. "Why am I going to need a real estate agent?"

My eyes met Constantine's and he crossed the room to stand at my side.

"I'm thinking I'll move out next summer," Mason began.

"Or sooner," Victoria said.

"*Christ,*" Leandra muttered, rolling her eyes at Victoria.

"I was imagining… *We* were imagining," Mason said, waving a hand to indicate Lauren and Leandra. "That you'd want to sell." He shrugged. "You hate this place more than any of us, and you only bought it from Moon-Flower so we'd have some stability—"

"Still can't believe you actually called her that," Con said in my ear.

I laughed shortly. "Still can't believe the names are the part that shock you," I mumbled back.

"So, yeah," Mason said, looking from Con to me. "That's all."

I nodded. "Okay. Where do you think you'll go?"

"Ah. Not sure," Mason said. "Not too far, but—"

"Somewhere with an art museum and faster broadband," Victoria said. "The city. Or the suburbs."

"Both of which Mason always hated," Lauren said. "'I'll never live anywhere but a small town.' Isn't that what you always said?"

Mason sighed. "Things change, Lauren. The move would be good for business."

Leandra fumed. "At least when Micah left, we knew exactly why he was—"

"Enough!" I held out a hand and everyone quieted. "Nothing's being decided today. Mase has a right to do whatever he wants. Let's go enjoy the party." I reached for Constantine's hand.

But when everyone else had filed out, including Victoria—who rolled her eyes as she left—Mason put a hand on my arm to hold me back. "You mad?"

"Mason, why would I be?"

"I dunno. Feels a little weird. I know you bought this house for us, so we'd always have a place to call home. It was such a big deal. Such a point of pride. And now everyone's moving on."

"It was never about the house. It was about stability. As long as you're moving on for the right reasons, it fulfilled its purpose, I guess."

"Yeah," Mason agreed. He summoned a smile and held out a hand for Constantine. "Sorry, we haven't even been formally introduced. I'm Mason, the cause of all Micah's gray hair."

"Nice to meet you," Con laughed, shaking it. "I'm Constantine, the cause of my mother's grays."

"We can trade stories sometime," Mason said. "Did Micah ever tell you about the time I used a construction chute and a giant vat of coconut oil to make a slip and slide off the roof of my high school?"

Constantine looked at me. "*No.* And I cannot imagine why he failed to do that. A slip and slide?"

"Mmm. Four of us greased ourselves up like piglets and slid down. *Oh,* important to note that we were three sheets to the wind at the time." Mason led the way back into the hall.

"Shit." Con winced. "Tell me you didn't land on the ground."

"No! God, no. That would be *stupid,* Constantine!"

Con snorted.

"We had a cheap-ass inflatable mattress and absolutely no understanding of how gravity works. What could go wrong?"

"What *did* go wrong? Did anyone—?"

"Die? No. Somehow. The guy who went first broke his leg. Badly. Lost a soccer scholarship. Pretty sure he still walks with a limp. I broke my elbow and dislocated my shoulder. Couldn't wipe my own ass for *weeks,* which made me seriously rethink my opinion of my own invincibility. One of the other guys broke two ribs and needed to have his fucking spleen removed." He shook his head as we made our way out to the back deck.

"And the fourth guy?" Con asked.

"Stood up and asked to do it again," Mason said, staring into middle distance. "I take it back, maybe he *was* stupid."

Constantine leaned against my arm, laughing without restraint.

"It's not funny, though," he said a minute later, wiping his eyes. "God. Did you get arrested?"

"Nope. Guess they figured at least three-fourths of us had learned our lesson. We weren't allowed to go to graduation or prom, but that was about it. And they were right, because the orthopedist who set my arm was so cool, I decided to go into medicine and actually applied myself for once." Mason shrugged. "So something good came of my idiocy… eventually."

"Huh."

Olivia came skidding onto the deck, her black hair flying behind her. "Uncle Con, come *now*. We're gonna play parade, and you're the tallest one, so you get to be in front."

"Whoa, front of the parade?" Con let go of my hand. "Catch ya later, Micah. I have a date with destiny." He pressed a kiss to my cheek. "And a date with you later."

"I meant, front of the parade after *me*," Olivia explained as she led Con down the stairs to the gaggle of unicorns. "Not *actual* front."

"Oh. Naturally. As befits the birthday unicorn." Constantine turned back to wink at me before letting himself be towed out to play with a bunch of little kids. Fitting into my family like he'd always been a part of it.

Mason slapped my arm and gave me a knowing smile as he followed them down the stairs, but I stood where I was and looked back at what had once been my grandmother's house. Nothing was the same as I'd left it—not the walls or the furnishings, not the smell of the place or the people who lived here—and that was a good thing. There was a lightness to the space that I'd never felt when I lived here.

Stability wasn't in the decorations or even in the house. It was in the family. It was in the things that you learned and the ways that you grew.

So maybe it was time to make my move to O'Leary

permanent, for all the right reasons. Maybe it was time to do exactly what Mason had said and start acting like keeping Constantine in my life was nonnegotiable.

Because I really didn't think there was another option anymore.

Chapter Twelve

CONSTANTINE

December

"Hey." Micah's weight dipped the bed. "Sleeping beauty." He nudged my foot and I groaned.

"Five more minutes," I muttered, pulling his pillow over my head.

"That's what you said half an hour ago when my alarm went off. What happened to the man who used to be wide-awake and giving me shit at four o'clock in the morning?" he chuckled.

My boyfriend was way too fucking amused for whatever hour of the night this was.

I pulled the pillow off my head to tell him so and saw daylight shining through the window. In December, that meant it was way later than I thought it was. Way later than it *should* be. The clock on the nightstand said 7:17.

I groaned as I flopped back down again and rubbed my eyes. "I only got home from the station six and a half hours ago and I have to be to work at eight-thirty."

"You've got a little over an hour. Coffee's ready." He

stood up again and for the first time, I managed to focus on the gorgeous man in front of me. He was naked from the waist up, and tiny droplets of moisture still clung to his shoulders from his shower, making *me* shiver in the chilly morning air, though Super Micah seemed impervious to it as he stood in front of the closet, rifling through his shirts.

Of all the naked men I'd seen, there were very few who looked as good from the back as they did from the front. And yes, that was not the kind of thought I'd share out loud with anyone, not even Micah, but it was really fucking true. There was something about those broad shoulders and the finely rippling muscles, the little freckles and the ridges of his spine, that I freakin' adored. And I wasn't shy about telling him so, especially when I topped him.

"You could come back to bed," I said, kicking off the blanket and stretching out fully. "Wake me up properly."

Micah glanced at me over his shoulder, a knowing little smile toying at his mouth. "Your back fetish amuses me to no end."

"Hey!" I tried to inject some outrage into my tone, which was difficult given the way my cock was tenting my boxers at the sound of Micah's voice. "It didn't seem to amuse you in the middle of the night when I was fucking you into this mattress." I slapped the mattress in question and wiggled my eyebrows in a hopeful sort of way. "Remember, I spent three hours out in the cold, busting a bunch of hardened teenage *criminals* who were drinking out at the campground?"

"And one of the teenagers vomited on your shoes, and you knew karma was real," Micah recited. "And I thanked you for your service, keeping the mean streets of O'Leary safe from sixteen-year-olds with Boone's Farm apple wine. I remember." His eyes heated and they trailed down my naked chest to my cock like a physical touch.

"They were my *favorite* shoes, Micah." I batted my eyelashes. "You could thank me again."

He licked his lips… then closed his eyes with a groan.

"I *can't*. I have a meeting. Meet and greet at the Scarlet Maple with a bride and groom, and I can't be late." He sounded like he was trying to convince himself as much as me, and I took pity on him, flinging the blanket back over myself.

"Okay, okay. I'm being good. It's safe to look again."

But Micah's eyes remained closed as he turned back to the closet. "Nope. If you think it's just your cock that gets me excited when you're practically naked in my bed, you've missed the point entirely."

Now what the hell was I supposed to do with a comment like that? Besides have my heart nearly beat out of my chest and my mouth go dry, of course.

I cleared my throat. "Another meeting with the Valentine's Day wedding woman? Wanting to check for the two-hundredth time that you haven't forgotten her?"

Micah laughed over his shoulder again. "Nah. I'm meeting with a new potential client today. Besides, Marissa doesn't set up meetings, she just calls at random hours of the day to check that I haven't died and O'Leary hasn't fallen into a sinkhole. She's not the first nervous bride I've gotten. Your mom must see the same, all the time."

"Happy to say I have nothing to do with that." I turned so I could lean on my elbow and watch Micah watch the closet like he thought a shirt might jump at him. "Wear the green one. It's lucky."

Micah laughed again. "Pretty sure *getting lucky* in a shirt makes it my *get lucky* shirt, not my lucky shirt," he informed me, even as he pulled the green button-down off the hanger and pushed his arms through the sleeves. "A subtle but important difference."

I grinned lazily. "No shit. You'd better *not* be getting lucky today. At least not until I get home and you can make up for denying me this morning."

Micah paused with his hands on the buttons of his shirt. "Home?"

"Oh." I frowned. When had I started thinking of Micah's little apartment as home? "*Your* home, I mean. Here. Tonight. If you'll be… around."

"You think I might not be around *tonight*, unlike every other night this week?" He resumed buttoning, that quirky little smile still on his lips. "And every night last week, too?"

"It hasn't been that often." *Had it?* I sat up, letting the comforter pool around my waist. "Shit."

Micah laughed. "I'm not complaining, Constantine. Just observing."

"I guess I should maybe go home tonight," I said, thinking out loud. "Like, to my *actual* home, where my mail gets delivered."

"Don't be crazy. It really *wasn't* a complaint." Micah took a step toward the bed and pushed my shoulders until I fell back. He leaned over me, smelling like shampoo and coffee and everything I wanted. "I *like* that you're here. I want you to be here."

I wrapped my arms around his neck, because I couldn't *not* when he was this close, and pulled him down so I could feel his weight against my chest. I nuzzled into the spot under his ear. I sighed. "I like it, too. But…"

"But…" He pushed himself up on his elbows and frowned down at me. "What if someone notices? What if someone sees your car parked outside, or down at the station, a little too often? What if someone guesses the horrible truth?"

Fuck.

I'd been waiting for this for weeks. In fact, it was a

goddamn miracle I'd been able to avoid the conversation this long.

I bit my lip and waited for the explosion.

But Micah just pushed himself off me with a roll of his eyes. He grabbed his shoes from the closet and sat down on the bed by my knee. "I don't even wanna *know* where your mother thinks you are, do I?"

I blinked, stunned by this nonreaction. "Um… no," I admitted. She hadn't asked me about it directly in a while, but I knew from various comments she'd made that she thought I was still seeing the woman she'd heard rumors about a couple months ago, and I hadn't corrected her.

God. I was such an asshole.

"It's just for a little while longer, I swear," I blurted. "I'm gonna talk to her this morning. Show her the business proposal we've been working on."

"Is it done?"

"Well, no. I still want to talk to banks about potential financing. But I'm tired of waiting. I know you must be—"

Micah finished tying his shoes and sat upright. "Babe, the only thing I *must be* doing is going to this meeting." He leaned over to kiss me, his lips warm on mine.

When he tried to deepen the kiss, I pulled away. "Ugh. My breath is awful," I said, covering my mouth. "Lemme—"

Micah pulled my hand away from my face and stared down at me. The short gray hair at his temples glinted silver in the morning light, and there were tiny little lines on his forehead, like he'd spent too long frowning. It made my heart lurch with the need to make him smile. I was so gone for this man.

And that was before he said what he said next.

"Constantine? I don't care about your breath. And I

don't care about your mother. Wait and show her the proposal when you're done."

"Really?"

"Really. And you know what? I've got an idea about getting you the financing, too, once your mom agrees to the rest. Something outside the box."

I narrowed my eyes suspiciously. "Where?"

"A group that specializes in small business lending. Angel investors."

"Yeah?" I blinked. "And you think someone would invest in my idea? Even though I have no collateral?"

"Yeah," Micah said slowly. "I'm positive someone will."

I grinned. "We can talk about it tonight."

"Yes we can. As soon as you get *home* from your shift."

Was it possible to feel like you were flying and crash landing at the same time? Because my stomach was doing a pretty solid attempt at merging the two feelings into one.

Thirty minutes later, after Micah had left, I'd gotten some coffee, complete with the cream and sugar substitute Micah kept stocked for me. I'd showered and shaved, using the razor I kept in Micah's bathroom. I'd looked at the pile of my laundry on the floor mixed with Micah's, and thrown the whole thing into the tiny washing machine tucked into the closet in the kitchen. And I realized that somehow, I really *had* gone from being the most devoted patron of The Hive to Micah's unofficial live-in boyfriend… and I was more than okay with it. Now I owed it to Micah and to myself to move things out of the shadows and into the light.

I drove out to Ross Landscaping and parked in the little lot by the office. Mama's little Ford was already there, along with Carlos's pickup truck and the ancient white van we used for deliveries. I could see Carlos walking around the closest of the greenhouses, likely checking out the systems, which meant my mother would be alone in her office.

Good.

I stepped out of my car and gave it a loving pat, because I'd never take my vehicle for granted again, then I stood in the silent morning and looked around at the place that was as much home to me as the house where I'd grown up or, apparently these days, Micah's.

The larger garage, where the summer equipment was stored, was all closed up—we'd officially cleaned our last leaves until spring—and the trucks had both been outfitted with plows, ready for Mother Nature to unleash on us.

I loved this place. The rhythm of it, the constancy of it, the permanence and legacy of it. Hell, sometimes even the routine of it. And I was determined to keep all of that, if at all possible.

But spending the day with Micah's family a few weeks back had crystallized a bunch of stuff for me about what family really meant, or what it *should* mean. About how mistakes could *propel you forward*, as Micah had once said, instead of holding you back.

The Blooms were every bit as loud and boisterous and *nosy* as my family could be. Every bit as prone to saying stupid shit. But they were open with each other and honest… more or less. Their closeness came from staring down adversity together, not because they all fell in line and did what was expected of them. There was no fear there. And I realized there *couldn't* be any fear, if you wanted to have a family like that.

One time, over the summer, Micah had tried to tell me that not everything in life was transactional, and I hadn't really gotten it then, but I was starting to get it now, especially after seeing Julian choose Daniel despite my mother's objections. Love and respect and support were supposed to be unconditional. Like the way Micah believed in me and saw me as something more than an immature fuckup or the unofficial court jester of O'Leary.

And if you'd told me a year ago that I'd be standing in this parking lot thinking deep, gooey thoughts about Micah Bloom, I'd have laughed my ass off, which just went to show that all kinds of things could change, if you had the right mindset.

The building we called the office was really only three rooms. The main room was dominated by a large, laminated-wood table, a giant whiteboard with important color-coded dates, and bizarrely colorful safety posters. At one end of the main room was a miniature kitchen, complete with an oven no one had ever used and a fridge that was always stocked with bottled water. My mother's office was at the other end of the room, the door propped open with a five-gallon bucket of rock salt, as usual.

"Mama?" I knocked on the open door. She looked up from her computer and took out her headphones.

"Morning, sweetie." Her eyes raked me up and down, and she smiled. "Looking rested."

"Yep." I scratched the back of my head guiltily, feeling disloyal to her for keeping a secret and disloyal to Micah for hiding the truth. "I wanted to talk to you."

Focus, Constantine. One step at a time.

"Does this rested, relaxed you have anything to do with whomever you were texting on Thanksgiving?" she asked archly. A second later, she waved away her own question. "I know, I know, you're twenty-four. But it's been a while now, Constantine. Don't you think it's time we got to meet her? Am I so terrifying that my sons can't bring their significant others home?"

She was joking, but it was no laughing matter.

I gave her an incredulous look. "You're asking me that,

even after the debacle with Jules and Daniel at Thanksgiving dinner?"

"Don't be dramatic." She rolled her eyes. "I already apologized to Julian for grilling Daniel. It's a mother's prerogative to—"

"It was more than grilling. You were rude."

"Stop. You're exaggerating the case. Julian knows." She nodded once, firmly.

Focus on your own problems, I told myself. *Focus.*

But I couldn't.

"*Does* he know? Or does he just want to keep peace with you so badly that he's not pushing the issue, even though he thinks you actually *were* rude, and to the guy he's in love with, no less?"

"*What?*"

"Don't confuse compliance with agreement, Mama. They're not the same. And if you haven't given Julian an actual apology, you owe him one."

"Constantine, what's gotten into you?"

"Do you know why Julian didn't talk about Daniel for months and months? Not because he was ashamed of Daniel, but because he worried that *you* wouldn't like him. Because he wanted to have something that was *his* without you questioning it and making him defend it."

"You're *way* out of line." She tossed her braid over her shoulder and leaned forward, her eyes glinting. "You, Julian, and Theo are my heart and soul. I have done *every-thing* for you boys. I would die to protect you. Sometimes when you love someone, you have to take a stand. I don't want to see Julian *hurt*—"

"I know, Mama. I know. But the only person who's hurt him in this scenario right now is you."

She shut her mouth with an audible *clack*.

"This isn't even what I came to talk about," I said,

pushing a hand through my hair. I dropped into the chair in front of her desk. "Look, I know you love us. But you asked me a second ago why Jules would keep a secret, and that's why. That's it. Because he loves you, but he can't live his life to please you. He doesn't want a life without risks. He doesn't want you to protect him. He's twenty-nine fucking years old and—" I held up my hand when she would have protested my language, "he doesn't need you to shield him, he needs to know he can share stuff without being judged or questioned like he doesn't know his own mind."

She blinked. "Julian told you this?"

I shifted in my seat. "Some. And some I… guessed."

"I see." She leaned back in her chair slightly, but the way her eyes roamed over my face, I wondered if she saw more than I wanted her to.

"So. On that note." I took a deep breath. "I'm putting together a proposal to add on a landscape design division to Ross. I'm going to show it to you in a couple of weeks. After the holidays."

"Oh, Con." She sighed wearily. "One family crisis at a time, please."

"Mama, Julian's relationship is not a crisis. And there will never be a good time. I'm not asking your permission. I'm telling you that this is what I'll be doing. This is what I want to do with my life. It's the thing I'm passionate about. And there is nothing I want more than to build this as a part of Ross Landscaping, to have you be involved."

"You know why—"

"Yes, I know finances are tight. So if you're not comfortable being involved, that's okay. I'll… start my own company if I have to."

Oh. *Wow.* There was that flying and crash-landing feeling again, and I didn't enjoy it any more this time than

I had earlier. I hadn't intended to say that. But saying it felt… right.

"What?" She leaned forward again, jaw open.

"That's not an ultimatum—"

"Sure sounds like one!"

"It's not. It's me saying that I care too much about our relationship to keep pushing and pushing and letting you put me off. I don't want to resent you, and I will." *I already kinda do.*

She squinted at me and made a helpless noise, like she'd been blindsided, and I understood. I'd held this back for too long.

"I'm sorry," I said, hoping she'd know how much I meant it. "For letting things go on this long and not showing you exactly how serious I was earlier. I know I fucked up when I was younger. I did some really stupid things, and maybe they're things you can never forgive me for. I mean, I hope you can—"

"That's ridiculous, Constantine. Of course I can! You know I already have." She rubbed a hand over her fore-head. "I don't understand how things got so off track. I don't understand why you're suddenly forcing things when we've been doing just… *fine.* Haven't we? I mean, I know things have been tight financially. I know this is hardly ideal for any of us. But things are already getting better. We've gotten a whole bunch of new orders—" She grabbed a sheaf of papers and waved them at me. "For the holidays. Way more than I'd planned. I was thinking I could finally get you and Theo your bonuses. And that we could have a nice, peaceful Christmas. The whole family." She hesitated. "Even Daniel, if he wants to come."

Jesus.

My resolve wavered. But I knew if I didn't take a stand now, once and for all, I'd be losing ground for the rest of my life. I'd always prided myself on never lying, but I had been. By not speaking up where it counted.

That was going to change. One step at a time.

I stood up. "We're *going* to have a nice Christmas. And I'm going to get that proposal to you in a couple of weeks. It's going to be *good*. And I really hope you'll keep an open mind about it. Not because I want to force your hand—even if you say no, I'll still give you as many hours as I can for as long as I can. I'll still care about Ross Landscaping, just like I'll still care about you. But I truly think it would solve a lot of problems for all of us if you agreed. Okay?"

She nodded. It was kind of wooden, not so much an agreement as a kind of end to the conversation, and I recognized it because I'd done it so many times myself.

But again, baby steps, right?

"I'm not doing this because I'm angry. I promise. I'm doing this because I love you, and I really want to have the kind of family where we don't have to hide things from each other anymore."

And then I gave her a smile—an honest, genuine one, for the first time in a long time—as I left the office and got to work.

Chapter Thirteen

MICAH

"Good morning, Micah!" Charlotte Fielding sang as I stepped into the business office at the Scarlet Maple Inn. "Thanks so much for coming down! The clients arrived, and I sent them down to the restaurant for coffee and pastries, but they should be back in just a couple minutes! They're really impressed with your portfolio, and they're eager to meet you! What a gorgeous shirt!"

I blinked and looked down at the green shirt Con had chosen for me. "Thanks?"

Charlotte was always cheerful—kind of a requirement of her job as the head wedding coordinator for the Inn—but she was rarely this over the top unless...

"Oh, Lord." I looked around the office to make sure we were alone, set my case on her immaculate desk, then leaned over and lowered my voice. "How bad?"

"What?" she said, eyes as blue and guileless as fucking Snow White in the forest with the woodland creatures.

I winced. "Damn. That bad, huh?"

"I don't know what you could possibly mean."

"I mean, the more obnoxious the client, the more

cheerful you get. And the last time you greeted me this cheerfully, the Sarah Palin look-alike was here planning the double wedding for her daughters."

Charlotte's nose wrinkled as she remembered.

"She wanted *the lucky winning florist* to create topiary busts of her daughters, Charlotte. And throw them in *for free*. She brought that yappy lapdog with her and laughed when it peed on your carpet." I'd never been so happy to tell a client I couldn't possibly live up to their expectations.

"*Princess Coco*," Charlotte spat, clearly still traumatized. She hesitated for a second, then looked out into the hallway to check if the coast was clear. She motioned for me to close the door.

"Okay," she whispered, once it was firmly shut. "Between you and me, this groom puts Mrs. Clemence *and* her Pomeranian to shame. He's plastered yet keeps drinking from his own hip flask when he thinks the bride isn't looking. I'm waiting for *him* to pee on the carpet and laugh."

"Oh, joy. What about the bride?"

"Not sure. I haven't heard her speak a word yet." She raised an eyebrow significantly. "She's very sweet and blonde and delicate. I was considering slipping her a note to see if she's here of her own free will, but she keeps giving the bastard these besotted looks, so..." She shrugged.

"Tell me there's a responsible adult in the room?" I begged. "Tell me there's a reason I climbed out of my warm bed?" My warm, *very occupied* bed.

"Sorta? Father of the groom is here. He's not drunk, that I can tell, and at least he's vocal. Erm. Possibly *too* vocal."

"The father of the *groom*?" That was unusual.

Charlotte threw up her hands. "Not a clue. Far as I

know, the bride's family is footing the bill, but the groom's family is making all the decisions."

I breathed in through my nose. The choice to leave Con in bed seemed dumber and dumber by the minute. "I'm not sure if this is the best fit for Blooms," I began.

Charlotte selected a sheet of paper from her desk and handed it over. It was a client intake form, with all the general information about the bride and groom, including the—

"Holy shit," I said. "This floral budget. Is that a typo?"

"Not a typo," Charlotte said with a grin.

"It's the gross domestic product of a small nation."

"Did I not mention that the bride is the heir to the Kelly Pharmaceuticals fortune?"

I glanced at her over the top of the paper. "You may have missed that critical fact."

"Suddenly more appealing?" she said wryly.

"I find myself marginally more inclined to deal with this shit show, yes."

"Funny how an extra zero can change so much, hmm?"

I sighed. *Seriously.*

"You can go and wait for them in room one," she said. "I'll show them in as soon as they get back and we can go over details so you can work up a proposal."

I nodded and got to my feet… then I had a thought. "What time is Angela coming?" Often potential clients scheduled appointments with several vendors for the same day, and it was always awkward walking out when someone else was walking in, especially when that someone was the mother of the man you'd been secretly shagging, oh, *eight hours ago.*

"She's not," Charlotte said.

I frowned. "Is she sick?" I wondered. I dismissed the

idea as soon as I said the words. For this amount of money, Angela would have dragged herself here even if she had Ebola *and* the plague.

"Nope. Clients absolutely didn't want her. Wouldn't even consider it," she said with a frown. I knew Charlotte and Angela were at least as friendly as Charlotte and I were.

"That's… odd."

"Odder than a groom who shows up inebriated at this hour, with an interfering father and a budget that could get me a down payment on a small island? Who knows why rich people do what they do, Micah?"

"Well, that's for damn sure." I tucked the sheet of paper into my case. "See you in a few."

"There's fresh coffee in there, too," she called. "Grab a cup and become as perky as I am!"

I snorted as I walked out. I didn't need coffee. All I had to do was fantasize about landing this contract, which would make Marissa Corcoran's Valentine's Day wedding seem like child's play, and give me exactly the boost I needed to move forward with my *new* financial plan. The plan where I stepped back, slowed down, and for the first time in my life, acknowledged that there was something more important than making my business successful.

My phone buzzed with a new email alert and I slid it out of my pocket as I walked into the meeting room. The little space was decorated with an understated luxury and smelled like chai tea, probably not by accident. Someone, somewhere, had no doubt realized the scent of fancy cafe drinks made it easier to convince clients to part with their money.

I sat in the chair furthest from the door and started skimming.

. . .

Hello, Mr. Bloom —

My name is Danielle Perry and I'm with Sherburne Realty. We'd like to order approximately three dozen holiday arrangements to be sent to our clients…

I considered it for only a second before hitting Reply.

Hi, Ms. Perry. Thanks so much for your inquiry. Unfortunately, due to low quantities of stock, we won't be able to fill your order. However, I highly recommend another local company, Ross Landscaping and Flowers…

Once upon a time, *that time being six short months ago,* I'd rather have chewed off my own thumbs than send a message like that to a potential client. Now, I hit Send with only the barest twinge of regret.

Fucked up, right? But this was the *eighth* polite refusal I'd sent since Olivia's unicorn party, and it was getting easier.

Admittedly, rational Micah wasn't even eating popcorn anymore; he'd graduated to silently rocking himself in his corner and hoping the trauma would end. But there comes a time when you stop fighting the instincts that try to overtake you. A time when you have to admit that, despite every probability curve and on-paper incompatibility, the only person in the whole goddamn world who makes you feel whole and happy is a provoking troublemaker with infinite blue eyes and an irrepressible smile. And when that time comes? When you realize you're in love with a man who happens to be your business rival's son, and who very badly needs said business rival to stay in business and, hopefully, become financially solvent at some time in the near future? You do whatever it takes to give that man what he needs to make his dream come true. Even if it means referring your prospective clients to Angela Ross.

This, as Mason called it, was the Micah Bloom philosophy of love.

And once I'd committed to it, it had felt *good*.

It wasn't even *that* irrational. Blooms, the business, had never been about *me* or even about being successful for the sake of it. It had always been about stability, about making sure I'd be able to provide for the people I loved. Now, Con just happened to be a part of that circle.

Even if he didn't know it yet.

Even if it was *killing* me to hold myself back from telling him, especially in the quiet times, like this morning, or even last night when he'd cuddled against me before falling asleep.

But the whole point was giving Constantine back his choices, right? And one thing I knew about this complex man I'd fallen for? He felt his debts *keenly*, whether it was owing his mother for shit that happened in the past or not wanting me to give him a single cent of financial support for the business he wanted to start. The last thing I wanted was to tell him how I felt and have him feel like he *owed* me some kind of commitment in return.

Step one, making sure Constantine could start his business by giving Angela the flexibility to let it happen.

Step two, getting Constantine the financial capital to *make* it happen by selling off MoonFlower's old house— literally the best use for that house I could think of, now that Mase no longer wanted it—and anonymously investing some of the proceeds in his business as an angel investor.

Step three, tell Constantine everything, and hope that when he was free to make a choice, when he was building his business and his career uncertainty was mostly settled, he'd choose to build something else, too.

A future. With me.

My phone vibrated again, this time with a text.

Con: *Welp. Talked to my mother. Told her I'd be giving her a formal proposal in a couple of weeks.*
Micah: *And?*
Con: *Eh. Could have gone better. Still alive. I'll tell you about it later.*
Con: *You still looking for a full-time employee? You could interview me for the position later. I'm very motivated.*
Micah: *And the boss already likes you. In any kind of position.*
Con: *Just for that, I'm making baked ziti tonight.*
Micah: *You're hired.*
Con: *Thanks, baby. Later!*

Yeah, it was safe to say I had no regrets about the path I'd chosen. Rational Micah could choke on his popcorn for all I cared.

"Micah?" Charlotte chirped as she walked in the door with a tablet clutched to her chest. "I'd like you to meet our beautiful couple, Violet Kelly and Trent Gaynor, who'll be celebrating their wedding with us in September!"

I gave them a broad smile as I stood and offered my hand.

Violet was exactly as Charlotte had described her. Blonde and lithe as a fairy princess. She was also dressed like something out of the 1950s, in a little cashmere twinset and pearls, with her hair pulled back into a bun. She smiled at me a little, but couldn't take my hand because her fiancé was currently wrapped around her like an octopus… or like a man who was having trouble standing on his own.

"Trent, honey," she said a little breathlessly, trying to disentangle herself.

Trent, who had similarly golden blond hair, an athlete's body, and a butt-dimple in his chin, straightened and lifted that chin at me. Then he looked around the room, sniffed once, and propped himself against the wall on the other side of the table.

I looked at Charlotte, whose eyes widened infinitesimally. *See what I mean?*

Oh, I saw. Violet had picked herself a winner, alright.

Bringing up the rear was a slightly shorter, slightly older version of Trent, right down to an obviously hereditary butt-dimple. "Vince Gaynor," he said, shaking my hand with a little more force than necessary.

Vince took the seat directly across from me and patted the chair next to him. "Violet, honey."

After a single worried glance at her fiancé, Violet obediently sat.

"So, we've heard good things about you," Vince began. He slouched in his chair. "Very good things."

I glanced at Charlotte, who'd taken the chair next to me, and she shrugged before smiling brilliantly at Vince. "I told you, I gave the Gaynors your portfolio to look over."

Vince smiled. "Actually, I was interested long before that. Website says you're doing Marcus Turnbull's wedding, aren't you?"

I cleared my throat. "Well, not Senator Turnbull, but his stepdaughter, Marissa—"

Vince waved a hand negligently. "Of course, of course. But we all know who's footing the bill."

I smiled blandly, then turned to Charlotte expectantly.

"Alright, well, if you'd like to tell me a little bit about the theme of the wedding—"

"Love," Vince said.

"Pardon?"

"The theme. It's *love*."

"Oh," I said. "Right."

"Isn't that what the senator's having at his wedding?"

I ran a tongue over my top teeth. *Think of the money, think of the money.*

"*Marissa*," I clarified, "is having a Valentine's Day theme, because her wedding is on Valentine's Day."

"Well, fortunately for us, love is a year-round thing!" Vince laughed uproariously at his own joke. "Good thing, too, or you'd be out of business, eh?"

Wow.

"So true." Charlotte's smile was brighter than the sun. "But you know, most brides want to put their own stamp on things. Is there any particular flower you really like or dislike? What are your favorite colors?" She pulled up a screen on her tablet and prepared to take notes.

"Well, I—" Violet began.

"Violet's a practical girl," Vince interjected. "She doesn't mind."

"And Trent?" I asked.

Vince snorted. "Trent's not concerned about flowers." He looked over his shoulder. "Are you son?"

Trent slid a little farther down the wall and folded his arms over his chest.

Super.

"You know, I always discourage my clients from following another bride's style too closely," I said smoothly. "Especially if there's any chance that there might be guests who attend both."

Vince frowned, like he hadn't considered that.

I turned my attention to Violet. "Let me show you some sample styles, and we can discuss what you like and what you don't."

For the next half an hour, Vince stayed mostly silent and watchful, Trent propped up the wall like it was his job, and Violet answered only direct, yes-or-no questions about her likes and dislikes. I'd had more painful meetings, but only rarely, and I felt like my brain was itching.

"I think I have enough to get started," I said. "I can get some more details from Charlotte and the staff here about the exact specifications as we get closer to the day." I gave Violet a smile and lied through my teeth, "I'm confident that your wedding will be a beautiful reflection of your personal styles and your relationship."

"Thank you." Violet's shoulders sagged, like she was relieved she wouldn't be asked any more difficult opinion questions.

"You're a good kid, Violet," Vince said approvingly. To me, he added, "Trent's had some difficulties, but finding the right person has really sorted him out. Isn't that right, Trent?"

Trent neither moved nor spoke, and I wondered if he'd fallen asleep against the wall, but Vince and Violet both smiled as though he'd enthusiastically agreed.

"That's so… *sweet*," Charlotte said. "Love really does put everything in perspective, doesn't it, Micah?"

That was something I could agree with.

"Well." Vince slapped the table with both palms. "I guess that takes care of one vendor, Charlotte. Please send us the contracts, Mr. Bloom."

Charlotte and I exchanged a glance. Clients rarely decided to sign a contract on the spot.

Vince must've seen our look, because he gave me a smug smile. "We considered a couple of other, smaller vendors, but none of them have a client list like yours, nor your integrity."

Don't ask, I told myself. *Do* not *ask*.

"My integrity?" I heard myself ask. "Don't get me wrong, it's always validating to hear that Blooms has earned a good reputation, but that's an interesting choice of words."

Vince steepled his fingers. "We have family in this area. In fact, we lived not far from here at one point."

"Middle of fucking nowhere," Trent said, speaking for the first time.

Vince's nostrils flared, but he forced a smile. "Yeah, the place doesn't have pleasant memories for us. But I believe you know my cousin Patrick over at HG Supply."

I felt my smile fade. "Yes. I know Pat."

"And I believe you also know the Ross family of Ross Landscaping? In fact, according to Pat, you've had your own share of trouble with them."

"Trouble?" I gripped the arm of the chair more tightly. I frowned. "Not really. They seem like very decent people. I admit they haven't taken too kindly to competition, but that's only to be expected."

Charlotte gave a tinkling little laugh. "Of course!" She set her palms on the table. "Alrighty, then—"

"Oh, you don't need to speak so diplomatically with *me*, Mr. Bloom. We have our own history with that family. One of the boys was a schoolmate of Trent's. Had some *deplorable* behavior issues, probably stemming from a lack of adequate supervision in the home." He sighed. "Trent tried to extend a hand of friendship to the Ross boy in a time of need, and the boy completely abused Trent's trust. And after a brief physical altercation, he nearly killed Trent in retaliation."

"He means Constantine Ross fucked my girlfriend

behind my back. And when I beat his ass, he wrecked my car like the little pussy he was. Fag shoulda stuck to fucking his own kind."

Charlotte gasped.

Vince said, "Trent. *Enough*."

Violet said, "I don't understand. Trent, what are you saying?"

And me? I said *nothing*.

Not one goddamn thing.

I didn't move a muscle.

For what might have been minutes or hours or millennia, I sat in stunned silence. My limbs felt weightless, even my *lips* tingled, as I realized exactly who was in front of me. Exactly who I'd been speaking to.

When the full impact of it hit, I stood up.

Vince gave me an assessing glance and whatever he saw on my face made him say in a placating tone, "Everyone, calm down. Mr. Bloom, Trent is still very upset by what happened. His… *derogatory language…* in no way reflects his actual beliefs or opinions."

Trent snorted.

"Wow. You really *are* a lawyer, aren't you?" I collected my case and walked around the table.

"What does that have to do with anything?" Vince demanded.

I ignored him.

"Charlotte." I turned to the woman whose cheerful attitude seemed to have deserted her, and she raised her troubled eyes to mine. "Under the circumstances, Blooms won't be able to accept this contract." I looked directly at Trent as I concluded, "I don't work with homophobes."

"Homophobe?" Trent gave an exaggerated frown. "Nope. Just one particular cocksucker I don't like." His half-lidded eyes glittered. "Though I heard he was really good at it."

"Trent." Vince's voice was laden with warning.

Trent didn't heed it. "Little prick got what was coming to him. Dad took them for practically everything they had." He smirked. "Justice is a beautiful thing."

"Yes," I agreed. "Sometimes it really is."

And then I punched the arrogant asshole in the mouth.

Chapter Fourteen

CONSTANTINE

January

"Hey, Ross!" Mitch's bellow rang through the squad room just as I was about to shut down the computer at the little desk I shared with Grace Ferdinand, O'Leary's other part-time auxiliary officer. "Come in here before you head out?"

I stifled a groan as I looked around the empty room. It had been a long, *cold* night shift, with not one but three separate callouts that had kept Carmen and me busy until sunrise. Hell, Carmen was *still* out. I'd been counting down the minutes to seven AM when I could finally get out of here, but it looked like that was going to be delayed.

"What's up?" I asked as I walked into his office. "Problem with my report?"

"Huh?" Mitch scrubbed a hand over his short cap of silver hair. The haircut was new, and based on his expression, not his idea.

I smothered a smile and nodded at his computer screen, where he'd been reviewing my work.

"Oh. No. Report's solid. Troubling, though. Who vandalizes what's basically an empty lot?"

It wasn't an idle question.

I sat down heavily in the chair in front of his desk. "When that lot is the remains of Parker Hoffstraeder's bar? A bar that mysteriously burned down, like, four weeks ago? It's not random."

"Exactly." Mitch sighed. "Insurance company's still not paying?"

"Nope. Which is *ridiculous*. They've got that fire investigator guy poking around, trying to get people to say shit about Parks. And you'll notice he was the fourth person on the scene, after me, Parker, and Jamie. Hanging around like a bad smell."

"Parker *and Jamie*?" Mitch raised an eyebrow. "Is there something there?"

"Who knows?" I shrugged. I couldn't handle my own *secret relationship*. I sure as fuck wasn't in a place to speculate on anyone else's.

"Maybe someone was trying to help Parker out," Mitch suggested. "Clear him of suspicion."

"I dunno. If someone wanted to throw suspicion off Parker, I think they screwed up."

"You think?"

I shrugged again. "Official cause of the fire at Hoff's is undetermined. There was plenty of speculation at the time, given how quickly the building was consumed, but it was under renovation, and there were a lot of valid reasons for chemical traces to be present in the debris, so there's nothing to prove it. Insurance company is doing their investigation, but there's no reason to believe they'll find anything more than Gideon and his guys found. So why vandalize the lot? Why give this fire investigator something else to turn over? Why give him another reason to put Parker under a microscope?"

"So maybe the person wanted exactly that," Mitch suggested. "To implicate Parker?"

"I don't know why they'd think Parker would vandalize his own lot, but if so, they screwed up there, too, because Parker has an alibi." I nodded toward my report on the screen again.

"An alibi who's also Jamie Burke."

"Still not speculating," I said, holding up my hands. "Ask Marci when you see her. She'll know." Our dispatcher was the repository of *all* O'Leary gossip.

"Marci? Why would I see Marci?" Mitch demanded, like this was the craziest notion ever.

I rolled my eyes. "Okay, first? Because you guys are totally together and people have been speculating about it since September. You're about as subtle as a brick through a window. And second, the woman works here." I jerked my thumb out toward the squad room. "First law of secrecy is never to look overly guilty."

"Fuck." Mitch ran a hand over his hair again, and I debated whether to give him shit about who was responsible for his new look, but I didn't.

Look at me, being all mature.

"You know, I've spent years learning detective skills from O'Leary's top investigator," I said instead.

"*Uh-huh.* Well, that's part of why I called you in here, actually." Mitch leaned back in his seat. "What would you say about becoming full-time?"

I frowned. "I... me? Here?"

"Yeah, you. You've worked here longer than anyone besides Marci and Si. And O'Leary's getting busier. After that business with Everett Maior last fall..." He shrugged.

"The town is finally ready to spend the money for an extra full-time spot."

"Oh. *Wow*. That's… a surprise." I forced a smile. "Love that you call an abduction, an attempted murder, and the unmasking of a serial killer *that business with Everett.* That's funny."

Mitch lifted an eyebrow. "You're not excited about this."

Not a question, but I answered it with one. "What makes you say that?"

"I've known you for too long, Con. Anytime you change the subject, it's a dead giveaway."

Jesus. Why did everyone in the world seem to realize this when I hadn't? It was seriously annoying.

"Okay, then." I took a deep breath. "No. I'm not really excited. I love working here, I do, but… This isn't what I want to do full-time."

"You've got another idea in mind?"

"Yeah. Landscape design. I want to create a division of Ross Landscaping specifically for that." I swallowed. "I actually went and got approved for financing, wrote up a business proposal for my mother, the whole nine."

I'd basically shit bricks for a week, absolutely positive that the funding wouldn't go through, but somehow, miraculously, it had. And it had been a total head rush to know someone out there had thought this plan was solid, besides me. But now, talking to Mitch, I felt a little of the same trepidation.

Mitch considered me for a moment, his eyes narrowed. And then he smiled. "I think that's an amazing idea."

"Really?"

"Of course! You know your dad and I were close, and I can tell you for fucking certain that there is *nothing* that would make him prouder than having you involved with the business."

I laughed a little in relief. "Thanks, Mitch."

"What'd your mom say about your proposal?"

"Mmm. I think it's safe to say she's not quite as excited as you are." I rolled my eyes to the ceiling. "I warned her it was coming back in December, but she still seemed surprised when I actually handed it to her last week."

"And?"

"And she hasn't said anything to me about it yet, except that she'll meet with me next week to give me her answer."

"Next week, huh?"

"Yep. And spoiler, it's not that long a proposal. But she couldn't just say, 'Yes, Con, I love it!' or 'No, Con, it's trash!' I have to wait until next week." I shrugged.

"And if she says no? You want me to hold this full-time spot?"

"If she says no, I'm going out on my own," I told him.

Mitch smiled again. "Good man. So should I plan to hire a full-timer *and* a part-timer?"

"Nah. You're not getting rid of me that easily. Gotta get some clients first. I'll give you plenty of warning before I give up the part-time gig." I stood up, rubbing a hand over my weary eyes. "And for now, I'm gonna go home and get some sleep."

"Home." Mitch tilted his head to the side. "You mean, *home*? Or to Micah Bloom's shop, where you spend an inordinate amount of time?"

My jaw dropped.

Okay, yes, I'd been getting a little careless about where I left my car when I was at Micah's, and I'd stopped sneaking in and out under cover of darkness a couple of months ago. But I'd sort of imagined that since no one had said anything, no one had noticed. Clearly not.

And I probably should have been more worried about that.

"O'Leary's top investigator, right here." Mitch pointed to himself. He grinned smugly and made a circle in the air with his hand, indicating my open mouth. "FYI, first law of secrecy is not to look overly guilty."

I shut it firmly.

"Micah's a good guy," Mitch said. "For what it's worth."

I hadn't realized exactly how much I needed to hear those words from someone, not because I didn't already know them to be true, but because the need to keep my feelings for Micah a secret was strangling me these days.

Next week, I told myself. Next week, once my mother had made her decision for better or for worse, I was going to tell Micah exactly how I felt about him, and let the rest of the world know, too.

"He really is," I agreed, grinning. And I decided my guy deserved some decent pastries.

I left my car in the lot at the station—I mean, since Mitch already knew, why not?—and walked the short distance to Fanaille.

The morning was a diamond-bright assault on my senses. Sunlight reflected off the snow banks piled on either side of the street, and off the icicles hanging from the rooftops, singeing my eyes. My hands were red and numb, despite being in my pockets, and the air was so cold, I could feel crystals forming in my throat as I breathed it in. For a moment I seriously considered whether Ross Landscaping could use a Florida branch. And then I remembered that everything—and every*one*—I loved was right here.

The line at Fanaille was predictably long as the weekday regulars grabbed their coffee and goodies before starting their days, and my stomach was grumbling as I took my spot at the back.

I spotted my brother Julian at one of the little tables in front of the window, and nearly called out before deciding not to interrupt. He was holding hands on top of the table with Daniel, his big, blond god of a boyfriend, and paying more attention to the man than to the muffin and coffee in front of him.

Christ, Jules looked happy. I'd been a tiny bit worried last month—not as bad as Mama, who'd been ready to rouse the villagers with their pitchforks and descend on Daniel's cabin out for blood, but still worried—when he and Daniel had seemed to hit a rough patch. But ever since the beginning of the month, when Daniel had gotten back from his trip to the city, he and Julian had been pretty much inseparable.

I wanted that.

Julian's muffin reminded me of the muffins Micah and I had shared out at the lake and—yeah, okay, I was basically the sappiest person in the entire universe—but it made me think of how everything had really started changing for me that day. That was the day I'd realized just how much I could trust Micah, not just to handle me when my own emotions were so knotted I couldn't think straight, but to handle my past and my future, too.

For the longest time—Christ, almost *ten* years now!— I'd been pushing back every negative emotion, thinking that if I was cheerful, positive Constantine, I'd somehow forget just how fucked up my life was. I'd gone from one day, to the next, to the next, never really wondering whether I was on the right path or on *any path at all*.

Then Micah had come into my world and messed me up. Made me remember that paths were a *thing*, challenged me to call things what they were, and believed that

I could be more than the robot I'd allowed myself to become.

"Morning, Con! What can I getcha?" Ash Martin greeted me, wiping his hands on a white towel he'd slung over his shoulder. "Got some raspberry cake things—"

"Lemon-raspberry breakfast rolls," Caelan James corrected without looking up from the cash register where he was ringing in a different purchase.

Ash grinned at Cal, his eyes tracking from Cal's red hair down to his face.

"That's what I said. Raspberry cake thingies."

Cal frowned and glanced at his boyfriend in annoyance, then rolled his eyes when he saw Ash's grin. "Pretty sure you're doing this on purpose to annoy me, Ashley."

Ash pretended to consider this. "Pretty sure you're right, *Caelan*."

Cal's lips twitched. "Remember you get what you pay for." He said this like it was a warning. Ash did not seem worried in the slightest, and I felt my own cheeks flush.

I really needed to get to Micah's.

"Two coffees—one black, one extra-extra. And four muffins. Any kind. Surprise me."

"Connie?"

I turned to find Jules behind me, grinning. "Hey! I saw you and Daniel over there, but I didn't want to interrupt."

Julian blushed. "Nah. You wouldn't be interrupting. You wanna come sit with us? I wanted to talk to you about something." Ash set a carry tray with the two coffees and a small box of muffins in front of me, and Jules blinked. "Oh. Meeting someone?"

This was the part where I was supposed to yell *squirrel* and distract Julian, but I was getting really weary of that.

"Yeah," I said. "Meeting someone."

"The girl you're dating?" I frowned, and he rolled his eyes. "Mama told me."

"Uh. No," I said. I hesitated. "And I don't know where Mama got the idea about that woman, but I've never met her, let alone dated her."

"Oh."

I grabbed my purchases and walked Jules back to his table. "I actually *have* been dating someone. I just… I'm not totally ready to talk about it yet. Okay?"

Daniel looked curiously from Julian to me and gave me a welcoming smile. "What's this about?"

"Constantine's dating someone he doesn't want to talk about," Julian said, taking his seat.

"Does it run in the family?" Daniel grinned.

"Not exactly," Julian said, giving him a knowing look and a raised eyebrow I didn't know how to interpret.

Daniel laughed and twined his fingers with Julian's on the tabletop again. "Well, if you need help getting your head out of your ass when it comes to your secret relationship, Con… Ah, actually, you know what? Never mind. Don't talk to me. I just got really lucky."

Jules rolled his eyes. "What he *means* to say is that we're here for you if you need anything."

Daniel nodded. "Yes. That."

I snorted. "I'll keep that in mind. What did you need to talk about?"

"Oh, that. Have you talked to Mama since yesterday?" Julian asked, sipping at his coffee. "Because I stopped by the house to give Theo some stuff Sam needed, and she was sitting at the dining table surrounded by papers, muttering something about loans and clients."

"Ugh." I closed my eyes and shook my head. "Remember I told you last week I was giving her a proposal to expand the business?"

"Oh," Jules said, wrinkling his nose. "Shit."

I sighed. "It's okay. It'll be fine. Just maybe avoid her for a bit. She's set up a meeting to talk to me about it. Doesn't sound like it'll go well."

"A meeting." Jules whistled. "Well, it looks like you got her attention, anyway."

"Pretty sure I've had too much of her attention for too long," I said wryly.

"Nah. I think Mama's been so busy trying to *protect us* that she stopped looking at who we are." Julian's mouth twitched up on one side. "Have faith."

I sucked in a deep breath and nodded, but I privately thought it was easier to have faith when you were someone like Julian, who never had a reason to doubt himself.

"Okay, I'm off," I said, hoisting my cups and bag. "I'll try to avoid Mama, and you do the same."

Jules laughed. "Well, watch out, if you're trying to avoid her. Her car's parked out front." He nodded out the window.

I winced. The last thing I wanted after a night like last night was a confrontation.

"Hey, Ash?" I asked, turning back toward the counter. "Can you do me a solid?"

A minute later, I was safely out the back door of the bakery, in the alley behind the street. Micah's truck and van were parked out there as expected, and he'd even left the door on the latch for me, despite the chill in the air, because he was the best boyfriend in the universe.

And if I got inside right now, I'd have nearly an entire *hour* to show him so before he had to open the store.

I pushed open the heavy steel fire door… and paused.

The lights were on, and a stunning half-finished arrangement was sitting on the steel workbench, but Micah wasn't there. I set my breakfast on the bench and took a breath to call his name when I heard his raised voice coming from the office.

"My choices, and the reasons for them, are my concern. They are most certainly not *yours!*"

I almost grinned, because my boyfriend in a temper was a thing of beauty, as long as that temper wasn't aimed at me, and I knew just how to calm him—

"It's my business when it involves my *son.*"

Oh. Oh, no.

No, no, no, no, no.

I froze in place. Was this a nightmare? Had I fallen asleep at my desk at the station?

"It's my *business,*" my mother continued, "when my son is suddenly giving me ultimatums and slapping business proposals like *this one* on my desk."

I heard the sound of paper slapping wood.

"Read it," she challenged.

I didn't hear a single sound that would indicate Micah moving.

"You don't even need to read the proposal, do you?" she said. "You already know every word."

"Angela—"

"What are you doing with Constantine?" she demanded. "Why are you trying to turn my son against me?"

Oh, Jesus. Drama, much?

"I told you last summer," Micah said gently, "what's between me and Constantine is none of your business."

"Oh, God. This has been going on since last summer?" she wailed.

I rolled my eyes and without letting myself think about the consequences too much, I stepped into the office.

Micah's eyes came to me first, since he was facing the door. He was leaning back with his hands resting on the arms of his chair, looking mostly bored. At least, until he saw me. Then, his eyes widened, and he looked a little panicked.

My mother spun around, likely following the direction of Micah's gaze, and when she spotted me, she looked angry but guilty, too.

"Hey," I said, because I really had no idea what else *to* say.

"Hey," Micah returned softly.

"Constantine, what are you doing here?" My mother tried to form this as a question, but it was really more like a plea. The look on her face said she knew exactly why I was there, she was just praying I'd tell her she was wrong.

I took a deep breath and glanced at Micah, who watched me intently, like he was almost as curious about what I was going to say as my mother was.

If I hadn't felt like vomiting, it might have been funny.

"I'm here because…"

"Because I've been helping him with his business plan," Micah interjected. He shrugged like this was no big thing. "Constantine helped me out last summer, and I owed him a favor, so I gave him some sample business plans to look over. Did you need more help, Constantine?"

God. It was kind of cute, him giving me an out like that.

It was also kind of annoying.

"Micah and I are dating," I told my mother, moving around the desk to stand closer to his chair.

Micah closed his eyes and sucked in a breath, and I couldn't tell if he was angry or excited. Honestly, I wasn't sure how I was feeling either. This wasn't the way I'd imagined this going.

"I don't understand," Mama said. She sounded confused. She *looked* devastated.

"Mama, try to understand. Me and Micah dating… it wasn't something we meant to happen."

"It was an accident? A six-month accident?" she demanded. "And what about the woman… Oh my Lord. There never was a woman, was there?"

"No." I took a deep breath. "I haven't dated anyone but Micah for a few months now. But I didn't lie, you assumed."

"And you *let me*. All the while asking me to consider this proposal?" She grabbed a sheaf of papers from the desk and smacked them down again.

"That proposal has nothing to do with Micah," I insisted. "I wanted that long before—"

"It has *everything* to do with him. His fingerprints are all over this, Constantine."

"Why?" I shook my head. "Because I finally stood up for myself? Because I finally demanded something I wanted?"

"Because he's manipulating you!"

"Christ," Micah said. "*Manipulating* him? How the hell—"

"Pretending you're being supportive," she spat. "Sending some minor business my way, working with lenders, that whole dramatic incident with the Gaynors that you engineered, just to make Con believe you were on his side—"

Micah pressed his fingers to the bridge of his nose and closed his eyes. He didn't say a word.

"The Gaynors?" I repeated, folding my arms over my chest because I suddenly felt very, very cold, even in my winter coat. "What the hell are you talking about?"

"The Gaynors," Mama said. "Trent and—"

"I know who they are!" I snapped, still looking at Micah.

Micah who hadn't moved.

Micah who hadn't said a word.

"I was going to…" he began. He cut off with a curse. "Okay, fuck it. No, I was never going to tell you." He looked up at me, green eyes swirling with emotion. "I had a meeting at the Scarlet Maple in early December. Wedding client."

I lifted my chin. I remembered. "The day you ruined my favorite green button-down."

"Yeah," Micah agreed. "You know, you never mentioned the guy's name when you told me the story last summer."

"Oh, this gets more ridiculous by the minute," my mother said, but I barely heard her. I was focused on Micah.

"They said some things that made it pretty clear who they were. Once I put two and two together, I refused the contract," Micah said shortly.

"You called him a homophobe and hit him in the mouth." My mother's cheeks were burning, and I swear she was standing on her tiptoes as she leaned toward Micah's desk. "The only reason you weren't arrested for assault and the whole sorry business between Constantine and Trent wasn't dragged back out into the latest town gossip is because Vince Gaynor convinced his son not to press charges."

"Because he knows his son uttered homophobic slurs more than once during the course of the meeting, and Charlotte said she'd testify to it!" Micah said, pushing his chair back from the desk and getting to his feet. "Which I guess she forgot to tell you when she was giving you all *this* information?"

For a second, my mother gaped like a fish—such an

unusual reaction for her that I would have enjoyed it… if I wasn't basically doing the same fucking thing.

"Charlotte thought it was good for me to know, since it involved the Gaynors," she sniffed. "And I appreciated her being forthcoming, since neither of *you* thought to mention it to me." She shifted her glare to me.

I shook my head. "Yeah, in case you hadn't caught it, Mama, I wasn't aware either. Until now."

Micah leaned against the file cabinet at the back of the room wearily. "Ironically, I didn't want you to be upset, Con."

"Yeah?" I huffed. "Good plan. Nice work."

"Constantine," Micah began, but I lifted a hand to cut him off.

"What's the rest?" I asked my mother. "The lenders? Sending you business?"

Mama looked from me to Micah. She hesitated a bit, like the wind had gone out of her sails. "He's been sending me referrals. More than one potential client over the holidays said *he* wasn't accepting new business."

"You told me things were slow," I reminded Micah. "No calls coming in, but that was okay because it meant you could spend time with me, and with Lauren and Leandra and the kids."

Micah watched me warily.

"The kids?" My mother looked between the two of us like we were some species of flower she'd never seen… and didn't particularly enjoy. "You've met his family?"

"Yes, of course." I waved a hand dismissively. "Micah, why would you do that? And why would you lie?"

"I wanted Ross to stay solvent and I knew you wouldn't let me help any other way. In my mind," he said slowly. "It wasn't much different from what I did over the summer, giving up the contract at the Crabapple so Ross could stay afloat."

"You did *what?*" my mother gasped. "You told him that, Constantine?"

"No," I murmured, feeling sick and scared and completely untethered to the ground. "I didn't."

"*Jesus Christ.*" Micah scrubbed a hand over his face and sighed. "I overheard you talking. At the farmer's market. Back in the spring. The day you were such a little shit, Constantine."

I forced a laugh because I wanted to cry. "God. Which time?"

Micah closed his eyes again, like my joke had made him sadder than anything else in this conversation. "The same day we met at The Hive."

"Ah, of course." I gave an exaggerated frown. "That makes sense."

He'd come to find me not because he actually needed skilled help—*Jesus, how had I ever let myself believe that?*—but because he knew I couldn't say no.

"Con," he started again, but I shook my head.

"Get it all out," I told my mother. "Rip the Band-Aid off. What else ya got?"

"Well, I..." She sounded unsure. "This lender on your plan." She tapped the page. "They're a broker that connects small businesses with angel investors."

"Yeah, I know." It was, like, the one thing in the universe I could say that about right now.

She licked her lips. "Well, that means it's not a sure thing. I don't know if *he* told you that. It could take a long time to find someone unless you already have an investor lined up. I've tried to use them in the past, and I've found..."

"It's a sure thing," Micah interrupted.

Mama looked at him with her eyes narrowed, then suddenly they widened in shock as some understanding passed between them.

"I'm missing something," I said to no one in particular. "I mean, I can't imagine why this is a shock to me, considering all that I've been missing for the last seven months. In fact, it's amazing that I manage to find my way home at the end of the day. It's amazing I remember how to dress myself properly, for I am surely the most idiotic idiot who's ever walked the face of the earth."

"No. *Christ*. Constantine, that's the last——"

Micah took a step toward me, and I could tell just by the look on his face that he wanted to wrap his arms around me. It was the thing I wanted most in the world and also the thing I wanted least. So I backed up until I was pressed against the giant whiteboard, and I shook my head.

"Nope. No touching."

Micah heaved a breath and scrubbed at his hair like he wasn't sure what else to do with his hands. "*I* am the investor, Con. I'm selling the house in Baxter."

"Of course you are." I nodded. "Just to be clear, you didn't tell me about this because…?"

He shook his head, just once. "Because I wanted you to have it. And I knew you wouldn't agree otherwise."

My mother gasped.

"So you were going to wait to tell me until… when? When I'd already signed the paperwork and it was too late to change my mind?"

"No. My name would have been on the paperwork as the investor before you signed it. It was just until…"

"Until I made a fool of myself, giving this business plan to my mother. Until I got myself in so deep, I wouldn't want to back out. Got it."

"*Fuck*. Constantine, please listen."

"I'm listening!" I insisted. "See me? Right here? Listening. She's listening too." I pointed at my mother, who was watching Micah unblinkingly.

Micah cast an angry glance at my mother, then looked back at me. "This was not part of some devious plot, Con. Come on! You *know* better. You know *me*. You know I…"

"I don't know shit!" I yelled, throwing my hands in the air. "Clearly, that's the theme of this day! I thought I knew things. I thought I knew all kinds of things, Micah. Like about who you were, and how you felt about me, and what we were… *building*."

On the last word, my voice cracked—fucking *cracked*, like I'd regressed into adolescent-Constantine, all pissed off because the world had taken away someone I hadn't realized was precious until he was gone. Or maybe he'd been inside me all along, just waiting for the next loss.

"You know," Micah insisted. "You *do* know."

"You lied," I said simply. "That's what I know. *You*, who told me that not volunteering information was basically the same as lying."

"I wanted you to have what you wanted. I wanted you to have… options. Choices."

"So you took my choice away by not telling me the truth." I ran a hand over my chin. "Yep. Sounds legit." Then I laughed because, you know, it was either that or bawl. "God, this has been the longest night ever, huh? I need to sleep for, like eighty-seven years." I turned to my mother. "I'm leaving. If you'd like to stay and yell at my… at *Micah*, feel free."

I walked out of the office. Mama followed silently behind.

"Constantine, don't leave!" Micah begged. "Yell at me, instead. Fucking *hit* me."

"Right." I snorted. "That's apparently your thing."

"Stop fucking deflecting!"

I turned around to find him standing in the doorway of the office. His eyes were wild with panic. He cared about me; I knew he did. But that didn't magically make things better. Not even marginally better.

"Walking away isn't deflecting. I'm not pretending I don't care. I care *a lot*. But you hurt me, Micah. I trusted you, and you *lied*, and now I feel stupid and shitty."

"I know. I'm *so* sorry," he said, and I could tell he meant it, too, but that didn't change my feelings. "I didn't get it. But I do now."

"That's good. I'm glad you get it. But… I don't care." I could feel my heart doing its porcupine-thing, curling in on itself, needing protection from the thing it wanted most. "I can't get more honest than that, Micah. So if you want to show that you respect me, even a little tiny bit, let me go." I turned to my mother, also. "Just leave me be."

Then I walked out to the alley and called Julian.

Chapter Fifteen

CONSTANTINE

February

"Knock, knock. You busy?"

I glanced up from my laptop screen and looked across the main room at Ross Landscaping to find my mother standing in the doorway of her office, knocking on her own door to alert me to her presence. She wore a thick red sweater, leggings, and boots, in deference to the February chill.

"Doors don't work that way," I informed her. "You knock when you want to go in, not when you want to come out." I took a bite of the apple in my hand and went back to plugging numbers into a spreadsheet.

"Haven't seen you in a few days."

"I left you a message. I told you I was taking some sick time." In reality, the only thing that had been aching was my heart... but after five nights sleeping on Julian's crappy futon, and four days binge-watching movies while eating cheese curls and ice cream, I actually *did* feel like shit. Amazing how that worked.

"You working on your business plan?" she asked, taking a few tentative steps toward the big table in the center of the office, where I'd set up my computer. She laid her hands on the top of the chair opposite me.

It was almost amusing. I mean, my mother was *not* a tentative person by nature, and she was acting like I was a wounded animal who might turn on her at any mo— Huh. Okay, maybe that was more accurate than amusing.

"Nope," I said, popping the "p" sound. "Going to place an extra order for ice melt, since we're running low, and trying to figure out how much we'll need to last the season."

"Oh." She drummed her fingers against the wood and watched me take another bite and chew it. It was very off-putting.

"Something you need?" I asked around the apple.

"To clear the air."

I swallowed. "Air's clear."

She tried again. "I was out of line, going to Micah."

"You were."

"Someday, when you have children, you'll—"

"God, can you imagine? I might just forget I have them and leave them someplace. Or trade them for a handful of magic beans." Another bite of apple. "Who knows what I'm capable of?"

She pulled out the chair and sat down. "Okay. *Enough.* You want the kind of family where we're honest, right? That's what you said to me, after Thanksgiving? Well, here's some honesty."

I watched her as I chewed and swallowed, but she seemed sincere.

"Okay, shoot." I set my apple on the table next to the computer, sat back in my chair and folded my arms over my chest.

"I was not always a cautious person," she began, laying her hands out flat on the table. "In fact, caution's not in my nature at all. You get that from me."

I snorted.

"You forget, Constantine, I was a girl who fell in love with a man she'd only known a couple of months. My parents were *not* thrilled." She shook her head, but smiled too. "I was the girl who followed this guy back to his tiny little town in New York a few months after that." She looked around the room. "I was the one who encouraged her husband to start his own business, even when Jules was a baby and we didn't have a pot to piss in."

"*Language.*"

She raised one eyebrow at me. "Don't you test my patience, Constantine."

I pressed my lips together. "Sorry, Mama."

"*Anyway.* After your dad died, things changed. *I* changed. Suddenly I had three boys to look after and a business to run. I think…" She hesitated. "I think I started focusing on the wrong things. On trying to *control* the wrong things. I guess I thought if I pretended we were done grieving and pushed through, it'd make things easier for all of us. And I did all of you boys a real disservice, Con. But especially you."

I snorted. "What the heck are you talking about? You didn't do anything to me. You were fine. I was the one who—"

"Who didn't have healthy outlets for his anger and grief. Who probably should've gotten help, if I wasn't too stubborn and proud to let anyone think I couldn't handle my boys and my family on my own." She toyed with the end of her braid. "I tried to tell myself it was teenage hijinks. You were fourteen, fifteen. I'd done wild things, too. And then Trent Gaynor happened."

"This is ancient history," I told her. "There is no need to hash over—"

"Oh, yes there is. Because we never really talked about it, so you made assumptions. And those assumptions have been festering inside you like shrapnel for nearly ten years. And I didn't understand that until last week. Until… that conversation with Micah."

She licked her lips. "I've told you already, I forgave you about thirty seconds after Mitch showed up at the house and told us what had happened to Trent. I had never seen you look so… small, Con. Not physically, but emotionally. You were so lost and so sorry, and I… I realized in that minute just how much I'd messed up. I hadn't seen your behavior for what it was. If there is anyone I've blamed all these years, it's myself."

"What?"

"And because I did, I accepted the settlement Vince offered. I didn't need you dragged off to trial. You'd already been through enough. That might have been my first mistake." She stared at her fingers as she knit and unknit them on the tabletop. "But then I made things worse when I decided to open the greenhouses."

She lifted her eyes to mine. "That was possibly my *biggest* mistake. And you can blame that impulsive nature of mine, because I thought bringing our flowers in-house would show those clowns at HG a thing or two, since we were one of their largest customers at the time." She grimaced. "It's safe to say there were many aspects I didn't consider. But once I'd committed to it, what else was there to do but make the best of it?" She shrugged. "Even now, I mess up all the time. I let Carlos handle the systems, and I make a decent guess about how much stock we're going to need, but I always seem to over- or under-produce. That's me being *honest*." She ran a hand over her braid and joked, "You know anyone who needs a couple gross of red and pink tulips? Cause I've got a bunch sitting in the greenhouse and I could give you a sweet deal."

I shook my head mutely.

"Yeah, didn't think so. What I'm trying to say is, my lack of enthusiasm for your plan has never been about you, Constantine. It's been about *me*. My worry. My fear. My insecurity. My wanting you to be free from all this. My inability to trust myself. My need to protect you, even though now I see I went about it all wrong."

"I… I don't get it," I muttered. It was like listening to a pop song in another language—my brain kept trying in vain to make English words out of the familiar tones and rhythms.

"I know. We've been talking in circles for a long time, hearing what we expect to hear from each other. But let me say this again, because this is the important part: I forgave you the minute it happened, Constantine. You need to forgive yourself."

I ran a hand over my forehead. "I… I think you might be right," I admitted. "*Damn.*" I sniffed a little. "You could've warned me it was going to be *this* kind of discussion."

"Oh, buckle up, kiddo." My mother shifted position, so one leg was bent underneath her. "Discussion's not over. We need to talk about…"

I expected her to say Micah, so when she finally said, "Julian," I swallowed my protest.

"What about Jules?"

"You've been staying at his place above the clinic," she said. Not a question.

"I haven't felt like sleeping at your house, and I have nowhere else to go."

Her lips quirked at that, but she said nothing. "Julian and Daniel are moving in together officially next month."

"It's pretty unofficially official already," I said. "I mean, the reason I'm at Julian's is because he's at Daniel's house." I peered at her more closely. "You worried about it? Think it's too soon?"

"Nope. I'm happy for him. When it feels right, it feels right."

I blinked. "Okay. Who are you right now?"

She laughed. "You know, when you have kids, and you get past the baby years, you think the hard part is behind you. Then suddenly, you have teens, and you think, '*Shit*. Miscalculated *that*.' And then, I think, for some of us, when our kids become adults, it's even harder. For better or worse, my parenting key words have been *control* and *protect*. Now, they *have* to be *respect* and *support*. It's hard to remember. But I'm going to do better. For you, for Julian. For Theodore, God help us all."

I laughed out loud. It was a cleansing, healing thing, and I felt at least half the anger I'd been carrying for the last few days evaporate.

"But, um, before I back a respectful distance from your personal life…"

"Oh, God. Here it comes. Look, I'm sorry I didn't tell you about Micah."

"I know."

"I felt like I couldn't tell you about it because you wouldn't understand."

"Oh, I wouldn't have. You were right."

I tilted my head and studied her more closely. "You look like my mother. You *sound* like her. But the words you're saying…"

"*Enough*." She rolled her eyes. "I was very biased against Micah. He was threatening my cubs. Or something." She waved a hand through the air. "He's not a bad person."

"He's not," I agreed. "Not *bad*. Just a misguided liar who needs to mind his own damn business. Literally and figuratively." I gave her a small, meaningless smile. "I appreciate the kind words, but Micah and I… aren't a thing right now. So that's one less thing for you to respect and support me on."

"Really?"

"Yes. We haven't spoken in days."

She frowned. "Because you told him not to call you."

"I know." But I hadn't thought he'd agree. "I haven't wanted to…" Okay, I couldn't finish that statement without telling the biggest lie of my entire life. "I haven't known what the hell to say." I shrugged. "You want the truth? I fell for him. But…" I shook my head. "We are very different people."

She laughed. "So?"

"Sooooo… We're incompatible. Obviously. We have very different ways of solving problems. Or not solving them."

"Right, like *you* give him an ultimatum not to call you, and when he honors it, you get upset. That's *different*."

I raised one eyebrow. "Mama, for a second there, we had a beautiful truce going. A real moment of mother-son bonding happening."

"But that's not the kind of family you want, Constantine. You want *honesty*," she reminded me blithely. "So let me tell you flat out: you need to give him a second chance."

I sighed. "Since when are you on Micah Bloom's side? A week ago, you were ready to hit him with your car and make it look like an accident. What gives?"

"Last week, I took all the facts and assembled them wrong. I thought he was trying to manipulate you. Instead, he was trying to *love* you. Just in a really stupid way." She grinned and pushed back a lock of her dark hair. "Look, for a long time, I thought you were happy, kiddo. Content. It wasn't until last summer, when I saw how…" she widened her eyes, "fired up you got, that I realized something inside you had been dimmed for a long time. And it scared me. That's honest, too. But life is about risk. It's about change. And there is such a thing as too much safety." She leaned toward me. "You can't protect yourself from everything."

"I'm aware of that. This has nothing to do with risk and change, Mama." I rolled my eyes.

"Dummy. Of course it does."

My jaw dropped open. "Did you just call me—"

"*Honesty*," she sang.

"Ugh. Is it too late to walk back the honesty thing?"

"Yep. Just like it's too late to un-fall for Micah." She wiggled her eyebrows.

"*Wow*. See, you're totally not getting the point here."

"He *hurt* you."

"Yes! He really did."

"He lied to you."

There was a lump in my throat that made it hard to swallow. "He did."

"He stepped back his business for you. He committed to lending you thousands and *thousands* of dollars. He punched a potential client in the face and dealt with the fallout without telling you. And he did it all in the stupidest way possible and managed to do the tango all over your manly pride in the process."

"My *manly pride*?"

She shrugged. "Your father was the same way. With the

pride, I mean. Not the stomping. That was generally my job."

I pushed to my feet and shut my laptop. "Okay. Well, this has been really interesting. I should go do a thing—"

"Your father wasn't perfect, Constantine. Just like I'm sure as heck not perfect. Just like *you* are not perfect. Just like *Micah* isn't perfect. He messed up."

I sighed and pushed a hand through my hair.

"You know the secret to marriage, baby?"

I shook my head.

"It's giving the person you love the benefit of the doubt."

The benefit of the doubt. Like Micah had given me.

"Who said *love*?" I protested.

She laughed. "I did. When I saw your face just now. Look, you *are* gonna mess up, both of you. In ways that are not cute. In ways that aren't even noble, like what Micah was trying to do, but are a *little* selfish, a *little* unkind. They're going to forget important things and remember stuff you wish they'd forget. But love is like a dance. You'll meet each other halfway, over and over and over again. Sometimes you'll miss a beat. Sometimes he'll step too far. Just keep going."

"That's the sappiest thing you've ever said. Like, ever."

"Constantine."

"No, I mean it. Sappier than when you said all you wanted for Mother's Day was for us to *behave*. Sappier than the heart-shaped pancakes you used to make us on Valentine's Day." I walked around the table toward her.

She looked up at me and shook her head in exasperation.

"I hear what you're saying. I promise I do. But how are you suddenly so okay with me and Micah? He's sixteen years older than me, and he's *still* your biggest competition."

"Your father was only six months older than *me*." She smiled softly. "Life's uncertain. But we had twenty really happy years together and three wonderful boys. And I wouldn't have traded any of it, even if I'd known how it would end."

Mama stood up. She was so tiny, but when her eyes narrowed like they did then, she was fierce, too. "Micah Bloom makes you happy. And that is all I've ever wanted for you. Life is short, Con. You've spent almost ten years dwelling on your *own* mistake. How long are you going to waste dwelling on Micah's?"

I frowned down at her. "I don't know. *Longer?*" I sounded whiny, even to myself, which was annoying because I'd been sure I had the moral high ground here until about twenty minutes ago, and now I wasn't so certain. I was hurt, damn it. *Hurt, hurt, hurt.* "I'm thinking things over."

She shook her head. "You're thinking too much. Tomorrow, you're going to Fanaille with me and Julian. I'll buy you a giant cupcake."

I rolled my eyes and smiled, just a bit smugly. "Oooh, no can do. Tomorrow's the thirteenth. We're gonna be slammed getting the Valentine's Day orders ready."

"Nope." She grinned. "Because the brand-new head of Ross Landscape Design is going to help me prep them now."

My smile fled. "That's not funny."

"It's not a joke."

"Without Micah's funding—"

"We'll make it work. *You* will make it work. I know you will. And I'm ready to get out of your way and let you."

"Shit," I said, and she didn't even correct me. "That is…"

"Well-deserved? About time? Long overdue?"

"Awesome," I told her, and I desperately wanted to call Micah and tell him this news… Which probably should have told me something, but I still wasn't ready to hear it.

"Good. Now let's go create some magic," Mama said, and she stood aside so I could lead the way to the greenhouse.

Chapter Sixteen

MICAH

"Micah!"

I stepped into the vanilla-sugar magic of Fanaille and spotted my brother immediately at a little table in the center of the room. The bakery was always funky and old-fashioned, with its lace window curtains and black-and-white checkered floors, but today it looked like Cupid had vomited all over the space. A million red and pink hearts dangled from the ceiling and a giant Cupid window cling on the front window gave the impression that the winged one himself was watching over the proceedings inside. It was charming.

I fucking *hated* charming.

I was heartily *sick* of hearts and romance. I was sick of Cupid. I was sick of flowers. I was sick of *love*.

And also, *Bah humbug.* Because why limit it to Christmas, really?

I made my way through the crowded room and over to Mason's table. The bakery was *packed* today, even more than usual, and everyone was decked out in reds and pinks because this was O'Leary, and Valentine's Day was tomorrow, so go big or go home, right?

That expression really assumed you weren't going to go big *and* go home. Which was what happened to some of us, who were total idiots and had no one to blame for our own misfortune but ourselves.

I spotted Julian Ross sitting alone at a four-person table by the window, and I took the seat facing away from him because really, too much was too much.

"And hello to you, too," Mason said as I stripped off my coat and laid it on the back of the chair. He pushed a paper cup and a heart-shaped cookie across the table toward me. "Happy Val—"

"Do not," I said in my most warning tone of voice. "Do not *dare* finish that sentence."

"*Whoa.*" Mason frowned. "I guessed based on your reaction when I asked about Con—"

"Don't finish that sentence either," I interrupted in a slightly softer tone.

"Okay," Mase agreed, wincing. "So, neutral topic. How's Blooms?"

I laughed, a little too loud, a little too desperately, a little too close to tears.

"Definitely, *definitely* do not ask me about Blooms."

"Micah, what's going on? I talked to you three weeks ago and everything was fine. You were laughing. Con— uh, *everyone*—seemed great. I called you yesterday, and—"

"Not *fine* three weeks ago," I admitted. "Not fine, but not awful. Now… Well, now it's bad."

"What is?"

I huffed. "Everything. Basically."

Mason shook his head. "Be more specific."

And I figured, *why the hell not?* It wasn't like I was going to be able to hide things from Mason anyway. Not for very long.

"I got into a fight a while back," I began. "Punched a guy in the face…"

"Wait, pause." Mason held out a hand. "I hate to stop you so early, but I have so many questions."

I sighed and explained the anthropomorphic gaping asshole that was Trent Gaynor, and how I'd hit him.

And how I'd fucking *liked it.*

"You remember Jonny once taught us how to punch?" I asked Mason. "And MoonFlower was pissed because she didn't want us being violent, but Jonny said once we learned, it'd come back to us when we needed it?"

He nodded. "Yeah! Did it?"

"Fuck no. Hit him with the flat of my fingers. Hurt like a *sonofabitch.*" I shook my head ruefully. "So, further proof Jonny was full of shit."

"As if we needed it."

"Yeah."

"And what happened after that?" Mason demanded.

I scratched my head. "Idiot threatened to call the cops, but Charlotte—the woman who works at the Inn—told Trent and his father that she would explain exactly what she heard, including the use of homophobic slurs. Turns out Trent's dad has high hopes for his son. Doesn't want this on his record. So he's keeping it silent. Mostly."

"Mostly."

I smiled. "Yeah. Little fact I knew but forgot in the moment is that Trent's related to the guys who supply my flowers."

Mason's eyes widened. "So they… aren't doing business with you anymore?"

"Oh, no. No, worse than that. They started making these little errors, exactly as they did with Constantine's mother back in the day. More and more and more, over the past four or five weeks. Passive-aggressive bullshit, and I'd thought I could just wait it out, you know? Let them get it out of their systems. Until this week. When I needed a giant supply of flowers for literally the biggest wedding contract I've ever signed—"

"The senator's wedding!" Mason said, eyes wide. "I remember this."

"It's the senator's stepdaughter," I corrected. "But yes *and* for a little holiday called Valentine's Day. The make-or-break holiday for my shop."

"And what happened?"

"Oh, they told me there's a shipping delay." I grabbed the cookie and took a giant bite out of the perfect little heart.

It was satisfying.

"A… what?"

"Shipping delay," I repeated around the mouthful of cookie. "Yeah. Apparently, a blizzard in Topeka has grounded my roses."

"There's a blizzard in Topeka?"

"Wow, how interesting that you should ask. No, Mason, there is *not* a blizzard in Topeka." I took my phone from my pocket and set it on the table. "As any idiot with a weather app would know."

"So, what did they say when you confronted them?"

I shook my head. "Pat—he's the owner—he said there was nothing he could do. And he told me, in a very loud voice, not to take my aggressions out on him."

"What?"

"I wouldn't be surprised if he had cameras in the office ready to record me hitting him or something." I rolled my eyes. "I was tempted but refrained. I used to say that fairness and respect went a long way in business, but apparently not when your asshole cousin tells you to blacklist someone."

"Shit. So… What are you gonna do?"

I took a sip of my coffee and thought about it. For the five millionth time since Monday, when Pat had spewed his candy-colored bullshit at me.

"Not sure," I said, coming to the same conclusion I'd come to the other four million, nine hundred ninety-nine thousand, nine hundred ninety-nine times. "There's exactly one major flower supplier around here, and they're it. I've been on the phone all week trying to source even *part* of what I need." I sighed. "This morning, I had to call the bride and explain the situation."

"Oh, God."

"Yeah, you have no idea." Marissa Corcoran's panicked voice was one I would remember for a really long time. I shuddered a little.

"What did Constantine say?"

"He didn't say anything. I didn't tell him." I took another long sip of coffee. And then I explained everything I'd tried to do for Constantine, and everything I'd ended up doing instead.

"Ohhhhh, Micah."

"And he told me if I respected him even a little bit, I needed to let him go," I said. "So I did."

"And that was how long ago?"

"Six days." The six longest days of my life.

"And you haven't called?" he demanded. "Not even a text? Not even to say, *How are you doing? Am I still slightly below plankton on your personal list of useless organisms? Nothing?*"

"He said not to."

Mason nodded. "I see."

"What do you see?"

"Nothing." Mason smiled. "Just… really glad I persuaded you to come meet me today."

I laughed. "Okay. Because I'm such great company? Or because you needed the cookie."

"Both. Just out of curiosity, how are you doing otherwise?"

"Uh. Besides my boyfriend possibly breaking up with me, losing a contract that's going to cost me thousands, and being basically paralyzed until I can find another supplier? Things are going great, Mase. Thanks for asking."

"I mean, no headaches? No heart palpitations? Numbness or tingling in the extremities? Anything that would make you prone to fainting?" he asked, studying me. "I'm asking this as your physician, I mean."

"Why would you ask that? Do I *look* sick?" I demanded. "I feel okay."

"Super. *Oh my God, Constantine!*" Mason said, jumping up from his seat and rushing to embrace Con, who was approaching the counter with his mother. "I haven't seen you in ages!"

Constantine squared himself against the attack but seemed to relax a tiny bit when he saw who it was and patted Mason on the back lightly. "Uh, hey, Mase. Pretty sure it's been less than two weeks, but… yes. Hi."

I was not jealous that my brother had more physical contact with Constantine this week than I had. That would be ridiculous. Even more ridiculous than everything else.

Angela Ross stood next to Constantine *beaming at me*. I swiveled a bit to the right and then the left, positive she must be looking at someone behind me, but there were no likely candidates. *Huh.*

"Hi, Angela," I said. "You look… well?" She looked about as she always did—long black braid, snapping eyes, body that was too small to contain the force of her personality.

"Happy almost Valentine's Day," she returned. And for the first time in my life, she smiled at me.

Maybe I really *did* look sick.

My eyes met Constantine's as he was still locked in Mason's embrace, and his look so clearly telegraphed, *What the actual fuck is going on?* I nearly laughed… before I remembered that Constantine probably still didn't want to see me.

"Mason, could you please let my… Constantine go? You're manhandling him."

"Oh. Geez." Mason backed up. "Sorry, Con. Just good to see you, that's all. I missed you. I mean, not as much as Micah here did, though. Just *look* at him."

I felt my face heat. "Mason. Sit *down*."

"That's funny," Angela chirped—which was enough to make my eyes widen, because I didn't know she *could* chirp. "I was just telling Con yesterday that he hasn't been acting like himself."

Con squinted at his mother in shock. "What the heck is going on right now? Did you set this up?" He looked from Angela to *me*, accusingly, like *I* had somehow helped engineer this meeting.

"Hey, don't give me that look. I'm here for *coffee!*" I said, lifting my cup. "It wasn't even my idea. And I certainly didn't think I'd run into *you*."

Con's brow lowered. "Well, sorry to disturb your *coffee*, then." He glared at his mother who in turn glared at me.

Lovely.

"Con, I didn't mean," I began, but he clapped a hand to his pocket and removed his vibrating cell phone instead.

"I need to take this," he said. Then he dashed out the front door with the phone pressed to his ear.

Angela looked at Mason and sighed, then turned around to take her place in line.

Mason got very busy eating his cookie in tiny, precise bites.

"Mason."

"Hmm?"

"You didn't seem very surprised to see Constantine."

"Didn't I?" He nibbled at the cookie. "I was."

"Really? Because I was thinking you'd orchestrated this."

"What? Me?" Mason pressed a hand to his chest. "Honestly, how likely is that, Micah? People show up in public places all the time. Like… bars. Shopping malls. Bakeries next door to your boyfriend's brother's vet clinic in a tiny town that has *maybe* four places to eat? Coincidence."

"See, somehow I doubt that."

"Or," he said, holding a finger in the air. "It could be *fate*. Throwing you two lovebirds back together."

"Right."

"Or, your boyfriend's mother was so worried about Constantine that she had his brother google 'Bloom' in Baxter, New York, since apparently you let it slip that's where you were from, and she contacted me at work, and I contacted Lauren and Leandra, and the four of us devised a plan to make it so that you and Constantine were in the same room at the same time, since you're a pair of idiots who hate talking about shit." He nibbled at the cookie once again. "Honestly, doesn't *coincidence* sound most likely?"

"I sincerely hope that someone comes along and interferes in your love life someday," I said sourly.

The bell on the front door jangled like the thing was being torn off its hinges, and Constantine came storming back inside, blue eyes blazing. He ignored his mother, he ignored his brother, and instead, he came directly to me, and stood looming over me.

"What the actual—" He glanced around the packed room. "The actual *flipping heck* were you thinking, Micah Bloom?"

"Thinking?" I blinked. "About what?"

He searched the ceiling—with its multitude of colored hearts—for patience. "You know what? We need to talk. We're leaving." He grabbed me by the arm, and hauled me from my seat, snagging the remains of the heart-shaped cookie off my plate and cramming it in his mouth.

"Where are we going?" I asked as he towed me out the door.

He shook his head. "No questions. This time, Micah, you're going to be quiet and follow *me*."

And since I would have followed the man anywhere, that's exactly what I did.

Chapter Seventeen

CONSTANTINE

I DIDN'T HAVE a clear plan in mind when I dragged Micah down the street, other than finding a place where I could raise my voice without giving all of O'Leary a free show— okay, fine, *more* of a free show than me hauling my forty-year-old, possibly former boyfriend down the street by his hand, in broad daylight, without his jacket already presented—but when I spotted the rainbow flag hanging outside Blooms, I realized where I'd been unconsciously heading the whole time.

The door was unlocked when I pushed it open, and the sight inside nearly made me cry. There were a variety of little plants—pothos and kalanchoe and tiny succulents in pots—arranged on the tables out front, but the refrigerator cases were nearly empty when they should have held a whole variety of pre-made bouquets and arrangements. I felt my gut clench nearly as much as I had when I'd taken the call from Tyler a few minutes ago.

Tyler and I had texted a bunch after our first meeting at The Hive—nothing remotely flirtatious, just fun, friendly riffs on our love lives. It had totally slipped my mind that he'd be in town over Valentine's Day for his sister's wedding until his name had come up on my phone back at the bakery, and I'd had a single, beautiful second of wondering whether Tyler could be just the distraction I needed from Micah *"I'm just here for coffee"* Bloom...

Until Tyler had opened his mouth and explained that his sister Marissa was freaking out because her Valentine's Day-themed wedding—*the wedding of the year*, the one my mother had been so pissed to lose to Micah last spring—was going to be *flowerless*, and that Micah had called her this morning to say he wasn't going to be able to supply her flowers for the wedding after all.

I dragged Micah through the back room, where Belle was constructing an arrangement out of some sorry-looking carnations, and up the stairs to his apartment.

"Great job, Belle. Be back in a bit," Micah called over his shoulder without slowing down.

When we got upstairs, Micah unlocked his apartment door and pushed it open, letting me precede him into the tiny kitchen.

The usually tidy space was a wreck by Micah standards. The sink was cluttered with dishes and the recycling bin overflowed with takeout containers. Sitting on top was a familiar ice cream carton—the same, exact caramel flavor I'd eaten my weight in this week—and I felt a stirring of sympathy because this week really hadn't been any easier for Micah than it had been for me.

Then I thought of Tyler and ruthlessly suppressed it.

I whirled around to face him. "Why didn't you tell me about HG Supply being shitty to you?" I demanded.

"Oh, that." He turned and shut the door.

"Yes, *that*." I squinted at him. "What did you think I wanted to talk to you about?"

"I dunno. I was hoping it was literally anything else."

Micah threw his keys on the counter and ran a hand over his mouth, watching me with those steady green eyes. "I'm kinda tired of thinking about it, honestly."

I frowned. "Tired of thinking about it? Of thinking about how the Gaynors went to Pat, that weak little *asshole*, and got him to fuck you over, since they couldn't figure out how else to get to you? About how Pat was probably only too happy to do it, since he wants your ass and you clearly haven't given it to him? About how your reputation will be so shot, after word gets out that you couldn't meet the terms of the Turnbull wedding contract, that you'll be lucky if you ever sell another bouquet of daisies, let alone get chosen for an entire wedding?"

Micah rubbed his temples with his fingers. "Such diplomacy. Such sensitivity. Such compassion."

"Fuck that!" I yelled. "You don't need compassion or diplomacy or any of that shit. You need some sense knocked into you."

"And of course, you volunteered. How the hell did *you* find out about it anyway?" he demanded, crossing his arms over his chest and leaning against the refrigerator. "I hadn't thought it was a topic of gossip yet."

"I don't know if it is or it's not. Tyler called me, and then I called Charlotte at the Scarlet Maple, and she gave me details." I pulled myself up to sit on the counter next to the sink, directly across from him.

Battle lines drawn.

"Tyler?" Micah scowled. "Who's that?"

"You remember, my friend Tyler? From The Hive, that first night? The night when you felt so sorry for my pitiful ass that you—"

"Pitiful!"

"Yes, piti—"

"Oh, for the love of fuck." Micah scrubbed a hand

through his hair. "Speaking of people who *actually* need their asses kicked. Who the *hell* would ever pity you? Huh? You are the hottest, most intelligent, most capable person—"

"Bullshit!"

"No!" He took a single step forward, and his long stride eliminated the distance between us, so he was standing way too close. "What's bullshit is that your own opinion of yourself is so fucked you can't see what I see. I have jumped to conclusions about you, I have been unkind to you, I have overstepped your boundaries, but I have never fucking *pitied* you, and it's insane you would think that."

He stared at me for a second, his chest heaving, then asked in a softer voice, "How do you pity someone you think can do anything, Constantine? Huh?" He shook his head. "You don't. You try to clear obstacles out of their path. You try to show them that you believe in them. You try to stand close enough to bask in their light without holding them down. You try to love them, and hope some-day, once they've achieved what they need to achieve, they'll love you back."

He swallowed hard, like he was as shocked as I was to hear that word coming out of his mouth, and he stepped back to his original spot, not looking at me anymore. "You know, this is counterproductive. When you said you wanted to talk, I thought..." He shook his head again. "Maybe you should go."

There are these moments in life when your brain finally grabs hold of a truth—when you learn the world is *not* always a fair place, for example, and that people die way too young, or when you find out that being *sorry* doesn't magically right all the wrongs you've done. And then there's the moment when you realize you've been looking at the world through the lens of your own fucking *guilt* for so fucking long, you've managed to distort the brightest and most beautiful thing in your life into something small and ugly, and you've turned someone's gift into a stick to beat them with.

Spoiler: it was not a comfortable feeling. Grabbing hold of that truth burned like holding a hot coal and snatched the breath away from me. It was so tempting to retreat from it. But Micah—*Micah, who could do anything*—looked so fucking bewildered and beaten down, I couldn't do it.

He needed me. *Micah* needed me. Possibly even as much as I needed him. And it wasn't weakness to lean on him or to let him help me.

Adversity was like a fire that could meld two metals into an alloy stronger than either component was on its own—I'd learned *that* on a science show, too, so maybe educational television wasn't *all* bad.

"So that's it?" I said softly. "You're just going to give up? On us? On Blooms?"

Micah threw his hands in the air. "Give up? I haven't *given* anything up. I've been an idiot, clearly. About you and *us*. About fucking *HG Supply*." He spat the words like they were the worst curse he could think of. "But I don't know where to go from here, Constantine. You don't want to talk to me or hear my apology. I can't find another supplier on this short notice." He made a sound that was halfway between a laugh and a sob. "I've contemplated driving around to every grocery store in the area to find the flowers I need. Hell, at this point I would take just about *any fucking flowers in the universe.* I'd make an arrangement of *dandelions.* But even if I took the time to do that, it'd be too late for me to assemble the arrangements." He leaned against the counter again, defeat in his posture. "I'm out of ideas."

I jumped down from my perch and crossed the small

space, laying a hand on his chest, as my mind whirled with an actual, honest-to-God, save-the-day plan.

"Well, guess what?" I said. "I'm not."

———

An hour and a half later, after meeting with Tyler at Fanaille to get his approval as "man of honor" for the wedding and Marissa's official representative, and after a long, detailed phone call with my mother, Micah and I stood across the shiny, metal table in the back room of Blooms.

"Let me understand, because I suddenly feel like I've been plopped down into an alternate reality," Micah said. It should be noted that he sounded really calm and looked incredibly sexy for a guy suddenly finding himself in an alternate reality. The little crinkles on the sides of his eyes just *did it* for me, and I knew they always would. "Your mother is on her way here right now."

"Yep." I leaned my elbows on the table.

"With a metric shit ton of red and pink flowers she just happened to have lying around your greenhouse—"

"Tulips," I clarified. "Yeah."

"And your brothers have called in favors with a bunch of florists in surrounding towns, like your mom is the head of some backwoods floral *mafia*—"

"I'm going to start a band," I mused, stacking my fists together and leaning my chin on them. "Even though I can't sing for shit. Just so I can call us Backwoods Floral Mafia."

"And you'd still be better than Pete Daley," he grumbled. "But seriously, Julian and Theo are going around to ten different places, collecting their unused stock."

"Yep."

"And bringing it here."

"Unless they get hijacked by a rival floral gang on the way, yes." I eyed him speculatively. "You *were* there when we discussed all this with Tyler, right?"

Micah ran a hand through his hair. "Yeah," he said weakly. "Didn't understand it any better then than I do now."

He was so fucking cute, I had to take pity on him. "We're getting you flowers for the wedding. Not the *right* flowers, but *some* flowers. And Tyler is cool with the change. He said Marissa trusts you, Micah."

He'd also said he was going to have a few words with his father, who just so happened to be Senator Marcus Turnbull, about how HG Supply had screwed us over under direction from the Gaynors. I wouldn't want to be Vince, Trent, Pat, or Donnie come Monday morning.

Micah frowned and shook his head. "But *your mother*, Constantine. The woman who's tried to ignore my existence like I'm dog shit on her lawn, the woman who's given dirty looks to anyone who dared to buy a potted plant from my stall at the market, a woman who assumed I was sending her business because I wanted to manipulate you —though I'm still not sure what I was supposedly manipulating you into doing—is now calling in every favor she's ever racked up, just to help me. Why?"

I took a deep breath and stood up straight. "Because I asked her to."

"Yeah," Micah said, running a hand through his hair. "I figured that much. But again, Con, *why?*"

"Well. It could be because I'm going to be the head of Ross Landscape and Design, so I'm kind of a big deal."

Micah's eyes widened and his face split into a huge smile. "No way. She agreed? Shit. I'm so happy for you, ba —um. Constantine." He shoved his hands into his pockets.

I nodded and pushed back from the table so I could walk around it in a wide arc until I was standing just a few feet from Micah. "With that epic business plan you helped me draft, how could she not agree? But I think she also sees an opportunity to redeem herself and welcome you the way she should have in the first place."

"Yeah?" Micah raised a skeptical eyebrow. "I don't see your mom rolling out the O'Leary welcome wagons for a business competitor who'd jeopardize her bottom line."

"Well, maybe she wouldn't ordinarily welcome you as a business competitor," I allowed, stepping into his personal space. "But she'd welcome you to our family. As my boyfriend. As the man I…" I swallowed. "I love."

Micah's hands clenched and unclenched at his sides like he wanted to put them on me, but wasn't sure whether he should. "Say that again."

"You heard me." But *shit*, it was such a relief to say it, and to see the dawning wonder in my man's eyes when I did, that I couldn't hold back, even to tease. "*I. Love. You.*"

Micah pushed me against the refrigerator door and kissed the ever-loving shit out of me. His hands grabbed my face so I couldn't move—*like I would have*—his entire body flattened against mine, and my heart, which hadn't beat right in days, started pounding.

He pulled back a moment later, breathless and almost shaking, and I wrapped my arms around him to hold him in place.

"Sorry." He rubbed my bottom lip with his thumb. "*Fuck.* I thought I'd done that for the last time."

"I know," I said. "I'm sorry I freaked out. I was looking at everything wrong and I—"

"So was I. I thought if I could help you get the other things you wanted, you'd be ready to—"

"You did the nicest things anyone's ever done for me.

You believed in me. You sacrificed your business for me. You defended me." I shook my head, because I legit still couldn't believe that he'd hit Trent Gaynor. More to the point, I couldn't believe I hadn't gotten *photographic evidence*. "You're the only person who's ever defended me like that, Micah. And that wasn't even the first time. Even my mother told me yesterday that I needed to get over it and give you a second chance. She accused me of having my *manly pride* bruised. She said you were trying to love me, even if you went about it the wrong way." I bit my lip and stroked my fingers along the curve of his jaw.

"I guess I did. But she was right." He squeezed me tighter. "I do love you."

"Damn, I really like hearing that." I laughed out loud. I'd always sort of figured that commitment would tie you down, weight you to the earth. But it was more like a tether that kept you balanced, that made it safe for you to soar. "Shit, who knew?"

"I love you," he said again, kissing me this time. "And I get that we are gonna have to take things slow. You're still working things out with your business, and—"

"Nah," I interrupted. "I mean, I'm cool with taking things slow, if that's what you want. But—" I bit my lip, tried to gather my courage, and found that I didn't need any, because telling Micah how I felt was as easy as breathing. "I know who I love, and I have for a while. I'm done screwing around, so… As much as you're ready to give me of you, that's what I want."

I wasn't surprised when he wrapped his hands around my ass, hauled me against him, and kissed me again.

The knock at the back door sounded more like a kick.

"That's gonna be Theo," I said, stepping away from Micah to open the door. "You ready for this onslaught?"

Micah grinned and those eyes, man. *Damn.* If my brother weren't on the other side of the door.

"Fuck's sake, Connie, this thing's *heavy*," Theo yelled, kicking the door again.

Micah winked at me, I opened the door, and… chaos reigned.

Theo and his friend Sam were the first to arrive. Sam, with her arm in a sling, was mostly there for moral support and what she called, "packing coordination," which had been necessary given the relative size of Theo's little car to the load they'd collected: buckets and buckets of flowers, boxes of green foam and test tubes, Mason jars, and even some kind of fake grass that Sam said looked more Easter bunny than Valentine's Day, but they'd taken everything that was donated gratefully.

Julian and Daniel came in next with even more buckets, these mostly filled with greenery. Boxes of tiny vases, dozens of candles, yards of tulle and ribbons galore. Once they'd carried it all in, Daniel perched on one of the counters with Julian leaning back between his legs, trading good-natured insults with Sam.

My mother arrived maybe ten minutes later, and she immediately mobilized Julian, Daniel, Theo, and Carlos to cart in sixteen metric shit-tons of tulips, until the entire space—the countertops and the floor around it—were covered with stuff. Then she stared around at the assembled goods, nodded once, and said, "Let's get organized before the others get here."

Micah and I looked at each other.

"What others?" I asked.

"Oh, a few people I ran into," she said with a little wave. "People who wanted to give Micah a hand. You know how O'Leary is."

Silas Sloane and his boyfriend, Everett Maior, were the

first to knock on the back door. "Angela said you and Con were looking for volunteers," Si told Micah when he answered the knock. "I don't know shit about flowers, but I've got two good hands. And God knows Con has saved my ass more than once. Happy to return the favor." He gave me a chin lift from across the room.

"Same on both counts," Ev said, tucking himself against Silas's side. "But I'm ready to learn."

Ash and Cal came over from Fanaille after closing time with trays of brownies and muffins and giant vats of coffee we had to set up out by the cash register in the front of the store, since there was no space in the back.

Lisa Dorian and Margo Martin, Ash's mom, came by with a bunch of folding card tables they'd used at the last library book sale, and stood gossiping with Henry Lattimer, Ev's grandfather, who'd hobbled in—without his cane— and had claimed the chair from Micah's office. Jamie Burke came by with Mitch Turner. Mackie and Rae Martin arrived together. Bill and his wife, Dhann, who ran the Books and More across the street, came by to see what the fuss was all about and stayed to help. Leandra and her husband Jared, who'd left their kids with Lauren and Chris, arrived with Mason and some friend of Mason's named Tobias, who Micah greeted with a giant hug. They set up the card tables and got to work, under my mother's careful instruction, making arrangements using tulips and greenery, packing them into boxes and then the boxes into cold storage.

If Micah was a little overwhelmed at the way my mother took charge of his back room, he gave no indication. He seemed bewildered but happy to let her conduct the troops like an orchestra, which was… unusual for him. But it hit me that Micah was used to working on his own. Sure, he'd had Belle help out, and he'd had me, but the majority of the work was done by his own hands. He'd probably never tried to organize this many people all at once and wouldn't have known where to begin.

My mother was standing against the refrigerator—the same refrigerator where Micah had given me a blowjob, and *Jesus*, that was not an uncomfortable realization *at all* —keeping an eye on the minions when Micah approached her for maybe the first time ever.

"Thank you," he told her seriously. "I don't know how you got so many people here, Angela, but I don't know what I'd have done—"

"Nonsense. O'Leary takes care of O'Leary, sweetheart," she told him. Then she patted him on the cheek like he was just another one of her boys and hurried off to do something else, leaving Micah blinking after her with a little smile on his face that made my heart melt.

With this many people, even unskilled as most of them were, we were able to crank out the arrangements we needed in record time. When the work was winding down, close to midnight, I grabbed a couple of brownies, caught Micah's eye, and nodded toward the alley. He joined me outside a minute later.

"Fucking cold out here," he said, taking the brownie I offered and cramming it into his mouth like a starving man.

"As opposed to inside, where it's sweltering."

"I had no idea we could fit that many people into such a small space." He looked at me solemnly. "Let's never try it again."

I laughed as I swallowed the last chocolatey bite. "Agreed. This will be the first and last time we let Mama take over," I proclaimed, almost believing it would be true. "But God. Can you believe how much work we got done in such a short time? My old boss would be so impressed. He taught me everything I know." I batted my eyelashes.

"Pretty sure you taught him a thing or two, too." He leaned into me, bowing me backward. "Lots and lots of things."

"Stop," I laughed against his mouth. "Business first, Micah, and… Oh my God, what am I saying? Kiss me again."

So he did, thoroughly, letting me sink into the flavors of Micah and chocolate, letting me finally believe he was *here* with *me* and that he loved me, too. I kissed him until I had *him* backed against the brick by the door and both of us were dying.

"We can't," Micah said. "We can't. We have—*fuck, that feels good.*" He tilted his head farther so I could kiss his neck, rubbing his jean-covered cock against mine. "Your mother is on the other side of this wall, Constantine." He pushed me away with a groan, but his green eyes promised all kinds of things that almost made up for it. "But later on, when all this is done? I am taking you upstairs."

"And?" I demanded breathlessly.

"And I'm going to reacquaint you with all the things you taught me." He leaned toward me and waggled his eyebrows.

"Oh, God." I bit my lip. "What kinds of things?"

I expected all kinds of intimate details. What I got was even better.

"Like, that life is about more than business," he whispered, holding my cheek in his hand. "And love is worth any risk."

"Shut up! You can't say stuff like that and not let me kiss you," I informed him.

He gave me that grin I loved, and *God!* How the hell had I gotten here, standing in an alley in February, looking up at this guy in the glare of a floodlight, and knowing without a shadow of a doubt that I was exactly where I needed to be?

"It's scary, you know? I'm on the cusp of having everything I wanted, and stuff I didn't even know I wanted, too, and like… what the hell do you do when you've gotten everything you want, Micah?"

With his hand in mine I felt stronger, bolder. Ready to make things happen, knowing I'd always have a soft place to land.

"You dream a new dream, babe," he said.

"Simple as that?"

"Simple as that."

I mean, what was I supposed to do then but press myself against him and give him the kiss of our lives? I didn't give a shit whether my mother and all of O'Leary came through the door and caught us—*let them* catch us—because what Micah and I had was not something I'd ever hide or compromise on again.

And I realized maybe Micah was right. Maybe it really *was* that simple. Maybe life wasn't about having a plan or having things figured out in advance. Maybe it was about finding the right person to figure things out with and dreaming along with them. Maybe love—finding it, wanting it, and learning how to *accept* it—was the secret all along.

Epilogue

MICAH

May
15 months later

"Hᴇʏ, everyone! Welcome to this year's first Rushton-O'Leary Farmer's Market!" Pete Daley's voice rang over the fairgrounds, loud as ever. "We're the Daley News and we're so happy to be back with you for the third year in a row!"

Ah, O'Leary. Where the more things changed, the more things stayed the same.

There was a polite smattering of applause from the gathered crowd... including from the man across the aisle, who leaned his arms on the top of his table and smirked at me.

"Enjoying the entertainment, Mr. Bloom?" the trouble-maker demanded, loud enough for everyone around us to hear.

Theo, who was working in the booth with him, rolled his eyes. Lauren snickered from the comfort of the lawn chair she'd set up behind my table. She was heavily pregnant with her third baby and due in a few weeks, but she'd insisted on coming today for "moral support," which was code for bearing witness to Constantine's shenanigans.

"Why, yes, Mr. Ross," I called back. "I was just thinking to myself how comforting the familiarity of this place is."

"Now that's not true," Con chided. "Lots of things change. For example?" He waved a hand over his head, gesturing at the Ross Landscape and Design banner hanging there. "*This* is barely a year old."

Constantine's company had taken a little extra time to get off the ground because he *hadn't* wanted me to be his financial backer. But the solution we'd figured out, one that involved his mother leaving the florist game entirely, had ultimately been the best thing for everyone.

I grinned. "I suppose that's true. But maybe that's just the exception that proves the rule."

"Well, there's this," Constantine said, pointing to the ring on his left hand. "You might not have heard, but I'm *engaged*."

"Pretty sure there's no one in Upstate New York who hasn't heard," Theo muttered, loud enough to carry.

I whistled appreciatively. "That *is* some nice hardware," I agreed. And I would know. I'd had the two-tone tungsten ring specifically designed so that Constantine could wear it while working without damaging it. And I'd given it to him three weeks ago, on our *second* beach vacation.

By now, Constantine had officially seen an ocean *and* the Gulf of Mexico, and I was hoping we'd expand that list when we took our honeymoon… which wouldn't happen until we managed to pick a date for the wedding, but I was trying to be patient. After all, Constantine's new business was still in its infancy, and mine was getting busier than ever.

"Nothing wrong with trying new things, Mr. Bloom," Constantine said.

"Yes, we all know you're a great lover of variety," I said blandly, pretending to be very busy tweaking the flower pots in my display by tiny, tiny increments. "In your stock, I mean."

I could practically feel my man's narrow-eyed glare singeing my skin, and I knew I was going to pay for this comment when we got back to our apartment over the shop. The little space had finally started to feel like a home once Con was there, and I was almost a little sad that we'd put a down payment on a pretty little Craftsman not too far from the store.

Almost.

"Oh, not anymore," Constantine said. "When you find a decent supplier, you stick with them. I mean, you'd know that better than anyone, right?"

No one around us seemed to be paying any particular attention to our conversation. And to the casual observer, we were talking about the long-term arrangements we'd made between Ross Landscaping and Design, Micah's Blooms, and Angela's company, which was now known as Ross Floral Supply. The arrangement we'd made to save Marissa Corcoran's wedding had worked so well, we'd expanded on the idea. Now Angela's greenhouses and nursery supplied nearly all my regular stock and most of Constantine's, too.

But I was much more concerned with another part of Con's statement... and the other side of the conversation we were having.

"Decent?" I glared right back. "I think your *supplier* is a little better than decent."

"Well, I mean, I hate to sound like I'm bragging, but my supplier *is* very consistent." He pursed his lips thoughtfully. "Some people worry that once their stock gets to a… certain age… it'll just *wilt*, you know?" He held his hand up straight then let his wrist go slack and gave an exaggerated frown as his hand sank. "So disappointing when you have limp stems. Fortunately, I haven't had to worry about anything like that." He smiled broadly. "Yet."

"Lauren," Theo piped up. "Would you like to go for a walk? To anywhere that's not here?"

Lauren laughed and rubbed her belly. "I would if I could, Theo, but you'd end up delivering this little boy along the way and that might be even more traumatic than listening to these two discussing their… plants. Besides, your mom'll be along in a little while. She'll keep them in line."

Lord knew the woman tried, but with limited success.

"*Your* supplier has never had an issue with wilting stock," I reminded Constantine. I folded my arms across my chest.

"That's what I'm saying," Con agreed. "I mean, I haven't been with my supplier long enough to guarantee that it would *never* wilt." He wrinkled his nose. "Wilty stock happens to everyone once in a while. It's nothing to be ashamed of. I'm sure you've gotten some, too."

"Not. Even. Once." I pushed each word out through my clenched jaw.

Con's head went back, and he stared at me appraisingly.

Lauren made a strangled noise. "Boys, you can whip out your… stocks… and compare them later. Micah, maybe now you could help the *customer*?"

Constantine snickered, and I rolled my eyes.

"I'm sorry about that. Can I— Oh. I know you. You're—"

"The man you were supposed to have coffee with,

months and months ago?" He gave me a warm smile and stuck out his hand. "*Robert*, in case you've forgotten."

I had. I'd totally forgotten. But I shook his hand anyway. "Of course. Nice to see you again."

"I'm going to assume you've been dying to call for the last year and just… misplaced my number." He grinned archly, and his teeth were very white and even. "So, this time I'll be a little more persistent. How about that coffee?"

"That's very flattering, but—" I began when my better half—my provoking, troublemaking better half—sauntered across the aisle.

"But that would be bad for Micah's health," he said with a rueful smile.

Robert frowned, looking from Constantine to me and back again. "Coffee would?"

"Coffee with *you* would," Constantine said. He came around the back of the table, wrapped his arm around the back of my waist, and held out his hand to Robert. "I'm Constantine. Micah's fiancé." The hand at my waist tightened, and I felt a stab of lust in my gut.

That was something that sure as hell never changed.

"Fiancé. Ah." Robert screwed up his mouth and nodded. "Next time I'll need to be persistent *faster*, I see. Best of luck." He smiled as he walked away.

I turned to my future husband, the love of my life, and stared into those blue eyes that took my breath away. "Would it help if you rub your scent on me? You could get me a t-shirt that says *Property of Constantine*. Or I could get it tattooed. On my *forehead*."

I was joking. Constantine wasn't often jealous—we never gave each other reason to be—and that little display had gotten me more aroused than angry.

But Con wrapped his other arm around my waist and

pretended to consider it. "Nah. I like this handsome face just the way it is. The t-shirt might work… But it'd need to be washed occasionally."

Lauren snorted. "Knock him up, Connie. Then no one will look at him."

Constantine gave Lauren a wink and a bright smile. "No way. With my luck, he'd take after you and Leandra, and then he'd be even more gorgeous when he was pregnant."

Lauren grinned back, then turned to me. "Constantine's my favorite brother now."

Theo yelled from across the aisle, "No give-backsies, Lauren. You want him, he's yours."

Constantine turned to give Theo a nasty look…

Which was, of course, when Angela bustled up, tying a Micah's Blooms apron around her waist.

Once upon a time, I would have thought that was a sign of the apocalypse. Now, it was just a typical Saturday. Since she no longer manned her own booth, she came to help out at mine… and to cluck over whichever of my sisters and their babies happened to be here with me.

"Constantine Luciano, did you just stick your tongue out at your brother? How old are you?" She threw her long braid behind her back.

"He's twenty-six," Theo volunteered. "*Old.*"

Con snickered. "Old enough to kick your…"

"Hush!" Angela said. "You're disturbing Lauren's baby."

Which was so ridiculous, none of us could argue with it.

"Let's go get you some coffee, while everyone's here to cover for us," I told Con, grabbing his hand and pulling him out of the booth. "Come on."

"Yes, because more caffeine is what he needs!" Theo yelled.

"*Come on*, Constantine. *Come on*, Constantine," Con said, even as he knitted our fingers together and leaned into my side. "Always the same thing with you."

"You complaining?"

"About coming with you? Nah." He smirked. "You know I love *coming* with you. Hey! Where are we—"

"I changed my mind," I said, pulling Constantine between two of the booths to the grassy lane that ran behind them, the place where I'd first stood and overheard a conversation that had changed… well, *everything.* "You don't need coffee."

"I could use another vacation," Con suggested. "If you're offering."

"Four days on the beach in Sarasota with all the Shirley Temples you could drink wasn't enough?"

He yanked on our hands and pulled me to a stop. "Never enough days with you, Micah Bloom," he said softly.

God. The man killed me sometimes, he really did.

"How the hell did I ever think I could resist you, Constantine Ross?" I wondered. "You make me laugh, you piss me off, you challenge me to do better, you love me even when I fuck up. You know, before you, I thought stability was the ultimate goal. That's all I wanted out of life. I didn't know I could aim higher or dream bigger until you."

Con frowned and swallowed hard, his eyes suspiciously shiny. "Why would you say something like that?" he accused. "Why would you make me fall in love with you even more, right in the middle of the fucking farmer's market, when I promised Mitch I'd cover my one shift a month at the station *tonight,* and I can't even—"

I kissed him, thoroughly and passionately, until he forgot what he was saying. I'd gotten pretty good at that, if I did say so myself.

"Your flirtation game," Con panted against my mouth a minute later. "Has gotten so much stronger."

"I try," I said modestly. With one hand, I sketched an oval in the air. "Imagine my flirtation game is like a seed."

"Hey! You can't just *use* that expression. That's trademarked."

"Trademarked?"

"Yes! I came up with it. Your *seed* is mine."

I turned both of my lips under and pressed them together hard.

Constantine frowned. "What? What did I... Oh! *God*. Really? Sperm jokes? I'm marrying a forty-one-year-old adolescent."

I burst out laughing.

"You're a troublemaker!" he insisted. "*Provoking*."

"That's my boyfriend's influence," I told him solemnly. "I used to be way more mature."

"You don't *have* a boyfriend anymore," he reminded me.

"That's right. And pretty soon I won't have a fiancé anymore either. If he'd ever pick a *date*."

"Oh, it's up to me?"

"Yup."

"Any day I say?"

"Any place, too," I agreed. "Anywhere, anytime."

"You don't have a single plan in mind, huh?"

I laughed. "My plan is to marry you. The details don't matter." I'd learned that much.

"Then I pick Wednesday morning. Paston Marsh."

"What?"

"It's the birdwatching paradise of Upstate New York," he informed me, wrapping his arms around my neck.

It still felt surreal to have someone I loved this much; it was beyond surreal that it was someone as perfect for me as Constantine. "And Wednesday is my favorite day of the week. So why wait?"

Why, indeed?

"Done." I grinned. "But *you* can tell your mother."

"*Fucking hell.*" Con groaned and leaned his forehead against my chin. "The things I do for love."

See Micah's brother Mason get his HEA in *Off Plan*, the first book in the Whispering Key series, available here →
https://readerlinks.com/l/1570165

After you do, don't forget to grab *Unicorns Forever*, an O'Leary/Whispering Key bonus story, here→ https://readerlinks.com/l/3143036

And don't miss the next Love in O'Leary novella, *The World*, available here → https://readerlinks.com/l/1570172

About May Archer

May is an M/M author who lives in Boston. She spends her days planning vacations, mainlining diet soda, avoiding the gym, reading M/M romance, and when all other forms of procrastination fail, writing it.

Visit her website at mayarcher.com to sign up for her newsletter to hear about sales and upcoming releases, freebies and behind the scenes info and more! Or join her Facebook group, Club May!

facebook.com/may.archer.author

instagram.com/mayarcherauthor

amazon.com/May-Archer/e/B075JQVGLX

bookbub.com/authors/may-archer

Also by May Archer

Love in O'Leary Series

Whispering Key Series

The Sunday Brothers Series

Copper County Series

The Way Home Series

Licking Thicket Series

(cowritten with Lucy Lennox)

Champion Security Series

(cowritten with Lucy Lennox)

Honeybridge Series

(cowritten with Lucy Lennox)